Fiona McCallum spent her childhood years on the family cereal and wool farm outside the small town of Cleve on South Australia's Eyre Peninsula. While she now lives in Adelaide, she remains a country girl at heart. Fiona writes heart-warming journey of self-discovery stories that draw on her experiences, love of animals and fascination with life in small communities. She is the author of seven Australian bestsellers: *Paycheque*, *Nowhere Else*, *Wattle Creek*, *Saving Grace*, *Time Will Tell*, *Meant To Be* and *Leap of Faith*. *Standing Strong* (which is a sequel to *Wattle Creek*) is her eighth novel.

More information about Fiona and her books can be found on her website at www.fionamccallum.com and she can be followed on Facebook at www.facebook.com/fionamccallum.author.

Also by Fiona McCallum

Paycheque
Nowhere Else
Wattle Creek
Leap of Faith

The Button Jar Series
Saving Grace
Time Will Tell
Meant To Be

STANDING STRONG

Fiona McCallum

HARLEQUIN® MIRA®

First Published 2016
Second Australian Paperback Edition 2016
ISBN 9781489223265

STANDING STRONG
© 2016 by Fiona McCallum
Australian Copyright 2016
New Zealand Copyright 2016

Published by
Harlequin Mira
An imprint of Harlequin Enterprises (Australia) Pty Ltd.
Level 13, 201 Elizabeth Street,
SYDNEY NSW 2000
AUSTRALIA

Creator: McCallum, Fiona, 1970- author.
Title: Standing strong / Fiona McCallum.
ISBN: 9781743693513 (paperback)
Subjects: Love stories, Australian. Country life—Australia—Fiction.
Dewey Number: A823.4

Printed and bound in Australia by McPherson's Printing Group

Acknowledgements

Many thanks to Sue, Annabel, Cristina, Michelle and everyone at Harlequin Australia for turning my manuscripts into beautiful books, for all the wonderful support, and for continuing to make my dreams come true.

Huge thanks to Kylie Mason, editor extraordinaire, for the guiding hand to bring out the best in my writing and the story, and for being so easy to work with.

Thank you to the media outlets, bloggers, reviewers, librarians, booksellers and readers for all the wonderful support. To hear that my stories, which really are from the heart, are being so widely enjoyed is amazing.

Special thanks to Jason Sabeeney and Duncan McCallum for providing some valuable insights into volunteering with the CFS. Any errors or inaccuracies are my own or due to taking creative liberties.

Finally, thanks to dear friends Carole and Ken Wetherby, Mel Sabeeney, NEL and WTC for all your love and support. I am truly blessed for having you in my life.

*To the men and women volunteer firefighters
who put their lives on the line every summer, and
the families who support them.*

Chapter One

Jacqueline hadn't been out for her daily walk for ages – certainly not while her parents had been staying. Actually, she realised with a jolt, as she rounded the edge of the rustic golf course, this was her first walk since Jacob Bolton had turned up and attacked her.

It was a glorious cool, clear summer morning. She hoicked her shoulders higher, squared her chest, and took a deep breath. Today she didn't have a worry in the world. Well, except for missing Damien, and what to do about replacing her car … And whatever that little nag pestering her was. She just wished it would reveal itself so she could deal with it and move on.

Normally, Jacqueline strode at a strong pace. Today she ambled and took the time to really enjoy her surroundings, even stopping to watch a few bees busy with the bottlebrush flowers. At the top of the hill, just past where the golf course ended and the now defunct pony club's cross-country course began, she stopped and looked back. She had a lovely view of the town laid out in its perfectly symmetrical grid below her. A few streets had broken protocol and were curved, with a few cul-de-sacs off some of the corners and sides. *How very rebellious,* she thought with a smile. Her mind wandered, imagining the council meeting for the proposed extension to the town, and some bold person suggesting a deviation from the original plan: 'Well, Colonel William Light's grid style is nice and neat and it's worked well for us, but wouldn't a few curves here and there be nice? Let's not forget, people, this is the twentieth century, not the nineteenth! What we need is a show of progress, a bit of independence!' Jacqueline chuckled. She could almost hear their voices, which were plummy English in her mind.

She walked on a few metres down the rocky rise and perched herself on the top rail of one of the jumps. It was nice to just sit. She really didn't spend enough time just sitting, being – certainly not lately. She'd been on the go the whole time since arriving in town. It was a relief to stop for a few moments and contemplate nature. She listened for birds. Nothing. The only sounds she heard were the rustle of gum trees overhead and the whisper of a car somewhere in the distance.

She unscrewed the top of her water bottle. *Life really doesn't get much better than this,* she thought, as she lifted the bottle to her lips and took a swig. She had a wonderful job she enjoyed and found rewarding, and where she was pretty much in charge. She was being warmly welcomed into a town of lovely, friendly people and had made a great friend in her neighbour, Ethel. More importantly, Jacqueline had found a good man and was sure their relationship would evolve smoothly. She wanted to savour it; didn't want to rush in and get the stages ticked off too quickly – engagement, marriage, honeymoon, kids – only to suddenly turn around one day and wonder 'What now?' She did think she wanted kids one day – no, she *knew* she wanted kids one day. But she had a career to better establish. She had spent too many hard years studying at university to take time out just yet. She was young; she could wait a few years before her fertility was at risk.

Jacqueline realised she was getting quite warm, and got up. That sun had some bite. No wonder there weren't any frolicking birds. She only hoped the snakes and lizards were still hidden away – she didn't fancy encountering any of them as she made her way across the creek and cross-country course around to the back of the hospital.

She thought again about Damien. She hoped he'd slept okay in his new surroundings, and that the joey was doing well. She wondered if he might drop by later in the day. She hoped so. During one of their deep and meaningful evenings snuggled up on Ethel's couch, they'd discussed communication. Jacqueline had been surprised when it had been Damien who had instigated the conversation. They shared the view that a relation-ship should not consist of a series of text messages, which seemed all the go these days. They'd gone so far as to outline a few rules: No ridiculous long text message back and forths. If there was something to say, say it – in person or by picking up the phone and calling. They were adults, not teenagers. Proper communication was what was important.

Damien was actually quite definite and strong with his views when you got to know him. Nothing like the shy, insecure fellow she'd first encountered in her office. He'd been so vulnerable just a few short weeks ago. Thankfully he no longer needed her; to see him both professionally and personally would be totally unethical. A big no-no.

Jacqueline stopped dead in her tracks. She felt her face go pale and her heart rate slow. Ethics. *Oh. My. God!* She brought her hands to her face, which was now starting to flame. *How could I have forgotten?* Did she have some weird form of selective amnesia? She stood there on the footpath feeling totally bewildered. *Christ. I've completely stuffed up. No, things are different out here, aren't they? Yes. Doctor Squire had been very clear about that. Yes. It'll be all right.*

No. it won't.

She started walking again, increasing her pace until she was almost jogging. She felt the overwhelming need to get home. She knew nothing would be different when she got there, but felt a desperate need to get back fast to the safety of her little cottage. Her heart raced, her mind spun. She had missed a stack of ethics classes due to an ear infection and the details of the few she'd attended were little more than a blur thanks to the distraction of the pain she'd been in, and the fug of painkillers. She knew you couldn't date a patient. That was obvious; a given. But how could she have forgotten the bit about there being an exclusion period of twenty-four months? Had she known? She must have – she knew now. *How could I have been so stupid?* How could her intuition have let her down so badly? But it hadn't, had it – she had felt uneasy about Damien putting his arms around her after the frightening Jacob Bolton episode. She'd pulled away. But he'd still officially been her patient then.

Jacqueline fumbled and struggled to get the front-door key into the lock. Once inside, she collapsed on one of the wooden kitchen chairs. She felt seriously out of kilter; as if she'd just come out of a coma and found she'd lost a chunk of her life.

Okay, calm down. Perhaps it hasn't gone too far. Now the wording came back to her, as if someone had turned a camera lens to improve the focus: the rule didn't say relationship, it said sexual activity: A two-year exclusion period on sexual activity with a former patient after terminating a professional relationship.

Now she remembered thinking the wording odd at the time, and that surely a line was crossed when an emotional relationship began, never mind sex. So how the hell had she managed to forget it until now?

Right, so technically I haven't crossed that line yet – haven't actually done anything wrong. She felt a glimmer of relief, but in a split second it was gone. It was only a matter of time before she and Damien did make love. There was no way she was waiting two years. If she was reported, would the board say she had crossed the line by starting an emotional relationship anyway? *Oh Christ.* What the hell was she supposed to do now? Should she discuss it with Doctor Squire? Oh God, he'd have a fit. But she had to, didn't she? He was her boss.

What bothered Jacqueline most about her realisation and predicament was that she'd managed to somehow block it out. She honestly, hand on heart, hadn't given the twenty-four-month exclusion period a thought. Not once. But how could that have happened? Did she have a brain tumour, or something affecting certain parts of her memory or thought processes?

She sighed. She didn't have headaches, blurred vision, or anything of the sort. It was highly unlikely she had a brain tumour or any other neurological disorder, except perhaps being swept up and blinded by love. But she didn't feel swept up and out of her mind with lust. She was functioning as a normal, rational human being; totally level-headed. Though, clearly not, she had to concede, given the situation she now found herself in.

To be fair, it is my first time being properly in love. How was I supposed to know what it would do to me? She almost laughed at picturing herself using that as her actual defence in front of a board hearing a complaint against her.

Would anyone complain? No, who out here would care? It seemed Damien was a favourite; no one would want to cause him grief. But Jacqueline knew it was not a chance she could take. She could not live her life looking over her shoulder – she'd done that with Jacob already. And, actually, there was a chance her stalker might figure this out and use it to cause her more grief. He had seen Damien there at her house. Regardless, she couldn't live with knowing she was doing the wrong thing – even if she did think the rule was a bit over the top.

Jacqueline actually felt sick to her stomach. She swallowed it down, made herself a cup of tea, then took it outside to the small garden table, along with a notepad and pen. She sat tapping her pen against her lip. What options did she have? She could end things permanently with Damien and save her career – though she could still get into trouble if someone dobbed her in. She could resign her job and psychology registration and stay with Damien. But then what would she do for money? She'd had a number of patients in who were out of work; with a town so small, the opportunities were very limited. Perhaps she could write and 'fess up to the board and beg them to allow her to both continue to see Damien and keep her registration. It could be argued that, technically, they hadn't breached the letter of the ethics clause – if it came down to it and she had a decent lawyer on her side. She almost snorted. Pigs would be more likely to fly. If she came clean to Doctor Squire – as terrifying as that would be – perhaps he'd be kind and keep her on as a counsellor and not a registered psychologist. That wasn't much less ludicrous than writing to the board. She was seriously deranged. And, anyway, no matter what Doctor Squire's reaction, *his* career might be in jeopardy if he covered it up and didn't report her. No, she couldn't mention it to him until she'd decided what she was going to do.

But really there was only one main concern: was Damien more important than her career, which she'd studied for years to acquire? She had so much still to achieve – so many people to help. But how much good would she be doing if she didn't know the basics, such as ethical standards? Tears flooded her eyes. What a mess.

She considered phoning Damien just to hear his voice, in the hope it might make her believe there was a way through this and that things would be okay. But he'd be busy by now. And he'd detect her angst. It wouldn't be fair to put this on him, he hadn't done anything wrong – it was she who had well and truly stuffed up. She should have known better. She *had* known better. She'd just let herself down.

She was the only one who could get her out of this mess – by resigning her job and giving up her psychology registration before she could get into any real trouble. It was the only way. She sighed deeply. All she could hope was that Doctor Squire might appreciate her work enough to keep her on anyway. Really, helping people was what was important. And she had the training.

She could give up her piece of paper to keep Damien, couldn't she?

Chapter Two

'Did you sleep well?' Damien asked the joey suckling on the teat attached to the bottle clutched between her tiny paws. None of them had got more than a few hours of sleep between feeds. He rubbed his slightly gritty eyes and looked around the van. It really was a surreal thing, this being homeless. Well, he wasn't homeless in the poverty-stricken sense – he just didn't have his own roof over his head. And it wasn't like he didn't have everything he needed thanks to the kindness and generosity of everyone. He'd been really too tired the night before to take much in beyond ascertaining the caravan's main facilities, but it was fully contained and even set up to run completely on solar power. He liked the idea of being self-sufficient – off-grid. Losing everything really did put life into perspective. His current most prized possessions – other than his ute and Squish and Bob and Cara, of course – were the packets of jocks and socks from the owner of the menswear shop in town. It had felt so good to put on his own underwear after his shower last night. And of course, Bruce from the store knew his size and what style he liked because he'd been shopping there for ever.

Damien kept being surprised about how the little things could become huge. Like Stan Richards going to the trouble of retrieving a copy of Damien's dad's house plans from the council. Damien wouldn't have thought of doing that and it meant so much to him. They could have just said they were building him a stock-standard weatherboard cottage and he would have been very grateful and happy. But to actually go and dig out the plans of his dad's hand-built house ... Well, that was something else entirely.

The question now was, did he want the house he'd had before or did he want something different? He'd need to discuss it in more depth with Jacqueline. If things went to plan, she'd be living in it at some point. He smiled, picturing them at the bench together, cooking. No way would he make the mistake of thinking she'd be doing all the cooking and cleaning. He might be a country guy not up with all the femmo mumbo jumbo, but he was smart enough to know you couldn't make assumptions about who did what any more. While he had to concede he didn't have much of a clue what she was like domestically, if Jacqueline turned out to be the sort of woman who wanted to take care of her man, he sure wouldn't argue. He bet she'd be tidy, like she was with her office and desk, he thought, picturing her professional surroundings. Everything in its place – that's what she'd be like.

His mum always went into a frantic cleaning frenzy when visitors were expected – despite the place always being immaculate. Damien wondered if this part of his mother had changed now she seemed to be a little less uptight. He hoped so, for his sister Lucy's sake, otherwise Tina's visit to her London flat, which was, apparently, minuscule, could end in tears. Tina and Lucy's relationship was best described as 'tense' and he wondered how Lucy was taking the news of their mother's impending visit. Had Tina stopped to consider that Lucy might have moved to the other side of world to escape her control-freak mother? *It's not my problem,* he thought, dismissing them and returning to Jacqueline.

The way he felt about Jacqueline, she could tell him she was the great-great-granddaughter of Hitler and didn't have a problem with what he'd done, and he'd probably shrug and say, 'Yeah, okay, whatever.' She was seriously under his skin and could do no wrong in his eyes.

'It's love, isn't it, little one?' he said, stroking the top of the joey's head. 'Right, all done? Back into bed then.' He held the baby roo against the homemade pouch hanging on the back of one of Ethel's wooden kitchen chairs. There wasn't a whole lot of room in the van for furniture that wasn't built-in, but there was also nowhere really to hang the pouch. Damien had briefly wondered if one of the cupboard doors might do the trick, but dismissed it. The last thing he wanted to do was damage the flash van he'd been loaned. The filthy black grime that already seemed to have seeped in despite him taking his boots off and wiping Squish's paws before coming in was bad enough. He really hoped the curtains were washable. The couch was leather and should be able to be wiped off. Auntie Ethel would know how to sort it out. Anyway, it was a problem for another day. He was doing his best.

Damien picked up the binoculars and peered outside. A light fog was hanging over the gullies. Pity it was all black from the fire, otherwise it would have been a lovely sight. He couldn't see the young buck anywhere. Hopefully that meant he was happily grazing over the rise or, better yet, had found his mob or joined up with a new one and was in company.

One thing that bothered Damien in all of this was reconciling his past views about kangaroos with how he felt now. Since he was a kid he'd loved spotlighting – hunting kangaroos. It was a uniquely country sport and entertainment. But now he was thinking more deeply, and had changed himself and his life so much, it was really troubling him. Looking at the joey and thinking of all the work he and his auntie Ethel had done bringing her and the young buck back from the brink and then how many kangaroos he'd shot over the years – and foxes, rabbits and wild cats too, for that matter – made his stomach turn and his skin crawl. But they were pests: in large numbers, kangaroos caused havoc trampling crops and eating pasture the sheep needed, and carnivorous predators preyed on lambs that were crucial to a farmer's livelihood. One good thing about a few years of drought was that pest numbers had been kept down naturally. If they got too high again, he didn't know what he'd do. There was no way he could live with saving their lives one day and going out shooting them the next night. Culling was always done humanely, but it still didn't sit right with him

at all. Why was life so full of compromises and contradic-
tions? Was it especially so out here on the land, or was it
just because that was what he saw day in and day out? In
many ways it was a wonderful life to live, but it could also
be confronting. The things he'd seen and done and taken
for granted ... Christ! He'd have to put it out of his mind
and deal with it when it came up, otherwise he might go
completely mad.

'Fancy a walk, Squish?' Damien asked quietly. The
dog leapt off the bed and was at the door in a split second,
wagging his little tail. 'I'll take that as a very enthusiastic
yes, then,' Damien said with a chuckle. 'You'd be useless
at poker.'

He grabbed the jumper of his long-gone uncle Gordon
that he'd been wearing the day before. He considered
leaving the joey in her pouch, but he couldn't bring
himself to let her out of his sight. Her pouch had straps
to wear it like a backpack, or as a front pack – thanks to
Auntie Ethel.

She was a thinker all right. And a doer. Damien
had quite often thought over the years that his auntie
Ethel had been wasted out here being a stay-at-home
housewife – she'd have been a great inventor or engineer.
It made him a little morose to think that if she'd been
young now – and not born into an era where women
stopped working when they got married – she could
have really done something meaningful with her life.
Not that being a mother wasn't meaningful. But perhaps
it was the way it was meant to be. And he'd certainly
never heard her complain. About anything; she was one
of the most positive people he knew.

And, anyway, there'd be plenty of people thinking I'm mad doing what I'm doing. But he was happy saving lives – even if they weren't human. And as far as he could see, giving something a chance was as important to the world as inventing something cool like a smartphone app. Well, maybe it wasn't. But it did feel good to be helping, no matter how small his actions might be in the scheme of things. Damien felt himself choking up. This was the first time since losing his dad that he could remember being truly content and feeling that he was okay with his place in the world. God, he wished his dad was here to see it. He swallowed hard.

'Righto,' he said boldly in an effort to rid himself of the downer threatening to engulf him. With the pouch secured to his front and the binoculars in hand so they couldn't hit the joey if she popped her head up, Damien let Squish out, then carefully negotiated the caravan's steps, and shut the door behind him.

Over at the new dog enclosure, he was greeted enthusiastically by his farm dogs, Bob and Cara. Their whole bodies shook and they whined and moaned as they waited at the gate to be let out.

'Okay, everyone, we're off. Bob, Cara, you stay close. No chasing anything,' he called as they loped off ahead. Squish was by his side, his little legs going a mile a minute to keep up with Damien's long-legged stride.

He skirted around the bare black earth that had once been his stubble and sheep feed for the next year. He hadn't thought about that particular loss as yet, but now his mind was clearing, it would make sense to plant a crop and cut hay. But he wouldn't do it himself. He had no plans to replace all his expensive equipment and go back into cropping. No, he'd keep that part of the insurance money and let someone else have the grief by contracting it out.

He called the big dogs back to his side as he climbed the small rise. He didn't want them tearing off out of sight and startling the young buck or sheep. He didn't have to worry about Squish; the pup was struggling to keep up. And, anyway, being so short, Damien doubted he saw anything beyond feet and legs. He took pity on the little guy, put the binoculars around his neck so he had both hands free, and then bent down and scooped him up. He draped the little dog around the back of his neck, retrieved his binoculars from under the dog, and carried on.

Damien was a little out of breath when he paused at the top of the rise to take in the gully stretching below. The joey and Squish together were heavy. Half of the gully was black. On the other half, a mob of about a dozen kangaroos grazed. He took a few deep breaths.

'Do you reckon our buck's down there?' he said, and received a lick on the neck from Squish. He put the binoculars to his eyes. He wished they'd put some sort of marking on the roo – from here they all looked the same. A gust of wind must have carried their scents down the gully, because suddenly all the roos lifted their heads and turned towards them.

'Stay!' he commanded Bob and Cara. 'At ease, you two,' he said, taking the binoculars away and looking directly at the dogs looking up at him expectantly, crouching and ready to give chase. The only way the dogs would believe him was if he got himself settled. He carefully lowered Squish and then himself onto the ground. It was nice to have the time to just sit and watch. There were a million things he should be doing, but it could all just wait for a bit. He really wanted to see if he could make out the young buck they'd released. He was actually quite anxious to know he was okay, and hadn't had a relapse and ended up going off into the scrub to die. He crossed his legs under himself. The joey's pouch was the perfect length to sit in his lap. Squish sat beside him, panting, and Bob and Cara gave a frustrated harrumph and lay down nearby. Settled, he brought the binoculars back up to his eyes. He was surprised to see one of the roos was out on its own, halfway between him and the mob, and making its way towards him. Damien could now see the bare patches of pink, healing skin on its legs.

'It's really you,' he muttered, a lump forming in his throat. To see this guy out here in his own environment when not much more than a week ago he'd thought he hadn't much of a chance was quite overwhelming. The roo was now just metres away; one or two decent bounds and he'd be on top of him. Damien wished he'd remained standing. He felt a little vulnerable, sitting down like this. The roo hadn't shown any sign of aggression while in their care, but you could never be totally sure what any creature with a brain might do.

He held his breath and put his hand out towards the battered-looking creature, which was now just a long neck and arm stretch away. They stared at each other. Suddenly the roo stretched its neck the final distance and positioned his head right under Damien's hand. He obliged by scratching the soft, slightly wiry fur on the roo's head. Tears rolled down his cheeks.

In a cloud of dust, the roo turned and bounded back down into gully towards where the other roos had resumed their grazing. Damien was left wondering if the encounter had really happened, or if his mind was playing tricks on him. His chest ached. After a few moments he gathered himself, rubbed a sleeve roughly across his cheeks, carefully got up, and set off back home with his menagerie in tow. God, it was all too much, too emotional. But, damn it, despite how sad he felt, it felt good – happy-sad, like the end of a movie.

Damien was desperate to call Jacqueline and tell her about his encounter with the young buck, but he restrained himself; it was one of those you-had-to-be-there moments. Sure, she'd be pleased for him and would ooh and ahh in all the right places, but the moment was already lost. Besides, they would share plenty together down the track.

He did want to see her today, though; he wanted to get her thoughts on the house plans. He'd pop in and surprise her for lunch at work. He knew she didn't schedule appointments between twelve and one.

Meanwhile, he had a stack of things to do. He thought he might get a bit bored now he didn't have all the farm jobs to do, thanks to the fire, but there was a lot of administrative stuff regarding Esperance to deal with. Ordinarily he hated paperwork and had been quite happy to leave the farm paperwork in his mum's capable hands, but Esperance was totally his venture.

And, anyway, this paperwork was a means to an end. It was an important part of things, not just a pain in the arse, like he'd usually viewed it. God, he'd really had a few things the wrong way around in his brain. But he'd got his shit together now and had a clean slate. Thanks to the fire, there was a nice clear line drawn in the sand, so to speak. It was filthy, actually. *Everything* was filthy, thanks to the soot and grime.

Chapter Three

Jacqueline's morning was quiet, with two people cancelling appointments; it seemed a cold was making its way through the district. While she didn't like the extra time it afforded her to think about her predicament, she was thankful to be spared the germs. The last thing she needed was to get sick.

It was almost lunchtime. She'd meant to pack something at home, but in her distressed state she'd completely forgotten. She really didn't want to head out to the bakery; didn't feel up to smiling and chatting when she was carrying this burden. But her stomach rumbled as if to remind her that life went on and she couldn't hide in here all day. She considered indulging in a few chocolate biscuits, but knew the last thing she needed was to feel sick from too much sugar – she already felt queasy.

She had run out of tears and sadness in the shower that morning. After all, it was only her job she was giving up – she still had Damien. She had briefly felt sad at losing the little cottage that came with her job. She hoped Ethel might put her up for a few days while she found another rental, and she hoped her parents might tide her over financially, if it came to that. She would hate not being independent, but she couldn't leave Wattle Creek now. Maybe she could get some bar work in the pub.

Having forced herself to stop with the what-ifs and the self-pity, she now just felt mostly numb, lost, and bewildered that everything could go so spectacularly wrong so quickly, that it was of her own doing, and all because she'd blocked something very important out of her mind.

But she'd written her resignation letter to Doctor Squire and printed it out. It was sitting in her in-tray – where she kept looking at it – in case any changes came to mind. Doctor Squire had got caught up at the hospital. She didn't want to give it to Louise and Cecile and risk them opening it, nor did she want to slide it under his door where they might find it first. Anyway, all those options were gutless. She needed to look him in the eye and 'fess up to her crime like the adult she was. She'd considered begging him to keep her on as an unregistered counsellor, but had decided she'd leave him to make that suggestion if he wanted to. She was the one who had done the wrong thing – she had no right to ask for any concessions. If he wanted to offer them, then that was up to him. Though, knowing what little she did of Doctor Squire, she figured he'd be keen to wipe his hands of her as quickly as possible. Jacqueline was startled from her thoughts by a knock on the door. She hoped it wasn't Louise or Cecile wanting her to head out for lunch. They both knew she was there, so there was no hiding, and no being rude. She plastered a smile on her face to help her voice sound cheery and called, 'Come in.'

The door opened and there stood Damien. Dear, sweet Damien with his brooding eyes and floppy dark hair, wearing what she knew was a joey in a pouch on his chest. Beside him was Squish. She couldn't help but beam at the scene, it was so cute. And yet also a painful reminder.

'We've come to have lunch with you. If you don't already have plans?' Damien said, carefully leaning across her desk to kiss her.

'No, no plans.'

'Excellent,' he said, placing two white bakery bags on her desk. He pulled the two chairs in front of her desk closer. Squish leapt onto one and sat there looking very pleased with himself. Damien went to sit down, but appeared to change his mind. 'Actually, do you mind if I hang this little one over the chair? I think she'll fit.'

'Go right ahead.'

Jacqueline looked on with amusement as he set about organising the bundle. Finally he settled in his chair.

'Right, egg, lettuce and mayo or ham and salad. Your choice.'

'Egg. Thanks very much.' Ham and salad was Damien's preference, she knew that – he was just being polite.

The joey's head popped out of the pouch like a periscope and she looked around, taking in her new surroundings.

'Uh-oh, looks like someone's awake. Damn, I was hoping I'd have another hour or so.'

'What's the problem?'

'She's going to want to hop out and stretch her legs.'

'I don't mind.' *It's not my office, and I won't be here for much longer, anyway.*

'Well, there's nothing we can do about it. If she wants to get out, she'll get out,' Damien said with a laugh.

Seconds later the joey had climbed out of the pouch, found her feet, and begun making her way around Jacqueline's office to check it out.

They tucked into their sandwiches – Damien with gusto, Jacqueline less so. She was pleased to see that Squish had his own lunch – a few crusts of wholemeal bread. She found herself struggling to be normal with Damien, to even look him in the eyes. But she'd sorted out the mess – well, as good as – so what was her problem?

Finally they were screwing up their paper wrappers and leaning back in their chairs, satisfied. An awkward silence loomed.

'So, how's it all going?' Jacqueline asked, and cursed how professional she sounded.

'All good. Coming together. Thankfully it's not as hectic as last week's whirlwind. Actually, can you look at the house plans and give your opinion?' he asked, reaching down and picking up a roll of papers she hadn't noticed. She'd been too busy thinking how good it was to see him, despite the fact he was a sad reminder that her career was over.

'Sure.'

They chuckled as the young roo did one more lap of Jacqueline's office before finding her pouch and somer-saulting back in.

'That's so cute,' she said, wistfully.

'It is. I never get tired of seeing her do that. Hey, are you okay?'

'Yes, fine. Why?'

'You don't seem totally yourself. You seem, I don't know, troubled.'

'Probably tired. It's been a crazy few weeks, though nothing compared to what you've been through.'

Damien frowned. 'Well, if you're sure. You'd tell me if something was wrong, wouldn't you?'

'Yep. It's all good,' she said, smiling, but unable to quite bring herself to look him in the eye. She felt a stab of guilt as sharp as a knife dig in under her ribs. Should she just tell him?

'Right, so,' he said, standing up to lean across her desk and unroll the plans. 'I just want to know if you think I need to make any alterations. I'm disappointed you didn't get to see through the place that day before …' Damien unrolled the large sheets without finishing his sentence and began collecting objects from her desk to hold the unruly corners down.

Suddenly they were both staring at the letter to Doctor Squire in full view on top of her in-tray. Damn it, she should have at least tucked it into one of the middle trays. But she'd become distracted by the cuteness of Damien and his small menagerie, and then hadn't really had a chance. Regardless, there, staring up at them in clear, bold, underlined type were the words: *Re: Resignation of psychologist position*. Jacqueline felt her cheeks heat up. Damien, frowning, looked from the piece of paper to Jacqueline.

'You're resigning?'

'It's okay. It's all good. *We're* all good,' she said, trying to sound bright.

'But I thought you liked it here in Wattle Creek.'

'I do.'

'So, why are you leaving?'

'I'm not.' *Well, I hope I'm not.*

Now Damien looked really confused. Jacqueline sighed, swallowed, took a deep breath, and opened her mouth. 'I've made a huge mistake …'

Damien sat in stunned silence as she told him everything. And then, just as she had that morning, he tried to find another solution. And to every suggestion, she shook her head. She'd been through every scenario, looked at it all from every angle.

'Resignation is the only way,' she said when they'd gone around and through it all for a second time.

Damien nodded a few times slowly. He clearly saw it now too. 'It's not fair,' he said sadly.

'I know it doesn't seem like that, but I should have known better.' *I still can't believe I managed to block it out.* 'I should never have got involved with you – well not for two years,' she said with a wry smile. It felt better to have it out in the open, as horrible as it was.

'I guess rules are rules. But you've worked so hard to get where you are. All those years of study just to …'

'Hey, it's okay, we've still got each other. This way there's no problem.' Jacqueline didn't like the look that crossed Damien's face. What was it – scepticism?

'But what if Doctor Squire accepts your resignation and doesn't ask you to stay on as an unregistered counsellor?'

It was the one option they hadn't discussed, as if voicing it might make it too real, or make it come true.

'I'll cross that bridge when and if I get to it.'

'But what about the town? We need you.'

'I'll still be here – nothing will change.'

'Only if Doctor Squire offers to keep you on.'

'Yes.'

'You're putting an awful lot of faith in him thinking of something out of the box.'

Jacqueline stayed silent. She knew that all too well.

'And you've said you've already been in trouble with him before ...'

'Yep.'

'I think you should be upfront about what you want. As it is, you're leaving far too much to chance. What does Auntie Ethel say?'

'I haven't had a chance to ask her. She's gone to visit her new granddaughter, Tilly.'

'Oh, that's right. But you could call her mobile.'

'I don't want to bother her with my problems.'

'Jacqueline, this isn't just your problem. This is potentially the whole town's problem – the whole *district's*.'

It was on the tip of Jacqueline's tongue to tell him he was being a bit melodramatic, but she could see how it might look to him. They'd never had a dedicated psychology service in the area before and now they were coming around to the idea of seeking help, discussing their problems – they wouldn't want it taken away.

They both sat silently for a few moments, Damien so deep in thought she could practically see cogs turning beneath his skull. She wondered what was churning there.

Finally, he looked up. 'Okay. So this is what I think,' he said boldly. 'We have to stop seeing each other.'

'What?' Jacqueline was engulfed by a mixture of fear and disbelief.

'I'm serious. We're no longer an item.'

'You're dumping me?' Jacqueline almost laughed. It was almost laughable. He was playing some kind of game. She wanted to tell him the room wasn't bugged – they didn't have to pretend in case someone was listening.

'Yes. We're not together. We're not doing anything wrong with regards to your ethics. I'm not going to be partially responsible for this town losing their psychologist and you losing your career after all the hard work you've put in.'

Jacqueline gaped at him. 'But ...'

'We'll just have to hope no one dobs you in. And then, in two years, or twenty three and a half months – or whatever it is – we'll be okay to take up where we left off.'

'Are you serious? You're prepared to wait two years for us to be together.'

'Jacqueline, I would wait a lifetime for you,' Damien said tenderly – so tenderly Jacqueline's throat constricted. 'In fact, I think I already have,' he added.

Tears filled Jacqueline's eyes and her throat swelled. *Shit. He's serious. Oh, my God, I really am being dumped.*

Damien shook his head sadly. 'You mean so much to me. I love you. But so does this town. Look what everyone's done for me. How can I repay them by taking you away?'

'But ... Surely ...'

'Surely there's another way? There isn't, not to keep you as a registered psychologist and here in town – you said so yourself. Please don't cry. We'll be okay. Just … not right now.'

Jacqueline was stunned, speechless, as Damien calmly rolled up the plans spread across her desk and replaced the rubber bands, and then hoisted the joey's pouch back onto his chest, all the time being careful not to meet her gaze.

'I guess we'll see you around,' he said with a shrug and wan smile. 'Come on, Squish.' The dog hopped off the chair with a little groan and trotted after his master.

Damien turned at the open door and paused. Jacqueline could see his eyes were filled with tears. Her heart lurched. But a moment later the door closed quietly with a metallic clunk.

Jacqueline yearned to have someone wrap their arms around her. She brought her hands to her face as if to keep the emotion at bay. She expected a flood of tears, but it didn't happen. Her whole chest was a painful ache, and she was so heavy she felt glued to her chair.

But as she sat there taking it all in, turning it all over, she realised she felt a little relieved. Gradually the feeling intensified into enormous gratitude and incredible awe towards Damien. He'd put aside his own feelings for the town, put her career ahead of his own happiness. God. Jacqueline knew there was no way she would have had such courage. She only hoped she'd find some way to be able to wait for him. Two years seemed a very long time.

She dragged the resignation letter from her in-tray and stared at it for a split second before poking it into the small shredder under her desk.

Chapter Four

Damien, settled in the safety of his ute, gripped the steering wheel hard. He took a few deep breaths to ease his painfully thudding heart. It had taken every ounce of his being to keep putting one foot in front of the other across the car park and not turn and run back to Jacqueline, take her in his arms and say he'd made a terrible mistake.

But he hadn't made a terrible mistake. No, definitely not. Sometimes sacrifices had to be made for a greater good. And Jacqueline was good for this town; look how much she'd helped him. He couldn't deny others that just to have a relationship with her. And really, if they couldn't survive two years apart, then there would be no forever.

They'd have to avoid each other socially, or else everyone would still think they were properly together and if anyone got wind that they shouldn't be, there'd be trouble. He knew of a number of people in town who didn't have enough to occupy themselves and who would love nothing more than to be responsible for upholding a rule or two, regardless of who got hurt. No, best it got around that they'd split up. Better yet, he could see if Auntie Ethel could put the word out that they'd never really got it together and his announcement at the launch of Esperance was just him getting caught up in the emotion of it all. That might work. He blushed slightly as he thought about how he'd stood up there in front of everyone and declared he and Jacqueline were an item. How bloody embarrassing. He really wished he hadn't done that. Perhaps if he hadn't, he wouldn't be in this predicament. But it was done. And, anyway, Jacqueline wasn't the sort to choose to do the wrong thing. That she seemed to have strong principles and integrity was something he found most attractive about her. And she wasn't exactly ugly, either.

Though he had to admit knowing she was in her little house right across the road from his aunt would make it a damned sight harder. 'Well, I guess that's that then, Squish,' he said. It was nice of Squish to have the good grace to look sad too. Damien took a deep breath. No point crying over spilt milk, Auntie Ethel would say, though probably not in this situation. 'God, listen to me; anyone would think I just lost the girl of my dreams. But I haven't. It's just been put on hold temporarily. Put on ice. Yeah, I'll be needing plenty of cold showers.'

Squish looked up and wagged his tail slowly.

'Well, lots to do,' Damien said, forcing his tone to be upbeat. He owed it to Jacqueline – and himself – to not fall apart. She didn't need to feel guilty for him losing his way again. With a heavy heart, Damien turned the key in the ignition and drove off.

He paused before exiting the car park and shook his head slowly, wondering how she of all people could have made such a big oversight. God, she must have really been shaken up by the events of the past few weeks. He felt a fresh wave of hatred towards Jacob Bolton rush through him. And of course Jacqueline's sudden immersion into the realities of summer in rural South Australia hadn't helped. The poor girl. He liked the idea of protecting her from more stuff, but he couldn't now. That made him feel even sadder than the thought of not sharing a bed with her for the next two years.

He got a fright and waved self-consciously as a white car drove around him to exit the car park on the wrong side of the driveway. He didn't recognise the driver – or the car – about two in three vehicles were white around here. He smiled to himself. In the city the person might have sat behind him and honked and got all hot under the collar. He watched the news and had seen the reports of road rage. Not out here. The only time you'd see two blokes stopped on the road was for a yarn. God, he loved the place, with or without Jacqueline Havelock in his bed or arms.

*

Damien managed to keep himself busy pondering his new venture, and adding notes to his growing Esperance Animal Welfare Farm operational folders. It had struck him on the way home from town that since the joey would never be able to be released into the wild, she really should have a name. He loved the name Jemima.

But better than him naming her would be running a competition, which would generate interest and raise the farm's profile. Better yet, if he could somehow raise some funds in the process …

He really should pull his finger out and get into Facebook properly, set up an Esperance page – see if he could get word of mouth going beyond the district. He'd had a Facebook account for ages, but he didn't go on it much. He'd quickly got tired of seeing people writing boring, stupid stuff like what they were having for dinner and where they were at any given time of the day. Who gave a shit if you'd just checked into Maccas at Port Augusta – how was that anything worth writing about?

But if he wanted to get word out about Esperance, he'd have to get on board; he couldn't rely on Auntie Ethel and the people in town to do everything for him. He'd accepted all the friend requests he'd received, and had quite a healthy number – another good thing about a district of fifteen hundred people all knowing each other and taking up a new fad like sheep. It might be quite useful for Esperance. He couldn't believe he hadn't thought about it right at the start. He wondered about a website. He knew he needed one – what legitimate organisation in the twenty-first century didn't have a website? – but he'd avoided looking into it. He didn't much play well with computers. What he needed was a twelve-year-old he could pay peanuts to, but the Facebook page would be a start. He got out his new laptop and opened Facebook.

At nine-thirty when it was time for bed – well, for a few hours until the next joey feed – Damien was tired and distracted. He hadn't done the page – he'd decided he'd wait until he'd taken some decent photos to put up before launching and bothering everyone with asking them to 'like' it. With a sigh, Damien made himself a Milo.

'Well, guys, it's back to the box for entertainment for us,' he said. Squish took it as a cue to stretch out beside him on the bed and get more comfortable, and the joey as a sign it was time to poke her head out of her pouch and rub her face with her paws.

'Yep, you're right, could be worse,' he said, scratching the tight belly Squish was presenting to him.

He picked up the phone to send a goodnight text to the love of his life before dropping it like a hot potato. It was amazing how quickly a habit could form. He felt stung and decidedly sad when he realised he'd have to wait two years to send Jacqueline another text.

Chapter Five

Jacqueline was getting on with things. She had no option other than to act as if her life was business as usual. Yes, she was sad about Damien, but it was her own doing, and she deserved to suffer at least a little. She felt guilty about what she was putting Damien through and every few minutes, when she wasn't adequately otherwise distracted, had to tell herself he was fine. He'd shown more spine than she had of late. Today, her packed morning of appointments had kept her mind focussed. She'd even remembered to pack her lunch.

Last night she'd busied herself with sorting out a replacement for the car lost in the fire that had destroyed Damien's home. She'd decided it was safer to avoid getting embroiled in any competitiveness between the two car dealers in town and just replace her VW Golf with another from the place in Adelaide where she'd got her original one.

Her dad was going to go in today and choose one for her and sort out all the paperwork. In her late twenties and supposedly an independent woman, she should be doing it herself, but it was quite impossible to do from so far away. Her dad had said he was happy to take care of it, and she secretly thought he appreciated being asked. Taking care of their children was what fathers enjoyed, wasn't it? Especially now he had so much free time on his hands.

It still bothered her that it had taken her parents so long to 'fess up about his arthritis and his plans to scale back his work commitments, but it was really none of her business what they did with their lives. Shockingly, she was actually quite thrilled they were moving to Wattle Creek just as soon as they'd sorted everything out. Perhaps she was growing up properly after all – monumental career blunder aside, of course.

Eileen and Philip were definitely going ahead with doing up the old cottage they'd found next to Damien's property. According to her father, they'd got it for a song. Apparently the few acres with it weren't large enough to be productive and the place had for years been a bit of a thorn in the side of the family who'd owned it.

'It's a win-win,' her mother had announced in the sort of tone that suggested she'd just learnt some new lingo. They hadn't decided yet if they would go ahead with opening a B&B. One step at a time. They'd renovate the cottage and then see how they felt.

Jacqueline thought they had rocks in their heads even contemplating it. They certainly didn't need the money, and wouldn't. But she supposed Eileen, after a lifetime of being a stay-at-home mother and wife, felt it was her time to do something for herself. And she would be a great host, no doubt about that. She also loved to clean. Jacqueline wished she'd inherited that trait.

She hadn't told her parents about her and Damien. It was more the sort of conversation to be had in person – especially since they'd be here soon enough. Well, that's what she told herself, refusing to accept she was being gutless. When she'd got off the phone to them this morning, she'd been concerned her dad might be in touch with Damien about Esperance. If so, would he tell Philip about the break-up? She didn't think so – they would talk business and Damien would leave it up to Jacqueline to spill the beans to her parents. Not having to tell them would be good but she knew it was, sadly, unavoidable. They'd have to know the full story sometime.

Jacqueline had just finished writing up the notes of her most recent client and was contemplating getting her lunch out of the little fridge when there was a gentle tap on the door.

'Come in,' she called. The door opened and Ethel's head appeared around it.

'Are you busy? I figure it's about your lunchtime. Or do you have plans?' she asked.

'No, no. Come on in.' Jacqueline stood and made her way from behind the desk to give the old lady, her dear friend, a hug. When she did, she didn't want to let go. Since discovering her career hung in the balance, Jacqueline had so craved the comfort of a hug – especially one of Ethel's. Oh God, it felt so good. She really didn't want to let go.

'Golly. I was only gone a day and a half,' Ethel said with a laugh as she extricated herself from Jacqueline's grasp. 'Anyone would think you missed me.'

'I did miss you.' *Like you wouldn't believe.*

'Right, well, I come bearing zucchini slice and salad. And then buttered date loaf for afters.'

'Oh, you shouldn't have.'

'Fiddlesticks. You provide the company – for which I am very grateful – and I'm only too happy to provide the food,' Ethel said, starting to lay a red and white gingham tablecloth across Jacqueline's empty desk. Ethel dropping in had become a bit of a ritual for them, starting as morning tea to welcome Jacqueline while she was finding her feet. Now she had so many more clients, Ethel kept any visits to lunchtime. And today, her timing had been impeccable as always. Jacqueline's lunch of leftover chicken risotto could wait another day.

'God, you're a sight for sore eyes,' Jacqueline said, letting out a deep sigh as she accepted her plate of food and cutlery wrapped in a linen napkin that matched the tablecloth. Shit, she hadn't meant to say the words out loud.

Ethel paused with her plate suspended and scrutinised Jacqueline sitting across from her. 'Why, what's happened?'

'Nothing, just a lot on,' Jacqueline said, trying for dismissive, even waving her bound cutlery for effect. 'Dad's sorting out my car,' she babbled in an effort to distract Ethel, who rarely missed anything. 'I'm just going to replace the hatch. It's easier than dealing with the politics of choosing one car dealer over another.' *And I don't need to consider a small four-wheel drive now there's no Damien and me and no back and forth to his farm.* That was the reason she hadn't rung the VW dealership straight away, she now remembered.

'Hmm, probably best,' Ethel said thoughtfully, and cut into the plate of food in front of her.

'So, how was the visit with your daughter and baby Tilly?'

'Exhausting! To be honest. She's a sweet baby and Sarah seems to be coping in her new role of mother very well. I thought being a grandmother was meant to be nothing but fun. But I'm exhausted, and I was only there for one night! Tilly's got a great set of lungs on her. I really don't have the patience I once had.'

'Nonsense, look at all you did for the injured buck and joey – and right through the nights.'

'Hmm, maybe I don't like human babies very much. And don't you dare tell my daughter that, if ever she deigns to visit!'

Jacqueline laughed. 'My lips are sealed,' she said. 'Did you like Sarah when she was a baby?'

'I think so. I always gooed and gahhed over baby animals, but I was never really clucky or desperate for a human baby, but back then it was what one did, no questions asked. If I had my time again I might have chosen a different path – not that Sarah hasn't brought me a great deal of joy and pride along the way. It's just that children do cause you a lot of worry – you never stop. Oh, listen to me, going on like an old crow. I'm just sleep deprived and it felt like a long drive. It's very good to be home.'

'And it's very good to have you home.'

'So you indicated. I'd like to know why, specifically,' Ethel said, narrowing her eyes to stare pointedly at Jacqueline.

Jacqueline shifted in her chair and kept eating.

'There is something going on with you. And don't you dare take me for a fool and say there isn't, that all is fine. Because it's not,' she said, waving her fork at Jacqueline across the desk. 'Come on, spill, as you young ones say.'

Jacqueline put her knife and fork down. 'Speaking of fools – oh, Ethel, I've been the biggest.'

'Oh? Are you in trouble with Doctor Squire again?'

'No. Not yet. I didn't know how I could have forgotten, totally blocked it out – that's the really worrying bit,' Jacqueline rambled.

'Dear, you're not making any sense.'

Jacqueline shook her head as if to get the jumble in her mind into some sort of order.

'Getting involved with Damien was a breach of my professional ethics.'

'But he's not a patient any more, and you weren't involved when he was.'

'It doesn't matter. There's a twenty-four month exclusion period. I'll lose my registration.'

'Oh, hell.'

'Exactly.'

'So can you ask someone for an exemption or something?'

'I don't think so.'

'Well, haven't you asked?'

'There's no need. Damien dumped me, so technically I'm not doing anything wrong now. I'll be fine if no one realises the rule exists and I don't get dobbed in.'

'Now, hang on. Go back a bit. Damien dumped you? Why?'

'Because of all of this. He doesn't want me losing my registration and this town losing their psychology services.'

'Oh, bless him. The poor boy.'

'Tell me about it.'

'So, what does Squire say about this?'

'He doesn't know. If I confide in him, the mandatory reporting clause as part of *his* ethics will mean he has to report me.'

'Christ, you really have got yourself into a pickle, haven't you? Did you know about this twenty-four month thing, or could you plead ignorance if it came to it?'

'Yes, I knew about it. But for some reason, I totally forgot, blocked it out or something. Not exactly a sound defence,' Jacqueline said, colouring with embarrassment.

'Well, dear, what with moving out here, having that thug turn up to stalk you and losing your car in the fire, I'm not surprised it slipped your mind. Could that be a defence? What do they call it – extenuating circumstances?'

'Yes, that's the right word. But I doubt it.'

'But you haven't asked?'

'No. Well, Damien's solved it.'

'But has he? You're okay with waiting for two years before you can be together? If you are, you've got better patience than me, my girl!'

'I don't have a choice. *We* don't have a choice.'

'But you're made for each other.'

'I thought so too,' Jacqueline said sadly.

'How could you have been so stupid?' Ethel suddenly scolded quite loudly.

'Don't worry, Ethel, you couldn't make me feel any worse than I already do.'

'I'm sorry. I'm just annoyed with the system, or your profession, or whoever's rule it is.'

'Rules are there for a reason – in this case to protect the vulnerable.'

'But he only saw you a couple of times.'

'Once would have been enough.'

'I still think Squire needs to know. Maybe he can offer a solution – write to the board, beg them to give you an exception because of being a vital rural service, or something.'

'Don't you dare tell him. While he doesn't know and I'm not involved with Damien, my job is safe, and the community service is safe.'

'But surely you can see that that's not workable – not in the long term.'

'It's early days, I know, but I don't have a choice. We'll have to wait to be together.'

'But you're still running the gauntlet, hoping no one dobs you in, because you'd still get in trouble for the past week or so, even if it's over, wouldn't you?' Ethel said thoughtfully.

'Yes.'

'That's no way to live.'

No, but it's now my reality.

'Poor Damien. After all he's been through,' Ethel said, and, after a shake of her head, she resumed eating her meal.

Jacqueline followed her lead. While she ate, she could see the intense concentration etched in Ethel's worn face. She was trying to find a way out of this mess. But there was no way. Well, there was – to come clean and resign. But Damien had taken that option off the table.

When the silence stretched into awkward territory, they automatically turned to talk of the weather – how it had been, what the forecast was predicting, and how most of the time the reports got it wrong.

Finally, Ethel had repacked her picnic basket and was ready to leave.

'Thanks for lunch. And I'm so sorry,' Jacqueline said, hugging her friend at the door. It was a much quicker, looser hug than earlier, but she was grateful. She only hoped her friend's new demeanour was down to being distracted rather than being angry at her. Poor Ethel was now as good as in the middle of everything. Being a fixer and a strong leader in the community, she'd struggle to sit back and leave well alone. Jacqueline really hoped she would. Any well-meaning intervention could have the opposite result. The trouble with Ethel – and Jacqueline was seeing a similar trait in many of her patients out here – was that she tended to consider things quite clear cut, black and white. Country people seemed to be practical people who thought things were simply right or wrong. In this case, she feared Ethel considered Jacqueline right for the town and right for Damien and the psychology board and its rules keeping them apart wrong, and might get it into her head to do something about it.

Jacqueline deliberately hadn't told her about the glimmer of hope that was renouncing her registration and begging Doctor Squire to keep her on as a counsellor.

Deep down, she was struggling with whether Damien was worth giving up her precious pieces of university paper she'd worked so hard for. She knew she loved him and was serious about making a life with him. Such a thought was very selfish. But she didn't want to one day resent Damien and their relationship for her sacrifice. She might be new at counselling people and having a proper adult relationship, but she knew enough to know that's how it went more often than not when tough choices had to be made. She knew Damien could see it and if he didn't he would when she pointed it out. So, while being apart was bad, it was best for the long-term health of their relationship. Perhaps she should have explained that to Ethel. But then she would have come off looking self-absorbed – making it all about her: What if *I* resent him later? And it probably showed a weakness in her character.

It was a mess, but at that moment it was contained. She only hoped Ethel would leave well alone and things would stay the way they were – not ideal, but workable.

But the reality was she had no control over what Ethel, or anyone else, was going to do. All she could do was hope for the best.

Chapter Six

Damien put Squish and the joey in her pouch in the front of the ute and clipped Bob and Cara on the back. He gave the two farm dogs an extra few pats, making a big fuss of them as he thought for the umpteenth time back to the amazing job they had done getting the sheep moved amid the smoke, chaos and stress of the fire. They deserved a bloody medal for saving all those lives. Yeah, the sheep were insured to the hilt along with everything else thanks to his mum, but Damien was pretty sure hearing the stock as they died in pain and seeing a whole mob of blackened corpses would have sent him over the edge. Sight was a powerful sense, but he reckoned smell and sound could even be worse for creating lasting memories. He'd never forget the smell of the singed fur of the young buck – that was etched on his mind. Thankfully there had been a good outcome, otherwise he'd have more, worse, nightmares than he already did. Thanks to these guys, he didn't have to close his eyes at night and see his sheep writhing around and hear them screaming out in pain.

'You guys did so well,' he said, rubbing their ears. 'Come on, let's take another look around.' Damien liked getting out and taking a drive around his place, even more so now after the fire. While he hated seeing the black areas where he'd lost valuable stubble and pasture, it was a good reminder of how much worse it all could have been.

He drove over the rise. There were the dozen or so kangaroos he'd seen the other morning happily grazing. They collectively raised their heads to determine the level of threat. Damien skirted around them, being careful to leave plenty of distance.

Paused at the top of the next rise, he watched his two thousand or so sheep down in the gully grazing as carefree as they'd always done. If only they knew how lucky they were. He hadn't lost all of his feed and his last crop had been good, so there was plenty of stubble. He'd always resented sheep until recently; he'd been angry at the world and they'd really just got in the way. But he'd changed. God, if someone had told him this time last year how different he'd be he'd have told them they were crazy.

'Well, they all look happy enough, eh, Squish?' he said, patting the little rotund dog stretched out on the seat beside him.

Satisfied that all was fine in his patch of the great outdoors, Damien headed back to his van, waving an arm out the window in greeting to the guys in the tip trucks and loaders who were cleaning up the remains of his house and taking it away. They should be finished today. He was glad for all the community support – left to his own devices, he might have just carted it up behind the scrub and dumped it just out of sight along with the several generations of dead cars already there. But this was a much better result.

He'd just got settled with a cup of coffee when there was a tap on the door. He was a little taken aback as he hadn't heard a vehicle pull up. But then he wouldn't would he, he realised, over the roar of the loaders. He got up and opened the door, fully expecting it to be one of the truck drivers needing him for something.

But it wasn't. Standing there just below the steps was his mother. Since when did she knock and not just barge in? Now there was a turn-up for the books. Tina never just dropped by, it was always for something to do with the farm or to tell him his house was a mess.

'Mum. Hi. Come in,' he said, pushing the door wide. She looked a little tired, but then she was going through a marriage break-up. That'd do it. Thank God she'd finally seen the light and turfed out the dickhead old shearer. Fancy the cheeky bastard having a bit on the side for months. So much for this town not being able to keep a secret. And he couldn't believe someone who had so clearly been hit with the ugly stick pulling two reasonably good-looking sorts. Perhaps Leanne – the other woman – had been lonely like his mum.

He sure hoped his mum wasn't wasting too much energy on Geoff. Oh well, it was none of his business. All he had to do was refrain from knocking the bloke's head off when he saw him next. Though, hell, he'd

been restraining himself from doing that since practically the day he'd hooked up with Tina. Then he'd kept
his opinions and fists to himself. Now he was a different
bloke anyway. A lover, not a fighter, as the saying went,
he thought with a chuckle to himself.

'Coffee?' he asked. 'I've just made one.'

'Yes, thanks.'

'So how are you settling in?' she asked, seated on the
lounge behind the small table and looking around. 'This
looks comfortable.'

'Yeah, it's good. Pretty small, but does the trick.'
And beggars can't be choosers. That thought ran through
his mind quite a bit these days – usually when he got
frustrated at not having his own stuff around him.
He'd walked past the framed photos on the mantel
every day for years and not paused or given them a
second thought. Now he'd give his right arm to have
them back. It really was the little things that were the
hardest to deal with. But he kept reminding himself
that he had his memories of his dad, was now fulfill-
ing his dream, and he had Squish, Cara and Bob, so he
was damned lucky. He needed to stop moaning and
dwelling.

'How's the trip planning going?' he asked for something to say.

'Slowly. I'm holding off booking flights until my
passport arrives. Apparently you can get some great last-
minute deals.'

Well, would you listen to that, Damien thought, *the world's
most organised person holding off for last-minute flights!* He
almost snorted at the unlikeliness of it. But she didn't look

uptight; that as-tightly-wound-as-a-spring-waiting-to-uncoil-at-any-moment intensity was missing. She seemed relatively okay in the circumstances.

'Have you spoken to Lucy?'

'I've left a couple of messages. I think I keep getting the time difference wrong,' she said, lifting a hand from her mug and then putting it back again.

Damien reckoned his sister, Lucy, was more than likely right by the phone each time, listening to the messages, pacing back and forth in her shoebox–sized apartment, trying to figure out how to stop her mother visiting.

He rarely spoke to Lucy – they really had nothing in common – but he'd actually been half-expecting a panicked distress call from his sister regarding Tina's impending visit. *Good to be kept out of it,* he thought. Anyway, it was Lucy's turn to put up with their mother – he'd had her dropping in, looking him and his house up and down, finding fault and criticising him for all these years. Let his sister have it for a few days. In his mind, it wouldn't go well.

He couldn't understand why Tina was doing it. Surely she remembered how they really didn't get on? Though Tina didn't tend to be the most perceptive person around. He was really beginning to see that, now his eyes had been opened by Jacqueline. But even he, with his limited knowledge of the human species, could see that his mother was totally self-absorbed and tended not to notice, or chose to ignore, the negative body language of anyone around her. Hence, the whole Geoff thing. *I rest my case.* He loved his mum – that was programmed

in from day one, right? – but he could also see that she
was her own worst enemy.

Auntie Ethel had said this trip to see Lucy was all about
what people think. One must go and visit one's daughter
if she's moved away. It was expected: impressions were
everything out here. And there would never be an utter-
ance of, 'Oh, no, I won't stay with my daughter, we don't
really get on.' You might get, 'Oh, no, I won't stay with
my daughter, she really doesn't have the space,' to save face.
People constructed all sorts of facades to avoid looking
like they had a failing. Heaven forbid one admitted to
having a problem, especially a dysfunctional family. He'd
been caught up in the mindset, too, and look where that
had nearly ended. He might be a clueless bloke when it
came to all this sort of stuff, but he wasn't blind or stupid.
And if Tina thought she was going to go off to London
and stay in her daughter's tiny flat for even a few days and
it not end very badly, then she clearly was blind and/or
stupid. Someone should point that out. But it wouldn't be
him. He'd stay well out of it. If she needed taking to the
airport down in Lincoln and collecting again, fine, but
that was going to be the extent of his involvement.

'She could at least phone me back,' Tina said.

'Well, I'm sure she's pretty busy with her job and
social life, and everything,' he said lamely. *And avoiding
her mother.* That was the good thing about numbers
appearing on phones these days – you could choose who
you picked up for.

'So, how's everything going?'

'Good. Good. Lots to do though,' he said. This was
getting bloody awkward. Any minute now and he

would have to resort to asking after her with regards the break-up, and he really didn't want to do that and risk tears. It wasn't tears, per se, he had a problem with, but Tina – always stoic – bursting into tears and needing comforting would completely freak him out.

Just as the awkward silence was descending, there was another knock on the door. *Saved by the bell – well, sort of,* he thought with relief and got up.

There stood a bloke he didn't know the name of but thought looked vaguely familiar. He held a cardboard apple box – the sort with a lid that slid over the top of an inner box and had air holes in the sides. 'Um, er, you take unwanted animals, don't you?' he said, thrusting the box at Damien.

'Yes, we do,' Damien said, accepting it.

'Cool, thanks.' The man bolted back to the old white Commodore parked nearby.

Damien stood wondering if he should do anything else. This was his first case of surrender. It would have been hard enough for the guy to front up without worrying about being asked questions. He shuddered as he thought about how it would have been far easier for him to drown the creatures or leave them to die somewhere – like on the side of the road, as someone had done with Squish. He felt a wave of gratitude towards the guy and on behalf of whatever was in the box. He really needed to set up something at the farm gate where people could remain totally anonymous, he thought. Perhaps he could leave a cheap mobile phone there – secured so no bastard could steal it – so people could alert him when they'd left something. Hmm.

He'd ponder it. There was a growing list of ponderings, he realised, as he turned and went back inside.

He put the box on the table and noticed his mother's nose wrinkle in distaste. He ignored her – if he wanted to put a box of puppies, or kittens, or whatever, on the table of his temporary home, then he bloody well would. He'd wipe the table down before he next ate from it – not that he ate *from* it; he used plates like a civilised person. What was important right now was the welfare of these animals.

'You're clearly busy. I'll get going and leave you to it.'

'Okay. Thanks for stopping in,' Damien said, already distracted by what was inside the box. He really hoped it wasn't dead bodies. He waited until the door closed behind his mother before sliding the lid off.

Four of the smallest kittens he'd ever seen were huddled on newspaper – one black and white, one tabby grey, one ginger and a dark motley one that his dad would have referred to as prunes-and-custard coloured. Okay, so this was now serious. It was one thing to rescue two roos off his own land after a fire and nurse them back to health, but this was the future. This taking in unwanted creatures, making sure they were healthy, getting them desexed before they went back out into the big wide world. Not to mention educating those out in the big wide world about Esperance Animal Welfare Farm.

'Okay, little guys,' he said, stroking them. But, shit, they were tiny, and he knew diddly squat about kittens. They needed milk, didn't they? But cats are lactose intolerant, aren't they? He'd read or heard that somewhere.

Panic gripped him. God, had he done the wrong thing going into animal rescue? Where was Auntie Ethel when he needed her? He had to pull himself together.

He was debating whether to get out his laptop and Google, phone Ethel, phone the RSPCA, or phone Philip Havelock when there was another knock at the door. Christ, it's like bloody Rundle Street here this morning, he thought, the stressful situation making him jumpy.

He nearly cried with relief upon seeing his auntie Ethel standing there. 'Thank God you're here,' he said, ushering his bewildered aunt up the steps and inside. 'I need your help.'

'Whatever is the matter?' she asked, but then peered into the box. 'Oh, look at you guys, what cuties. So, what's the problem?'

'What do I feed them? They're tiny.'

'Dear boy, do calm down.'

'It's my first real case,' he said, rubbing a hand through his hair. He couldn't believe how undone he'd become. He really needed to get a grip – for the sake of the kittens, if not for himself.

'They need formula. Remember, I put a tin in the top cupboard along with instructions and some bottles and teats for when this day arrived?' Ethel said kindly, patting his hand.

'Oh, God, that's right. Maybe you should be running this show, not me.'

'Fiddlesticks. You'll be fine. You just need to get into a rhythm. And stay calm. It's early days. You know you can always ring me – day or night.'

'I was just about to, actually,' he said sheepishly. 'So why are you here, anyway?'

'Let's just get these guys organised.'

Damien acted on Ethel's instructions and soon they each had two kittens happily suckling. Food, warmth, tender loving care; it's all they need, he told himself. He couldn't really get it wrong; whatever he did was better than them being abandoned to die a slow, lonely death. He really had to remember that next time, and remain calm. He was cut out for this.

'Right, now, what's this I hear about you ending things with Jacqueline?' Auntie Ethel said when the kittens were back snoozing in their box to which Damien had added some softer bedding.

Damien sighed. He needed an interrogation like he needed a hole in the head. He passed a mug of coffee to Ethel and sipped from his own.

'Auntie Ethel, it's for the best. If you know, then Jacqueline's told you, and you know the full story. I don't have the energy to go through it again.'

'But ...'

'But nothing. We've gone through the options. This is the only way. I don't want her losing her career after all her hard work or the town losing its service – I know first-hand how much she can help. And, anyway, the last thing I need down the track is her resenting me for choosing me over her career. I know a bit about resentment ...

'She's worked hard to be where she is, Auntie, and she shouldn't be punished. Yes, she stuffed up. But we've all stuffed up one time or another. Granted, probably not in such a big way. When we get together, I don't want there to be any roadblocks or any chance of resentment. I'd wait five, ten years for her if I had to. I wouldn't want to, but I would,' he said wearily. 'So, please don't make me feel any worse about it than I already do.'

'Okay, consider me put back in my box,' Ethel said, raising two hands as a gesture of surrender.

'Sorry, I've just …'

'It's okay. No need to apologise. I really just wanted to make sure you're okay. I'm sorry for seeming like I was going at you like a bull at a gate. I'm just sad and frustrated about it, which I'm sure is nothing compared to how you're feeling.'

'It's okay. *I'm* okay. Honest. We'll get through, it'll just take some time. Meanwhile, I've got my hands full here thanks to my growing menagerie.' He offered Ethel a smile to reassure her.

Chapter Seven

On Friday morning there was a knock on Jacqueline's closed office door. Since the Damien and then Ethel visits, she was surprised to find herself becoming a little jumpy when a knock sounded. In some ways she wished she'd carried on with tendering her resignation and coming clean about everything to Doctor Squire, because now every time there was a knock on her door she didn't recognise, like now, her heart rate spiked. It was ridiculous, she kept telling herself. She was fine. As if anyone out here would figure out about her breach of ethics, let alone care enough to dob her in. She really had to just settle back into life and work and stop giving it all so much thought. At this rate it would become a self-fulfilling prophecy.

She swallowed and called, 'Come in.' Then breathed a slight sigh of relief when Louise from reception entered.

'Got a minute?' she asked.

'Sure.'

She watched as Louise made herself comfortable in one of Jacqueline's padded vinyl chairs.

'Sorry to hear about you and Damien not working out.'

'Thanks,' she said, dropping her head. So that was how quickly word got around.

'He's always been a bit of an odd one – in a quiet, brooding way.'

Jacqueline briefly toyed with telling Louise the truth and defending Damien in the process. Just because someone was careful with their words and used them sparingly, it did not make them odd. But she thought better of it. The fewer people who knew the truth, the safer her job was. And she didn't know Louise – or Cecile for that matter – well enough to know just how much she could trust them.

She idly wondered who had told her. Only three people knew: Jacqueline, Damien, and Ethel. She knew she hadn't told anyone else and Damien wouldn't have said anything to anyone, she felt certain of that. She was disappointed to think Ethel would have gossiped about her – and her own nephew – but she had been pretty annoyed when she'd left the other day. Perhaps she'd needed to vent to someone.

Or, she suddenly thought, relaxing slightly, perhaps no one had said anything. Perhaps Damien had gone into the pub and, with him suddenly appearing again out on his own, people had put two and two together … Jacqueline forced her attention back to Louise, who she now realised had continued speaking.

'Sorry? What?'

'Tonight? Tea at the pub? Get you out and about again.'

'Oh, I don't know,' she said, remembering the telling off she'd got from Doctor Squire the night she'd overdone it out with Louise and Cecile. Though it might be nice to have some company and leave the house for a bit.

'Just a quiet meal. Promise we won't lead you astray again,' Louise said with a laugh. 'Be good for you to be seen out and about – show the blokes you're available again.'

Matchmaking seemed a favourite pastime out here. There seemed to be a high level of suspicion about people who were under sixty and not paired up. Or perhaps it was just Louise and Cecile. No doubt they were settled in their own lives and didn't have enough else to do, so they meddled in others'. Perhaps if Louise was so concerned about pairing people up she should work on her own circumstances. She refrained from pointing it out.

'Who's going?' Jacqueline asked.

'You weren't listening to a word I said. Just you, me, Cecile and Rob.'

'Sorry.'

'So, straight after work – five-thirty. I'll come by and collect you?'

'Sounds good,' Jacqueline said, trying to muster some enthusiasm.

'Well, have a good day.'

'You too.'

As she considered the closed door after Louise's departure, she thought back to the last time she'd been to the pub. It was the night Jacob had turned up, and the night she'd realised there was a lot more to Damien McAllister … She shuddered and pushed it all aside.

★

True to their word, Louise, Cecile and Rob took good care of Jacqueline, and she was home by eight. Rob had had a quick dinner – had apparently phoned through his order so it was ready right at six when the pub's kitchen officially started taking orders – so he could get to his SES meeting on time. The girls weren't in a hurry, so it was better this way, they said, when Jacqueline expressed her surprise. Yes, maybe it was more convenient for Rob, but it certainly wasn't polite. She really had to get used to how differently some things were done out here – like everyone being in your business.

She'd spent the first half-hour being grilled about Damien: who had dumped whom and why, et cetera. She'd deflected as best she could and managed to get away with saying it was mutual, that the timing was wrong, what with her being new in town and he being busy with his new venture. Eventually they'd seemed satisfied and gave a collective shrugging of shoulders and moved on to the next topic of gossip – a young lad who'd crashed his car and lost his licence for twelve months. Louise and Cecile had tutted and shaken their heads, but as far as Jacqueline could see, they were operating on a double standard. While they weren't staggering drunk when they'd left the pub the couple of nights she'd been out with them, there had never seemed to be a whole lot of thought given to driving home, and everyone had had more than she thought would keep you under the limit. Tonight she was pleased to see Rob had only been sipping water – on account of him heading off to

SES. But Louise and Cecile had downed three bourbon and Cokes to Jacqueline's one glass of wine, which was disgusting and lukewarm by the last sip. Oh, well, they were adults, they knew the risks. She couldn't nag them and come off looking like a wowser. Other than Ethel, they were the only real friends she'd made in town.

When Louise dropped her home – she'd half-heartedly tried to decline the offer, on account of the drink-driving risk, but her fear of walking alone when it was almost dark, thanks to Jacob Bolton, won – Ethel was out watering her front flower beds. Jacqueline waved Louise off and went across the street to say hi.

'You've been out,' Ethel said, with her hose trained at the base of a rose bush. 'Good to see you're not sitting home pining.'

Jacqueline felt a bubble of annoyance burst inside her. 'Did you tell anyone about me and Damien splitting up?'

'Of course.'

Jacqueline was taken aback. She'd been expecting a denial, or a confirmation and a sheepish look. Certainly not a cheerful admission.

'Why? Who?'

'I told Madge down the road, who is one of the biggest gossips in town, and also happens to be young Louise from the surgery's gran.'

Jacqueline frowned. Why the hell was Ethel looking so damned pleased with herself? She grew more annoyed. 'Why can't you stay out of other people's business?'

Ethel sighed, went over and turned off the tap, wound the hose up on its reel, and took it back to beside the house. Jacqueline stood there not knowing if she was expected to stay or if this was Ethel signalling she wasn't wasting any more breath on the topic and their conversation was over. For Jacqueline, it was far from over.

Finally Ethel looked up at her and spoke. 'Sounds like you need a cup of tea.'

I don't need a bloody cup of tea, Jacqueline wanted to snap, *I need an explanation or for you to mind your own bloody business*. But instead she meekly followed Ethel inside.

'Now, don't go getting all uppity with me, missy,' Ethel said, pointing her finger at Jacqueline as she waited at the bench to tend the pot. 'I did it for your own good.'

Jacqueline opened her mouth to protest.

'Uh-uh, just hear me out,' Ethel said, raising a silencing hand.

Jacqueline shut her mouth and clasped her hands tightly together under the table.

'You need the town to know there is nothing between you and Damien so no one gets wind you've done anything wrong with regards your career, right?'

Jacqueline nodded.

'So, what better way than to get the news going through the oldies and the young ones at once?'

Jacqueline wondered if Louise and Cecile had invited her out of their own accord or been manipulated by Ethel. She really didn't like all this meddling going on around her and involving her. But she was starting to see it was being done for the right reason. Ethel's heart was in the right place. But it still rankled.

'Yes, Louise's invitation tonight was off her own bat,' Ethel said, startling Jacqueline slightly. Did the woman have psychic abilities as well? 'Not that I wouldn't have pulled a few strings in that direction, too, if need be.' Ethel grinned naughtily. When that grin came out, Jacqueline could never be annoyed with the old lady.

'God, Ethel, you're incorrigible,' she said, smiling and shaking her head slowly, rolling her eyes as a steaming cup of tea was placed in front of her.

'Friends again?'

'Yes, but you have to stop meddling.'

'Now, that I cannot promise. Not when it's for a good cause. And you, my dear, are a good cause. But, seriously, it's one thing for a rumour to go around about you and Damien, but it's even better to back it up with a sighting, actual evidence.'

'You make me sound like the Loch Ness monster, or Big Foot, or something.'

'Well, you are a local attraction.'

As she sipped her tea, it struck Jacqueline that creating the news around her and Damien might have the opposite of the desired result; that putting their names in the front of people's minds again might get people thinking, and then someone might … No, she was being paranoid. No one cared about her private life – well, they did if you asked Ethel … But still. She reminded herself of a quote she'd heard a few times: No one thinks of us nearly as often as we think they do. Well, she thought that was how it went. And, anyway, whatever was going to happen, was going to happen. She'd done her best to right a wrong situation for the good of all concerned. She really just had to put it out of her mind and get on.

In the next breath, Ethel changed the subject. 'It's time you went and did some community talks over at Hope Springs. How would next Tuesday work – seven p.m.? CWA?'

'It's very short notice, isn't it? And I thought they only met during the day.'

'Ah, doesn't take much to rally the troops. And they do usually only meet during the day. But I said you're far too busy now with your growing list to go gallivanting around the countryside during work hours,' Ethel said with a wave of her hand. 'It'll be organised by the CWA – so you can be assured of a good spread! – but it'll most likely be open to all women of the town and area. Hospital auxiliary, church ladies of various congregations, et cetera. So are you in?'

'I'm in. On one condition.'

'Name it.'

'No, actually, two conditions.'

'Now don't you go getting all demanding on me,' Ethel said.

'One, you come with me. And, two, you squirrel away a plate of the best sweets and savouries for me like last time.'

'I have to go – you'll need a car on account of you not having got one yet. Remember? And on point two, consider it done.' Ethel clapped her hands together. 'Good, all sorted. I'll start properly rallying the troops.'

They lapsed into silence, lost in their own thoughts.

'Damien is fine, in case you're wondering,' Ethel said. 'He's busy with all his stuff. Plus he's taken delivery of four kittens needing round-the-clock feeding – dear little things. Just when the joey was about to be put on a more convenient meal schedule, too. He's just thrilled someone had the courage to deliver the little blighters, rather than leave them somewhere to die. He's going to do great.'

Jacqueline knew Ethel wasn't having a go at her, and hadn't actually added, 'No thanks to you,' but she still felt the words stab painfully under her ribs.

'Yes, he is,' she said, only sure she'd uttered the words when she heard them with her own ears. She was sad not to be a part of it, not to be able to phone, give him encouragement, go out and help with the workload. Four tiny mouths to feed at once must be difficult with just one pair of hands.

When Ethel began yawning, Jacqueline took it as her cue to leave. They hugged tightly at the door, their friendship clearly restored. Not that it had been completely severed, thanks to Ethel's firm hand.

Chapter Eight

Damien thought back over the past week, and felt a great sense of achievement. He'd settled into a routine and the kittens were doing well. He'd officially named the joey Jemima, having decided running a competition was too complicated and would take too long. The poor little thing was part of his growing family, so needed a name. She was now spending more time out of the pouch. He'd tried to start leaving her for short bursts in one of the smaller runs, though when he'd peeked through the caravan window after half an hour and she was still scratching at the wire door and trying to get out, he'd felt sorry for her and brought her back inside. The last thing he wanted was for her to be distressed. It would be different if she had other kangaroos for company, but she didn't.

Each morning and evening, he'd taken to making the three-kilometre round trip to the gate to check the depository, new enclosure he'd set up so people could make donations of food and bedding, and surrender unwanted animals. He'd set up an old phone he'd got from the second-hand store in a box attached under the little verandah and had left clear instructions on how to turn it on, send a text advising of delivery of an animal, and then how to turn if off again to preserve the battery. He thought it was pretty straightforward, and hoped it would make people feel more comfortable doing the right thing by the creatures of the district – maybe even beyond. He was going to try to rig up some sort of solar recharger for the phone, but at this stage he was still pondering how. Nonetheless, he was pleased with his efforts. It would be time-consuming and a bit of a pain to keep checking the enclosure, but he couldn't bring himself to totally trust the phone, or that people wouldn't just leave animals without notifying him. But it was a start.

He'd also figured out a contraption for feeding the four tiny kittens at once. He'd wrapped a shoebox in foam and then a towel – that could be washed – and poked holes through so the teats could stick out. Then he'd placed a rolled-up small towel in the shoebox so the bottles attached to the teats would be raised enough to keep the flow going right to the end. He'd put the whole thing in the large box with the kittens and, voila, he had a self-feeder, a pretend mother cat, for his little kittens. He'd work on perfecting his design, but for now it did the job, and he could always add more holes for more teats along the way if necessary. He was satisfied that his creation wasn't too far off feeling like their mother's tummy when the kittens paddled, if they used their imagination. But best of all, because it was contained in the larger box, he could take the kittens wherever he went and they could be fed on the move while he was out in the ute.

It had been a good few days, he thought as he had breakfast and checked the new Facebook page he'd set up. It had photos of the tiny kittens drinking from their self-feeder and a cute shot of Jemima with her head poking out of her pouch – he liked that he had a name to add to the caption. He'd even managed to get a great photo of Squish peering into the box of kittens as if overseeing proceedings. He'd got lots of 'likes' and even a few shares. He was beginning to see how Facebook could be a valuable marketing tool. When he got organised to do a major fundraiser, he might be able to save time and money by doing most of the advertising via Facebook.

Damien was starting to really enjoy the PR and marketing side of things. He'd never had to do anything like this to sell his grain and wool; you just took your load of grain to the silo or put your wool into the next sale. There was no having to suck up to people to get them to buy your produce. Perhaps, if he had his time again, or if this all went tits up – which he wouldn't let happen because the animals needed him – then he figured he wouldn't have minded giving this marketing caper a crack. He idly wondered if he should look into doing some short course or something to learn more. He was serious about Esperance Animal Welfare Farm being a huge success. And for the next two years he wouldn't have a relationship to distract him or take up his spare time.

With that thought in mind, he gathered his troops – Squish, Jemima, Bob and Cara – and set off to check the depository. On his walks, he always took Jemima's pouch – she insisted on tagging along, but only ever got a few metres before she was panting and unable to keep up. Damien would stop, bend down so she could hop into the pouch, and then they would carry on until the next time she decided she wanted to get out and hop, though she also spent plenty of time with her head out of the pouch, enjoying the sights. Damien knew this wouldn't last for much longer – soon she'd be too big for the pouch and too heavy for him to carry. She was growing like a weed, so he was determined to enjoy it while he could.

Squish's little legs struggled to keep up too, so he often had the pup perched on his shoulders. He was sure when Bob and Cara paused to look at him it was with pleading expressions for them to be carried too. Not a bloody chance! He felt like a pack horse as it was. Anyway, they needed the exercise, they were starting to look like lard-arses thanks to all the extra human treats – like little bits of cheese – he was giving them out of gratitude, despite telling himself they didn't expect it and had probably long forgotten the fire.

His little menagerie sure did bring a smile to his face and put a spring in his step. As he traipsed along, he pictured the four kittens, grown up, following in a line. But he had to stop himself – they were temporary visitors. Not all creatures who came his way could stay – he'd rehome them when he could. He wasn't going to be in the business of just collecting.

But he had plenty of space, and if he could earn enough, perhaps horses and donkeys could retire here. He stopped in his tracks. Where the hell had that come from? He hated horses. No, not hated horses, had hated having them on his property. After the last of his mother's and Lucy's horses had gone, he'd vowed there would never be another horse there again. He couldn't think of a reason why, except that it was the view of most farmers around here. And of course, while he'd been so unhappy he'd had a negative opinion on most things. He was starting to see that. His dad had loved horses. Now he quite liked the idea of the challenge of working with a spooked or mistreated horse to see if it could be retrained and then sold on to a good home.

One step at a time, Damo, he told himself. *The universe is going to send what the universe is going to send. Sit back and let it happen.*

He walked on. That was the trouble with being raised by a control freak − you weren't very inclined to stop and let the plan unfold. It was taking some reprogramming, but he was getting better at going with the flow. He wished his mother would see how uptight she was and how life could be better, easier, if you just sat back a bit.

She'd phoned him last night, all miffed because Lucy still hadn't called her back. It had been on the tip of his tongue to ask what she wanted him to do about it when she'd gone on to say that because of this she'd decided to take a tour rather than just book flights and do her own thing, and only spend two days and one night in London. The funny thing was that she'd said it in a haughty tone as if to say, 'That'll teach her.'

Damien had come close to pointing out that Lucy probably didn't consider her mother choosing to not impose for a week or so the punishment that was clearly intended. He really was beginning to see just how his mum made everything about her. Most likely Lucy would whoop with joy at learning she only had to spend a dinner and maybe an hour or so over lunch in her mother's presence. It was all too funny.

'People,' he told Squish, Bob, Cara, and Jemima, 'are weird. Now you guys have it all sorted. Food, sleep, only get cranky for good reason and when necessary …'

Damien wondered if his mother was seeing Jacqueline professionally. He hoped not, because if she was, Jacqueline clearly wasn't making much headway. But then he wondered if people could change such a major part of their makeup. Was a control freak destined to always be a control freak?

'All too much for me,' he muttered as he reached the boundary and his new little shed and enclosure. He checked the mobile and everything else before turning around and heading back home.

*

The phone rang when Damien was enjoying his first mug of coffee for the day and adding and subtracting things from his to-do list and copious sheets of notes. He didn't recognise the number.

'Hello, Damien speaking.'

'Hello. Damien, this is Irene Timms from the Wattle Creek Hostel. Your auntie Ethel tells me your baby joey and rescued Jack Russell might like to visit and add a bit of interest to the residents' day.'

Since the little roo seemed so happy in the company of humans and was still nice and small and manageable – not to mention cute – Ethel had suggested it might make a nice interlude to the oldies' day. Damien had wondered if there would be health department regulations against livestock in such places, but Ethel had assured him these things were at the discretion of the person running the facility and that she knew Mrs Timms well. 'Of course you do,' Damien had said with a smirk. His auntie Ethel knew everyone around here well. He knew Mrs Timms by sight and to say g'day to, but no more than that.

'We would. I mean, I'm sure they would.' He looked down at Squish and Jemima laying on the mat together. Squish gazed back up at him, wagging his tail. He was always up for any attention. 'Jemima, that's the joey, has only been in contact with a couple of people at a time so far,' he warned. 'But we can see how she goes. Squish – that's my little Jack Russell – loves everyone. He'd be great.'

'So when would suit you? I'm thinking just half an hour for the first visit to see how it goes.'

'Okay. Well, I'm easy. You choose a time.'

'How would two p.m. Wednesday suit?'

'That would be great. I'll look forward to it,' he said, scrawling a note on the nearest piece of paper.

'As will we,' Mrs Timms said.

'Is there any paperwork I need to fill out or anything beforehand?'

'No, that's okay. We'll just play it casual.'

Even better, Damien thought. Esperance was already starting to generate a hell of a lot of paperwork. He hung up, feeling decidedly chipper. Another step in the right direction. Yippee! He'd take Bob and Cara too. They

were just the right height to sit beside a chair or wheel-
chair for a pat. They'd never spent any time inside, but
they were smart and followed basic commands – well,
most of the time. Damien refused to entertain the notion
that his visit could turn into something resembling a
scene out of a National Lampoon movie. Though, if
it did, the oldies couldn't complain they hadn't been
entertained or hadn't had an interesting interlude to
their day. He grinned to himself. He hoped Jemima
wouldn't disgrace him by leaving a smelly deposit on
their commercial carpet squares. Though she hadn't had
any diarrhoea for days now and was regularly leaving
nice piles of firm little pellet-shaped poo. And if Jemima
wasn't keen to entertain the oldies of the district and
submit to having bony, arthritic fingers poking and
prodding her and being run through her fur, then Squish
was sure to be happy to oblige. Damien idly wondered
if he could teach the dog some tricks to entertain them
with. And perhaps the facility might like one or two of
the kittens when they were old enough and had been
desexed. Jacqueline was all for pets as therapy.

He wished he could go and discuss these things with
her. The more he thought about it, two years was a
bloody long time. But he had no choice, he'd just have
to keep busy. No worries there, he thought, picturing
his growing to-do list. God he was getting good at lists.
He couldn't believe he'd tried all those years to keep
so much in his brain. No wonder he'd become a bit
unhinged – his bloody head had been full of stuff it didn't
need to be full of. He was probably actually becoming
a little obsessive with his list-making, but figured there

were worse problems to have. And anyway, they helped keep him organised. Organised? Him? Who would have thought? He wished again that he could share all these revelations with Jacqueline and get more of her insights. She really was a smart cookie, as his father would have said. Damien thought they'd make a pretty good team if given the chance.

God, I've really got to stop thinking about her.

Chapter Nine

Ethel and Jacqueline set off nice and early for Hope Springs so they could have a bit of a tour of the area. Jacqueline had only visited the town the day she'd driven through on her way to Wattle Creek. Now, as they drove into the wide main street, she marvelled at what a pretty little town it was: lovely old homes and a few larger commercial buildings all in beautiful pale stone. The place was generally very neat and tidy, and the parking area in the middle of the street was adorned with large trees that she guessed were probably Norfolk Island pines. There were two old limestone hotels on corners – one at one end of the main shopping strip in the main street and the other overlooking the small harbour. It was really quite the perfect seaside setting.

As they drove around and explored the town more, Jacqueline became a little disappointed. Just a street or two back from the hub, the town became bare, paddock-sized blocks with brown weeds waving in the breeze or industrial-sized sheds in shiny steel and various shades of Colorbond. Everything was so desolate, brown and parched. She much preferred Wattle Creek, where more people seemed interested in gardening and keeping a green lawn.

They were too late for the local artists' exhibition running in the second storey of the institute and to visit the café-slash-haberdashery-slash-homewares store for a coffee. Ethel apologised profusely for not checking, she had just assumed that everything would be still be open later because of daylight saving. She explained that during the summer holidays, the town's population swelled threefold. Now school was back in, Hope Springs was back to being its sleepy self.

They went into the small convenience store that was also the takeaway shop and newsagent. They were greeted by a cheery 'Good evening,' and a broad smile that Jacqueline couldn't help returning. It was infectious. Ethel brought a copy of *The Advertiser* and Jacqueline the *Woman's Day* to while away the next half-hour or so. The town didn't have its own paper – its news was covered by the weekly *Wattle Creek Chronicle*.

Being in the store with its creaking floorboards, grey and shiny from over a century of feet coming and going, reminded Jacqueline of her own summer holidays as a child, when she and all the other kids around her age in her street hung out together and would visit the corner store to blow their pocket money on bags of mixed lollies. She felt really old when she peered into the glass case behind a handwritten sign that read, *Mixed lollies $2*, and saw just how small the bags were. In her day, twenty cents would have bought more than that!

She licked her lips as she spied the stainless steel milk-shake mixer and line of pump nozzles attached to huge bottles of flavourings.

'Do you fancy one, dear?' Ethel asked, following her line of sight.

'Sorry? What?' Jacqueline said.

'Milkshake? You were licking your lips.'

'Was I?' Jacqueline said, blushing slightly. 'Oh, no, I couldn't.' Jacqueline hadn't had a milkshake since … Well, she couldn't recall when she'd last had a milk-shake. Eons ago, most likely.

'Well, I am,' Ethel said forcefully. 'I haven't had one for donkey's years. Owen, I'll have a strawberry milk-shake with the works, thanks – and a …?' she said, nudging Jacqueline. 'Come on, won't kill you. My treat.'

Oh, why the hell not! 'Chocolate, thanks,' she said to Owen, who was patiently waiting with a pink anodised aluminium milkshake cup in hand. 'And let me get these. It's the least I can do, since you've driven me.'

'Well, I'm not one to argue, so if that's what you prefer, thank you very much.'

Not one to argue, my foot, Jacqueline thought with a smirk.

They drove to the end of the street and sat overlooking the harbour, watching a few boats come in – some small private vessels and some clearly larger commercial enterprises. Most likely belonging to the oyster farmers that had made the town famous right around Australia, and probably beyond. It was nice to sit calmly and watch the world go by.

Jacqueline was a bit nervous about her talk. She always was. Not hugely, just a little jittery; enough to keep her on her toes and not become complacent, she always thought. It had been what her dad had said when she'd once complained of nerves before one of her university tutorial presentations, despite having done several. He'd hoped she'd never totally quell the butterflies because if she did, it would mean she'd have lost her respect for her subject and her audience. She could see his point. A part of Jacqueline hoped the milkshake wouldn't leave her feeling sick. Another didn't care – it was oh so good.

Ethel was clearly enjoying her blast from the past as well. 'Sorry in advance for my slurping like a child, but it has to be done,' she said with a grin as she sucked on her straw and moved it about, trying to get every last drop.

Jacqueline laughed. 'I was wanting to do that, but thought I'd better not.'

'Can't not, the best bits are at the bottom,' Ethel said with a laugh.

'They are! Just hope my nerves don't cause me to throw it all up.'

'You'll be fine. Might be good for you to have your stomach lined so well. Well, miss, guess we'd better present you before we start getting frantic phone calls,' Ethel said, starting the car.

Jacqueline was given a warm welcome by the CWA President, Mrs Lisa Bishop, who explained they'd opened the evening to all the women of the district, and any who were visiting for the summer holidays. She was then taken onto the stage and introduced to the audience of at least one hundred ladies of various ages seated on rows of old wooden chairs. The room was nice and cool – clearly the building had been shut up for several days and the warm weather kept out.

Jacqueline's spiel was similar to what she'd used for each of her other community talks, she just tailored it a bit to the particular audience with the examples or stories she told. She didn't use notes; she was talking about herself and the profession she was passionate about – she could talk for hours unaided. She didn't see herself as a comedian by any stretch, but was usually able to get a few chuckles from her audiences by uttering some self-deprecating stories. It was important for her growing business to be seen as down-to-earth and approachable. And she'd seen that country people saw through any inauthenticity and bullshit as quickly as a hot knife went through butter.

Tonight, as always, she talked about how a psychologist could help with a problem and that it wasn't the same as airing one's dirty linen. Everything spoken about within the walls of her office remained confidential. At least this time around, Jacqueline had the benefit of a little more knowledge of why she thought people were reluctant to seek professional help: they didn't like to show themselves as being weak. From what she'd seen – and heard from Ethel and Damien and a few others – country people generally seemed a very resourceful group. They wanted to sort out their problems on their own. To seek help was to show weakness or to complain. And another thing country people tended not to do was openly complain.

Once she explained that to seek help might actually be seen as being smart – using all the resources available – she left the subject so it might sink in, and turned to a lighter topic. She spoke about her tidy life, tidy mind principle and how lists could help to make an overwhelming amount of things to do feel a lot more manageable.

Finally she got to her favourite subject of learning to listen to one's intuition or inner voice more to avoid making mistakes that turned into regrets. Intuition, she explained, was there to protect you. It was your soul, governed by the universe – or God, if that's where your faith lay. Personally, Jacqueline detested organised religion – it was control through fear, in her opinion. But she kept her religious views to herself. She was very spiritual, it just didn't manifest itself in her through being Catholic, Anglican, or whatever. While she'd been raised to believe religious and political views should not be openly discussed, she'd also learnt that a high percentage of country people still went to church each week. It was important to have faith in something – even if it was yourself, your ability to get through what life tossed your way or that the universe – or God, if that was your view – would have your back. This she did say.

Jacqueline explained that intuition was the little voice deep inside or a feeling that makes you pause ever so briefly. When you keep going without acknowledging the intuition or acting on what it's telling you, chances are it will turn out to be hindsight that kicks you in the butt.

'Like sometimes you might think briefly, hmm, I probably should fill up with fuel, but dismiss it. You don't have time, can't be bothered. Then the next thing you know you've run out and end up having to walk miles thinking, if only I'd just filled the damned thing up. That's hindsight kicking you up the butt, my friends.'

The ripple of tittering and head nodding told her plenty of people here related to her example.

She went on to explain that these days, with people keeping so busy, it's easy to not hear the great voice of intuition. Didn't she know that all too well? She paused for breath and a sip of her water. She certainly wasn't going to use her blunder with Damien as an example. Though it was a bloody good one.

'We need to stop regularly and sit quietly for a while to calm the mind so it can pass on messages that keep us safe,' she said. 'It's important to not let all the other noise drown out the voice of intuition and the subconscious – it's possibly the most important tool we have.' She was verging on sounding melodramatic, but she didn't care. It was what she believed, what she was passionate about. If more people stopped to listen to their kind inner voice (not the negative one that put them down – that was a whole other thing) and acted on what they heard and felt, they would have a much happier and calmer life. It wasn't hard, it just took some concentration and effort in remembering what to do.

'Your intuition and subconscious know everything. You just need to give them a chance to show you, to tell you. Like, say you went into a room to get something, but because you were in a rush or thinking about other things, you get there only to wonder why you had come in in the first place. Who hasn't done this plenty of times in their life? Me, certainly. Anyway, if you clear your mind and go back the way you came, you'll remember what you went in for. It works every time if you still your mind enough to let your wise inner voice come through loud and clear.'

She ended there and was rewarded with hearty applause. Mrs Bishop appeared beside her and when the chatter and applause had died down, invited the audience to ask questions.

There weren't many, and those who did put up their hand did so to offer up their own experiences of listening to their intuition. On a few occasions, the room erupted into laughter and chattering and had to be brought back to order by Mrs Bishop. Finally the time had come to wrap things up and Mrs Bishop asked for one final question.

It came from right at the back of the room, from a tall, well-presented woman Jacqueline guessed to be in her sixties, with grey hair cut into a rather severe chin-length bob.

'Is it true that you're now seeing one of your patients – in a romantic sense – and is this really ethical?'

It took all Jacqueline's strength to keep her expression neutral and not let her mouth drop open. She willed her colour not to rise, but didn't need to worry; she had just felt her blood drain away.

'No. I did see a *former* client socially on a few occasions. And, no, a practitioner can't have a personal relationship with a current client. That's against the rules.' She chose her words very carefully and was sure she hadn't actually lied. She'd left out the word sexual – no need to get into specifics or be crass.

'But if the person was vulnerable – because that's why they'd be seeing you in the first place ...' the woman persisted.

But Mrs Bishop had clearly run a few meetings in her time and dealt with pesky types and curly questions before – and for all Jacqueline knew, this woman might be a serial pest at these sorts of events – and she shut proceedings down quick smart.

'You're welcome to discuss it privately with Ms Havelock. There are stacks of her business cards on the supper tables with her contact details on. And now let's show our appreciation to Ms Havelock for giving up her evening to come along and give us the benefit of her expertise. I know I've got a lot out of it and will be taking extra care to listen to my inner voice in the hope I get fewer kicks in the butt from hindsight. Thank you very much, Ms Havelock,' she said, smiling warmly at Jacqueline and handing her a bottle of wine wrapped in cellophane. She then led the crowd in a round of applause.

Phew. And bless you, Jacqueline thought, as she dipped her head and mouthed, 'Thank you,' through the noise.

'And now, supper is served out in the supper room,' Mrs Bishop said, when the noise had subsided and the clapping had been replaced with chatter. Jacqueline exited the stage with Mrs Bishop, who left her in Ethel's capable hands while she went to double-check all was well with supper.

'God, can you believe that question at the end?' Jacqueline hissed.

'It's fine. Don't worry about it,' Ethel said. 'Just continue to put on a brave front, smile, and mingle.

It'll be fine. You'll see.' Ethel squeezed her elbow reassuringly.

Jacqueline wished she could muster Ethel's confidence. Everything had been going so well until that last question. Oh, well, nothing she could do about it. If the woman caused her further grief, she'd deal with it. She squared her shoulders and entered the sea of people balancing cups of tea and plates of cake. She accepted a cup and an empty plate just as she was swallowed into her first small group of people. She slid the plate under her saucer – it wouldn't feel quite right eating while she was talking.

Jacqueline was exhausted when she finally collapsed into the passenger's seat of Ethel's car and accepted the paper plate of goodies covered in cling wrap. 'Yum,' she said, grabbing a cream cake. She wasn't hungry by any stretch, thanks to the milkshake still sitting in her stomach, but the cake was too irresistible. Thank goodness she hadn't encountered the lady with the curly question again. She suspected Ethel might have had something to do with that. She stayed silent and let Ethel concentrate on driving until she could hold her tongue no longer.

'God, Ethel, fancy that lady asking that. Do you think she'll dob me in?'

'No. I know she won't dob you in.'

'How can you be so sure?'

'I spoke to her.'

'Oh no, you didn't.' Jacqueline knew only too well that when it came to human nature, reverse psychology was a powerful thing. If Ethel had warned the woman to leave it alone, then chances were she would wonder about all the fuss and pursue it with vigour when she might otherwise have dropped it.

'Don't worry. I didn't warn her off, or anything. Just explained that Damien was my nephew and that he had called off the relationship with you because he was too busy with his new venture. She seemed to accept it and that there was nothing untoward going on. Thankfully she'd heard of Esperance Animal Welfare Farm. So, you have nothing to worry about with her – of that I'm certain. I actually think she has a suitor for you in mind – a grandson. I think she might have offered you his number if Lisa Bishop hadn't shut her down so quickly,' Ethel said, grinning cheekily at Jacqueline.

'Oh dear.'

'Well, you're new blood, dear. Every second person is going to want you paired up with their son, brother, nephew or grandson. Sad, but true, I'm afraid. You'd better get a decent thanks but no thanks story sorted, missy, if you're going to stay true to Damien.'

'Of course I'm going to stay true to Damien. How could you even question it?'

'Well, two years is a long time when you're waiting for something, someone. And your generation is not known for its patience,' Ethel said sagely as she pulled into her driveway.

Jacqueline said no more than, 'Thanks so much again for driving me,' before giving her friend a tight hug. 'Goodnight. See you soon.'

'Sleep well,' Ethel replied.

Chapter Ten

After doing a check of his property, Damien spent a few hours preparing for his visit to the old folks' home. Bob and Cara had been highly insulted to have been subjected to being washed. They were so well-behaved they'd merely stood and scowled, and then shaken themselves off furiously, as though shaking off the embarrassment of it all. Damien had laughed at how they had enjoyed being towelled off, especially having their ears and heads rubbed, even to the point of groaning with pleasure. They were now lying on the caravan floor; Damien hadn't wanted to tempt fate by letting them go anywhere that would undo his hard work of the past hour. Anyway, it was a good test to see how they liked being indoors. If they freaked out and leapt all over the place in a frenzy to find a way out, then they'd be staying here, locked up in their run. He needn't have worried – they were sprawled out calmly as if this was how they spent all their time.

Damien told them to stay and tempted fate further by leaving them unsupervised so he could take Squish outside for a wash. The little dog was small enough to be done in the caravan sink, but he didn't relish wiping all the droplets or soap suds from every surface when Squish decided to shake himself off. For a small body, he sure did get a decent shake up.

The kittens were in their box on the small outdoor table nearby so as not to inadvertently become a snack for the kelpies inside. Jemima was out of her pouch and getting in the way. A few times Damien gently splashed her nose in an effort to discourage her, but she was becoming very bold. And she had developed quite an attachment to Squish, so she wanted to be nearby.

Finally Damien had his exhibits presentable for their trip into town. He hoped Mrs Timms realised what she was letting herself in for. He figured the kittens might enjoy a bit of a cuddle. Or they could stay in their box in a corner out of the way. He wasn't leaving them home alone or in the ute.

He chained Bob and Cara on the back of the ute, settled the kittens in their box on the passenger's seat and encouraged Jemima, who decided she didn't fancy going back into her pouch right at that moment, to sit on the floor on the passenger's side. He hoped she would stay put. She was growing so quickly, it would only be a matter of weeks before she started causing chaos in the cab if she chose to. Squish sprawled out on the seat beside Damien.

He was a little nervous as he turned out of the property after stopping to check he hadn't had any new arrivals dropped off in his enclosure. *Fingers crossed you guys don't disgrace me,* he thought with a deep breath as he put the ute into gear.

At the home, he realised he must look quite the funny sight, standing there holding a box with four squeaking kittens – they did that most of the time when they weren't sleeping or feeding. Beside him Jemima hid in her pouch with Squish standing close by to protect her. And sitting at Damien's feet, as though they were the best trained, most obedient dogs in the world, were Bob and Cara – farm dogs extraordinaire! They seemed to get that this was important. Like the day of the fire, Damien thought wistfully, while he waited for the door to be answered.

Mrs Timms greeted him warmly. 'Wow, you've brought quite a menagerie,' she said, looking Damien and his charges over. 'What do you have in there?' she asked, pointing to the box.

'Kittens. I couldn't leave them. They're pretty tiny – maybe too small for socialising …' Damien introduced her to the dogs and just as he was saying the joey called Jemima was hiding in her pouch, she popped her head out and looked about.

'Oh, aren't you a cutie?' Mrs Timms said, bending down to give Jemima a pat, only to be licked by Squish, demanding his share of attention.

'Is there anything I can do? And do you want to go straight in and meet the residents or do you need to do anything first?'

'No, we're good to go, thanks. And if you could take the kittens, that would be great. I'll bring Jemima. Thanks.'

As Damien crossed the threshold into the slightly musty-smelling building with Bob and Cara looking up at him quizzically, he felt a bolt of apprehension and nerves surge through him. *Well, this is it, Damo, your first real test. Too late to back out now and not look like a dickhead.* Squish had no such apprehension; he bolted inside.

'Come on, guys, in you come,' he urged the farm dogs. They seemed to look at each other and shrug before following their master in.

Mrs Timms took him into a large room that, judging by the piano in the corner, was the recreation or entertainment room. What looked like most of the residents were arranged around the edge of the room in chairs, a couple of wheelchairs, and a few mobility scooters.

He was thrilled when Mrs Timms not only introduced him, but gave his new business a plug by name and spoke a bit about what it was all about. She must have read the write-up in the paper about the launch the other week. He damned near shed a tear when she told the group he'd lost everything in the recent fire and that he'd decided to go on a more meaningful path; she'd obviously been talking to Auntie Ethel in depth. All this attention took Damien by surprise. He'd just brought the animals along to give the residents something a bit different to look at – bring some interest to what he imagined might otherwise be a pretty boring day. But at least the shock had quelled his nerves.

'How about you introduce us to each of the friends you've brought along and tell us a bit about them, Damien,' Mrs Timms suggested.

'Okay, great,' he said, smiling and nodding at her. *This I can do.*

He decided to do it in chronological order, starting with Bob and Cara. They stood solemnly beside him, behaving perfectly.

'This is Bob and this is Cara,' he said, pointing to them in turn. 'They're kelpie work dogs.' He figured plenty of the residents were most likely off farms, or at least got the gist of what work dogs did, so didn't feel the need to elaborate. 'They're great at what they do, and were responsible for saving my two thousand head of sheep during the fire.' *God, I'm choking up. Damn it!* He swallowed hard and forced the lump back down. 'They love to have their heads and ears rubbed,' he added with a laugh.

'Shall I ...?' Mrs Timms said, patting Bob. Damien nodded. Bob and Cara were taken to each end of the row of people and Damien watched for a moment to make sure all was well before continuing. He picked Squish up.

'This is Squish. About two months ago I found him on the side of the road in a sack. Sadly I was too late to save his siblings. I don't know why I stopped that day, but something made me, and I'm so glad it did. I was going through a tough time emotionally.' Again, he was annoyed to find himself choking up. Oh well, at least they would see how much these animals meant to him. 'This little guy gave me something to care about and be responsible for. And I really needed that at that time,' he finished with a shrug. Squish rewarded him with a big lick to the face. When he put Squish down, the little dog ran over to an old man who clapped his hands and called him by name, and hopped up into his lap. Damien's heart lurched at seeing the old man's eyes light up and a grin spread across his face.

'In here is Jemima, a female eastern grey kangaroo joey,' he said, holding up the sack. 'She must be sleeping. Oh, no, she's not, here she is,' he said with a laugh as Jemima, as if on cue, popped her head out. A few of the residents clapped and Damien cringed and hoped she wouldn't be frightened. She'd become used to the big dogs and Squish hanging around and a bit of banging of pots and pans in the caravan and while in Auntie Ethel's kitchen. 'I found her in a bad way after the fire. She still has some bare, sore patches, but her recovery has been amazing. A young buck was injured too, and my auntie, Ethel Bennett, and I nursed him back to health. He's been released back into the wild near where he was found. Unfortunately for Jemima, she was too young when she lost her mum, so will always have to live in captivity. Well, it seems she's keen to meet you all,' he said with another laugh, as Jemima fought to exit her pouch. There was silence as they watched her make her way around the room, going up to the residents in turn and sniffing them. 'As you can see, she loves a bit of attention. And like Bob and Cara, she loves her ears and head rubbed. And a tickle under the chin.

'And, finally, I've brought along four orphaned kittens – only really because I didn't want to leave them alone. They've been with me a few days, and they're doing well. Once they're old enough to be desexed, and have been fully vaccinated, they'll be looking for new homes. I'll be sad to see them go, but I want to help as many animals as I can, so those who can will need to leave eventually. They're pretty small and quite noisy, but I'm sure they'd love a cuddle.' Damien opened the box and took the first kitten out. There was a series of oohs and ahhs as he crossed the room to find a lap for the creature. He found himself drawn to an old lady who sat expressionless, just staring ahead. He didn't know why he chose her.

'Would you like to hold this one?' he asked, squatting down beside the old lady's chair. The woman held out her hands and accepted the kitten, then gently brought it up to her chest. The kitten snuggled in and, yet again, Damien felt his heart strings being tugged painfully. He had the feeling he was seeing something really special, as the old lady's mouth had turned up ever so slightly into a smile.

Before long, the animals and residents were settled and everyone was getting on well. The room was a sea of excited chatter and soothing tones. Damien stood back and marvelled at it all. *This is what life's about,* he thought, *the simple things.* He reckoned he'd brought some real joy to these people. And the animals were loving the attention.

'It's going great. A huge success,' Mrs Timms said, appearing beside him.

'Yes. I'm so pleased.'

'Fancy a cup of tea?'

'That would be lovely, thank you.'

They stayed an hour and a half, even delaying the residents' afternoon tea by half an hour. But no one had wanted to see the animals go.

'It's okay, everyone. Mr McAllister will bring them back again next week, won't you?'

It was the right time to leave. A few people were starting to yawn. And Damien was beginning to think he might be pushing it with all the bladders and bowels – of his charges, not the residents.

He lavished praise and thanks on the big dogs as he settled them on the back of the ute, and then Jemima, and finally Squish, before heading home. He stopped at the butcher for some bones as treats for Bob and Cara and Squish. He'd see if Jemima would like to share one of his peaches.

He was on a high as he drove out of town. It felt so good to do something for someone else, just because. 'Did you see how their eyes lit up, Squish? They loved us. Well, you, Bob and Cara, the kittens, and Jemima. I was just the hanger-on. But that's okay. Mission accomplished.'

While he'd sat having a cuppa with Mrs Timms and keeping an eye on everything, she'd mentioned that there might be a grant she could apply for to pay him to come and visit with his animals. God, he'd do it for nothing, but if he could be paid, that would be awesome. She'd said there were government grants and funding for all sorts of things if only you knew where to look and were prepared to deal with the paperwork. She'd even offered to lend him a hand with that side of things, since she'd done heaps of them and been quite successful over the years. Apparently there was quite an art to successfully applying for funding.

Mrs Timms had also suggested that perhaps kindergarten and primary school kids might like a visit and that it would be good for teaching them about responsible pet ownership. He'd definitely look into that too.

Since it was all going so well with Mrs Timms, Damien had almost got bold enough to ask if the hostel might be interested in a kitten or two as permanent residents, but she'd got in first. She thought they might like two and they could see which ones seemed to fit in best. Damien hoped that if all the kittens proved themselves over the coming weeks, she might decide two weren't enough to go around and keep them all.

Chapter Eleven

Jacqueline had finished her lunch and gone through a stack of private emails and was getting ready for her first afternoon session when she remembered the letter Louise had delivered to her earlier. She should read it and she had a couple of minutes before Mrs Smith's appointment – if the woman showed; she made it to around two out of three scheduled visits, and never really seemed to realise she had missed one. She'd just turn up the next week as if nothing was amiss and carry on where she'd left off last time. Blissfully unaware, Jacqueline often thought. Mrs Smith was a patient who treated her more as someone to pass some time with. Jacqueline had a few of them. She didn't mind. Whatever helped. They were pensioners: if they wanted a free chat session on the government via Medicare, then who was she to argue? And, anyway, any interaction was good for a potentialy lonely person's emotional and mental wellbeing, and that was what she was there for. And Jacqueline was learning a lot about the ways of the town and its attitudes from these clients. So she figured it was a win-win.

She retrieved the letter from her handbag. The simple 'If undeliverable, return to GPO Box 5899, Adelaide, SA, 5001' in the top left-hand corner wasn't familiar, and shed no light on the contents. No doubt an invitation to a conference, or something else she couldn't be bothered attending. She slid a nail under the seal to open it and drew the crisp sheet of paper out, unfolded it, and laid it out flat on her desk in front of her. There at the top of the letter was the letterhead of the Australian Health Practitioner Regulation Agency. As she read, she felt the blood drain from her head and the pit of her stomach turn molten.

Dear Ms Havelock,

Re: Notification of breach of Australian Psychological Society Code of Ethics, item C.4.3 – sexual activity with a client.

It has been reported by a concerned member of the public, who wishes to remain anonymous, that you have engaged in sexual activity with a client named Mr Damien McAllister.

Before proceeding with further investigation, the board requires your response to this serious allegation in writing, postmarked no later than fourteen (14) days from the date of this letter.

Regards,
Dr Alastair Douglas
President

Oh shit. Shit, shit, *shit*! The words swam before her eyes and she couldn't get her brain to formulate anything coherent.

When there was a tap on the open door, she plastered a smile on her face and looked up, ready to welcome Mrs Smith in and get on with her job. But it wasn't Mrs Smith.

'You must be waiting for a client – since your door is open,' Ethel said, looking like she was about to back away.

Jacqueline leapt up. 'No, don't go.'

'Is there something wrong? Only, you look a little pale,' Ethel said, stepping into the room. 'Have you had some bad news?' she said, pointing to the letter.

Jacqueline nodded and swallowed. 'Oh, Ethel,' she said, putting her head in her hands and slumping back down into her chair. 'Thank God you're here.'

'Whatever is the matter?' Ethel moved a step inside.

'Come in. Please. And can you close the door?'

'But what about your next patient?'

'Most likely a no-show – if she was coming she'd be here by now.'

'So what is it that has you so rattled?' Ethel said, sitting in one of the chairs in front of Jacqueline's desk.

Jacqueline silently turned the letter around so Ethel could read it. It seemed to her to take an age for Ethel to get her glasses out of her handbag, put them on, pick up the paper, start reading, and then for her mouth to fall open, for her to take her glasses off again, fold them up, and look up at Jacqueline with concern etched across her face.

'Oh dear.'

'Yes.'

'So, what are you going to do?'

'What I was going to do a week or so ago – hand in my resignation and suffer the consequences.'

'You're not going to fight it?'

'What's there to fight? I've been through this with you,' Jacqueline said wearily. 'I've done the wrong thing.'

'Now, dear, tell me if I'm completely out of line here, but *have* you actually had, quote, "sexual activity" with Damien? It's just …'

'Ethel!' Jacqueline said, aghast.

'I know it's a very delicate subject, but if this goes anywhere,' she said, pointing to the letter, 'it'll be out anyway.'

'Which is why I'm just going to resign. Plead guilty. But to answer your question, and there's no way to put this delicately, no, Damien and I have not had a sexual relationship. We didn't get a chance. We weren't going to do *that* on your couch or when my parents, or you, were in the next room,' she said, blushing furiously.

'It's as I suspected. So there it is.'

'Sorry?'

'Your defence.'

'Ethel, I have no defence,' Jacqueline said with a sigh. 'It's all about crossing the line. An emotional relationship or a physical one – regardless of actually having, er, intercourse – would still be considered wrong, a violation. It's all about protecting the client, who is considered vulnerable – hence them seeing a psychologist – and messing further with their already fragile state of mind.'

'But it says here in black and white: "sexual activity". Therefore, the way I see it, that's the only charge you need to answer. And in this case, you are not guilty. It is not asking you if you've had an emotional relationship, a non-sexual physical relationship or any of that wishy-washy stuff open to interpretation, is it?'

'But …'

'Get with the program, Jacqueline. Start playing by their rules. Or do you just want to give up your job, your career?'

'No.'

'Well?'

'But it would still mean I couldn't have a relationship with Damien for two years. Nothing would have changed,' Jacqueline said, unable to hide her frustration.

'Oh. Right,' Ethel said, looking clearly deflated.

They sat back in their chairs and were silent for a few moments.

'Could you write and ask for permission to have a relationship with Damien?'

'It would be a very long shot.'

'But worth a try, right?'

'I don't know, Ethel. Why would they grant permission – effectively a breach of the rules? It's no skin off their noses if they quash my love life. They're all about keeping their profession squeaky clean. And fair enough, too.'

'Well, I bet this sort of thing happens all the time – relationships forming with past patients before two years is up. You can't help who you fall in love with, or when.'

'Yes, it probably does happen all the time, but most likely in a city where you're so much more anonymous than out here. I wonder who dobbed me in – that lady at Hope Springs CWA?'

'No, I doubt it. I can't imagine these organisations act so quickly. She only raised it the other day.'

'But she could have already written to them, or phoned them.'

'Yes, she could have. But if that was the case, she wouldn't have been able to resist telling me she had the other night. Of that I'm sure.'

'Hmm, you're probably right. So, who?'

'No idea. Maybe that nasty Bolton fellow? He was pretty upset at being dragged off in handcuffs. And he did see how Damien was there for you. Probably put two and two together.'

'But he wouldn't know Damien had ever been to see me professionally.' The cold finger of fear traced a line down Jacqueline's back. She shivered. Had Jacob been in her office? She felt her blood disappear again while she looked around her room, scrutinising every item. All appeared just as it should. But she'd moved everything and dusted just the week before, when it had been quiet. Anyway, Jacob would have been careful not to leave any sign. When he'd been in her house in the city he'd left a sign – subtle, but noticeable for someone tidy and observant. He'd wanted her to know he could get in any time he liked.

'It could still have been him,' Ethel said. 'What if he didn't know anything, but has reported you just to cause you grief – payback? If only you could find out who made the report.'

'It will all be kept confidential for now. And rightly so. People need to be able to make complaints without fear of retribution.'

'I suppose so. So you're really going to resign? And write and plead guilty?'

'I don't see any other alternative. I've got to cop it on the chin, Ethel, as much as I don't like it.'

'Well, at least discuss it with Doctor Squire. Perhaps he can help,' Ethel said, shrugging her shoulders helplessly.

'I doubt it. But I won't just hand in my resignation without an explanation. That would be too strange. He'll probably be pleased to see me go. I can just hear him, "Oh, the young of today",' she mimicked.

'He might surprise you.'

Yeah, and pigs might fly, Jacqueline thought.

'I wish there was something I could do to help,' Ethel said, lifting her hands and dropping them again in a gesture of helplessness.

'I do too, I do too,' Jacqueline said sadly.

There was a feeble knock on her door. They both looked up, startled.

'I'd better leave you to it,' Ethel said, jumping up. She grasped Jacqueline's hands, gave them a squeeze, then offered her a grim smile before letting them go.

Standing at the door was Jacqueline's next patient, Mrs Smith, flushed with embarrassment, and ten minutes late.

'It's okay,' Jacqueline said. 'Come on in. Ethel was just leaving.'

The two old ladies exchanged greetings as Ethel left and Mrs Rose Smith entered.

'I'm so sorry I'm late. I clean forgot. Well, almost,' she said, clearly flustered.

Jacqueline struggled to concentrate for the rest of the afternoon. Thankfully each of her patients was like Mrs

Smith and didn't seem to want any more from her other than for her to listen to them. Some were there for a natter and some were there to hypothetically discuss problems their friends were having. Jacqueline urged them to get their friends to make an appointment.

She went through the motions until five p.m. and then she was free. She practically bolted out the door. She'd meant to get a few things from the supermarket, but couldn't face the extra walk up there and back and putting on a cheery front to all the people she might meet along the way. She'd live without milk. She just hoped there was another portion of her mother's lasagne in the freezer.

Oh God, she thought, as she collapsed on the couch, *what a bloody mess.* She yearned to call her parents, hear their words of comfort, but feared coming clean and disappointing them.

Ethel must have seen her arrive, because just a few minutes later she was on Jacqueline's doorstep, ringing her bell, steaming casserole in hand.

'Oh, Ethel, bless you,' she said, ushering her friend in and giving her a tight hug.

'If you want to be alone to think things through, I'll completely understand,' Ethel said.

'No, please, come in. I could do with the company. There's nothing really to think through. I'll do the letters tomorrow. Glass of wine? I'm opening a bottle, seeing as I might not be here much longer,' Jacqueline said wistfully.

'Fiddlesticks. We'll have none of that negative talk. It'll work out. You'll see.'

Jacqueline couldn't muster the energy to point out that it couldn't possibly be fine, and wouldn't work out. It was a done deal. She thought she could practically hear the cogs turning in Ethel's brain, searching for a solution. She could knock herself out, meddle anyway she liked, but there wasn't anything that could be done. At least whatever Ethel did, she couldn't make the situation any worse. Jacqueline tried to force it all out of her mind – she wanted a quiet evening with her good friend for company and a nice glass of wine or two and a decent meal. She'd deal with the mess that was her professional life tomorrow, or maybe bury her head in the sand for a few more days.

Chapter Twelve

On Friday morning, Damien was surprised to hear a knock on his caravan door. He'd heard a vehicle arrive, but had stopped taking notice days ago on account of all the coming and going for the house building project. He thought they must be close to pouring the slab any day now the site was cleared, but he was staying well out of it and letting those who knew about building deal with it. He had enough on his plate.

He was further surprised to see his auntie Ethel standing just beyond the steps, and even more so to take in her slightly haggard appearance. Usually she was so bright and bubbly; today it seemed each of the steps was like climbing Everest for her. A jolt of fear ran through him as he reminded himself she was no spring chicken. What would he do if she got sick and/or died? The thought filled him with terror. But that was life, wasn't it? People got old and died. He shook it aside. Everything was going so well, the last thing he needed was to start worrying about something he had no control over.

'Good morning. Lovely to see you,' he said, taking care to sound extra cheerful. 'Cuppa?'

'A cup of tea would be much appreciated, thank you,' Ethel said, taking a seat on the wraparound leather couch behind the table.

'Are you okay?' he ventured, leaning on the bench while waiting for the kettle to boil. 'It's just you seem a little down, or something.'

Ethel flapped a hand, as if in frustration or dismissal, he couldn't tell which.

'Fine. Just one of those nights. Didn't sleep too well.'

'Anything I can help with?'

'No, afraid not,' she said quietly. 'But, thanks anyway,' she said, offering him a feeble smile.

He turned back to the bench to prepare their mugs, wondering why she was there at nine o'clock in the morning, or even out for that matter. It was forecast to be a hot windy day – a 'shocker' in CFS terms.

'But sure could do with a cuddle with one of these guys,' she said, looking about the van. Squish took it as his cue. He hopped up onto the couch, threw himself into Ethel's lap, and gave her a hearty lick. 'Yes, thank you, that's lovely, Squish,' Ethel said, looking less impressed than her words suggested, wiping the slobber off.

Next, perhaps sensing that there might be some fresh fruit on offer – which she seemed to have developed a liking for – Jemima hopped forwards and sniffed Ethel's leg.

'Aren't you growing up fast?' Ethel said, leaning down and giving the joey's ears a rub.

'Yes, I'm going to miss her when she's too big and has to spend all her time out in the run. Not letting her inside is going to be hard.'

'Well, you won't have a choice. This place is too small to have her thumping around. Sometimes you have to be a little cruel to be kind – to both her and you,' she said, smiling sadly. Where was the brightness that always shone from Auntie Ethel's eyes and provided so much light and hope?

'Fancy a bikkie? Oaties, Anzacs, or whatever you want to call them. Not sure where they came from. Must have been leftover from the working bee. They've gone a bit soft,' Damien asked as he placed the mugs on the table.

'Oh, what the hell, yes, thanks. Could do with a bikkie to cheer me up.'

'So, what's the matter?'

'Oh, nothing specific. Just a bit tired and ragged around the edges.' And there was that hand flap again.

Damien felt as if his concern was being dismissed. Oh, well, he'd tried. He'd just have to wait now and see if she decided to tell him.

'Well, these little guys will cheer you up,' he said, bringing the box of kittens from his bed. Ethel, Jemima and Squish peered in. The little dog, deciding they weren't food, and thus weren't interesting, vacated the couch and curled up on the floor beside Jemima.

'They get on well, don't they?' Ethel said, nodding at the unlikely pairing.

'Practically inseparable. I wouldn't be surprised if Squish takes to spending his nights out with Jemima when she goes. It's as if they've formed a club – the saved – or something. I wonder if the kittens will join when they're bigger.' He chuckled, but he felt a little sad every time he thought of the kittens being bigger, because that meant they'd be leaving. For the first time he could see how hard this running an animal welfare charity might be on his emotions. But he couldn't shy away to protect himself. That would be selfish. He took two of the kittens out and handed them to Ethel.

'Oh, aren't you gorgeous. They've grown a lot already. You really have found your calling, Damien. I'm so proud of you.'

Damien wanted to kindly tell her to shut up before he got all teary. He wasn't used to such kind comments. His mum had pushed him hard over the years – now, having taken a step back, he was starting to see just how hard. There had been very few glowing endorsements.

'Speaking of which,' Ethel continued, 'your new enclosure out at the gate is genius. I stopped and had a good look. I reckon: even an oldie like me could figure out the instructions on the phone if needs be.'

'Thanks, Auntie Ethel, that means a lot. It's a bit of a work in progress. I'm sure I can improve it heaps, but it'll do for now.'

'Oh, and I completely forgot. How did the visit with the oldies up on the hill go? I was going to phone you. Sorry about that.'

'No worries. It went brilliantly. Oh, Auntie Ethel, I really think the animals made their day. It felt so good to see their faces light up as they interacted with the animals. And Bob and Cara and Squish and Jemima loved it too – they behaved so well, like they'd been doing it for years. The kittens went down a treat too. I'm hoping down the track the hostel might adopt a couple. Fingers crossed. And fingers crossed Wednesday wasn't a fluke, because we're going back again next week.'

'Oh, that's great. Everything is really coming together. I'm so pleased. Your dad would be so proud, too.'

'Thanks. So, I thought you'd be home battening down the hatches against the heat,' he said, desperate for a complete change of subject to lighten the mood.

'Just felt the need to get out. You know how it is: sometimes the same four walls that you love suddenly feel oppressive?'

Oh, yeah, he knew all right. He hoped his aunt wasn't slipping into a depressed state like he had; he doubted she'd consult Jacqueline properly now they were such good friends – just like he wouldn't if he needed to now. He was pleased to be ripped from his thoughts of Jacqueline by his mobile phone going off.

'Oh shit, this can't be good,' he said, looking at his phone. It was the captain of his CFS brigade, Keith Stevens. Summer had officially ended but there were still bursts of hot weather, which was why the fire season didn't end until the fifteenth of April – still a month away.

'Hey, Keith,' he said.

'Hey, Damien. We're sending two trucks out to the Peak. Hopefully just a matter of monitoring and cleaning up by the time we get there. I know you're busy, but I just wondered if you could come along? We're having trouble fielding two teams. There seems to be a heap of guys and gals still off on their beach holidays. That or just not answering their mobiles or pagers.'

Damien remembered he'd left his pager in his ute. Oops. 'Yeah. Look, hang on a sec.' He put his hand over his mobile. 'Auntie Ethel, it's a CFS callout. Would you …?' He nodded towards the kittens.

'Of course. You go. I'll take care of these guys. If I get bored I'll take them home with me and put Jemima in the run. But I've got my knitting in my bag, so I should be fine to stay.'

'You're the best. Thanks so much.' He uncovered the phone. 'You there, Keith?'

'Yep.'

'Count me in.'

'We'll be going past the end of your road in twenty. We'll put you on truck two one. Can you get there by then?'

'Yep. No problems. See you then.' He hung up. The adrenaline was already starting to pulse. He hadn't been in touch with CFS properly since he'd lost his house, mostly because the loss had sparked such a sudden change in direction for him and then brought up so much to sort out to follow his new path. He hadn't even thought to turn his pager on until yesterday when he'd seen smoke way off above the horizon while out checking the troughs. He was planning to get back in touch today and let them know he was available if needed after seeing the weather report and extreme fire warnings and bans on the telly. They'd need all hands on deck, or at least available on standby. He'd meant to call Keith first thing, but it had slipped his mind.

It felt good to be back in the loop again. And bless Auntie Ethel for stepping in. She even seemed to have got a bit of her old sparkle back, he thought, turning around and sneaking a peek at her cuddling the kittens.

'Thanks so much for this. Sorry, guys, but you're staying put,' he said, bending down to give Squish and Jemima a farewell pat. 'Bob and Cara are locked up in their run. They should be ...'

'I'll take care of everything,' Ethel said. 'You just get going.'

'Thanks so much.' He hovered in the open doorway for a moment and looked back at Squish, who was sitting to attention with his head cocked, waiting to be called. He felt a stab of sadness. He couldn't remember a time when the dog had been left behind since the day he'd found him. But it was for his own good; he'd be safe here with Auntie Ethel. On a call out, all hell could break loose at any moment and if it did, the last thing Damien's teammates and the landowners whose properties were under threat needed was a guy with his mind elsewhere.

'See you,' he called, as he raced out the door, down the steps and into his ute. The UHF radio was full of chatter. Four other units were on the scene and another four from around the district – not including Damien's – were on their way. From the urgency in the voices, he could tell this was bad – seasoned CFS personnel didn't get jumpy for no reason. He felt his heart slow momentarily as he remembered *that* day, not so long ago.

As he drove, he wondered how this fire had started. It was usually one of only three causes: vehicle accident, farm equipment, and lightning. He'd never heard of arson being a cause, unlike a lot of the fires in the more densely populated areas. Out here the community was tight-knit, and every kid knew that if anyone caught them doing something dodgy they'd be given a clip around the ear before being delivered home to face the music, which might be worse. There seemed to be an unwritten rule that anyone could be punished by anyone; none of that it's-my-kid-stay-out-of-it-I'll-deal-with-it nonsense. If a kid – or anyone else for that matter – did something that had wider community implications, like graffiti or playing with matches, it was considered okay for the wider community to sort it out. And, as far as Damien could see, it worked. The only two instances of graffiti in his time had been done by outsiders who'd moved into town. They'd been shut down pretty quick and their antics not repeated.

'G'day,' he said, getting into the first of the two trucks that had pulled up just off the side of the highway.

As they drove in silence, all concentrating on the radio chatter, it became clear that things were really bad. Two houses and a stack of sheds had been lost, but thankfully no lives. He felt for the landowners and for the firies. He knew all too well that houses could be rebuilt and stuff replaced. But he doubted the guys and girls who battled the flames only to lose something as precious as someone's home would ever be totally the same again. They were proud, they worked hard; to fail was hard to swallow. Especially when it happened so rarely. Out here, houses were so few and far between and most of the land cleared so there was a lot more opportunity to get the upper hand before buildings were threatened. In his almost twelve years with CFS, Damien's house was only the second that had been lost as a result of bushfire.

He'd seen how upset and deflated the guys had been when he'd arrived and found his place in a molten, smouldering mess. And now, just weeks later, some of those same guys would be going through it all again. He wondered if the CFS had started to include Jacqueline in their debriefs at the end of incidents, or was at least promoting her services to members. Plenty of them would have been at her talk the other week, but it was different coming from your leader. Out here, as he well knew, people, blokes especially, were loath to seek help without a decent shove. But while losing more houses indicated a new era, this having a psychologist on hand, and one who was warm and friendly and who wasn't all about textbooks and theory, was a new era too.

As the black and brown smoke loomed larger and then took up the horizon in front of them, the mood in the vehicle became more subdued. Even the radio chatter seemed to have died, although Damien suspected Keith might have turned the volume down.

After turning off the main road, they made a series of turns, the dirt roads showing less and less maintenance as they went on. The journey was vaguely familiar to Damien – he might have been out here to a clearing sale or even another fire in the past few years, though in this area, the scrub, roads, groups of buildings and driveways into them tended to all look pretty much the same. But as they turned off the road onto a private track and bumped their way over a cattle grid, Damien was sure he'd been here before.

Two trucks were leaving. The first rolled to a stop beside the one Damien was in – the second of his brigade – and the four drivers conferred. Damien, sitting in the back, could only hear the odd word, but the tension and weariness in the other drivers' voices were unmistakeable. All the crews waved to their comrades in farewell as they headed off again, but there was no cheer, no boisterous ribbing – they were clearly exhausted, and they might be out here for several hours yet. Firefighting regularly pushed people beyond their limits. Adrenaline helped.

The drivers parked the trucks on the bare area in front of a large implement shed a short distance from a cream brick house. Everyone got out and gathered around Keith. Damien's pulse raced a little and he was already sweating under his gear.

'Right,' Keith said, 'so it started two properties over. They got it contained about three and a half clicks away over there to the north-east.' He waved an arm. 'The landowner has a grader and was able to respond quickly. The good news is the wind has died down and looks like being nowhere near as gusty as forecast. And they're now saying the change won't come though until tomorrow arvo instead of tonight, so that'll help keep things stable. Sorry, guys and gals, it's going to be a hot one and just a matter of keeping an eye on things until we hear otherwise. The guys who've just left have headed out to check the perimeter again on their way home. Trent, I want you to take your truck and team back over the ridge and keep an eye on things there, just to be sure. I'm going to head out and check the lie of the land to the east and south. Damien, can you and Kate stay here and monitor anyone coming and going? If any other brigades and farmers come looking for water, there's a standpipe behind this main shed over there. Okay, so everyone's clear on what they're doing? Any questions?'

They dispersed, murmuring, leaving Damien and Kate behind. He knew Keith was probably easing him back in gently, and that Kate, with as much experience as him, was probably there to keep an eye on him. Actually, maybe she was being eased back in as well; she'd been at his fire that day when they'd all been taken by surprise and outwitted by the wind and flames.

They stood in silence for a few moments, watching the trucks disappear from view. Damien felt a surge of vulnerability and wondered if it was just him or if Kate was feeling that way too.

'Right, well, I think we should take a good look around, see what's what,' Kate said, clapping her hands together. Damien thought what Kate was really saying was that she didn't trust the forecast and wind and weather reports and that if she was going to be left here without a truck for protection she was damned well going to figure out an escape route or some other contingency plan. Well, that was what he was feeling, anyway.

'Yeah, good plan. Hey, any idea whose place this is? I'm sure I've been here before ...' He was starting to feel a little jittery. Perhaps that was just because he couldn't put his finger on why this place was tugging at his memory. He frowned.

'No, but I know I've never been here before, I'd
remember that tank,' she said, pointing.

A large corrugated tank was perched high on top
of a tall steel structure. Damien shuddered slightly. He
wasn't at all a fan of heights. Growing up and working
on the farm and being involved with CFS saw him
regularly facing that particular fear, but he'd never quite
conquered it and he certainly wouldn't be volunteering
to climb up there in a hurry.

'I'll go left and check out the standpipe and water
situation, you head that way and we'll meet back here in
around twenty minutes. Okay?'

'Yep, sounds good.' Damien checked his watch as
Kate strode off with her shovel.

He did a full turn to take in the sights, sounds and
smells. There was not a breath of wind. It was eerily still
and quiet. All the birds must have already fled – that
wasn't a good sign. He looked around. It was too still.
Too quiet. Something didn't feel right. Or perhaps he
was just being a little paranoid, hypersensitive. He tried
to shake it aside. His stomach churned. He told himself
he'd feel better when he'd checked out what his immediate surroundings had to offer. Maybe if he could find a
farm fire-fighting unit he'd feel more comfortable.

He moved off towards the front of the house, looking
for anything that might be a hazard if the fire came this
way. But Keith wouldn't have left him and Kate here if
there was any possibility of them being in any danger.
Damien suspected this was the house of a bachelor – the
only garden to speak of was a bed of neglected roses
near the front door, mulched with gravel. There were

no weeds and no dried-off neglected lawn – whoever lived here was either very fire-safety conscious or not much interested in aesthetics. He could relate to that. The only reason he'd had a garden was because his parents had planted it all those years ago when it was the family home and his mother had always kept up with the pruning and mowing of grass. He'd sprayed a bit of weedkiller around occasionally, but hadn't done much else in the way of gardening. Now, if he'd had someone to do it with, make a home together with, that would have been a different story. Well, he liked to think so.

As he headed around the side and then back, the feeling that he'd been here before became even stronger. He wished he could remember – it was beginning to annoy him.

A gust of wind whistled past him. He tensed and looked up. The trees were still. That was odd. He felt even more uneasy. At that moment a rooster started crowing, destroying the silence and startling Damien a little. And then he remembered: he'd come here with his dad years ago to get some chooks. If it was the same man they'd come to see, he bred prize-winning Rhode Island Red poultry. He'd been an old man then; he must be ancient now. Or perhaps his son had taken over, or maybe every adult looked old to a child. Damien felt a little better now that mystery was solved. But he still didn't feel completely at ease. He walked on a few steps. In front of him was a large wire enclosure surrounded by trees. He could see that the trees were there to provide shade and shelter but, Christ, it made it a fire hazard. He frowned. It was all in a wide-open, bare space, but he'd seen fire jump highways twice the size of that gap. He quickly finished his circuit and went to check on Kate. As he rounded the other side of the house, she rushed towards him.

'What's up?' he asked. They weren't due to meet for another ten minutes and she was looking a little harried.

'I don't know,' she said, gnawing on the inside of her lip. 'I don't like how close it looks from up there.' She indicated the tank with her head. 'I can't help thinking they've got it wrong.'

'Well, there're no certainties where fire and wind speed and direction are involved, as we both well know. What do you want to do, radio in to Keith?'

'Nah, better not. I'm probably just being paranoid – you know, after …' She sighed. 'Someone would have called us if things had changed – Trent should be nearly on top of it by now. I guess we'd better just sit tight. What do you think?'

'I'm feeling a bit on-edge myself, though that's probably just because we're without a vehicle. I'm going to take a look myself. Is that definitely the highest point around here, do you think?'

'Yup.' They walked in silence over to the tank and Damien paused and looked up before gripping the ladder with both hands, gritting his teeth, and putting his foot on the first rung. It seemed to take him an age, but eventually he was up there, and fighting vertigo, to take a good look around. Kate was right: the orange glow did look awfully close. And he'd swear the cloud of smoke was rolling ever so slightly in their direction. He could see one CFS truck in the distance. And he could see a big cloud of dust rising to join the smoke – most likely the grader doing its work. He looked around further and tried to judge the direction by the sun. It was difficult in the dark haze rising from the horizon. He estimated that what little breeze there was was heading towards them – completely different to what they'd been told. From what he could see, all that stood between him and Kate and the fire front was a few paddocks of stubble – a couple of thousand acres, tops. *Have I got it wrong? Have they?*

A strong gust hit him, causing him to sway slightly and his heart to race. He clutched the top of the ladder tighter. *Christ, that's all I need!* He carefully started heading back down.

'I reckon the wind's changed,' he said, once safe on the ground. 'And it seems a little gusty. I'm sure they've got things under control out there, but I don't like it at all.'

'No, me neither. What do you think we should do – ask them to come get us?'

'Nah, they're busy, let's see if there's a firefighting unit here first. Also, if the landowner's out on his grader, there should at least be a ute here somewhere. We'll be fine.' He said the words, but he didn't believe them for a second. The unease in his stomach was getting stronger. Satisfying his curiosity should have made him feel better, but it hadn't.

'Come on, let's stick together.'

Kate seemed relieved. They looked in the large shed. There was a tractor with spray unit attached, a truck, header, chaser bin, and what looked like space that would fit a grader. He was disappointed to find the truck and tractor doors locked. They walked to another, smaller, shed. He wondered if Kate was as worried as he was that no one had called them on their handheld radios with an update. There was plenty of chatter going on, but their names hadn't been called. Though the others had only been gone ten minutes or so, and they were probably still sussing things out themselves.

They peered into the shed, needing a few moments for their eyes to adjust to the darkness.

'Thank God!' Kate said when she saw a fire unit trailer hooked onto a ute. When Damien found the keys in the ignition he let out a deep breath he didn't realise he'd been holding. They checked the unit over. It was full and the ute started first go, as did the pump.

They stood leaning against the trailer and ute for a moment and then wandered in separate directions to check out the rest of the shed. Their relief was clear; things didn't feel so bad now. There was also a quad bike in the shed – with the keys in the ignition – and over in the corner a few large plastic drums. Chook feed, Damien surmised.

'Hey, whoever lives here must have trial or show dogs, or something. Isn't this a dog trailer?' Kate asked, standing in front of what looked like a squashed caravan.

'Show poultry,' Damien said. 'I finally remembered why I knew this place – I came out here with Dad as a young tacker to get some chooks. If it's still the same guy, he's a prize-winning breeder – like, Royal Show–prize–winning.'

'Right. Good for him. Personally, I don't like them, except for their eggs. I got attacked as a kid,' Kate said.

At that moment the rooster crowed again.

'And roosters give me the heebie-jeebies,' she added with a tight laugh.

They both looked up, frowning, at hearing the flap of iron above them. Suddenly the chatter on the radios changed pitch and there was a flurry of crackling, earnest voices, hissing radio static, people cutting in and out and talking over each other. Among the chaos they heard the words, 'Christ! Get back!' and looked at each other with wide eyes as they pulled their radios free and ran out of the shed into the open to improve their reception.

'Kate, Damien, this is Trent, you there?' The voice was breathless.

'Here,' Kate said, and then Damien. The fact radio protocol had been abandoned was not a good sign.

'You're going to need to prepare to take shelter or get out if there's a vehicle there. Sorry, but we're a bit stuck here. Wind's turned and getting a bit gusty. It's just a precaution. It's not heading in your direction. Not yet, but worst case, you've got around twenty minutes if it swings around any more.'

Kate looked at Damien with an expression that seemed to be asking if he was happy for her to answer for both of them. He nodded.

'Thanks. We're fine. There's a ute and working fire unit here. Out.'

'Great. Thanks. Be safe. Two one over and out.'

'Out.'

'Well, that doesn't sound good,' Kate said, hanging up her radio. 'But not entirely unexpected.'

'No,' Damien said thoughtfully. The rooster started up again. He had the distinct feeling its timing was no coincidence, but tried to tell himself he was being melodramatic. But then again, nothing to do with animals could be taken for granted. He knew that.

'What do you want to do?'

He knew exactly what he wanted to do, but was just trying to process how. He was damned if he'd come this far with his recovery to not listen to his gut now, especially when it had already given him several minutes' warning on the changed circumstances.

'I want to move the chooks – and rooster. Put them somewhere safe. There's a bank of trees behind their pens and if it comes this way, they won't stand a chance.'

'I was afraid you were going to say that,' Kate said, with a sigh and exaggerated eye roll. But she was smiling too. 'Come on then, let's see if the trailer will hook onto the quad bike. Best we leave the fire unit on the ute in case we need it.'

They attached the trailer to the bike and pulled it up near the hen house then stood silently for a few moments. Damien was surveying the enclosure and trying to ascertain how many chickens there were and how many to put in each of the ten compartments of the trailer. Kate was trying to look brave. The chooks were pacing about clucking, clearly on edge and sensing danger, or at least a disturbance.

Suddenly dust rose up around their feet. A whirly-whirly raced away off to their right.

'Come on, let's get cracking. The wind's definitely picking up,' Kate said. 'If you catch them and hand them to me I'll put them in the trailer boxes.'

'You sure you're okay to do it?'

'No, but it'll take too long if I just stand here being a wimp.'

'Okay, just leave one box free for the rooster. It looks and sounds like there's only the one.'

It seemed to take them an age before they had all the brown hens contained and Damien left the rooster's separate enclosure with the clearly unimpressed bird held close to his chest.

'Right, now what?' Kate asked when all the small doors were closed.

For the first time they paused and looked in the direction of the fire. The smoke was definitely thicker and getting closer.

'I don't like the look of that at all. And I don't think we should waste time climbing the tank again to check.'

'I agree.'

'Come on, let's just get out of here. I'll take this, you take the ute and fire unit. I'll wait out the front of the house so we can head out together.'

While Damien waited the minute or so it would take Kate to get to the ute and drive it out to him, he pondered if he was doing the right thing. He hated how hot the birds would be crammed three to a compartment. And where the hell was he going to take them anyway? Where was safe? All he could do was drive. He didn't like that he was so exposed on a quad bike – not to mention on an uninsured and unregistered vehicle, but there was nothing he could do about that. He was probably being overcautious and they'd all laugh at him later – or maybe they wouldn't because of all he'd lost – but he really did feel he needed to do this.

'I'm going to head left at the driveway and see if I can help the guys,' Kate announced when she pulled up alongside him. 'You go right back the way we came. When you get to the bitumen, turn right. I'm pretty sure you'll find shade and shelter for the birds at the old railway siding a few kay up. And you'll be well out of any danger.'

Damien nodded as he took in the directions. He hadn't been out this way for years, but he did remember the old, disused railway siding. And, if he remembered rightly, there was a large stand of gum trees just off the road not far from where he'd join the highway that might provide enough shade.

The trip along the dirt road felt endless, even though Damien knew it only seemed worse because of the wind in his face. The trailer of birds wasn't too heavy for the bike and he was able to average around forty kilometres an hour. When he was on the bitumen he was able to do sixty, and soon the stand of trees came into sight. He pulled over.

He was safe; time to check on the birds. He just hoped they hadn't expired in the heat and all this was for nothing. He crossed his fingers as he did a circuit of the trailer, lifting the main doors from the mesh sections so the breeze could flow through. There was a bit of fussing and clucking, which he took as a good sign – at least some were still alive. Buoyed, he peered through the mesh into each compartment in turn. Beady eyes blinked or stared back, little heads tilted as if to ask what was going on. He almost laughed when he got to the rooster, who seemed to be glaring furiously at him, clearly insulted by his treatment.

He didn't like feeling so out of the loop, but from the flurry of voices on the radio, he knew it was best he stay out of it. Reception was pretty crackly anyway, he was probably almost out of range. He was sure he could hear Kate's voice in the mix. She would have given them a heads-up. From what little he could hear, it was clear they were in the midst of a serious emergency.

'So much for just cleaning up and monitoring,' he said aloud. Suddenly he felt loneliness grip. He missed having Squish beside him and wondered if his auntie Ethel was still at his van or if she'd taken the kittens back to her place. His thoughts strayed to Jacqueline. Oh, to have her to go home to, to wrap his arms around after a long, stressful day. Why did things have to change, damn it?

Something in the corner of his eye drew his attention. He turned to see flashing blue lights coming towards him. *Uh-oh*. He always got nervous when he saw flashing blue lights. He got up and swallowed a few times, readying himself to explain why he'd been riding a quad bike on a public roadway – one that belonged to someone he didn't know – and without a helmet; he doubted his CFS helmet would pass muster. As he made his way over to meet the car he was surprised to see not a policeman alight but an old man. He was even more surprised when the old man flung his arms around

Damien's neck, almost throwing him off-balance. His eyes began to prickle at seeing the tracks of tears through the deep lines and streaked grime on the old man's face. He held the man tight as he sobbed and muttered, 'Thank you,' over and over. Damien tried to hold his own tears at bay, but the exhaustion and tension caught up with him and he soon found himself sobbing too. Over the old man's shoulder he noticed the policeman standing by his vehicle wiping his face with the back of his hands, staring at the ground and shuffling his feet in the dirt.

An hour or so later, the old man's son arrived with a ute complete with ramps to load the quad bike. They attached the trailer to the ute and Damien and Pete, the policeman from Charity Flat, waved them off. The birds were being taken to the showgrounds at Wattle Creek where there were pens to keep them safe for the time being. The old man, Bruce, had lost his pens and his house – he and his chooks and rooster were now homeless. Damien hoped he was well-insured.

Pete drove Damien back to the fire ground, travelling mainly in silence. The news had settled as a hard, painful ball in Damien's stomach. He felt tired, heavy and sad as he stared out the windows, watching the countryside fly by. A part of him wished he was being taken straight home. He didn't want to see the devastation.

They eventually turned in and crossed the cattle grid to find six fire units and several farmers and their units. Hoses were trained on the flames still chewing their way through the smouldering trees and ruins. If only the clearing had been bigger and extended right around the house and sheds. Damien was greeted warmly and given lots of manly back slaps. He blushed when Kate, clearly caught up in the moment, kissed him on the lips before pulling away quickly when everyone started cheering.

'Yeah, yeah, nothing to see. Move along,' Damien said, trying to sound light and laugh it off. He and Kate had shared a moment – two or so hours ago, not just now – but he only had eyes for Jacqueline. He ignored the protestations of his weary body, grabbed a rake leaning against the nearest truck and walked over to the chicken coop. Anything to get away from the scrutiny and appear busy.

He couldn't help but marvel at the beauty of the orange flames burning on the black trunks of Bruce's trees and at how his intuition had saved more than just him and Kate. Tears prickled again as he stood there watching, unable to pull himself or his thoughts away.

*

Damien didn't get home until after ten-thirty that night. He was wrecked, and filthy, and looking forward to a nice cool shower. As he drove in, he paused to check the depository with his torch.

He was surprised to find Ethel stretched out on his bed with the kittens and Squish beside her. He smiled and stood watching for a few moments, enjoying the peaceful sight and wishing it was Jacqueline he'd come home to – no offence to his auntie Ethel. It would just be so nice to come home to someone. For the first time, he thought he really understood the significance of the expression 'keeping the home fires burning.'

Chapter Thirteen

Jacqueline got to work early Tuesday morning in the hope of catching Doctor Squire before he went and did his hospital rounds. She was exhausted from fretting about the difficult conversation they had to have, so much so that when Ethel had phoned to check on her the previous evening, Jacqueline had promptly burst into tears. She wasn't much of a crier, ordinarily.

Doctor Squire's door was open and he had his head bent, reading something on his desk. She knocked gently, barely eliciting any sound at all. A part of her hoped he might not hear her and she could leave, telling herself she'd tried.

But he'd heard her – his head jolted up with shock, his eyes wide. He clearly hadn't expected anyone to be in the building at this time of day, let alone at his open office door. *Oh God, off to a bad start already.*

'Ms Havelock!'

'Sorry, Doctor. I didn't mean to startle you.'

'What are you doing in so early?'

'I need to talk to you, and yesterday …'

'Yes, yesterday was hectic. As are most days, really,' he said with a sort of pained smile, taking his glasses off, carefully folding their arms in, and laying them on the desk.

Jacqueline felt for him. Being a country doctor, especially being the only doctor, was clearly tough. She saw the hours he put in and that he was never actually off call. He did his rounds, saw to patients here, and attended the hospital whenever someone turned up out of hours.

He motioned for her to have a seat, which she did. She sat on the edge of the chair, but allowed herself to relax ever so slightly. She was here. Whatever was going to happen was going to happen, and then she would be free of this yoke that was weighing her down.

'It must be important. So, tell me. What has you in my office at seven-thirty on a Tuesday morning?' Doctor Squire asked, leaning back in his chair and linking his hands in his lap. His expression was neutral, bordering on friendly, and expectant. At least he didn't have his arms folded across his chest.

Jacqueline had gone over and over in her mind how she would approach this, so she only had to remain calm and follow her plan. She took the letter she had received from AHPRA out of her handbag and laid it flat on the desk so he could read it. He seemed to take an age to get his glasses from the desk, unfold their arms, and put them back on his face. The clock on the wall ticked its seconds in a hard plastic rhythm. *Clack. Clack. Clack.* His chair squeaked.

After what seemed another age, he took his glasses off, handed her back the piece of paper and said, 'Right, I see. Um. Well.'

Without a word, Jacqueline pulled from her handbag the letter of resignation she'd written and handed it over. He put his glasses back on, peered over them at her, smoothed the sheet of paper flat, and began reading.

When he'd finished and taken his glasses off again, he sat back in his chair, linked his hands and gazed at her with his lips pursed, clearly thinking things over.

'Of course I'm also sending a response to their letter, explaining myself and resigning my registration,' Jacqueline said slowly. The words were like barbed wire slicing through her, shredding the career she'd studied long and hard to achieve, and which she'd enjoyed – as short as it had been.

'Can I read that letter please?' he said, holding out his hand.

Jacqueline was taken by surprise. This wasn't how it had played out in her mind at all – there he accepted her resignation, told her when to vacate the cottage, that he was sorry it had come to this but rules were rules, and she left his office, hopefully with her dignity intact through having kept any threatening tears at bay.

She pulled the letter from her bag and handed it over.

He read with pursed lips, nodded a few times, then folded it back up and returned it to her across the desk. Jacqueline sat silently as he brought his clasped hands to his face, raised his two index fingers and began tapping them against his top lip while staring beyond her to a space above her head. She tried to remember what was on the wall there.

It seemed hours had passed, but sneaking a look at the clock told her the minute hand had only moved three places. If not for the loud ticking, she might have thought the clock had actually stopped.

'So, let me get this straight,' Doctor Squire finally said. 'You began a relationship with Damien McAllister after you had stopped treating him. He only saw you officially for treatment on three occasions. And you are of the opinion that the main problems that led him to seek treatment were that he hadn't adequately dealt with the grief surrounding the loss of his father some years before and that he was feeling overwhelmed by the pressure being brought to bear by his dominant mother. Furthermore, you are of the opinion that his emotional and mental state would not have been adversely affected by your personal dealings with him. Is this all correct?'

Jacqueline nodded. She hated that Damien was a part of all this, but she had decided she would be totally upfront. She realised she still needed to make a couple of things totally clear.

'Damien and I are no longer seeing each other. He, er, ended things when I realised the error I had made. He felt it was in the best interest of the town that I not resign. Otherwise I would have come to see you a week ago. We were, I was, er, hoping it wouldn't come out,' she said, blushing right up to her forehead. She stared at her hands.

'I see. But you still love him. This isn't just a whim, lust, is it?'

'No, it's not. We have agreed to wait, have nothing to do with each other until the two years is up,' she said.

'That is some commitment. I'm not sure I would have your resolve. Believe it or not, I was young once, too,' he said, smiling warmly. 'It will be next to impossible in a town this size to have nothing to do with each other,' he added.

'I know. And I'm sorry I didn't confide in you. I didn't feel I could ask your advice. Because then you would have been compromised and under mandatory reporting required to ...' she blurted. He was being so understanding, and she felt guilty about the mean thoughts she'd had about him since her arrival in town.

'Yes, rightly so. It is a bit of a pickle you find yourself in, isn't it, and of your own doing?'

'Yes. And I will take full responsibility. I *am* taking full responsibility.' God, she just wanted to get out of there now, not go over and over everything. It was like being slowly tortured. And the end result would be the same – the death of her career.

'While your letter is succinct, and gives a good account of your actions, et cetera, what is the point if you are just handing in your psychology resignation? If you're guilty of having a sexual relationship with a client or a former client before the twenty-four months have elapsed, which is the allegation they have made, why all the explanation?' He waved his hand. 'It's unnecessary. They won't care. Did you do it, or did you not, that is their only question.'

Now she did turn beetroot red. Of course, he was absolutely right. They would accept her resignation and the matter would be ended. So what had she been doing?

'Well, the thing is, I wanted to explain to them that while I've done the wrong thing, I haven't *technically*. We didn't, er, actually, um, have sex. We, er ...'

Doctor Squire held his hand up. 'Dear, I don't need to hear details. But what you are saying is that you have in fact *not* engaged in a *sexual* relationship with this former patient?'

'No. But ...'

'Well, why the hell are you pleading guilty in response to their letter?'

'Because *technically* it could be argued ...'

'We're not in court, Ms Havelock, you are not a lawyer, nor are you expected to behave like one. You either did what they are accusing you of or you did not.'

'Oh.' Jacqueline studied her hands. 'Well, I'm being honest. Owning up to my indiscretion. Trying to do the right thing. They will be concerned about Damien McAllister's state of mind and my impact on it through becoming personally involved with him so soon after being his practitioner.' She was quite taken aback by Doctor Squire's splitting of hairs. She'd taken him to be straight down the line, less interested in blurred edges than he clearly was.

'But they're not asking you if you were or are having a personal relationship with him. They're asking if you're involved in *sexual activity* with him. I can't believe you're throwing away the career you've worked so hard to achieve without fighting this.' He stared at her, aghast. 'Oh, Ms Havelock, I took you to have more mettle than this,' he said, shaking his head slowly. 'And what about this community? Young Mister McAllister is right, the district needs you. You're doing a good job. Sure we've had our hiccups, but this town needs you. *I* need you.'

Jacqueline was stunned to hear the passion in his voice. 'But I've done the wrong thing.'

'Yes, you have. But I happen to think it's a matter of degrees here.'

'But I should have known better. I *did* know better.'

'So, then, how did it happen?'

'I don't know,' she said with a sigh. She settled back into her chair. It was one thing to have Ethel's support, but it was a huge relief to have unburdened herself to Doctor Squire, her boss, and amazingly, not have been sent on her way to pack up her office. 'Honestly, it's as if my brain totally blocked it out. Then, after a week, I suddenly remembered. I don't understand it.'

'Well, you have been through quite a bit with having that stalker fellow turn up and then losing your car in the fire. And all that on top of moving halfway across the state to start a new job. Let's face it, suddenly finding yourself living in a fishbowl after the relative anonymity of city life can be very daunting. You were vulnerable. Mister McAllister was there when you needed him because his aunt lives across the road. You're young, you need at least a bit of a social life. I'm not surprised you blocked the exclusion period out. The human brain is a magical yet baffling thing. And what AHPRA needs to understand is that, whether they like it or not, some things are done differently out here and are often beyond our control. I know their rules are in place for the right reasons, but sometimes, like with your case, there's room for a little leeway, a little understanding on their part.

'I'm not condoning your breach of ethics for a second, but I can see some extenuating circumstances to at least try to fight this with. And I'm not sure if you're aware of this or not, but a couple of years ago, the Supreme Court overturned an AHPRA ruling and reinstated a psychologist's registration. It wasn't exactly the same circumstances as yours, but it might make them a little less likely to act so hastily when challenged. So, please, for God's sake, don't send this letter. At least not just yet. And, as for this resignation, it is not accepted.'

Jacqueline watched as he folded the paper back up and tore it in two, and then two again, before handing it back to her as a bunch of rough square pieces. She couldn't believe that Doctor Squire, who had reprimanded her for drinking and socialising not so long ago, was right behind her on this very serious matter.

'Right,' he continued. 'This is what I think we should do. Most of your letter to AHPRA is fine – the supporting evidence, that is. Take out the offer to resign your registration and change the main focus to a denial of the accusation based on the facts. I will write a letter of my own in support of you, outlining your value to this community. Golly, we don't have long,' he said, as if to himself before addressing her again. 'You rewrite your letter and drop it in to me at seven-thirty Friday morning. Sorry to have you come in so early again but it's really the only hour I get to myself before the chaos begins,' he added with a wan smile. 'Any questions?'

She was feeling a little stunned. If he had asked her to kiss his feet and then lick the dust from his leather shoes, she would happily have done so right then. 'Um, just one.'

'Yes?'

'Um, would you ever consider having an unregistered psychologist stay on as a counsellor?' she asked shyly.

'Of course. That is plan B, my dear. Plan A is to avoid that course of action. You've worked too hard and it seems the people here are warming to you. I don't want you to lose your piece of paper. Yes, you can still help people and do a lot of good without it, but I know how important the pieces of paper are. They are our credibility – even if only in our own minds. Many see them as just pieces of paper, and they are on some level, but I know as well as you do that they give us our confidence, our pride. I understand all too well.'

Jacqueline almost wept with relief. It was actually how she felt about her registration. 'Thank you. Thank you so much. You've no idea what it means to have your support.'

'I think, if they knew, you would have the support of the whole community. They know they are in safe hands with you here. You're just what has been missing and I'm damned if I'm going to give you up without a fight. And just because you're new around here – and will never truly be considered local because you're not third-generation born and bred,' he added with a laugh, 'doesn't mean you are not appreciated even, to some degree, loved.'

Jacqueline nodded as she replayed his words slowly. Damien had joked a number of times that he wasn't a true local because his grandfather hadn't been born there, but look how the community had got behind him and his new venture.

She stood and reached across his desk, gripped Doctor Squire's hands, and squeezed them.

'Thank you.'

He nodded and said, 'See you on Friday. Try not to worry too much.'

Chapter Fourteen

Damien was out taking a drive around his stock, as he did most mornings. It was important to him to make sure there was plenty of water during the warm months, and that the sheep or roos – or anything else – hadn't stuffed up a ballcock valve and drained the trough, or a pipe somewhere hadn't sprung a leak.

He also liked to set eyes on the young buck he'd saved. The roo now seemed well and truly part of the mob that was living in the next hollow over from where the fire had gone through. He was becoming harder and harder to pick out from the others now his wounds were almost completely covered with new hair, but if Damien got out the binoculars he could spot him. When all the hair had regrown, he'd most likely become completely anonymous, though he was always the last one to begin hopping away when the ute got too close. Damien liked to think his bounding off was only so as not to receive a ribbing from his mates for being so friendly with humans. He had no idea if those sorts of conversations went on between animals, or if they even had the capacity to think like humans, but he liked to believe they did. He'd often sit with the ute idling, watching them – had even been known to get so mesmerised he'd turn the engine off and let twenty minutes pass – before they bounded away. He'd imagine them formulating their getaway plan and agreeing where they would meet up later.

Perhaps he was still screwed in the head, he thought, shaking it all aside and driving away. As he did, a voice came on the UHF radio. He recognised it as once as Keith Stevens – captain of his CFS brigade.

'Damien McAllister, Robbie Olsen, Trent Baillie, Jack Smith, Andrew Olsen, you on channel? Over.'

'Receiving,' Damien said, as did the others.

'Just letting you guys know, we're having a combined CFS groups debrief at the Wattle Creek shed tonight at six, including a barbie, if you can make it. Sorry about the short notice, but that's life. Over. Oh, and partners welcome. Over.'

'Right,' Damien said, getting in first. 'Do we need to bring anything?'

'A salad or a sweet would be good, if you want. Otherwise, no drama. I'm sure there'll be stacks of food, as usual. Over.'

'Righto, count me in. Over.' Damien said.

The others confirmed and Keith said, 'Great. See you all then. Over and out.'

'Over and out,' Damien signed off.

He hung the receiver handset back on its hook beside the air-conditioning vent and as he did, he wondered when the powers that be would ban the use of these while driving too. It seemed a bit ridiculous that mobile phones couldn't be used while at the wheel but UHFs still could. They were great if you were happy for the world – or whoever was on that particular channel and listening at the time – to hear everything you said. And they were free. Perhaps the authorities feared too much of a backlash from the truckies. Plenty used their mobile phones these days, but Damien still used his UHF when it was appropriate. Though he often had to keep it turned down during busy times on the tractor because far too many people engaged in far too much chatter. Damien thought conversations should be kept short and sweet on the UHF. But of course there were no rules. And plenty of people seemed to forget the world was listening, or didn't care. Damien had spent years changing channels looking for less chatter, but had given up. So many times he'd wanted to add his own twenty cents worth, as his dad would say, and tell them to just shut up. Thankfully there was usually someone else listening who was less backwards in coming forwards and who'd politely point out that the UHF chatter should be kept to a minimum so everyone could get through.

He wondered if Keith had taken up his suggestion of bringing Jacqueline in for one of the debriefs, or just to talk to the guys. While it would be painful to sit there and look at her knowing there would be no snuggling up together or deep and meaningful conversations or lovely lip-locking sessions afterwards, tonight would be the perfect occasion to bring her in. All involved were devastated about the loss of houses and sheds yesterday.

He kind of wished he hadn't been so quick to agree to going, but it had been his idea to bring her in so it wouldn't look good to not turn up. He sighed as he pictured Jacqueline's eyes, which were sometimes browny-green and sometimes bright emerald. God, he missed her.

'But it's the right thing to do,' he told himself, and Squish and Jemima sitting beside him. He'd left the kittens at home sleeping safely in their box. He was only going to be out for half an hour, max. He had wanted to leave Jemima in the run, but because he'd brought Bob and Cara along, he hadn't been able to bring himself to leave her there alone. And she had followed him out to the ute and then stayed there, insisting she come along. He'd laughed when she'd scrambled up onto the seat from where she'd been put on the floor. Now she sat beside Squish. It was too funny, and oh so cute. He'd pulled the seatbelt around her because she hadn't looked too stable.

He was just pulling up to the van when his phone rang. He still got a flush of hope, thinking it might be Jacqueline every time it did, before telling himself not to be an idiot. His auntie Ethel's name was on the screen. He smiled. *Next best thing.*

'Hi, Auntie Ethel,' he said.

'Oh. Hi, Damien. Sorry, it still takes me by surprise that you know it's me,' she said, sounding flustered.

'How are you?' he asked, thinking she still wasn't sounding any chirpier. He wished she'd tell him what was on her mind and hoped all was well with Sarah, her daughter, and her new baby. 'What can I do for you?'

'Could you drop in after you've been to entertain the oldies? There's something I want you to do.'

'Oh. Okay. No problem. Actually,' he said, his brain kicking into action, 'would you be able to keep an eye on Jemima, Squish, and the kittens for an hour or so this evening from six? There's a CFS shindig. I could leave Jemima and Squish here, I suppose, and take the kittens and ...'

'Nonsense. I'd love to babysit. Are you going home and coming back again after the hostel visit or do you want to come here and have a bite to eat?'

'Thanks, but they're putting on a barbie. And I'd better head home and check the depository. But I'll leave plenty of time to help you with your thing. Half an hour okay? And do I need any tools?'

'Half an hour's fine and, no, no tools. Just yourself.'

'Any clues?'

'No. I'll tell you all about it when you get here.'

'Okay. A bit after five?'

'Perfect. See you then. Good luck with the oldies – not that you'll need it.'

'Thanks.'

★

His second visit to the hostel went just as well as the first. Mrs Timms even gave him some guff she'd printed out on government funding and grants, saying that perhaps if he got creative and thought outside the box, he might be able to convince the powers that be that he was a worthy recipient. He whizzed home and, after satisfying himself that no creature was expiring in the enclosure, was soon on his way back into town. He'd have to start trusting that people would be considerate and smart enough to follow his system. This running back and forth – especially from town – was a waste of fuel, and time, and a pain in the arse all around. He probably should have gone into the van and got changed, but he was presentable enough. He was keen to get in and see what Auntie Ethel needed him for. Hell, he'd been known to turn up to fight a fire or attend a meeting straight from the sheep yards or shearing shed in filthy, greasy clothes and with a face brown with dirt!

'Right, so what can I do for you, Auntie?' he said after giving his favourite relative a hug.

'Come in,' she said, ushering him and his hangers-on in.

'Stay,' he commanded Bob and Cara.

'Cuppa?' Ethel said at the bench.

'Milo would be good, thanks.'

Finally, with a mug in front of them both, the box of kittens on the floor and Jemima and Squish sprawled beside them, Ethel seemed ready to get down to business.

'Remember how I agreed to leave well alone with this predicament of Jacqueline's?'

'What have you done?'

'Nothing, yet. But …'

'It's her business, Auntie. I don't think …'

'Hear me out. There's been a development. Someone has reported her indiscretion and she's received a please explain letter from the medical board.'

'Oh no.'

'Yes.'

'Is she okay? God, she must be freaking out.'

'I haven't actually spoken to her since she spoke to Doctor Squire. All hell broke loose yesterday, apparently. She went in really early to talk to him ...'

'Hang on. How do you know if you haven't spoken to Jacqueline?'

'Because Doctor Squire, John, came to me.' Ethel puffed up ever so slightly with pride. 'He rang and asked me to pop around last night on the quiet.'

'I'm not sure it's a good idea to be discussing Jacqueline behind her back like that.'

'No, no, it's not like that. Hear me out. He asked me to ask you if you would write a letter of support for Jacqueline, indicating you are not adversely affected by the brief relationship, that you haven't actually had sexual relations ...'

'What? Now steady on. That's a bit bloody personal, don't you think?' he said, feeling the heat begin to creep up his neck.

'Now is not the time to get all coy, Damien. Jacqueline's whole career is at stake.'

Damien had the selfish thought that if it had come to this anyway, he could have been enjoying being with her all this time. God, what a bloody waste.

'Right. Got it. When does it need to be done by?'

'In the post no later than Tuesday. He's going to see her again first thing Friday morning. He said he doesn't want her having the time to stew on it too much. Oh, and we're keeping all this on the quiet.'

'I don't know ...'

'It's not me, Damien. It's on the advice of Doctor Squire, and I wasn't about to argue. If anyone knows what they're doing, it's him.'

'Hang on. Why didn't he call me himself?'

'He didn't want you getting worried about being called in to see him – like you were being called up before the headmaster for being in trouble, or something. Here's the reference number for her case you need to include,' she said, handing over a scrap of paper with a four-digit number scribbled on it.

'Okay. Fair enough.' Damien was glad for the doctor's sensitivity. That would have been exactly how he would have felt. He probably would have become a nervous wreck and more than likely put off turning up to see the good doctor at all.

'I'm thinking a letter of support from the local constabulary, Apex and CFS wouldn't go astray, either.'

'I can do that. I'll be seeing those blokes tonight.'

'Good. I'm going to do a ring around – CWA, church groups. Just make sure you give everyone the reference number and make sure they understand how important it is, and when it needs to be sent by. And that it needs to be kept on the down low.'

Damien almost smiled at seeing how animated Ethel was becoming. There was that light in her eyes that had disappeared for a bit. He would have ribbed her about it if this wasn't so serious, didn't involve Jacqueline.

'Hey, we could do a petition via Facebook,' he said, becoming a little excited himself. 'I know we don't have long, but do you think it'd be worth a shot?'

'I don't know. We don't have long. And we need to keep this quiet. Jacqueline wouldn't like a fuss and won't …'

'She's not on Facebook.'

'Really? Even *I'm* on Facebook!'

'Since when?'

'Oh, the other day. Madge, Doris and Janet insisted. Apparently Nancy Squire is too, so I thought, what the hell? Are you sure she's not on it and won't see what we're up to?'

'Positive. I've searched for her.' Damien was a little embarrassed. There was no way he'd own up to just how much time he'd spent searching, trying to cyber-stalk Jacqueline. She was on LinkedIn, but that was all he'd been able to find. He wondered if she had a particular objection to Facebook and Twitter or if she just hadn't been interested enough to get involved in the more social sites. Would it bother her if they put some-thing up about her on Facebook? Even if it did, she'd appreciate it was for the right reason, wouldn't she? She wasn't too proud to accept help, was she? And she was on LinkedIn, so it wasn't as if she had a serious aversion to having an online presence – that's what it was called, wasn't it? Fancy all the local wrinklies being into it. He'd better send Auntie Ethel a friend request and keep an eye on her!

'I'll have to have a think about Facebook,' Ethel mused. 'But in the meantime, you're clear with what you need to do?'

'Yep. Write a letter of support and get some others to, but keep it quiet. Got it,' Damien said.

'Because I don't need to tell you how important this is.'

'No, you don't.'

Chapter Fifteen

When Rob and Cecile picked Jacqueline up that evening she was more nervous than usual about her talk. It wasn't that she didn't know what to say, but she did feel a little rushed after only having been approached that morning. She couldn't exactly refuse the request – the head of the CFS had practically begged her. He said he was seriously concerned that yesterday's destructive blaze, coming so soon after the recent loss of the McAllister house, might be the straw to break his team's back. How was he to know she was dealing with her own disaster? She certainly hoped word hadn't got around – and wouldn't. Her mind was still processing the surprising turn her conversation with Doctor Squire had taken and she was feeling quite disconcerted about her life. It didn't help that she'd be seeing Damien in person – and in public – for the first time since their break-up.

If she'd been the one who'd ended things between them, she might have gone across the road to Ethel's, where his ute was parked, and made sure the air was clear. But it wasn't her call, it was his. She was a little hurt that he was so close yet apparently so far away, even though she understood – well, she was trying to. If only he wasn't going to be there tonight, but the universe wouldn't let her off the hook that easily.

As she walked with Rob and Cecile from the car to the brightly lit shed carrying the plates of food Cecile had prepared, Jacqueline told herself that she would put her predicament out of her mind for a few hours and focus on helping the community she was now part of, like Damien would want her to. Anyway, she might need this night to go well so as to insulate her against her clients drying up if word did get out about her blunder. Determined to be sociable and enjoy being out of the house, she pushed the negativity away and focussed on having a smile on her face when she entered the shed.

Keith Stevens hugged her so tightly she thought she might run out of air, but she was grateful to be so enthusiastically welcomed. He introduced her around and made sure she knew plenty of people. She felt welcome, not too much of an outsider, and didn't get the impression people were talking about her behind her back – you could always tell.

As she turned to take in the crowd to see who else she knew, she caught sight of Damien in the far corner, talking in a small group. Not wanting things to be awkward between them, she raised a hand in friendly greeting. He either didn't see her or he deliberately avoided making eye contact: instead of returning her smile and gesture, he turned away and raised his beer bottle to his lips. She felt a surge of disappointment the likes of which she didn't think herself capable.

Keith had her speak before they enjoyed their barbecue, joking that it was the only way they'd get the group to listen. She made a mental note to keep things even briefer than usual – hungry people were rarely an attentive audience.

Her part of proceedings seemed to go well. She kept her head, remained focussed, and spoke confidently. The restless, almost bored-looking expressions of her audience appeared to grow into understanding, a look that flowed right across the large space. She urged people to talk to each other, explore their feelings, and share them with their loved ones, their mates, their colleagues.

'Everyone reacts differently to each situation. Everyone *feels* differently afterwards. For some people the grief, guilt, sadness and fear hits straightaway. For others it can happen slowly, over quite a long period of time. And for others still it can hit later, but hard, like a bolt of lightning out of the blue. There are no rules. You feel what you feel, when you feel it. But it's important that if you don't like what you feel or if it's having a negative impact on your life, then it's important to get some professional help. Sometimes just knowing you're not going crazy and what you're feeling is completely normal, and being experienced by others, is all the help you need.

'Partners can sometimes be affected almost as much by what you've seen and been through,' she continued, 'even if they weren't there. Often our moods and behaviour change when we have a lot on our minds. And quite often we don't see the changes because we're too close to the situation or we think we're doing a great job of behaving normally, carrying on as usual. So it's important to gauge the reactions of those around you, listen to their feedback. Even if it seems like criticism, and you don't want to hear it. Be careful not to shut people out and think you can deal with these things on your own – you don't need to. Just remember, there is help available and, as my favourite saying goes, a problem shared is a problem halved. There's no shame in saying, "You know what, I'm not sure what's going in my head, but I don't feel quite right. And I don't like it." Even if you don't want to come and talk to me or another professional – a conversation that would be entirely confidential – talking to someone, *anyone*, will help. It's not about burdening them. In my experience, people genuinely want to help. And by listening, they are helping.'

There were plenty of thoughtful expressions and heads nodding among the crowd. And when she finished and was walking to her chair amid rowdy applause, there seemed to be a lot of animated chatter going on between audience members.

After the debrief was complete, she joined them for a wonderful barbecue meal that was a far cry from the sausages in white sliced bread covered with onions and tomato sauce she'd been expecting. There were baskets of what looked like homemade sourdough rolls and more interesting and delicious-looking salads than she would ever have imagined. She tried to sample so many she ended up with her plate heaped embarrassingly high. But she'd eaten everything and then lined up for dessert – another fine-looking spread, as Ethel would say. Again she'd ended up with a rather full plate. And to make matters worse, when she turned away from the table, she almost upended it into the chest of the man who'd been standing right behind her. The *gorgeous* man who'd been standing right behind her. Jacqueline had to forcibly stop herself from gasping. He had the longest lashes she'd ever seen above the deepest, darkest brown eyes, all highlighted by his fine dusting of even darker stubble. She almost dropped her plate.

'Oops, careful there. You don't want to lose that now you've done your gathering,' he said jovially. He flashed her a brilliant smile while helping her to right her plate and avert disaster and embarrassment.

'Sorry. I do seem to have quite a lot, don't I?' she said, forcing her gaze down to her plate. Did she really think she could eat custard slice as well as pieces of cheesecake and pavlova *and* a brandy snap? If only Ethel was here to get her a doggy bag. 'There's just too much choice,' she said, blushing, despite praying she wouldn't. Jacqueline's gaze moved back up and locked on his eyes. Golly, he was tall. And golly, the man looked good in a uniform, even if it was yellow. If she'd got this close to Damien she'd have said the same about him, she thought, reality hitting and disappointment surging.

'You're allowed to come back for seconds, you know. Food is where the country folk really come into their own, I think.'

'Oh, are you not from around here?'

'Yes and no. Sorry, forgive me, I'm Paul. I'd shake your hand, but …'

'Nice to meet you. I'm Jacqueline.'

'Yes, I know. We all know,' he said, grinning cheekily.

'Oh. Of course. Silly me,' she said, trying to laugh it off, but feeling the heat creeping up from between her breasts.

'Sorry, that was cruel. I enjoyed your talk, by the way. You made a lot of sense. And I liked how down-to-earth you made it – not at all preachy.'

'Great. Thanks.'

Now it was Paul's turn to look embarrassed.

'It's okay, I know what you meant,' she said, putting her left hand out and touching his arm. As she did, she noticed people were hovering nearby with empty plates, clearly attempting to not look impatient.

'I seem to be holding up the works, I'd better get out of the way,' she said. 'It was lovely to meet you, Paul.'

'Likewise. I'll see you around, I hope,' he said, flashing another dazzling smile before moving aside.

Jacqueline spent much of the evening feeling surprised at how she'd been sucked into the fold. She was sure the CFS crowd weren't just being polite and reserved around her – she was really being welcomed. She'd been welcome at every other event she'd been to, but this somehow felt different – and had seemed different even from before her talk – she just couldn't quite put her finger on how.

Later when Rob, Cecile and Jacqueline were preparing to leave, Paul appeared beside her.

'It really was lovely to meet you, Jacqueline,' he said, holding out his hand.

'Yes, likewise, Paul. Lovely,' she stammered, returning his handshake.

'If you'd like to stay a little longer, I could give you a ride home,' he offered.

'Oh. Thanks very much, but I'd better get an early night.' She wouldn't have minded talking with him more, but while she'd enjoyed being distracted and sociable for a few hours, she was suddenly feeling very weary. She was thankful Rob had an early start in the morning – something to do with lambs, he'd said – and was keen to head off early.

'Thanks, Paul, but we've got it. She came with us so we'll see her home,' Cecile said.

'Okay. Well, goodnight then,' he said.

As she alighted from Rob and Cecile's car, Jacqueline sighed to herself at seeing Damien's ute still at the kerb outside Ethel's. All evening she'd longed to go up to him and ask how he was and get all the latest news on the joey and everything that was going on with Esperance. She wouldn't have shared her latest news, but to be close to him might have provided some comfort. But whenever she'd thought she was getting closer to him she'd look up and he'd be on the other side of the big shed, talking to a different group. And as at the beginning of the evening, every time she thought she'd caught his gaze and smiled, he'd turn and be deep in conversation. It was probably for the best. They weren't together. And her life was messy enough.

After waving Cecile and Rob off, but before putting her key in the door to her cottage, Jacqueline toyed with popping across the road to see Ethel. Damien was sure to still be at the CFS barbie. She wondered if Ethel had told Damien about the latest development. Probably. She wasn't so keen on having her business discussed behind her back, but it saved her doing it. Anyway, she trusted Ethel and Damien to respect her.

She was still to tell her parents. She really wanted to tell them in person, but could see she'd have to resort to doing it over the phone – she couldn't put it off any longer. Apparently the car was taking a little longer than anticipated so she wasn't sure when they would be coming back.

Inside, Jacqueline found she suddenly wasn't tired or in the least bit ready to go to bed. She thought of Paul and felt a little chuffed that a handsome man had shown an interest in her. Had he been flirting or just being friendly? Whatever it was, it had been quite nice. But what really had Jacqueline on a bit of a high now was feeling such a part of things and her presentation going down so well. She'd made it clear that she was happy to be part of any debriefs after major incidents or whenever the brigade captains or group captain thought she could add value. And she didn't care about drumming up more business for the clinic. These people regularly put their lives on the line to save people's properties, for no pay and often when their own were at risk; the least she could do was contribute her expertise. She really was beginning to see how these small communities banded together to fight for a common cause. Of course she'd seen it in the news numerous times, but she harboured a healthy scepticism for the media and their ability to skew a story to suit their own needs. But to be a part of it, see it with her own eyes, *feel* it, was something else. She wasn't kidding herself, knew deep down she wasn't really a part of the community yet, was just being shown a courtesy, though a courtesy that perhaps ran deeper than before.

Jacqueline was beginning to see how the country seeped into your soul when you weren't looking. She'd come out here for a year to escape Jacob, but now she couldn't see herself wanting to leave. And she hadn't even been born and bred out here. She just wished she could share her epiphany with Damien. Though he would probably just look at her quizzically and say, 'Well, yeah, I know.' He did know. He had always known.

She'd tell her parents instead. But just as she picked up the phone and began dialling their number, it vibrated and rang. 'Mum and Dad Home' appeared on the screen.

'Hello?'

'Hi, darling. How's my favourite daughter?' Philip Havelock said.

'Dad, I'm your *only* daughter, only *child*, remember?' Jacqueline said, rolling her eyes at their little ritual.

'So, how's things?'

'You first. To what do I owe the pleasure of the call?' It was a valid question. Her parents tended to be creatures of habit and usually only rang to say hi and for a catch-up chat on a Sunday evening.

'Well, I have your new car out in the driveway. I think the dealer got sick of me asking and finally put the hard word on someone. We're going to drive over with it on Saturday.'

'Oh, that would be great. Thank you.'

'We'll only be able to stay for a few days – a week at most; we're meant to be having the house painted, but the heat has upset things a bit. But we thought you should have your car, and we'd like to check up on Damien, and start looking at rental properties.'

'Sounds good. It'll be great to have transport again.' It was on the tip of her tongue to tell her father about Damien, but she didn't. They'd be here in a few days – it could wait. And it would be much better to tell them in person. She doubted they could help, but their support would be a huge relief.

She turned her attention back to her father, who was telling her about their going a day without power at the surgery thanks to the wild weather that had swept though. That got her attention and she suddenly felt guilty – she should have rung to check they were okay. But she'd seen the map of damage on the news and it hadn't been anywhere near the house. She hadn't given any thought to the surgery being right in its path.

'God, Dad, that's terrible. Thank goodness you only lost power and not the roof.'

'It got a bit chaotic in the dark, but everyone scrabbled through okay. Anyway, enough about our dramas. How's everything with you?'

'Well, I've just got home, actually. I've been part of a big CFS debrief. They lost a couple of houses this week. Did it make the news?'

'I didn't see anything about fires over your way. Goodness. The Barossa fires still seem to be getting all the airplay.'

'It was amazing, Dad …' As Jacqueline relayed her evening, she thought how good it felt to share it with someone who didn't take for granted what she'd experienced.

'Wow, you really sound like you're becoming part of the place,' Philip said when she'd finished. 'That's great. And they say you have to be born into these rural communities to be fully accepted. I guess being so close with Damien is a big help.'

'Yeah.' Jacqueline almost let it go, but stopped herself. It wasn't fair to keep them in the dark. Especially now her father had brought Damien's name up. Hadn't she just been telling the audience at the CFS shed not to put things off? One of her mother's favourite phrases came to mind: 'Do as I say, not what I do.' She took a fortifying breath.

'Dad. There's something you should know ...'

'Oh, you poor thing,' Philip Havelock said after she'd spilled the beans on the whole tale: her and Damien; the letter from the board; Doctor Squire's support. Her face had begun flaming as if she was a teenager being subjected to a sex education class when she'd had to mention they'd not actually had sex, but she'd decided it was all or nothing. And it felt good to get it out in the open. 'You should have called us. But I understand why you didn't.'

'Thanks, Dad. I'm still working through it all myself.'

'Well, it sounds like you've got a good ally in Doctor Squire. And you've got Ethel right across the road for support. I'm grateful for them. But, tell me, how's Damien in all this?'

'I honestly don't know. Since he ended things, we haven't had any contact. I haven't told him about the latest development of the letter from the board, though I imagine Ethel will have.'

'The sad thing is you could have been together all along and had his support if it was going to end up like this anyway,' Philip said.

'Yes. It's frustrating.'

'But it's done now. You just have to work through it. These things have a way of sorting themselves out. You'll see.'

'Thanks, Dad.' She didn't tell him that she thought it right that she suffer as a result of her stupidity.

'Now, are you okay with me phoning Damien to let him know we're coming over?'

'Of course, Dad. You have a separate relationship with him because of Esperance. That's your business. And I wouldn't mind knowing how everything is going out there.'

'Well, hopefully this will all blow over soon and you can take up where you left off.' His unspoken words – *But I'm not going to be your go-between* – hung in the air. 'We'll talk about all this more when we get there Saturday. Are you okay if I update your mum?'

'Probably best you do.'

'Right, well, expect us mid to late afternoon. It'll be a slow trip with lots of stops since your mum isn't used to long-distance driving.'

'If it's a problem, I'm sure you could put the car on a car carrier.'

'It'll be fine. I think your mum is secretly quite relishing the chance to feel a little liberated,' he said in a whisper.

'Well, drive safely. I can't wait to see you,' Jacqueline said, a wave of emotion sweeping through her.

'And us too. Love from Mum.'

'And back from me. Thanks, Dad. See you soon.' She ended the call feeling decidedly choked up.

Chapter Sixteen

Damien felt bad about avoiding Jacqueline at the CFS do. God, how he'd itched to make his presence known when she'd been standing so close to Paul bloody Reynolds, who was known for his smooth moves and snappy dressing. At least he'd been in yellow like the rest of them. Shit, maybe that was worse. Wasn't it well known that women were attracted to men in uniform? Maybe yellow didn't count. He hoped not. Christ, this would all do his head in if he let it and he was already doing it tough. Bloody Paul bloody Reynolds. He hadn't minded the guy until he'd seen him practically drooling over Jacqueline! Damien sighed. He couldn't blame him; she'd been the best-looking girl in the room, in the district, by far. But she wasn't his girl and until she was in the clear, he wasn't about to do anything to get her in more shit.

He hadn't even risked meeting her gaze. One look into those eyes and he'd be spellbound. And if he'd got close enough to get a whiff of her hair, he'd have been a goner. He would've wrapped his arms around her and never let go. And she'd been wearing that top – or one the same colour – that made her browny-green eyes look bright emerald. Nope, no way he was going anywhere near her until she could be properly his again.

Not that she'd ever *really* be his, even if they were an item. He wasn't stupid enough to think a woman such as Jacqueline – well, any woman, really – was something to be owned. They were free spirits to be admired, adored and treasured. The idea that if you loved something then you should set it free and if it came back then it was yours, or however it went, had it sort of right. He reckoned most people had the wrong end of the stick about this love business: you had to set it free and welcome it back every waking second of every day. Being together was mutual, equal. Though, hell, look where he was on the old love wagon. Absolutely nowhere.

Squish hopped into his lap and snuggled up. *But I do have you,* Damien thought, as he scratched the little dog behind the ears. Humans really could learn a thing or two from the animal kingdom. Animals were good judges of character and didn't seem to go in for this cruel emotional manipulation crap that humans seemed so good at and seemed to do just because they could. He was sure Jacqueline hadn't been deliberately trying to bait him at the CFS meeting, though. She was a free agent and twenty-three and a bit months was a very long time to expect her to stay true to him. This wasn't the 1950s.

Damien had the sudden thought that if he couldn't have Jacqueline, he didn't want any woman. And it wasn't just a woe-is-me moan; the knowledge had settled upon him like any other major conviction, like his new venture, and the need to stand up to his mother. He chewed it over for a few moments, testing how he felt – really felt. Fine. Good. Okay. He knew all the women around here and it wasn't like he had the time or energy to go looking for love elsewhere. Most new arrivals came already attached – Jacqueline had been the one exception in many years and she really seemed to fit in, even down to the classy but understated way she dressed – and they usually only stayed just long enough to make their men miserable before realising this country thing wasn't for them.

As far as Damien could see, most men failed when choosing a wife, especially those who brought back a slick, well-made-up girl strutting around in white and tottering on high heels. Who in their right mind wore white out here and expected it to stay clean? And how could these men not see that the look they were attracted to – the one most likely to impress their mates and mothers – took maintenance and cost money? So it stood to reason that if you were happy to pay for the upkeep – which you would when you married and what was yours became hers – then a dolly bird would be a fine thing. But if you weren't – and let's face it, farmers were known for only spending their money on what could make them more money – then they were in for a rocky road and eventual heartbreak. And a substantial loss of funds.

Perhaps it was because he had a sister who fancied herself as a bit of a sophisticate, but from where Damien was sitting, it all looked crystal clear. Year after year, he'd watched the well-to-do farmers – or those who liked to think they were – trot off to the city and return with a lovely ornament. And then, after the lavish wedding and interest from the local ladies had died down, so did the girl's love for her farmer and her tolerance of the dust, flies and lack of decent shopping centre within cooee. If only the men put them through a bout of shearing, seeding and harvest first, they'd be much better off. A girl who could support you through all that without much complaint, few hissy fits, and only the odd mistake, like pranging into an auger and denting it, was a keeper in Damien's mind.

When it came to Jacqueline, however, his theory was totally shot. He couldn't believe she didn't at least have one grandparent who had been born and bred on the land. 'Yep, she's a really special one,' he told Squish wistfully. 'So, how are we going to get her back?'

He'd set the day aside to write his letter of support and get the Facebook campaign to keep Jacqueline in town up and running. It was forecast to be a stinker – 42 degrees. It was meant to be autumn, for goodness sake! He was planning to hunker down in the caravan with its little air-conditioning unit. Hopefully it was up to the task. The idea of sitting down and writing a letter, let alone one where he had to spill his guts on his private stuff, didn't exactly fill him with joy. But it had to be done.

'Whatever it takes, Squish,' he told the dog. It would be hard and would take him ages, but he'd do it. What he was more concerned about was the Facebook petition.

They didn't have time to get a big enough response. But his biggest worry with it was the wording. How could you ask for votes for Jacqueline to stay without telling everyone what she'd done wrong and embarrassing her? You couldn't ask people to get on board with half-arsed, wishy-washy wording. And it would still have to be expressed well enough to gain credibility with the medical board people, whoever they were.

He needed more coffee to nut this one out, he thought, getting up.

Back at the table, he added a few more notes to those he already had from his discussion with Ethel about what to include in his letter. His main problem was how to write it so he got everything across without sounding like a dumb hick farmer. And, worse, doing more damage to Jacqueline's cause. If he came across desperate or pleading, she'd be screwed.

He felt a stab of anger and frustration towards her. It wasn't too strong and was fleeting, but it was there. How could she have so badly fucked up? Yet if she hadn't, he wouldn't have had those couple of nights where he'd got to hold her in his arms and taste those sweet lips of hers … *Oh, God. This is so not helping.*

Damien almost leapt on his phone with joy when it began ringing. 'Hi, Auntie Ethel.'

'How are you going with your letter?'

'Um. Er. Bit slow actually.'

'As in, you haven't started yet.'

'Yes, that. I'll get there.' *I have to.* 'But, hey, how do we word a Facebook page and status post to drum up support for her without letting the cat out of the bag and embarrassing her? No one can know what she's done or that she's in deep shit.'

'I've had the same thought. That's why I'm ringing.'

'So what are you writing for your petition? Please tell me you've come up with the perfect thing and I can steal it.'

'No. I'm actually thinking of scrapping the petition and suggesting you scrap the Facebook petition too. You're right, there's no way of handling it delicately. The best I've come up with is, "If you think Jacqueline is an asset to this town and district, then sign below." But that will make it look like her funding is being cut and her job is in jeopardy, which then puts Doctor Squire in the firing line. And which runs the risk of sending people to Jacqueline to personally offer their support, which totally defeats keeping it on the quiet.'

'Hmm. So what else can we do? You've got a plan B, right? You always do.'

'Not really. The only thing I can think of is getting more individual letters from the right people. Yes, we have to broaden the inner circle a little, but I think they can be trusted. Did you get a chance to speak to Keith at CFS last night?'

'Yep. He's on board.'

'Good. I've got the others we talked about. Hopefully it's enough to get her over the line and it won't backfire on us. Oh, what a mess! How did last night go, anyway?'

'Good. She was great.' Damien was fully aware his tone was dreamy, but he didn't care. His auntie Ethel knew the score.

'We all know she's great, Damien, but how was she received? It was a slightly different talk than what she's been doing.'

'It went well. She was brilliant. And that's not just me – everyone was going on about how good she was afterwards. She really does make a lot of sense and does it without all the textbook-sounding crap.'

'Yes, Damien, we all know you're in love with Jacqueline,' Ethel said with a laugh.

'That obvious, huh?'

'Yep. Don't worry, we're going to do our best to remedy the situation.'

'Thanks, Auntie Ethel, for everything.' But the thing that bothered Damien was the two-year waiting period. They might be able to get her out of trouble and keep her in her job, but the rule would still be there. And he was feeling so much worse about that now he'd seen the sharks starting to circle. But best he keep that to himself; saying it out loud would make it so much more real, and no doubt give Ethel another cause to try to fix.

'Oh, before I forget. I had a call from Philip, Jacqueline's dad, just before. They're heading over with her new car tomorrow. He was checking on her on the quiet – she apparently told him everything last night over the phone. Anyway, I've invited them for dinner Saturday night. So now I'm inviting you – and your furry friends, if you like.'

'Are you sure it's a good idea for me to be seen socialising with Jacqueline?'

'I don't know,' Ethel said wearily. 'But the way I see it, the damage is done. And we're all friends. It will be good to be together again.'

'Has Jacqueline agreed to this?'

'Um, no, not yet.'

'What are you up to?' he asked, having noticed her cagey tone.

'Well. I'm going to notice their car in the driveway and pop across and invite them to dinner. Philip has agreed to play along and get Eileen on board too.'

'I'm not sure about tricking Jacqueline like that.'

'It's entirely up to you if you come or not. If so, be here at six-ish. Your choice. I'd better go and get the groceries. We're having trifle for dessert, if that helps your decision-making process,' Ethel added with a laugh.

'It does. Though trifle is hardly last minute if you're wanting everything to look spur of the moment to Jacqueline. But that's up to you.'

'Hmm. No, she'll be fine. And we've got her parents as back-up.'

'Well, I guess if her parents are on board, it can't hurt too much. At least we'll all be in trouble. And, Auntie, if anything can win her over, it's your trifle.' *At least I'll know she won't be out with Paul – or anyone else.*

'So I take it you're in.'

'Yep. Count me in.'

'Good boy. As I say, in for a penny, in for a pound. Now go and write that letter.'

'Okey dokey. See you then, if not before.'

Damien hung up feeling a little icky about being part of the subterfuge around dinner, but much better about the whole campaign to help Jacqueline. He reckoned Jacqueline would have said if the Facebook page was causing him so much grief then maybe that was a sign it wasn't meant to be. She was big on listening to your intuition, said it was there to protect you – you ignored it at your peril. Phew. He was glad he hadn't. Deep down, he'd known it wasn't the right thing to do. If Jacqueline hadn't come into his life, he'd still be a miserable git getting into all sorts of trouble through ignoring the little voice in his heart or soul, or wherever it was located.

That's where he'd begin, he suddenly realised, grabbing his lined pad and pen. At the start.

Chapter Seventeen

Jacqueline was in her lounge room, eagerly awaiting the sound of a vehicle pulling into her drive. She couldn't sit still, and for the last hour had regularly leapt up and gone to the window every time she'd heard a car drive past or just to check she hadn't missed their arrival.

Finally there was the *toot toot* of a car horn. Jacqueline raced outside to find her mother emerging from a VW hatch that looked identical to the one she'd owned before, though much cleaner and shinier.

'How was it?' she asked, hugging her mother, who looked a little dishevelled and travel weary.

'Exhausting. It's a very long way,' Eileen Havelock said, patting down her hair, as was her habit when things were a little off-centre in her world. 'I've never driven so far in my life.'

'Well, you did it. Well done,' Jacqueline said, trying to build her mother's spirits and reduce her own level of guilt for putting her through the ordeal. She should have insisted on having the dealer put it on a truck.

'It really is a nice little car to drive, though,' Eileen added.

'That's good. Thanks so much for bringing it over for me.'

'It's our pleasure. I just need to catch my breath. There were a lot of trucks out that last stretch – quite unnerving,' she added with a nervous little laugh.

At that moment her parents' familiar Holden Statesman pulled into the driveway. Her father got out and she hugged him, overcome by the familiar feeling that everything would be okay. She struggled to let him go and lose that sense of security, but did so reluctantly when he gently eased himself out of her clutches.

'Let me look at you,' he said, holding her by the shoulders and staring into her face. 'You look worried.'

'I am worried, Dad.' She tried to laugh it off, but failed, almost to the point of bursting into tears.

'So, what are you doing about it, other than not sleeping? That won't do you any good.'

'Dad, can we discuss this inside? Better yet, after I've had a chance to check out my new car? Thanks so much for taking care of it all.' Jacqueline wasn't too fussed about looking over the car – it would be just like her other one – but she welcomed the reprieve from her father's scrutiny. She leapt inside and had a quick look around. The only difference she could see was a little bluetooth symbol and what looked like an inbuilt GPS. She couldn't even be bothered to turn the key and check. The major difference was the smell and the state of cleanliness. She wished she could get more excited, but she had this other business taking up most of her brain power. And, anyway, the fire had been an all too stark reminder that a car was just a car – something that could easily be replaced if anything happened to it.

Finally the Statesman was unpacked and her parents installed in the bedroom she'd given up, moving into the spare room with the single bed, as previously. She'd toyed with buying a double bed for the room, but as the house was being rented fully furnished, she'd have to find somewhere for the single. And if she left, she'd have to take the new bed with her, and leaving was looking like it might be on the cards.

In the kitchen, hands wrapped around mugs of tea and coffee, they discussed all the goings on in each other's lives while carefully skirting the elephant in the room that was Jacqueline's job. She was actually feeling a little more positive about it now her parents were there, despite telling herself they couldn't actually help. There was nothing quite like feeling taken care of by your mother, and Eileen Havelock was very good at it. As usual, she had arrived with two large eskies full of assorted meals, cakes and biscuits.

They were just discussing whether to have her lasagne that night and invite Ethel over when the doorbell rang, followed by, 'Yoo hoo!' from the open front door.

'Speak of the devil,' Jacqueline said, and got up. She hugged her friend and apologised profusely and admitted she had forgotten to ring her back.

'It's quite okay,' Ethel said. 'I know you've had a lot on your mind and you'll call if you need me,' she said. But Ethel sounded a little hurt.

'Thanks. I'm still getting my head around it all. But I do want to tell you about Doctor Squire. He's been amazing.'

'Oh? That's nice to hear.'

'Come on through. I'm guessing you've seen the cars in the drive.'

'I have indeed. Thought I'd pop in and say hi,' Ethel said, making her way through to the kitchen.

Once all the greetings were out of the way and another cup of tea had been poured, Ethel invited them over for dinner.

'Mum brought a lasagne. We were going to have that,' Jacqueline said. 'Why don't you come over here?'

'No, that can wait,' Eileen Havelock said almost before the words were out of Jacqueline's mouth. 'We'd love to come, wouldn't we?' she said, looking expectantly at her daughter and husband. Philip Havelock was nodding enthusiastically.

Jacqueline frowned to herself. She had the distinct impression there was something going on here.

'I do have trifle,' Ethel said.

'Oh, well, that's it then,' Philip said, clapping his hands. 'Decision made. Thank you, Ethel. We would love to come. Six o'clock, did you say?'

'Um, she hasn't actually said a time yet,' Jacqueline said. 'What's going on?'

Ethel, Eileen, and Philip shared sheepish glances.

'This is not you coming across and inviting us on the spur of the moment, Ethel. Not if you've made trifle, which I know for a fact you do the day before,' Jacqueline said indignantly.

'Guilty as charged,' Ethel said.

'It's the only way you get any flavour from the port,' Eileen Havelock said.

'That and quadrupling the quantity of alcohol.' Ethel put a finger to her lips and pursed them.

'So you've been on the phone for days organising this then?'

'Oh no, just …' her mother said.

'That's not the point. Why not tell me? Why all the subterfuge? Come on. Spill.'

'Because Damien is coming,' Ethel said quietly.

'Oh. Look, we didn't break up because we've had a falling out or anything and need an intervention to bring us back together. It really wouldn't be a good idea to be seen socialising with him before my, um, situation is resolved.' *And probably not even then.*

'It'll be fine,' rang as a chorus around the table.

Jacqueline frowned. They didn't seem to see how serious the trouble she was in was. She was on the cusp of losing her licence to practise – and her credibility, for Christ's sake – years of study down the drain. And here they were going behind her back, orchestrating meetings with the one person she shouldn't be seeing.

'You don't have to sleep with him, Jacqueline. That's what the issue is, isn't it?' Eileen said.

Jacqueline almost choked on her tea. She stared at her mother, aghast, staggered that she'd say such a thing, and apparently so casually. Her whole world was seriously out of kilter.

'Look, you'll be chaperoned and we'll have you home by nine thirty. And if necessary, we will bear witness,' Philip said. 'We want to see Damien.'

God, so did she – desperately. She wanted to see how he was coping and hear how everything was going at the farm.

'You could stay here. I'll send over a care package,' Ethel said, smiling cheekily at her.

'Well, as long as you're okay with me moving back home and freeloading if I get fired,' Jacqueline said after a few moments. Maybe she was being a bit uptight about it all. She had dropped her letter in to Doctor Squire the day before and now had to do her best to put it all out of her mind until she heard back from the board.

'Good girl,' Ethel said, patting her hand. 'So I'll see you all in a couple of hours,' she added, draining her mug. 'No need to get up. I know my way. Cheerio then, see you a bit later.' She gave a wave, and was gone.

'Great. I'm glad that's settled,' Philip said. 'You really do make a lovely couple. I hope you can put this business behind you soon and get back on track.'

'Hmm,' was all Jacqueline could say without snapping at them. There was no point. It was all her own fault. They were right to be disappointed when they had become so attached to Damien. He really had, in just a few short weeks, become the son they'd never had.

'Right, there's time for us to go over this predicament of yours. Have you written your response yet?' Philip asked.

'Yes. I'll just go get it.'

Jacqueline sat nervously watching as her father and then her mother read her letter, waiting for their feedback.

'Why aren't you asking to be released from the two-year exclusion period?' Eileen asked, handing the letter back.

'Because I want to look like a professional worthy of keeping my status, not a lovesick teenager,' she said, trying to keep her annoyance at bay. 'What do you think, Dad? You've been on professional disciplinary panels before, haven't you?'

'Not for many years, and not for something like this. But I'm afraid I tend to think your mother might have a point.'

My mother who has always been a stay at home wife and mother, Jacqueline wanted to snap. But she was just angry and disappointed with herself – that was usually the reason for people lashing out at others. She tried to be more patient and less annoyed as she listened to her father.

'I'd be inclined to go for broke. You're already looking down the barrel of a reprimand and/or losing your registration. I don't think you could make things worse by asking. If you don't ask, you don't get.'

'If you love Damien, really love him – and I know it's early days – then why aren't you fighting for him, for your relationship?' Eileen said. 'Are you okay with waiting for two years? Is he? By not asking, it looks like you're happy to wait. That doesn't say much about your relationship to me.'

'I *am* fighting this, for *us*,' Jacqueline said, unable to hide her exasperation and astonishment at her meek and mild mother being so opinionated.

'No, dear,' Eileen said kindly. 'You're fighting for your career, not your relationship. Well, that's how it looks from where I'm sitting.'

'Sorry, sweetie, but I agree with your mother. How would Damien feel if you didn't say how important he is to you? Better yet, put yourself in his shoes: how would you feel if he was writing this letter and not mentioning how much you mean to him?'

Jacqueline felt the shame beginning to creep up her neck. They were absolutely right. She would be mortified if the situation were reversed. But it was too late. And this was business. Damien would understand that, wouldn't he? Just as she would.

'Of course he'd understand,' Eileen continued, 'because he's that sort of fellow. But he'd be deeply hurt, as would you.'

'The question is, could you survive that level of hurt? Relationships recover from disappointment, but few recover from deep hurt and betrayal,' Philip said.

If it wasn't so serious, she might have laughed and said something like, 'Listen to you, Doctor Phil and Mrs McGraw.' She wanted to tell them they were being melodramatic. But they weren't, really. She was beginning to see that if she left the relationship out of her letter then she was essentially ending it.

'It's too late, I've already handed it in to Doctor Squire ready to send. This is just a copy,' she said.

'Oh, I'm sorry, I didn't realise. I thought you were asking for our opinion,' Eileen said, her cheeks colouring.

She took the letter back to her room to close the topic and make an attempt at keeping her tears at bay. She was so disappointed in herself. She was being selfish, trying to resurrect her career without trying to get her relationship sanctioned too. She couldn't say it was for the money, because she knew Damien wouldn't hesitate – nor would her parents for that matter – to offer to take care of her financially while she found another source of income.

Jacqueline fought the urge to throw herself onto the single bed in her temporary bedroom like a petulant teenager and sulk, and instead set about getting changed for dinner. Her parents were entitled to their opinion and even if she did think they had a point, what was done was done. The letter had been sent. She'd been proud of her professionalism and objectivity before her parents had weighed in. She just had to focus on that; to start second-guessing herself now would do her in. And, anyway, Doctor Squire had agreed with what she'd written and, while the disloyalty to her parents stung a little, his opinion was the only other one that mattered in this situation. Of that she was certain.

Chapter Eighteen

Damien was pleased that the other guests were immediately drawn to Squish and Jemima and the box of kittens he'd placed out of the way on the hall table. All except Jacqueline. She stood back and let her parents come forwards and hug him and then ooh and ahh over the animals. He didn't think he'd ever get tired of being hugged by the Havelocks – they gave great hugs.

Jacqueline offered him a shy 'Hi' and a warm smile. He smiled back, wondering if they'd had to work hard to persuade Jacqueline to come, but instead of going over and giving her a hug, he offered a shrug and stuffed his hands further into his pockets. Given the state of play between them, that's what he figured was probably warranted. If he was going to greet her properly, it would be by wrapping his arms around her, pulling her in tight, burying his head in her hair, and telling her he loved her and that this exile had to end because he couldn't bear to be without her for another day.

Oh how he ached. He'd heard about how love and longing could actually physically hurt. He wouldn't have believed it before, but now he knew only too well. It also pained him to see how drawn and tired the love of his life looked. If only he could take all the pain away from her. But other than writing a damned good letter in support of her and getting the CFS head honchos involved, it was out of his hands. He felt as helpless as he had watching his dad die of a brain tumour all those years ago.

Ethel ushered them into the dining room and urged them to sit, pointing out who was to sit where. Damien was pleased to be seated where he wasn't in Jacqueline's direct line of sight, nor close enough that he could hold her hand under the table or brush it accidentally. Auntie Ethel had clearly thought this through. He was relieved when the bread came out and they busied themselves with breaking and buttering it and the atmosphere seemed to lighten.

'Any progress with the house, Damien?' Philip asked.

'Yeah, they're going great guns. The site's been cleared and the concrete slabs poured. I just hope the heat doesn't cause anything to crack. But I'm staying right out of it – the builders know what they're doing. And there's no great hurry. The caravan's good, though it's starting to get a little crowded now Jemima is growing and thinks she's an inside pet,' he said with a laugh. 'She and Squish have become quite inseparable.'

'Oh, that's so adorable,' Eileen cooed.

'And how are your plans coming along?' Damien asked, looking from Eileen to Philip.

'Slowly,' Philip said. 'We were hoping to be packed up and ready to move into a rental but we've had delays with the heat. We want to get the house painted and freshened up, but the painter won't work while it's really hot. But it'll all work out in due course.'

'So what do you have planned for this trip? How long are you staying?'

'Probably just the week. We really came over to bring Jacqueline her new car. But while we're here we're hoping to do some serious rental house hunting. And of course we'd love to come out and see how things are with you.'

'Damien's been very innovative,' Ethel chimed in. 'Tell them about the depository.'

Damien flushed a little with the attention. 'Well, it's not a huge thing and it's a work in progress, but ...' He told them all about it.

'That's a brilliant idea,' Philip said.

'Yes, how clever you are,' Eileen enthused.

Damien noticed Jacqueline nodding her agreement. He wished she would look happier about being there.

'Well,' he said, 'as good an idea as it is, having the mobile there still hasn't stopped me going up and checking it a couple of times a day.' He gave a tight laugh.

'It's a start. That's the main thing. You'll get used to it. I'm sure if people have made the effort to bring creatures to you, then they'll make the effort to follow the directions,' Philip said kindly.

'I hope so.' Damien turned finally to Jacqueline. 'So, Jacqueline, it'll be great to have transport again. I still feel awful ...'

'Don't. It's certainly not your fault,' Jacqueline cut in. 'And, yes, I hadn't quite realised how not having a car cramps your style around here. Though, of course, Ethel's been great. It'll just be nice to be able to be spontaneous again.'

'And to celebrate, we're going to do a few wineries, op shops and antiques stores tomorrow after the house hunting,' Eileen said.

'That sounds like fun,' Ethel said.

'Would you like to come along?' Eileen asked.

'Oh, no. Thank you, but I couldn't. I'll come and have a nosey at houses with you, but I've, um, got a few things on later in the day. Not really my thing anyway, I don't think.'

'I'm not sure it's mine either,' Philip said.

'Oh, come on, Dad, you loved it last time,' Jacqueline said. Damien was pleased to see her finally light up a bit.

'The wineries, maybe, but the op shops and antiques shops played havoc with my sinuses.'

'Oh, come on,' Jacqueline teased.

'Yes, since when do you have sinus trouble, Philip? What rot!' Eileen added, with a *pfft*.

'Well, why don't you girls go and send Philip out to visit Damien?' Ethel said. 'I'm sure you could find something for him to do, couldn't you?'

'Sounds good,' he said. What he had in mind was that Philip could help him fine-tune his letter, but he wasn't about to bring that up with Jacqueline in the room. 'Hey, if you come out early, say, get to my place by a quarter to seven, you might get to see the young buck you helped fix up. He's usually grazing with the mob. But I'll understand if you don't want to get up that early.'

'No, that would be great. How's he doing?'

'Brilliant. Almost completely healed. I haven't bothered him since we released him – I just look through the binoculars. Once the last of his hair's grown, we won't be able to pick him out.'

'That's amazing. And all down to the hard work of you and Ethel.'

'Well, you helped too,' Damien said.

'Okay, so that's all sorted. Thanks for getting me out of a shopping trip.'

'Sure you won't come with us, Ethel?' Eileen said.

'Quite sure, thank you.'

Damien smiled to himself. They clearly didn't know his auntie Ethel well enough to know shopping was not her thing. And other than the odd sherry or red wine to be polite, her preferred tipple was a cask of Coolabah.

Dinner was a triumph, as always, but the trifle was a particular hit and Eileen and Jacqueline began demanding Ethel write out the recipe for them. Damien loved the trifle too, but he'd had it dozens of times over the years, so wasn't quite as enthusiastic as the others. Many a time he'd been lucky enough to drop into his auntie Ethel's and scored a bowl for lunch, or just because.

Tonight they'd only managed to make their way through just under half of the huge bowlfull. Ethel joked that she'd be eating trifle until it came out of her ears.

'Hey, why don't you come to my place tomorrow night?' Damien found himself blurting. Where the hell had that come from? 'We could have the trifle for dessert. I can do a barbie. If the weather's okay we can sit outside, but if not, I'm sure we'll be able to squeeze around the table.' He hadn't really meant to, but the thought had come to him as the night was wrapping up.

Jacqueline was looking at him a little startled. Almost, perhaps, a little fearful. He was sorry about that. But now he'd seen her, been in such close proximity, the thought of not being near her stabbed him hard under his ribs.

'You'd better invite your mum in that case,' Ethel warned.

Mum? Oh shit. What's the date? What's the date tomorrow? He coloured again as he realised his blunder. *Uh-oh.*

'What's wrong?' Philip asked.

Damien shifted in his seat. 'Sorry, dinner's off. And catching up in the morning might be cutting it a bit fine, Philip. Sorry, but I've just remembered I have to take Mum down to Lincoln to catch the plane. She's off on her overseas trip.' It was pushing it a bit to get to Lincoln and back, deal with the animals, and get all the food for a barbecue sorted in time. He'd be a wreck and probably not very good company.

'Lucky you remembered in time,' Ethel chided.

'Oh well, next time. Do please wish her safe travels from us,' Eileen said.

'No problem at all. Best we leave it until you've got plenty of time to show me around. And, yes, please pass on our best,' Philip said.

'Do you want to leave the kittens with me, rather than drag them all the way down there and back?'

'Oh, that would be great, thanks.'

'And if you're back in time and feeling up to it, you can come for tea and pick them up. But I'll leave it entirely up to you.'

'Okay. Thanks.'

Conversation went on around him as Damien thought about how much nicer the one hour and twenty minute trip to the airport would be with Jacqueline in the car beside him. This separation was excruciating. What had he been thinking, believing he could do this?

He stood at the door with his aunt and saw the Havelocks off, putting on a brave face, but feeling his heart ache harder with each step Jacqueline took away from him. Then he bundled his animals into the ute, did a second headcount, waved to Ethel and drove away. For the first time in ages he felt really down and not at all like going home alone to his empty temporary house. Squish bumped his leg.

'Yes, I've got you, Squish. And you, Jemima,' he said as the roo leant over to copy Squish.

He had to pull himself together. He had a great life and was damned lucky. So what if he didn't quite have the girl of his dreams? They were working on that. He just hoped Jacqueline still wanted him as much as he wanted her.

Chapter Nineteen

Jacqueline struggled to get to sleep that night. She tossed and turned in the small single bed in the spare room while the odd snore and rustle came from her parents in her room. She'd eaten too much, and was unable to get Damien out of her mind, and there was the shadow of her imploding career always lurking for when her defences were down. She'd even wondered if her few cancellations recently were the result of people having found out the truth about her, but she knew she had to keep that thought at bay or else it would consume her and destroy her fragile confidence.

If only she had Damien to confide in. While she missed holding him, she thought she missed his intellect and their conversations even more. Being so near to him at the dinner table but not being able to touch or talk properly had been excruciating. He'd looked tired and she hoped that was only from getting up to feed the kittens rather than the recent fire and loss of property bringing back painful memories. Was he putting on a brave front or was he really okay with it all? She'd heard how he'd saved a flock of valuable and much-loved chickens and she desperately wanted to tell him how impressed and proud of him she was. She was only mildly surprised that his actions hadn't been singled out as part of the CFS debrief, or even tonight at dinner, but it could have been at Damien's request – he was humble and didn't crave the limelight. Jacqueline hadn't wanted to embarrass him by bringing it up. She knew, if pressed, he'd say the people who mattered knew and to please leave it at that. The fact that the house and other property had been lost didn't help – he might consider his victory small in the scheme of things and feel uneasy about not being there to at least try to save the house. She knew the firies were all gutted by the result. She'd learnt how rarely such losses happened and how hard they hit the volunteers. Twice in one season was almost unheard of, so it must be utterly gut-wrenching for them. She hoped they saw value and felt some comfort in her being involved.

At least she knew Damien was listening to his intuition more and following his instincts. That helped ease her mind a bit, but she was still worried about him. Several times she thought about saying 'screw this', and getting dressed, and heading out to see him. She had a car now and could be spontaneous. But she was always brought back to the same point: he had ended things with her for the good of the community and she had to continue to respect that. And there was Doctor Squire to consider – he was putting his reputation on the line to help her too. Giving up, not fighting for her job and her career, wouldn't get her anywhere. And Damien clearly wasn't prepared to have a clandestine relationship with her and put her more at risk; he had too much integrity for that. Jacqueline thought she did too and was surprised by the strength of her feelings and thoughts in favour of doing the wrong thing. Was it lust? Was what she had with Damien just a passing infatuation? If so, why was she craving just spending time with him? She'd have loved nothing more than to spend a few hours sitting beside him in the ute, driving to Port Lincoln and back. Even having to spend half the journey beside Tina would have been worth it.

Jacqueline finally fell asleep still feeling disappointed about being separated from Damien, but very grateful for having her parents in the next room. It would be so nice to be mothered for a few days, and that was something Eileen was very good at.

*

As Jacqueline followed her parents into the third nondescript, cream brick, late-seventies house, she thought about Damien. She longed to sit with him and feed and play with the tiny kittens, and Jemima, Squish, Bob and Cara, rather than spend time travelling around with her parents. Jacqueline felt like a hanger-on, despite doing the driving. Here she was, going through rental properties, knowing full well she might be moving back in with her parents. It meant she couldn't be totally objective; she looked at each place for her own needs. A few times she'd almost asked her parents if perhaps they should reconsider their move now her circumstances might be changing. After all, why would they move all the way out here if she was just going to end up back in the city? It was clear from the number of unemployed clients she had that jobs were few and far between. It was a town with only one hotel, one bakery, an insurance broker, a hardware store – there weren't many employers, full stop. But she had to remind herself it wasn't all about her, her parents had their own lives to lead. She felt like a petulant teenager at the thought that despite her crisis nothing had changed with them. But she was adult enough to keep her thoughts to herself.

The mood in the car was sombre as Philip, Eileen and Ethel compared the three homes they'd gone through. Philip expressed his disappointment at the lack of decent choice. According to the real estate agent's website, there were about a dozen places available to rent in town, but Ethel had assured them these three were the best of a generally drab lot. Anyway, they were all very similar in features and price.

'It's okay. It's clean and tidy enough,' Jacqueline said finally. 'Really, that's all you need in a temporary rental.' God, she sounded like her mother. One thing was for sure, the rental accommodation out here was cheap compared to the city.

'Are you sure you want to carry on with your plans to move out here when I might not be here?' she said on the drive back to drop Ethel home. There, she'd finally got it off her chest.

'Oh you'll be here,' Ethel said firmly.

Jacqueline looked across at her in the passenger's seat with raised eyebrows. 'You seem to be forgetting the pickle I'm in.'

'Ah, you'll get through it and be just fine.'

While Jacqueline normally appreciated Ethel's optimism and sunny disposition, today it annoyed her. Was no one but her, Doctor Squire and Damien taking this seriously? She wished she'd stayed home in front of the TV, wallowing in her self-pity and dire circumstances.

'It'll all work itself out, one way or the other,' her father said, reaching between the seats and patting her shoulder.

She smiled weakly at him in the rear-vision mirror, trying to look grateful for his supposedly buoying words. She just wanted it over with, whatever the outcome. She could deal with it, put it behind her, and get on with her life. It was the waiting that was killing her. Worse, waiting while being expected to carry on as normal, pretend nothing was up. Only her whole career – her life – was up in the air, she thought sardonically. No big deal. She almost snorted aloud as she pulled into Ethel's driveway.

'How about we do fish and chips at the seaside to cheer us up instead of going to a winery?' Philip suddenly announced.

'Good idea. You know, I think I've quite gone off the idea of shopping too,' Eileen said.

'Hmm, me too,' Jacqueline added.

'I read there's a nice café at Pigeon Bay. What do you say, Ethel? Will you join us?' Philip said.

'Yes, do, please,' Eileen pleaded. 'We'll wait for you to feed the kittens.'

'Oh. Well, okay then. If you're sure.'

'Absolutely!' Eileen cried.

'Yes, a bit of fresh sea air and a stroll along the jetty might be nice. Thank you.'

My poor parents. They are clearly desperate not to be left alone with their mopey daughter. I'd better make more of an effort.

A little over an hour later Philip and Jacqueline were waiting at the counter for their order and Eileen and Ethel were sitting in the car with the windows down, enjoying the sea breeze. Being at the seaside had even perked Jacqueline up a little – turning the radio up when ABBA had come on and them all singing along loudly to 'Chiquitita' had helped. It was quite exhilarating to sing out loud and have nobody care if you were a bit out of tune. Jacqueline loved singing loudly in the car, but had always been careful to keep it private. She thought she didn't have a bad voice, but wasn't entirely sure. The old hits had continued and their whole journey had been filled with raucous singing. Jacqueline couldn't remember her parents being so fun – Ethel really did bring out the best in people. She was so grateful for that and had to remember to be in the present, appreciate the moment – even if just for an hour at a time. That was what she advised clients going through tough times to do. She really needed to remember to follow her own advice, she thought, as she gathered up the bundle of fish and chips and turned away from the counter.

Straight into a chest. It was the same chest she'd almost crushed a plate of dessert into at the CFS shed.

'Well hello there, Jacqueline, you really know how to get a man's attention,' Paul Reynolds said, flashing that gorgeous smile.

'Shit, sorry,' Jacqueline blurted, blushing wildly.

'Paul Reynolds, nice to meet you,' he said smoothly to Philip, and stuck out his hand.

'Philip Havelock, the pleasure is all mine,' Philip said a little quizzically as he rearranged his armful of cold drinks and accepted the hand. While Paul was distracted, Jacqueline took the opportunity to take in his wet, mussed hair, thicker stubble, large, tight muscles on tanned arms and lovely lean legs beneath his navy and white striped board shorts. Christ, the man's feet even looked good in thongs!

'I'd better leave you to your lunch while it's hot,' Paul said, nodding to the paper-wrapped bundle she held tightly to her chest, trying to ignore how warm it was making her. She wished she was the one who'd grabbed the drinks – she needed one or two to put to her forehead and chest right about now.

'Thanks. Yes,' Jacqueline blustered.

'I'll see you 'round.'

'Yes. Right. See you.'

'Are you okay?' Eileen said, as Jacqueline handed everything over to Ethel in the passenger seat.

'Fine. Let's get out of here,' she muttered, avoiding looking anyone in the eye.

'It might be nice to sit here,' Eileen said, pointing at the picnic table under the verandah.

'No,' Jacqueline said, a little too sharply. It was only a matter of time before Paul came out again and she didn't like what seeing him did to her.

She sensed Ethel chuckling beside her and turned to look at her friend. If she wasn't so intent on getting away from here – fast – she might have smiled at the knowing, cheeky expression on Ethel's face. Instead she looked back to the windscreen.

'What's going on, Philip?' Eileen asked as Philip got in beside her. 'Jacqueline is acting strangely.'

'I think you'll find your daughter is blushing and flustered as a result of just having been flirted with by a nice-looking young man,' Philip said.

'Oh. Right. Lovely,' Eileen said, looking almost as flustered as Jacqueline. In the rear-vision mirror, Jacqueline noticed her mother open and then close her mouth, very much like she was about to say, 'But what about Damien?'

'Yep, Paul Reynolds strikes again,' Ethel said, grinning and nodding. 'Bit dishy, that one.'

'The young man who walked past?' Eileen asked. 'Yes, he was rather a fine specimen.'

'Mum!'

'Dear, I'm not too over the hill to appreciate a fine set of tanned muscles. Sorry, Philip.'

'Hey, don't stop on my account,' Philip said, laughing, 'I'd be worried if you didn't notice a fine-looking man.'

'As you still are, dear,' Eileen said.

'You're all too much,' Jacqueline said, shaking her head in consternation, but smiling.

'I heard you met him the other night,' Ethel said. 'He's a nice young man, as well as nice looking.'

Jacqueline blushed again and opened her mouth to say she'd never cheat on Damien, but Ethel got in first.

'We know you love Damien, but it doesn't hurt to keep your eye in.' She paused. 'Well, you know what I mean.'

'Yes, dear,' Eileen added. 'Sometimes it's nice to enjoy a piece of art, even if you wouldn't necessarily want it hanging on your wall.'

'Okay, thank you all for your advice. Right, to the jetty, unless there are any objections?' she said, glancing left and right before driving off. While she was sure she would stay true to Damien, her mother was right, what harm did it do to admire the scenery?

Chapter Twenty

Damien pulled up outside Dorothy's house per Tina's instructions. Despite him being ten minutes early, there his mother was, sitting on the step at the end of the path like a school kid waiting for the bus. Why wouldn't she wait inside with her friend? It wasn't as if it was a ridiculous hour of the day – it was ten in the morning. He'd wondered why Tina had asked to be picked up here since she'd announced her plans and requested his taxi service. She'd told him sharply that she'd be leaving her car in Dorothy's yard out of sight. It just didn't make sense – why would his mother leave her car out in the weather when she could have left it in her own garage? But he didn't ask – to do so would be like the inter-rogations Tina rolled out. There was clearly something going on with her that she didn't want to tell him about and he wasn't sure he wanted to know.

God, I hope she hasn't suddenly got Alzheimer's, he thought with a start as he stowed her luggage in the back and tied everything down. But if she was confused, she wouldn't have arranged for him to be here and wouldn't have her bags, ticket or passport. And she did, pulling the items out and showing him in response to his query.

Tina got into the vehicle and sneered with distaste at finding she would be sharing her space with Squish. Damien wanted to point out that it was his ute and he could have whomever he liked in it, but he couldn't be bothered.

She'd have a fit if she knew Jemima had most likely left roo fur all over the seat where she was sitting. Did roos shed like dogs and cats? He didn't know, but he was sure Tina McAllister wouldn't be impressed. He probably should have given the cab a vacuum. It was a bit stale smelling, now he thought about it. Squish, seeming to sense the hostility, snuggled up close to Damien's leg and put his head on his master's thigh.

They set off, waving to the few people walking the streets of the tiny town. While Damien drove, his mother chattered non-stop, even going so far as to get out the brochure and point out things in London she was looking forward to seeing and doing. He focussed on the road ahead, occasionally nodding and murmuring in a vague show of interest. She was clearly nervous. It was understandable, given she was leaving Australia for the first time ever. Damien wondered what the dickhead shearer thought about his estranged wife blowing a heap of dough on such a frivolous thing as an overseas trip. Perhaps she was nervous because she'd emptied their bank account without Geoff knowing, he found himself suddenly thinking. Perhaps she was not only fleeing her crumbled personal life and going to visit her daughter in order to draw some sort of line in the sand – perhaps she was actually becoming an international fugitive.

Christ, where did that come from? Clearly he hadn't had enough sleep. He almost laughed at the absurdity of it all, but did literally shake his head slowly in an attempt to be more sensible. Anyway, he had plenty of his own stuff to think about. These days his brain was constantly whirring with ideas for ways to make money for the farm. It was all quite exciting – he felt he really had found his calling. And there was all the other not so interesting stuff to do: he had to phone Steve Smith about putting in a crop for hay, and organise for the sheep to be crutched before too long. And then there were the fixtures and fittings to choose for the house. He'd once looked forward to making these choices – when Jacqueline was in the picture. He reminded himself that it was technically his mother's house and perhaps she might like to make these choices – or should be making these choices. Thank goodness she'd come to her senses and gone home and turfed the dickhead shearer out, otherwise he might have been facing the horrible prospect of her living back at the farm with him. He actually shuddered at the thought. God, if that happened he might really shoot himself. No, he shouldn't say such things, even in jest. Suicide and thoughts of suicide really were not laughing matters, as he knew only too well. He was past all that now and had himself together and his life sorted. But the truth was, without Jacqueline, he wasn't feeling one iota of interest in this homemaker side of things. While he was very grateful for them rebuilding his house and would love having all that space again, if it was left up to him, he might just stay put in the caravan until the owner made noises about wanting it back.

He should really be staying on in Lincoln for a few hours to clear some decisions away, but he felt very uneasy about leaving Jemima in the run and was keen to get home. She was safe enough, but he still felt guilty. Squish had whined at leaving her behind too, which had made it all so much worse. He felt bad about leaving the kittens and imposing on Auntie Ethel too, not that she seemed to mind. He'd hoped to bring them along, but there really wasn't enough room and Tina would have had kittens herself if asked to nurse the box on her lap. While she was being supportive of his venture, that support clearly didn't stretch to developing an affection or even, it seemed, a tolerance for the furry creatures in his care. Thank God he had Auntie Ethel and Philip Havelock. He was so disappointed – far more than he thought he should be – at missing Philip's visit. His feelings were ridiculous, given Eileen and Philip would be moving over permanently before too long.

Damien had asked Ethel if she'd drive Tina down to the plane instead, but while she'd sympathised, she'd refused, pointing out that it wouldn't pass muster with Tina. It was part of the politics of the place: just like one must stay with one's own flesh and blood, one must ferry one's flesh and blood to airport and return, else the tongues would be set wagging. Absolutely mortifying for the likes of Tina McAllister. There were reputations to uphold and social norms to conform to. Sometimes it did Damien's head in, but he always went along with all the palaver because that was less painful than a glacial, purse-lipped glare of disapproval from the ice-queen, his mother.

'I'm still disappointed Lucy wouldn't have me stay,' Tina suddenly said with a huff before folding her arms tightly across her chest.

'I think it's more that she couldn't, rather than wouldn't.' Damien felt the need to defend his sister. While they didn't have much of a relationship these days, Lucy had rung after the fire and they'd had quite a nice chat – better than they'd had in years. Anyway, while he thought it high time Lucy put up with their mother for a few days, he did feel for her. He got the distinct feeling Lucy really didn't like Tina. And Lucy wasn't as good at putting her head down and not taking the bait, just shutting up, as he was. He'd had way more practice.

'And can you believe I have to find a taxi and then her office on my own? She couldn't even meet me at the airport!'

'Hmm. It might be fun – an adventure,' Damien ventured. *God, I really am getting better at thinking positive. It's even starting to come naturally.*

'Yes, well!' was Tina's response – the fallback when she couldn't find a decent retort to carry on an argument. They descended into silence.

'So how's everything going with you? How's the romance?' Tina said suddenly, shattering Damien's peace.

He thought about lying rather than opening himself up for more questions and a possible interrogation. Just the thought of Jacqueline made him glow warmly with happiness and feel very sad and annoyed all at once. He said: 'Everything is fine. But Jacqueline and I … we're no longer seeing each other.'

'Oh. I'm sorry to hear that. She seemed nice enough. Probably for the best, though.' Damien noticed out the corner of his eye that she was staring at her hands and fidgeting with the strap of her handbag.

'Why do you say that, Mum?'

'Oh. Well it's probably not really right, is it, you seeing her when she's been your therapist?'

Damien's antenna shot up and a split second later the blood froze in his veins. *No, surely not.*

'Is there something you're not telling me, Mum?'

'What do you mean?'

'You tell me.' He'd have loved to have stared her down until she answered, but as he was driving, all he could do was shoot her a quick, icy glare.

'I heard it's not allowed – relationships between patients and therapists. And for two years even after the professional relationship has stopped,' she said, a little defensively.

'Where did you hear that?'

'Um, I'm not sure now. But it doesn't matter if you're not seeing each other, er, romantically. As I said, it's for the best. Jacqueline could have got into a lot of trouble.'

'She did,' he said quietly. And then louder: 'She *has* got into a lot of trouble, Mum.'

'What? No, but …' Tina McAllister's head shot up and there was a second before she managed to compose herself where Damien saw the truth, confirmation of what he'd been beginning to suspect.

'You dobbed her in, didn't you? How could you?'

'It was for your own good. I did it for you. But I fixed it. I took it back, wrote another letter straight away when I saw how much she was helping you.'

'Well, she's received a please explain letter from the medical board. You've got her in deep shit, Mum. Why couldn't you just leave well enough alone? I was happy. For probably the first time in my life, I was truly happy.' His heart clenched, but he was too angry for tears to form.

'I was upset, angry, worried about you …'

'Worried I might be happy, more like. Worried I might learn to stand up for myself. You can't fucking control everyone and everything, Mum. You just can't.'

God, he so badly wanted to pull over and yell at her to get out. He couldn't look at her, didn't want her anywhere near him. He was so angry. Worse – disappointed. He thought they'd turned a corner.

'I was worried. I still am.'

'So why? Why would you do this to me, to us? You've put Jacqueline's whole career in jeopardy. She might lose everything. And the district. She's good for this place. She saves lives. I can't believe how fucking selfish you've been.'

'But I tried to put it right. I wrote again straightaway.'

'So you said. And as I said, it doesn't matter. Jacqueline's in trouble and it's all because of you! What did you think would fucking happen?'

'But …'

'Don't fucking speak to me. Just shut up.'

Damien was disappointed in himself for being so fired up, and for how he'd spoken to Tina. No matter what she'd done, she was still his mother. His father would have clipped him across the ear if he'd been alive to hear it.

They drove on in silence. What was done, was done. But still he felt white hot with rage.

He found a spot in the shade for Squish, parked, then poured out some water in the bowl he always carried and put it on the floor. He told the dog he'd be back in a bit, gave him a pat, and left the vehicle with a window open several inches. Tina waited beside the ute for him to retrieve her heavy bags from the back.

He strode into the terminal and up to the vacant check-in counter, Tina hurrying to catch up. He went and stood by the far wall while she checked in, nodding and smiling and grunting greetings to the five or so people he saw that he knew. He wanted to be anywhere else doing anything else. He cursed the eastern Eyre Peninsula for being such a small, isolated place. There were only two towns serviced by commercial airlines – here and Whyalla. No matter what time or day you set foot in here, you were almost guaranteed to bump into someone from your own district – or that you knew from outside it. Thanks to his CFS work and the recent Port Lincoln fires, he knew a lot more people from down this way. Today he reckoned he would have considered giving up his left arm to have stood there anonymously, not knowing a soul. He wanted to leave, but once more good manners demanded he stay put and see the plane into the air.

He felt a right bastard thinking it, but right then he hoped his mother would leave and never come back.

What the fuck had she been thinking? *Trying to protect me, my arse. Trying to deal with your petty insecurities more like.* Fuck. What a fucking mess.

He found himself making small talk with a group of people. He had no idea what he was saying but he must have been doing okay because he wasn't getting any funny looks. And even better, his mother was talking too and they didn't have to speak or let on there was tension between them.

Finally he was watching the trolley of luggage being dragged across the tarmac, and then hugging his mother awkwardly goodbye as a show to those around.

'I'm really sorry,' Tina said into his shoulder.

'Have a safe trip,' he said through gritted teeth.

Then he watched as she and all the other passengers made their way across the asphalt towards the plane in a ragged line and then, after a final wave, climbed up the steps and out of view in the winged machine. Damien found himself feeling strangely sad as he waited by the window for the door to be closed, the empty trolley brought back, and then the flick of the propellers. But he reminded himself of what she'd done, and felt a renewed sense of disappointment.

He itched to get back to Squish in the ute – better yet, to have stayed out in the car park with him and watched from behind the chain-link fence. But, again, you couldn't. Oh no, it was another of the unspoken rules of existence – was it just country people, or city folks too? You had to wait until the plane actually left, had taken off and was in the air. And if you didn't, you would somehow be caught out – like the plane not taking off after all and your loved one being stranded. It was easiest to just conform.

It seemed to take an age for the droning, roaring engine to warm up and for it to then taxi out, turn around, and finally tear down the runway and lift up into the air. It felt to Damien that there should be a round of applause or something to conclude the slightly tense wait. But no, one by one, everyone turned from the window and earnest chatter ensued as they made their way out of the terminal and into the car park to retrieve their vehicles and get on with their lives. Damien was swept along with them, waving and mumbling his goodbyes.

He climbed into his ute cab and settled heavily into the upholstery. Squish climbed onto his lap and tried to lick his face. Damien wanted to push him away, wanted to push something away, expend some of his angry energy, but didn't. He rubbed the dog's face automatically, still in a trance. He felt totally betrayed, bereft. He put the key in the ignition, but sat back again. God, the last time he'd felt like this was the day of 'the Incident'. But, no, this was different, wasn't it? This was pure anger and disappointment – and not of his doing and out of his control. The day he picked up the gun he'd had a feeling of being completely out of place and out of sync with himself and the world. And he'd had the courage to do something about those feelings. He didn't need the actions of one person to control him, consume him, drag him down now. He'd come too far for that. But fuck, he was angry with his mother. Thank God he wouldn't be seeing her for a while.

Damien slowly started to feel a little better, calmer. He turned the key and carefully manoeuvred out of the car park and onto the highway. He really should have turned left instead of right and gone and chosen some taps and carpet and stuff, but it was the last thing he felt like doing. He just wanted to get back home, where nothing had changed.

As he drove, he wondered whether he should tell Jacqueline what his mother had done. But what good would it do? If he kept silent, it would be less embarrassing for him. If he didn't, she might spend her time wondering who'd dobbed her in, looking over her shoulder, scrutinising everyone. It might even stop her really settling into town. She had to be wondering if that Jacob creep was a part of all this. No, he thought, with a deep sigh, I'll have to tell her. And soon.

Chapter Twenty-one

Philip, Eileen, Ethel and Jacqueline sat under a big shady tree on the lawn at the end of the jetty overlooking the sea. They all groaned with bliss through their first mouthfuls of food, agreeing that the fish and chips were the best they'd had in a long time. Maybe even forever, Jacqueline thought.

'Sorry, seagulls, too good for you,' Ethel said, shooing away the first of the pesky birds. They were the one thing about the seaside Jacqueline didn't enjoy – she tended to give in to them. Clearly Ethel wasn't such a pushover.

Jacqueline stared at the waves rolling in, and became mesmerised. She thought she could sit here all day in this meditative state, pretending she didn't have a care in the world.

'I wonder what the other half are doing,' Philip said, leaning back after finishing his lunch. It was something he often said when content and enjoying the simple pleasures of life.

'Not having nearly as much fun as us, I'll bet,' Ethel said, taking the words out of Jacqueline's mouth. 'Thanks so much for this.'

'Pleasure,' Philip said.

'Yes, what a good idea,' Eileen said.

Before long they had bundled up their rubbish and were lying back on the grass, letting their food digest while watching the world go by. Jacqueline couldn't remember feeling so relaxed and fought to keep the negative thoughts and worries from ruining it. That was the only trouble with sitting so quietly: the tendency of her mind to wander. They were all so still and silent that at one point Jacqueline thought the others might have fallen asleep.

'I sure could go an ice-cream,' Eileen said suddenly, shattering the peace. 'But I'm too comfortable to get up. Philip, would you be a dear?'

Since when do you say, 'could go' anything, Mum? Jacqueline thought. Her mother was full of surprises these days. And she expected her father to say, 'What did your last slave die of?' but he didn't.

'Of course, my darling. What would you like?'

'Did they have tubs back there for scooping, did you notice?'

'No, I don't think so.'

'I don't remember seeing any,' Jacqueline added.

'Well something in a packet would be lovely – anything, surprise me.'

'Okay. Ethel, Jacqueline? My treat.'

'Oh, yes please,' Ethel said. 'I haven't had an ice-cream in donkey's years. I'm happy to be surprised.'

'Righto, four ice-creams coming up,' Philip said, easing himself to his feet.

'Do you need a hand, Dad?'

'No, I'll be okay. You sit and relax.'

'Okay. Thanks'

'Yes, thanks Philip,' Ethel said.

'You're a darling,' Eileen said, waving her husband off.

It seemed like only a minute later when Jacqueline heard her father's voice again. Had she actually dozed off?

'Look who I found,' he said.

Could it be …? How long did it take to get to Port Lincoln and back again? She sat up quickly, anticipation building.

'Hi,' said a deep voice.

'Oh, hello again,' Jacqueline said, pulling herself together and trying to decide if she was pleased or disappointed. She looked away from watching him slowly running his tongue around something icy sticking out of a tube. It was probably best the older ladies were sitting and couldn't fall down in a swoon.

'Mind if I join you?' Paul asked, of no one in particular.

'Make yourself at home,' Ethel said, patting the grass beside her.

'Yes, please do,' Eileen said. Jacqueline thought she heard her mother licking her lips.

Philip handed out ice-creams and they all sat in silence unwrapping them. Jacqueline tried hard not to look at Paul, but his careful actions were as mesmerising as the coming and going of the waves. She realised she was eating far too quickly – her ice-cream was disappearing fast. She stopped and took a deep breath.

'Thanks, Dad. This is lovely,' she said.

Eileen and Ethel followed suit, mumbling their thanks and agreement.

'So, are you a surfer?' Eileen asked after a few moments of silence.

Jacqueline glanced across and for the first time realised Paul wore a wetsuit pushed down to his waist, empty arms hanging by his sides, leaving his chest bare. In place of a T-shirt was a very impressive set of abs. How the hell had she missed that two minutes ago? She devoured her ice-cream, while trying really hard not to stare and also wondering when she'd become so shallow. She reminded herself of her mother's earlier words. *No harm in looking, enjoying the view.*

'Yes, when I get the chance and the waves are half decent. Here's not the best place, but I thought I'd pop by for a look. Not bad for beginners. Jacqueline, do you surf?'

'Me? No. Never tried it.'

'Do you want to?'

Without a swimsuit? You're kidding, right? No, no bloody way! 'Um. No, thanks. I've just eaten.' It was the first thing that came to mind.

'You do know that's a myth, waiting twenty minutes after eating before swimming, don't you?' Ethel said, idly plucking at her wrapper.

'Yes. Go on, be a devil,' Eileen said.

'Not without a swimsuit, I'm not. I'm not ten!'

'I've got spare boardies and a wetsuit that should fit you,' Paul said, leaning over and sizing her up. 'And the change rooms are right over there. But, hey, no pressure,' he added with a shrug.

'Thanks, but we have to go. Don't the kittens need feeding soon, Ethel?' she asked pointedly.

'Yes, we'd better head back, if that's okay with you, Philip?'

'Fine with me.'

'Maybe Paul can give you a ride home, though?' Ethel added. It was one thing for her to get the word out that Jacqueline and Damien had broken up, but this …? Jesus! Jacqueline wanted to give her a piece of her mind and tell her to damned well stop speaking and stop meddling!

'Wattle Creek? Sure thing, it's on my way.' Jacqueline suspected he would have said that regardless of where he lived. She wouldn't admit it out loud, but she was enjoying the attention. And maybe it was time she was a little impulsive. But she still couldn't get her head around putting a wetsuit on over her knickers and bra and letting some guy she barely knew wrap his arms around her while he held her steady on a surfboard. She'd seen enough movies to know where that went. But some harmless human touch would be nice … And she never did anything very daring. Maybe it was time she did. Suddenly it was ridiculously important to Jacqueline to not be seen as a stick in the mud.

'Okay. I'll give it a go,' she declared, taking everyone by surprise. 'As long as you've got some sunscreen too.'

'Sure do.'

'Right, well, kitten duty calls,' Philip said, getting up. He gathered the rubbish and put it in the nearby bin.

As she collected her handbag from the car, Jacqueline couldn't believe she wasn't chickening out and was actually going to stay with Paul and try surfing. With Ethel clearly knowing and approving of Paul, she wasn't concerned for her safety.

'Right, well, have fun, you two,' Philip called.

Jacqueline cringed in preparation for Ethel calling, 'Don't do anything I wouldn't do.' It seemed something she'd say, and her friend hadn't seemed to have any qualms about embarrassing Jacqueline before. Thankfully Ethel just waved and winked instead.

Butterflies of nervous excitement were fluttering deep in her stomach as her parents and Ethel drove away, but Jacqueline was pleased to find that Paul was the perfect gentleman and she soon stopped feeling self-conscious about not being appropriately dressed. Anyway, covered in a light wetsuit – that did almost fit her perfectly – no one would be any the wiser. Not that there was anyone else around.

Never being very sporty, Jacqueline was surprised and a little excited to actually stand up after a few attempts, with Paul's help. When he told her she was a natural, she laughed and said, 'That's what you say to all the girls.'

'No, seriously, you're not bad for your first go. But we'd better end it there for the lesson or else you'll be too sore tomorrow. You'll probably find muscles you forgot you had. I've got to get home, anyway.'

It seemed like only minutes had passed. The sun was still high in the sky. 'No worries. Thanks again so much for this. I really enjoyed it.'

'I'm glad.'

Back at his ute, Paul gave her a towel and she headed off to rinse the salt off at the outdoor shower. She had no choice but to put her jeans and T-shirt on over her wet underwear – there was no way she was going to sit beside Paul with him knowing she was braless and going commando! Too bad if she showed wet patches.

'I think you're right. I'm already starting to feel like I've had a workout,' Jacqueline said as they headed out of town. Her stomach muscles and thighs were feeling tight. No wonder he looked the way he did.

'Yes, it uses a lot of muscles. I'm serious about you feeling a bit sore. Sorry about that.'

'No worries. It was worth it.'

'You might not be saying that in the morning, or two days from now,' he said with a laugh. 'But, seriously, have a hot shower when you get home, it should help.'

'Thanks for the tip. And thanks again, I really did enjoy it.'

'That's great,' he said. 'I didn't think you'd have the guts to do it.'

'No, me neither.' She was still a little surprised that she had.

As they neared the outskirts of town, Jacqueline began praying that it was too early for Damien to be at Ethel's for dinner and wouldn't be there to see Paul dropping her off. She really didn't want to hurt him.

'So, can I call you?' Paul asked as he was idling in her driveway behind the VW. Damien's ute was not on the other side of the street.

'Oh. Well, I …'

'Hey, I know about Damien McAllister. That you two were an item, briefly. If you need time, or it's complicated, or whatever, that's cool with me. I can do casual. But we had fun, didn't we?'

Jacqueline found herself nodding, enthralled again by his lashes. 'Yep. Sounds good,' she said. She got out and waited as he reversed, and then waved him off before heading inside.

Chapter Twenty-two

Damien turned off the bitumen and onto the dirt road that took him to the edge of his property. It felt good to be almost home; he could imagine not wanting to leave for days. He should let Ethel know he wouldn't be there for tea, but didn't want to speak to anyone. He definitely wasn't up to socialising after his mother's bombshell. And, anyway, how was he ever to look Jacqueline in the eye again, knowing what he knew? Fuck, he was angry with his mother. How could she? He sighed deeply.

He pulled up at the depository and got out slowly. 'Stay there, Squish, back in a sec.' He felt dead on his feet, didn't even have the energy to push the ute's door closed behind him. Every step was a huge effort.

Damien peered through the wire to see if he needed to go inside. *Oh God.* He opened the door and stared, trying to take in exactly what he was seeing. Two pups, young brown kelpies by the looks of them, were against the far wall on their hind legs, their front claws hanging in midair. Two ropes stretched up, one end of each tied

223

to the four-by-two timber frame of the shed and the other around a dog's neck.

Damien pulled himself together and burst into action. He whipped out the multi-tooled pocket knife he kept on his belt. Tears filled his eyes as he got up close and saw the bulging, haemorrhaged eyes staring back at him. He was too late. *Oh God, you poor little things. I'm so sorry.* His heart hurt so much he thought it might actually be splitting in two.

'I'm so, so sorry.' He cut the ropes and then sank to the floor weeping, cradling the two lifeless bodies. There was nothing more he could do. Squish appeared beside him, licked his hand once, sniffed the bodies, and curled up beside his sobbing master.

★

'Hey, what's going on? What's happened?'

Damien looked up. Ethel stood in the doorway and his spirits lifted just the tiniest bit.

'I wasn't here,' he said, lifting his hands and dropping them helplessly. 'They hanged themselves.'

'What? How?'

'Someone tied them up with slip knots.'

'God.'

'I should have been here. Bloody Mum. If it wasn't for her, I would have been.'

Ethel eased herself onto the ground in front of him, giving Squish a pat. 'You can't save them all, Damien. You know that. I know it's hard, but it's the price you pay for caring.'

'It just hurts so much.'

'I know it does. I know it does,' she said, pulling his head towards her soft, ample chest. They were silent through a new bout of tears. Ethel's eyes were glistening too when they stopped and she released him.

'How bloody stupid? There's a secure door, so nothing needs to be tied up. Couldn't they bloody see that?'

'Damien, you're never going to be able to control what other people do. Come on, let's give them a decent burial. It's all we can do now. I've got the kittens in the car. You saved them and they're doing well – focus on that.' Ethel got up slowly and put her hands out for the bodies. Damien got up and followed her out.

'You got a spade in the back?'

'Yep.'

'Here's a good spot – just under that one,' she said, pointing to a lone native pine tree surrounded by broom bush.

Damien got the spade out of the huge toolbox on the back of the ute where he kept tools he might need on his rounds checking stock, fences and water pipes. Holes he could dig and right now that was all he thought about. It felt good to burn up some of the emotion. God, what a fucking day! He needed this like he needed a hole in the head.

Finally they were standing in silence, side by side, looking at the small mound of bare earth, with Squish standing nearby. Damien felt so sad and low he could barely stand.

'Why can't people just be bloody nice, do the right thing by animals – and each other, for that matter? It's not fucking rocket science!' It was only when Ethel put a hand on his arm that Damien realised he'd uttered his thoughts aloud.

'Perhaps they did think they were doing the right thing, dear. They brought them here, didn't they?' she said gently. 'It's up to us to educate them.'

He nodded and hugged her.

'Come on, I sure could do with a cuppa,' Ethel said, tugging at his sleeve before returning to their vehicles.

Back at the caravan he called home, Damien let Jemima and Bob and Cara out of their runs and gave them all a big dose of affection. Ethel carried the box of kittens in. Jemima hopped into the van before they had a chance to close the door. The small roo standing there in the middle of the van looking around her as if to say, 'Hello, look at me, I'm here,' brought the slightest smile to Damien's face.

One by one, he took each squeaking, purring kitten out of the box, gave it a cuddle, and returned it. Ethel was right, they really were doing well. He'd have to get used to not winning all the battles. But telling himself that didn't improve his mood. He was becoming sad and depressed. Even his anger towards his mother had been overtaken.

Ethel put two mugs down and took her usual spot on the bench seat.

'So, Tina got off okay then?' she said.

'Yeah. But you'll never guess what.'

'What's that?' she said, overly brightly. Too quickly, Damien thought, looking at her. She was staring down at the table, running a finger across it, following a pattern in the Laminex.

'You know, don't you?'

'What's that?'

'What Mum's done.'

Ethel sighed. 'Yes. She rang me from the airport in Adelaide. That's why I'm here. She asked me to check on you.'

'Oh. Right.' Damien was momentarily stunned. Now he thought about it, it was odd that Ethel was there. Thank goodness she was. 'Well, lucky for her we were busy driving and then surrounded by people in the airport because I swear, Auntie, I just wanted to wrap my hands around her throat and choke the living shit out of her.'

'I can imagine.'

'How could she have done that to Jacqueline – to us?'

'She thought she was doing the right thing, protecting you.'

'Well, she's a fucking interfering control freak – excuse my language.'

'Yes, she is that. And I've heard worse. But we all have to cut her a bit of slack. She's going through a tough time with Geoff.'

'I can't believe you're so calm. Jacqueline's your friend.' *And what about being angry for me?* 'I'm fucking furious.'

'Well, I'm pretty disappointed, but I'm not quite as emotionally involved as you.'

'How embarrassing. After all Philip and Eileen have done for me. How am I ever going to look them the eye again, knowing this is all my fault?'

'It's not your fault, Damien, it's your mother's doing. They're smart enough to know you can't control the decisions someone else makes.'

'Can you believe she went to dinner that night with us all – strolled in with her pavlova and sat around, happy as Larry. Yet just days before, she'd dobbed Jacqueline in.'

'Well, she did send the second letter. As far as she'd have been concerned, they would have cancelled each other out and no one would ever have been the wiser.'

'Fuck, I'm angry.'

'Understandably. I'm sure Jacqueline would say it would be a good idea to write it all down, get it out.'

'That's the one good thing about all this.'

'What is?'

'I now know how to write the letter in support of Jacqueline. I've been tearing my hair out about it.'

'What are you going to say?'

'What an interfering, controlling, cold, cow of a mother I have and how that was why I was seeing Jacqueline in the first place. My life was shit before I met her – and not just my love life. Jacqueline totally got me to sort everything out in my head and get on a different, better path, just by getting me to think about everything and analyse how I was feeling and why. The letter's not really about me, but her: how her being good at what she does helped me.' Damien stopped, suddenly aware he was ranting.

'Sounds good to me. Have you seen the Facebook page for her yet?'

'What? No. I thought we agreed it wouldn't be a good idea to go public.'

'Well, lucky for us Nancy Squire has fully embraced the Facebook phenomenon. Coming from her, it will be totally fine. Last check it's already had around five hundred likes. Amazing.'

'That's brilliant.'

'Yours is doing well too.'

'I struggle a bit with finding interesting stuff to post about. And I probably should stay off it while I'm so fucking angry – at Mum and whoever left the dogs to hang themselves.'

'Perhaps it might be useful to post about it – help you deal with it and educate people about the dangers of using rope and slipknots instead of a proper collar.'

'I should have taken photos. Maybe I could have used them to find the bastards.'

'No,' Ethel said thoughtfully. 'They were delivered to you. Someone took that bold step. It might not have worked out well in the end, but if you start using things like that as an example, then you might frighten people off from doing the right thing. I've heard the police use Facebook to help find missing persons. You use it for good too, Damien. By all means educate with articles and examples, but I reckon save using photos you've taken for helping people be reunited with lost pets or for finding new homes for those who've been given a second chance, eh? I hear it can go like wildfire – even around the world in a matter of minutes.'

'You're so wise. What would I do without you?' he said, putting a hand over one of hers.

'And what would this old duck do without you keeping me young by making me feel useful?' She smiled weakly back at him. 'Well, since you're sounding a little better, I'll leave you to it. I just wanted to make sure you were okay and bring these little guys back. I figured you wouldn't be up to socialising. I tell you, I won't miss their squawking – they're noisy for such small things.'

'Thanks. I do feel a little better. But I'm still pissed off with Mum.'

'And rightly so. Make the most of it, though, and get that letter written. We've got to do all we can for Jacqueline.'

'How am I going to tell her it was Mum?'

'Do you want me to?'

'Would you? Seriously? Would you mind? But would it look too gutless of me?'

'She'll understand. If not, I'll make her. Really, it should be Tina. But I don't think we should wait until she gets back.'

'No, you're right. You're always right.'

'That, my boy, is certainly not the case, but thanks anyway for your vote of confidence. Now you get on with your letter. The kittens are due to be fed in around an hour, but they'll be sure to let you know.'

Chapter Twenty-three

Jacqueline's legs felt leaden as she and her parents made their way across the road to Ethel's for dinner. She'd have loved to be staying home and having a quiet night in – not that spending time with her dear friend and neighbour wasn't relaxing. And it wouldn't be a late night. But if she'd felt like cooking or had already pulled one of Eileen's meals out of the freezer that morning, she would have invited Ethel to bring her leftover trifle to them and stayed put. She vowed to have a decent walk in the morning before work and stretch her muscles so she wouldn't seize up completely. While she'd been enjoying her surfing lesson and wouldn't have minded keeping going, she was now pleased Paul had called an end to it so soon.

'Long time, no see,' Philip said jovially as Ethel answered the door.

'Yes, come on in,' Ethel said.

Jacqueline's antennae went up, noting Ethel's lack of retort. As she retreated from Ethel's hug, she scrutinised her friend a little more closely. Something wasn't quite right. Perhaps she was just tired; she was in her seventies and they'd had a pretty packed day. Jacqueline wished they weren't imposing on her for the second night in a row.

'Hmm, something smells good,' Eileen said. 'Can I help with anything?'

'No, it's all under control. Nothing fancy, just apricot chicken and salad. It'll be ready soon.'

Ethel took them straight through to the dining room, which Jacqueline thought was also a little odd. Usually they milled in the kitchen for a bit, especially when there were animals to make a fuss of.

'Can I have my cuddle of the kittens, since I missed out earlier?' Jacqueline asked, trying to lighten the mood. The atmosphere wasn't gloomy, she thought, just different – not quite as light as usual.

'They're not here, I took them home to Damien.'

'Oh, okay.'

'Did all go well with …' Philip started before Ethel cut in quickly.

'So how was the surf lesson?'

'Great. Apparently I'm a natural,' Jacqueline said, rolling her eyes. 'I told him I bet he says that to all the girls.'

'He's certainly a smoothie, that one,' Ethel said.

'And very dishy. I wouldn't mind a surf lesson and having those arms wrapped around me,' Eileen said, dreamily.

'Mum!'

'You've always got me,' Philip said, making a show of wrapping his arms around his wife and kissing her.

'Speaking of smooth,' Eileen said, kissing her husband back. Jacqueline looked on with amusement while thinking that her father's semi-retirement really seemed to be doing wonders for their relationship. She hoped that might be her one day – her and Damien.

They sat, but Ethel remained standing. Jacqueline almost stood up again. Things were becoming awkward.

'So, where's Paul from, what does he do?' Eileen asked.

'Well, he's from up near Charity Flat – the other side of where the fire was the other day.'

'Golly, no wonder he was keen to head off – he was miles from home,' Jacqueline said. 'Isn't Charity Flat about an hour's drive?'

'Yes, but travelling long distances is part and parcel of living out here. It's nothing to drive a few hours for something like a surf.'

'Is he a farmer, like Damien? Well, like he was before Esperance, I mean,' Eileen asked.

Ethel nodded. 'Yes and no. He's a stock agent – buys and sells livestock. He owns land inherited from his parents and lives in the house but leases the property out. Now, just excuse me while I get the food organised.'

'I'll help,' Eileen said, getting up.

'No, you stay put. Please. It's all done. I won't be long. Though, I warn you, it's very casual.'

'Well, I think it's very good of you to have us two nights in a row – we should have been having you,' Eileen said.

'Ah.' Ethel waved off the comment while leaving the room. 'Open the wine you brought, Philip. I could do with a drink,' she said over her shoulder.

Jacqueline frowned. That was a bit unlike Ethel, too. 'Do you get the feeling something's not right?' she whispered as soon as Ethel had left the room.

'You know her better than us, dear,' Eileen said.

'Yes, and I think something's up.'

'Perhaps she's worried about the kittens,' Philip offered.

'Did she say anything was wrong when you saw them?'

'No, they were fine. And, you're right, she would have asked me to take a look,' he said thoughtfully. 'Maybe she's tired, I know I am. When you get to our age, Jacqueline, you don't have the stamina you once had. I know looking through those houses nearly did me in.'

'Hmm,' Jacqueline and Eileen said in unison. Jacqueline wondered if her mother was trying, like she was, not to think about the rental options on offer. Jacqueline had a lot she was trying not to think about.

'Hmm. That must be it.'

Philip poured them all glasses of the white wine he'd brought and Ethel delivered the food in two trips – again refusing any help – then announced dinner was served. 'Tuck in, everybody,' she said.

Jacqueline thought Ethel seemed like she was making a huge effort to be cheery. If she was, she was failing. And now she was hopping into the wine. Jacqueline watched with surprise as half the glass disappeared down Ethel's throat in one gulp.

'We'll serve. Mum, how about you do the chicken and I'll do the salad?' Jacqueline held her hand out for Ethel to pass her plate.

'I won't argue,' Ethel said, taking another drink, a smaller sip this time. Jacqueline wondered if she was already drunk.

After murmuring their gratitude and compliments, they settled into their meal in silence, punctuated by the odd inane comment.

'I can't believe I'm so hungry after that ice-cream, but I am,' Eileen declared.

'Yes, it must be all that sea air – always increases the appetite, doesn't it?' Philip said.

'Hmm,' Ethel agreed.

'At least Jacqueline has an excuse for being ravenous – all that surfing,' Eileen added.

'I didn't think I did much – I wasn't out there for long – but I sure can feel it. Paul's right, I am finding muscles I forgot I had.'

'Well, you only have to look at him to know it's good exercise,' Eileen said.

Jacqueline tried to laugh to lighten things, but it came out as more of a snort.

'So, how did Damien's trip down to Lincoln go? Did he get Tina off on her plane okay?' Philip finally asked.

Ethel let out a long, deep sigh. 'I'm glad you're all sitting down, because there's something I need to tell you.'

'Has something happened? Is something wrong?' Eileen said.

'Yes, very, very wrong. Tina, Damien's mother, was the one who dobbed Jacqueline in to the medical board. She wrote to them.'

There was stunned silence. Jacqueline stared at Ethel.

'Oh, poor Damien,' Eileen said, bringing her hands to her face.

'Yes, the poor fellow's beside himself. He couldn't face you.'

'But he has no control over what his mother does – or anyone else, for that matter,' Eileen said.

'Why would she do such a thing?' Philip said, clearly bewildered.

Jacqueline closed her mouth. *No, you've got it wrong. She'd apologised. We all had a nice night together. She made a pavlova.* She looked across at the floral curtains and set her gaze on one of the pink roses. *When I look back, this won't be happening.* She blinked and looked back at the table.

'Jacqueline, dear, are you okay?'

She looked down at her mother's hand on hers. The voices sounded like they were in a tunnel: distorted, echoing.

'But,' she said. And stopped. The words just wouldn't come. *If I'm feeling this betrayed, how must Damien be doing? Christ, I hope he's okay. How can he be? I need to go to him. But I can't, I'm technically just the ex-girlfriend – and the dumpee, not the dumper – it wouldn't be right.*

'I'm afraid it's true, Jacqueline,' Ethel said kindly. 'She told Damien herself.'

'How could she do that to her own son? What was she thinking?' Eileen asked.

'She claims she was protecting him,' Ethel said.

'From what? Our daughter?' Philip said, clearly becoming angry.

'I really thought she'd come around,' Jacqueline said, in barely more than a whisper. 'I wouldn't have invited her over if ...'

'You weren't to know,' Eileen said. 'It's Damien I feel sorry for.'

What about me? She's probably completely fucked up my career. But the words wouldn't form.

'She wrote to them when she was angry. She assures Damien she wrote again to retract her complaint straight away, as soon as she realised how you were helping,' Ethel said, looking at Jacqueline.

'Well not bloody quick enough!' Jacqueline blurted.

'It'll work itself out, Jacqueline, you'll see,' Philip said quietly.

'It wouldn't have to if she wasn't an interfering, controlling bitch.'

'Jacqueline, I know you're angry, and you have every right to be but ...' Eileen started.

'It's not your bloody career on the line, is it? Sorry.' She took a sip of her wine, but had trouble swallowing. It burnt like acid down her throat.

'It's okay. It's upsetting. Of course you're upset,' Eileen said. 'But I really do think all will be well.'

'I hope you're right, because it sure isn't now. It's all a fucking mess. Sorry about the language, but it's the truth!' Jacqueline looked at the curtains, blinking back tears and wishing she was still surfing or under the hot shower in her little house. Who would have thought simply crossing the road like she had so many times before would have brought with it this? Whoever said the truth hurt was so right about that. Fucking Tina fucking … whatever-her-name-now-is!

'The letters must have crossed in the mail and just need some time to be sorted out,' Philip said. 'You know what admin can be like.'

'Should we go out and see Damien and let him know we have no hard feelings?' Eileen asked.

'Give him a few days. His day got even worse after Tina inadvertently dropped her bombshell – he returned home to two dead dogs.'

'What?' Eileen said.

'Oh no,' Philip said.

'Not Squish or Bob or Cara?' Jacqueline asked, feeling panic rise.

'No, they're all fine. Someone dropped two pups off, but was stupid enough to tie them up using slip knots and they … Well, you can guess.'

'In the long run, sadly, this might actually be a valuable lesson for him,' Philip said sagely.

'Yes. And, of course, he's doubly furious at Tina because she was the reason he wasn't there.'

'Well, I hope he gave her a piece of his mind,' Eileen said. 'But he seems such a quiet fellow, I can't imagine him getting too hot under the collar. Even though she certainly deserves it.'

'Oh, don't you worry, Tina knows exactly how he feels. And he can be a right firecracker when he gets going.'

'Hopefully he won't hold it in and let it fester and make himself sick. The poor fellow. Are you sure we can't do anything to help him?'

'Not right now. I think he needs some time to deal with it.'

'We understand, don't we, Eileen? But please let him know we don't hold him responsible for his mother's actions and that we're here for him if he needs anything – he only has to ask.'

'Yes, exactly, well said, Philip,' Eileen said, nodding her head in agreement.

Jacqueline wasn't sure leaving him alone was the right approach. But if Ethel had been out to see him, then she was in a better position to know how he really was than them sitting here around a table speculating. And Jacqueline certainly shouldn't be going out there.

'You look completely done in, Jacqueline. It isn't surprising, but are you all right?'

'No, not really. I'm pissed off. Excuse the language.'

'It's okay, under the circumstances. Quite understandable,' Eileen said, and patted her daughter's hand again.

She was upset, angry, disappointed, but she couldn't say she wasn't surprised. Insecure people were threatened by the smallest things and lashed out in all sorts of ways. All she could hope was that – as misguided as her actions were – Tina really had done it with Damien's best interests at heart and not out of spite.

'Thank you for being so understanding,' Ethel finally said. 'I've been at my wits' end, stressing about how to tell you.' She began to clear the table.

'You poor thing. I'm sure you've been putting yourself through the wringer,' Eileen said, leaping up to help.

After they'd left the room, Jacqueline caught her father's eye. His pained, sympathetic smile made her heart lurch, but thankfully no tears sprang forth. Perhaps the sea air had dried them out.

'Can anyone stomach trifle?' Ethel asked as she and Eileen re-entered the room.

'I can,' Philip said.

'And me,' Eileen said. 'I bet it's even better today than it was last night.'

'Okay. Thanks,' Jacqueline said. It was the last thing she felt like, and she wouldn't mind betting her parents were of the same view, but sometimes sacrifices had to be made for the greater good. And right now the greater good was letting Ethel off the hook and making sure she knew all was well between the two families.

Chapter Twenty-four

Damien struggled to get out of bed. He lay there curled around Squish, patting the little dog. The more he told himself what will be will be, the louder the voice in his head asked him who he was kidding. No matter what he'd said to Ethel, the truth was he was terrified and sad. He wished he wasn't, wished he could be philosophical like he'd started learning to be, with Jacqueline's help. If only he could call Jacqueline up or knock on her door to talk this through. If only he wasn't going to lose her forever, thanks to his selfish, interfering mother.

He was annoyed at his father for dying. He didn't believe in God, but if he did, he'd blame him, too, for leaving him with the one parent who would never understand him. After their fight, perhaps Tina might just care enough that she'd trashed her only son's dream. But his mother was stubborn. She might hold firm, convinced she'd done the right thing just through sheer stubbornness.

Damien reluctantly got himself up and dressed, had a breakfast of cereal that tasted like sodden cardboard, and left the van. He fed Jemima a snack to ease his guilt over her bewilderment at being locked up, and chained Bob and Cara on the back of the ute. He made the quick trip into town in a daze. It was a bit of a waste of fuel to go in just to post a letter, but it was an important letter. And the way he was feeling, he might just forget. At least now it was done and he could put it out of his mind.

God, he hoped he'd said the right thing. He wasn't sure of anything these days. He'd been clear, concise, to the point. He'd stuck to how Jacqueline had helped him and why she was so important to the town. He'd explained about how controlling his mother was and how it had got him into the state that had seen him needing Jacqueline in the first place. While he'd desperately wanted to beg them to let him and Jacqueline be a couple again and say he'd definitely choose her over his mother if it came down to it, he'd refrained. He didn't want to come across as unhinged, desperate or disloyal. He figured the people on the board would be older, and older people tended to view loyalty to one's own flesh and blood as more important than most things – family is everything, blood is thicker than water. But Damien was starting to see that as a load of bullshit. His mother had thought she was doing the right thing, protecting him. *Pffft.* If only she'd bloody well thought to not interfere!

He drove, fuming, while at the same time telling himself he had to put it all out of his mind and start focussing on drenching his sheep. It was good that he'd have a distraction and some physical work for the rest of the day and part of tomorrow. He was quite at ease working with sheep these days. Surprising, when just the thought of it used to make him go purple with rage, but he'd changed – thanks to Jacqueline. She'd been able to get him to see that his frustration and anger lay nowhere near the sheep, but within himself – that living a life of compromise was coming out in this way. It had to come out somehow, she'd said. He was lucky he hadn't turned to drink or dope, like many around had.

Damien opened the gates to the yards that had remained intact thanks to the ground being so bare, though they were a little scorched around the edges. He had to show Bob and Cara, who were quivering all over with excitement, where the stock was expected to come. Other than taking a drive around them daily, he hadn't done anything serious with the sheep since the fire and the dash to move them to safety. As he drove, he tried to blink away the flashbacks: the smoke on the horizon; fear and bewilderment etched in Jacqueline's gorgeous face and later the tears that stained it, running channels through the soot and dust. Oh, how he'd wanted to be the one to ease her pain, especially after she'd done so much for him. But when he'd turned around from thanking the firies she was being escorted away by Auntie Ethel.

As he got out and pulled the wire gate open and hard back against the fence, he tried to tell himself he was just being a big wuss, and to pull himself together. His heart was racing and his legs were like jelly. Thankfully Bob and Cara didn't seem to be affected. They were squirming and whining, keen to be let off their chains to get on with it. He still had the odd nightmare – not that he'd tell anyone that – but this was worse than the worst of them. He could wake up from nightmares. But here he was in broad daylight, eyes wide open, and seeing it all before him again. And there wasn't a damned thing he could do about it, except just get over it. Get on with it.

On his command of 'Go way back,' the dogs leapt off the ute in a flurry of excited yelping and bounded across the paddock. All Damien needed to do was park out of the way and wait. As he did, he felt the already heavy clouds in his mind descending, closer and closer. He didn't feel particularly tired, just leaden and struggling to care – about anything. He wanted to go back to the van, close the blinds and hide from the world, hide from his problems. But he knew only too well that wouldn't help. The shadow always followed. He had to keep moving, keep busy, keep accomplishing.

He looked up as the mob of sheep raced towards him, dust suspended above them.

'Good dogs,' he croaked, getting another flashback of the day of the fire. Tears stung and his throat felt blocked and dry. 'Get a grip, soft cock,' he told himself. 'Not you, Squish, you're a good dog.' He patted the panting dog sitting to attention beside him then pushed the ute into gear and slowly eased it in behind the sheep as the tailenders ran through the gate.

Damien went through the motions of drenching the large mob; it was taking far longer than ever before. Usually he had his mother helping. He cursed himself for missing her. If he'd thought about it, he could have got a neighbour and mate over. They all swapped labour from time to time. But while it was taking forever – would stretch well into the next day – Damien knew he didn't have the strength to put on a happy face in front of anyone or pretend he was fine. He just wanted to be left alone with his worries and his black mood.

About a thousand times that day, thanks to the monotony of a task, he had cursed how fickle life was, that you could feel great about everything one minute but feel a hopeless desperation about your situation the next. Or perhaps it was just him. Perhaps he really was sick in the head. Regardless, he'd throttle the next person who said, 'What doesn't kill you makes you stronger.' He believed it, of course it was true – he was proof. It just wasn't a helpful thing to be told when the chips were down, and the only time anyone said it was when you were at your lowest.

Chapter Twenty-five

Jacqueline had intended to go for a decent walk before work to try to stretch her tight muscles, which seemed to be getting worse by the hour – God, she was seriously unfit! But when she'd seen Eileen in the kitchen getting pots and pans out, it didn't seem right to leave. It was lovely having her parents around to take care of her, but if she ended up having to move back in with them she'd have to tactfully ease Eileen away from mothering her. Though she was always telling clients to be extra kind to themselves when going through difficult periods in their lives; perhaps bacon and eggs for breakfast fell into that category. Hopefully Eileen wouldn't do too much damage to Jacqueline's waistline in a week.

After breakfast, she kissed her parents goodbye and headed out the door, deliberately leaving her car keys in the house so she couldn't duck out of walking. For the first time since her career began teetering on the edge, she felt almost normal – almost good, even. She even found herself humming.

She'd just settled in her chair when Louise appeared at the door.

'Good weekend?'

'Yes, thanks. You?'

'Not bad. There were some voicemail messages — eight cancellations for the week. Three today. It's a bit odd, because usually a cold going through means we get inundated,' she mused before handing the phone message slips over with a shrug.

'Thanks.' Jacqueline went through the slips and updated her calendar. *This can't be good.* It was now looking like a very slow week indeed, and just when she'd begun to seriously build her business. She tried to quell the rising panic by telling herself it was a coincidence. But she couldn't shake the feeling that the cancellations were because word had started to get around the district about her position being tenuous. Disappointment settled in the pit of her stomach and began to gnaw.

And then panic gripped again. Had Tina put word out as well as dobbing her in? Ethel had said she'd written to retract her complaint straightaway, but she could have still told people of Jacqueline's breach of ethics. Would she have? She was certainly spiteful enough to go bragging about it to make herself feel more important for knowing something others didn't. That wouldn't surprise Jacqueline at all.

Should she tell Doctor Squire about the cancellations? She'd really rather not. And he probably wouldn't expect her to. He'd made it clear he wanted her to be a self-starter, to essentially run and build the practice on her own — he was too busy to hold her hand. She felt the slightest glimmer of relief at not having to front up and be the bearer of further bad news. She was damned lucky he was being so supportive of her; anyway, the last thing he needed when he was already so busy was for her to run to him with every little thing. He might already be close to losing patience where she was concerned.

Maybe she was panicking unnecessarily about the bookings. It wouldn't surprise her – she had a lot going on and was feeling quite highly strung as a result. She hadn't had any calls from the Hope Springs evening, though maybe some would soon start trickling in from that. And maybe some of the CFS crewmembers might start approaching her. People needed time to get their heads around the idea of counselling and then more time still to actually act. She tried to ignore the little voice that told her she'd seen a spike in bookings the day after her other talks.

Okay, so she wouldn't tell Doctor Squire about dwindling numbers – that his side-business might be going down the tubes – but should she tell him that it was Tina McAllister who had dobbed her in to the board? Would him knowing make any difference? Hmm. Would it change what he wrote in his letter in support of her? She supposed that was the pertinent question. She tried to come at the problem from all angles. It wasn't as if he'd put in a paragraph discrediting Tina. That would be unprofessional, not to mention verging on defamation. God, she could see an even bigger can of worms opening up before her. No, she would not reveal this either. No doubt he'd find out soon enough – as far as she could tell, not many secrets were kept for long around here.

All the toing and froing in her mind was making her head ache. She got up to make coffee, wondering as she did how she was going to find more clients and keep from getting bored in the meantime. She wished Ethel were there to provide some advice, but she was spending the day acting as tour guide for Eileen and Philip.

'Knock, knock.'

Jacqueline turned from making a coffee to see Paul Reynolds leaning against her door frame. She lit up, despite her efforts to stay neutral; while she'd enjoyed her time with him, she had to be wary of leading him on. She took in his appearance and almost sighed with disappointment: he was still just as good looking as she remembered. Worse, she knew what he looked like under his clothes – well, sort of.

'Are you going to invite me in or are you busy?'

God he's smooth. 'Sure, come on in.'

'Fancy making me a cup?' he said with a cheeky grin, nodding at the teaspoon in her hand.

'How do you like it?'

'Just a dash of milk would be perfect, thanks.'

Jacqueline half expected him to add, 'I'm sweet enough,' and was strangely relieved when the moment passed and he hadn't revealed himself to be totally predictable – not to mention cheesy.

'So, you're out and about early. Ethel Bennett told me you live out past Charity Flat,' Jacqueline said when they were seated with mugs in hand.

'Checking up on me, were you?'

Jacqueline looked down at her cup and silently cursed, feeling the slight blush rising.

'Sorry, that wasn't fair. I'm only teasing. I've clearly been spending too much time alone out there and am forgetting my manners. Forgive me. So how are the muscles feeling?'

'Sore. I didn't realise just how unfit I am.'

'Not necessarily. Surfing uses a lot of different muscles. Don't be too hard on yourself. You just need to give it another go and work them out again – it helps.'

'I'll take your word for it,' she said, taking a long sip of coffee.

'I hope you don't mind me dropping in unannounced like this – I was in the neighbourhood. But while it's wonderful to see you again, my visit is sort of professional.'

'Oh. Okay.' Jacqueline felt her heart sink. Could a surfing lesson where he'd held her hands and waist to help her balance count as a breach of ethics if she took him on as a client? Why was she feeling disappointed, anyway? Was she hoping for there to be more between them? Or was she hoping he was free of emotional problems?

'Not me, personally, as such. I was hoping I could convince you to come out to Charity Flat and talk to the community. Morale's pretty low after the fire.'

'I'd be happy to. I'm actually needing to build the practice and any opportunity for publicity would be good. I don't know anyone out that way.'

'Well, you do now – know someone out that way, that is. Sounds like a win-win to me,' he said, beaming at her.

'Yes,' she said. 'Sounds good. When do you think?'

'One evening this week? You're welcome to stay so you don't have to worry about hitting a roo.'

'Oh.'

'All totally above board,' he said quickly, raising his arms and holding out his palms. 'If you don't want to stay with me, I'll book you into the pub. You're welcome to bring your parents – it's a nice little town worth a look. And maybe you'd like a chaperone.' He grinned cheekily.

'Very funny,' she said, unable to stop herself rolling her eyes at him. 'But, seriously, any night would work for me.' She felt an overwhelming sense of relief that he wasn't wanting to engage her services for himself, though she wasn't sure why.

'I'll think about it, speak to a few people.' He paused. 'I thought you would be run off your feet after your debrief and other talks about the place.'

'Unfortunately not. I had a stack of cancellations waiting for me when I arrived this morning.'

'That must have been a bit disappointing. But don't take it personally – people change their minds, get busy, feel better, I guess, too,' he added, shrugging. She liked the easy way he did that. She liked him, full stop. She smiled warmly at him.

'Thanks, but it might be a little more serious than that.'

'Oh. What's going on?'

When Jacqueline opened her mouth again, it was like floodgates had opened instead. She told him everything, right down to not actually having had sex with Damien. She couldn't stop herself. How bloody embarrassing!

Even worse, a few tears accompanied her account. She was pleased Paul stayed where he was. If he'd got up and comforted her, she might just have lost it completely.

'God, I'm so sorry,' she said when she'd finished speaking and regained her composure. 'See, I'm not much of a psychologist if I can't keep my own shit together.' She attempted a laugh, but what came out was more of a snort. 'I shouldn't have told you. Please promise you won't tell anyone.'

'Don't worry, I won't tell a soul. What a thing to be going through, especially when you haven't actually done anything wrong. Please don't be embarrassed you told me. I'm honoured you opened up to me. And I certainly don't think any less of you for having your own problems and needing to confide in someone. It shows you're human, which is a good thing. I hope it's helped.'

'Thanks. I really appreciate it. And, it has. I've got my parents and Ethel to talk to, but ...'

'It's okay, I understand. And I promise your secret is safe with me. You'd be surprised at the secrets I'm holding. I'm a very good vault.'

Jacqueline smiled at his attempt to be lighthearted and put her at ease. He really was being a good friend. She toyed with telling him she didn't want them to be any more than friends to avoid any awkwardness down the track, but the timing wasn't right. She just hoped he wouldn't take advantage of her vulnerable state.

'Would you mind if I made a few calls and arranged your visit while I'm here?'

'Go right ahead. Use my phone,' she said, pushing it towards him. 'It's not like it's ringing off the hook.'

It took just two phone calls for Wednesday to be the evening Jacqueline would visit Charity Flat.

'Every small town has a mover and shaker like Ethel Bennett,' Paul replied when she expressed her surprise.

They shared a chuckle. Jacqueline felt better at having her talk to prepare to distract her for the next few days.

'Right, I need an early lunch, then I need to go and see a man about some sheep,' Paul said. Jacqueline watched as he checked something on his smartphone. 'Fancy joining me or do you have other plans?'

'No. No other plans.'

'Excellent. Fancy being daring and accompanying me to my favourite secret spot?'

'Oh, sounds intriguing.'

'Well, it's not really a secret. In fact, you've probably already been there.'

'Where?'

'The lookout just out of town. Stunning views. Quite breathtaking on a clear day like today.'

'Sounds great. I haven't been to any lookouts yet.'

'You're in for a treat then.'

★

'So, what do you think?' Paul asked. He'd backed his ute up to the safety barrier, undone the tailgate, and helped Jacqueline to stand in the tray.

She gasped as she took in the 360-degree view. Below them was the town and beyond that lay farmland in a patchwork of earthy colours. The sky was a brilliant blue above them. After a few minutes, Paul sat with his feet dangling over the edge of the open tray. Jacqueline followed suit.

'It's a perfect day. You can see right to the sea. Over there,' he said, pointing.

'It's amazing,' Jacqueline said, in barely more than a whisper. As clichéd as it was, the view really had taken her breath away.

They unwrapped their rolls and lapsed into an amiable silence while they ate, both staring at the view, lost in their own thoughts. Jacqueline was thinking about bringing her parents up here before they left. A trip at night to see the town's lights twinkling might be worthwhile too. She thought it was probably the place local lovers came to 'park', but wasn't about to say that to Paul.

'You know they come here to make out – the local lovers?' Paul said with a wink before taking a large bite out of his roll.

'Really?' Jacqueline tried very hard not to blush. 'I suppose you did in your day?'

'What do you mean, in my day? Do those days ever end? I sure hope not,' he said wistfully.

'Sorry, I didn't mean ...' She felt the heat rise under her shirt.

'Hey, I'm just teasing,' he said with a wave of his hand, and resumed eating.

Jacqueline wondered what he was up to. Was he flirting with her or as he said, just teasing – like a friend would?

'And, no, the answer is no.'

'The answer to what? Ah, if you came here to make out or not. Really? I don't believe that for a second.'

'I did, once or twice, but not that. That wasn't what you were asking.'

'I didn't ask you anything else.' Jacqueline's heart beat very slowly.

'But you want to.'

'Do I now? And what, pray tell, is it I want to ask you?' Two could play at this game. Her heart rate quickened.

'Okay, so maybe it's not actually a question, but a pondering.'

'You've lost me,' Jacqueline said, being deliberately obtuse. The heat was rising between her breasts and she could feel the prickle of tiny beads of sweat. Whilst it was thrilling and tantalising and fun, she wasn't sure she wanted this to go in the direction she felt it was heading.

'No, I'm not going to kiss you, Miss Jacqueline Havelock,' he said, suddenly leaning across and kissing her on the nose. 'I never kiss a lady on a first date,' he added with a wink.

She was so taken by surprise, she let out a little, 'Oh,' which she thought might have sound ed very much like disappointment. She hoped not, though she wasn't exactly sure what she felt, other than embarrassed and completely out of her depth.

'You're fun. I like you, Miss Havelock,' he said suddenly, taking another bite of his roll.

'I like you too, Mr Reynolds,' Jacqueline said, shooting him a smile before resuming eating. *I don't have a clue what you're about, but you're fun and I like your company*.

'Look, wedge-tailed eagle,' Paul said suddenly, pointing to their left.

Jacqueline turned and her mouth dropped open with awe as she watched a magnificent brown bird gracefully gliding through the air. 'Wow,' she said.

'Largest raptor in Australia. But don't worry, they don't prey on humans.' They watched as the bird hovered, dove and then rose again and began circling slowly again.

'Sadly we can't sit and watch him all day,' Paul said a few moments later and started screwing up his lunch wrapper. Jacqueline was disappointed – it felt like they'd only been there ten minutes, but a check of her watch revealed half an hour had passed. She gathered her own rubbish.

'I could have, you know, sat and watched that eagle all day,' Jacqueline said with a laugh. 'It was mesmerising.' *And so much better than having to go back and be reminded that my life is imploding.*

'Oh, well, all good things must come to an end. Work to do,' he said jovially. Moments later he was out of the tray and had his feet back on firm ground. She reluctantly joined him, accepting his hand to help her down.

'Thank you, that was really lovely,' she said, when a few minutes later they were parked behind her office and she had her handbag in hand, ready to get out of his vehicle.

'I'm glad. Thanks for joining me,' he said, beaming.

'Good luck with your meeting,' she said, and got out.

'Thanks. Good luck with drumming up business. And if you decide you want to stay over on Wednesday, let me know. No pressure, seriously.'

'Thanks. I'll see what Mum and Dad want to do.'

She stood and waved as he backed out and left the car park area. As she made her way towards her office, she began wondering if she was pleased or disappointed he hadn't wanted to kiss her. As she put her key in the lock, she decided she was relieved. Paul was becoming a good friend. It would be a shame if it became awkward between them.

Chapter Twenty-six

Damien made his way quickly through the supermarket on his way back from the latest hostel visit. The last thing he'd felt like doing was heading into town in the middle of the day, but he'd had to visit with the oldies on the hill. It was only the second time he'd left the property since finding the dead pups. If he left, he feared what he would find when he returned. The rational part of him would have said he'd come and gone for weeks before that incident and all had been well, that it was just one of those things. But that part of him was functioning well below full power. Worse, he was starting to wonder if it was a sign that his venture, his life, was doomed. But he couldn't bring himself to let them down, no matter how shit he was feeling, no matter how much he wanted to be alone with his dark shadow. And he knew he had to keep moving, trying to outrun the black cloud threatening to completely suck him in.

He'd toyed with not washing the dogs, but one whiff and he'd realised they were putrid after being in the yards. And there was a thick layer of sheep shit stuck in between the pads of their paws. And while they'd given no trouble, washing them took longer than usual. Everything Damien did at the moment felt like he was wading through molasses. What should be quick and easy was slow and hard. And he was vacant in the head. He regularly found himself feeling bewildered and wondering what he was meant to be doing – it was almost like he was losing chunks of time. Over and over he told himself to get his shit together, get with the program, but it didn't seem to help. He felt worse than useless. Tears would appear without warning.

And then he got angry with his mum – this was all her fault. Why the fuck couldn't she have left everything alone? And why couldn't she have married someone who wasn't a complete loser? *And why, Dad, did you bloody well have to die?* He wished he could roll back time to a couple of weeks ago when he had life sussed and it all seemed so doable. *For fuck's sake, get a grip, Damo!*

It was a relief that the supermarket was unusually quiet and he was finished in quick time without seeing anyone he was expected to offer more than a simple nod and grunt of hello to.

The girl on the checkout was a different matter.

'Hey, you take all animals out there at your rescue farm, don't you?'

'Yes, I do.'

'And you don't kill them, do you?'

'No, definitely not – unless they're in pain or distressed and their suffering can't be eased any other way.'

'Cool. Thanks. That'll be sixty-five dollars and fifty-five cents.'

'On cheque, thanks,' Damien said, handing over his card.

As he drove out of town, Damien felt a little guilty for not stopping in to see his auntie Ethel, but he was keen to retreat back into his own world.

He approached his gate and the depository with unease. He was terrified of what he might find today, but also keen to see a sign – a sort of look into the future that might calm his fear. He'd take anything he could get right now, he couldn't think or make decisions for himself. He almost cried with relief to see it empty.

With a mug of coffee on the table in front of him, Damien went through the mail – all bills and bank statements, except one. He pulled out the folded piece of paper and read. He had to go through it twice before it sank into his doughy head: his application for tax-deductible donation status had come through. With this news he could start his serious fundraising. While a lot of local people had contributed to get him started, he knew that others would be more inclined to be generous with this added incentive. His mum, for one, only ever made donations she could get a tax deduction for as well.

He knew he should be ecstatic, but he just felt glum, disinterested, and unable to muster any enthusiasm. He should be leaping up and down, phoning Auntie Ethel and Philip Havelock and announcing the reaching of this milestone, and announcing it on Facebook and upgrading his website. Yet he just sat there feeling numb. He needed to think things through, get a few things straight in his mind, but his brain refused to work. It was as if it had turned into a tangle of spaghetti and he couldn't find an end to grasp to undo the knots. He stared at his mug, not quite able to muster the energy to deal with drinking the cooling liquid either.

Damien's phone rang. The screen read: *Lucy.*

'Hello, Damien speaking,' he said, despite knowing who was calling.

'Hi.'

'What's up?'

'God, I'm so sorry to hear what Mum did to Jacqueline. Even for Mum that's insane. Is it true Jacqueline's been hauled up before the medical board?'

'Not quite. She's received a please explain letter. Did Auntie Ethel phone you?'

'No. Mum did – said you're a bit upset with her.'

'That's the understatement of the century. Glad she's your problem for the next few weeks, I can't even look at her.'

'Sorry, what?'

'I'm so fucking furious at her, Lucy, I want to murder her! And I'd be pretty justified, I'd say.'

'Yeah. But what do you mean she's my problem for the next few weeks?'

'There in London,' he said.

'What, she's turning up here?!'

'Er, yeah.' *Der.*

'I don't know anything about it.'

'What? I took her to the plane. She should be there by now.'

'She's just split with Geoff – thank God – but as if he'd be authorising her to spend a stack of money on an overseas trip.'

'Hmm. Good point. But she's got money of her own.' *And access to the farm accounts.* Damien felt his blood run cold. *Shit! Would she?* He pulled himself together. They were operating on an overdraft and the insurance money wasn't in yet. She couldn't do much damage. And she wouldn't do that to him. But he didn't think she'd dob in the woman he loved, either, but she had.

'Hey, you don't think she's cleared out their bank account and skipped town, do you?' Lucy said.

'Nothing he wouldn't deserve, but I doubt it.'

'Yep, he's a creep all right.'

'That's a bit strong. He's an idiot, and I don't like the bloke, never have, but …'

'Well, clearly you didn't wake up from a snooze on the couch one day to find him leaning over you and reaching for a breast like he was going to cop a feel.'

'Surely not. You must have misunderstood …'

'God, thanks a lot. You sound like Mum. Seriously, Damien, take it from me, he's a creep. Jesus, I can't believe you didn't notice all the lewd comments, the sexual innuendo.'

'Did you tell Mum?'

'Yes, and well before she married him.'

'And?'

'Laughed in my face. Told me he was just messing with me, winding me up. Why do you think I live so far away and rarely visit, and why I have so little time for my mother? She's not exactly supportive.'

'God, you should have told me.'

'And you'd have done what? Come on, Damien, you would have sided with Mum – you're as thick as thieves. You're the favourite, everyone knows that.'

'I would have knocked his bloody block off.' Damien liked to think he would have defended his sister, but Lucy was right: until very recently he had been well and truly under his mother's thumb, thanks to depending on her for his livelihood, the roof over his head. Not to mention needing to keep the farm running for her and his dead dad, which he now knew was all ridiculous, of course.

'Yeah, well.' Lucy clearly didn't believe him either. Oh, it was easy to say you'd do the right thing after the fact. Truth was he'd always sided with his mother over Lucy. He wasn't sure why – maybe deep down he envied his sister's freedom, the fact she'd had the guts to leave the town, the district, their oppressive mother.

'So what do you think is going on with her? What did she actually say?' he asked.

'Just that she'd really upset you, and what she'd done. No idea why she'd call me – she should have known I'd tell her what I thought. I wasn't very sympathetic.'

'She doesn't deserve any.'

'So, what are we going to do?' Lucy asked.

'Well *I'm* not going to do anything. I'm too pissed off with her – selfish, control-freak cow. Anyway, it's about time you had to deal with her – I've had years of her pulling my chain, turning up here, breaking my balls. You're on your own.'

'Gee, thanks a lot. At least you've had a guaranteed job for all those years, and a rent-free, mortgage-free roof over your head. Small price to pay, I'd say. Some of us have had to pay our own way, not get a handout, no matter how hard it gets.'

Damien stayed silent. While he wanted to point out that farming was hardly guaranteed – just to start with – he didn't want to fight with his sister. And how was he to explain that really what he'd been in was a prison, even if he could have walked away years ago and been free – the only lock had been his own fears and inse-curities. Life was all about choices. But he could see how it must look from Lucy's point of view. She didn't know how much and how often his mother phoned or turned up without warning to tell him he was doing everything wrong and not working hard enough or fast enough.

'Right, so I suppose I'd better ring her, find out where she is and get to the bottom of it – whatever *it* is,' Lucy said with a deep sigh.

'That's up to you. Frankly, I think she's made her bed and she should lie in it – that's probably what she'd be telling us if the situation were reversed.'

'Well, I'd like to know why she lied to you about visiting me.'

'Okay, let me know what you find out,' he said. Let their mother pull Lucy's chain for a bit and give him a break.

'I'll call you back.'

'Righto. Good luck. See ya.' Damien hung up the phone and sat scowling for a few moments. He was glad he'd kept it together, but Christ, Lucy made his blood boil! She clearly thought he'd had everything handed to

him on a plate and without any strings attached. And
what the bloody hell was his mother playing at now?

'Oh, Squish,' he said with a sigh. And then he
surprised himself by crying. Great heart-wrenching sobs
swamped him.

What seemed minutes later, the alarm for the kittens'
next feeding sounded. Two hours had passed while
he'd just laid there, being angry and disappointed with
himself for being so damned pathetic. Thank goodness
for the kittens and the other animals that needed him,
he thought, dragging his heavy bulk off the bed. Otherwise he might just stay there forever, feeling useless,
being useless.

As he organised the kittens' formula, he realised that
other than the Scotch Finger biscuit he'd had with the
oldies, he hadn't eaten since breakfast. It was now five in
the afternoon. He wasn't hungry, couldn't be bothered
deciding what to eat, let alone organising it.

Lucy's name appeared again on the screen of the phone
vibrating on the table in front of him. He snatched it up
before it could start ringing.

'Hey, what did you find out?'

'Well, she's not coming to London, and never was.'

Damien thought his sister sounded very relieved.
'Lucky you.'

'She's in Adelaide, holed up in some caravan park
cabin.'

'Why? Why isn't she staying with one of the relatives?'

'She's too ashamed.'

'*She's* too ashamed – God, I haven't faced Jacqueline
yet!'

'Damien, not about that. Though I'm sure that's a big part of it.'

'Then what? And hang on, why wouldn't she just drive to Adelaide? Why fly?'

'If you'd shut up and listen for two minutes, I'll tell you what I found out.'

Damien said nothing.

'Right. So apparently Geoff has thrown her out of the house ...'

'But ...'

'Damien!'

'Sorry. Go on.'

'And wouldn't let her take the car ...' *So the car hadn't been in Dorothy's yard? Had she walked there? Hell, what do I care?* '... He's threatened to make her sell the farm as part of the splitting of assets. She's quite beside herself. He wants the house. All they really have is the house and the farm. I'm sure even you could see what a loser he is with money. And apparently he's gone through what little savings they had managed.'

'Auntie Ethel offered a place to stay for as long as she needed it. Why run away to Adelaide?' Damien said.

'Again, ashamed, I guess. You know what Mum's like.'

'Yeah, wouldn't want anyone to know the true score.'

'Exactly.'

'So, hang on, what exactly is the problem? That she doesn't have anywhere to live? So she moves back to the farm – in a caravan while the house is being rebuilt.'

'But Geoff is threatening to make her sell the farm. I don't think she'd have a problem with it, but she's worried about what you'd do.'

'I'll be right,' Damien said, more upbeat than he felt. 'She can't run her life around what I, or anyone else, thinks.' He nearly laughed – it was exactly what he'd done for the past goodness knows how long; since his father had died and he'd felt the pressure to step in, and then the pressure to stay.

'But what would you do?'

'No idea. But I'm not going to as good as hold my mother hostage like she did me.'

'Wow. Well, I think she'll need to hear that from you.'

'I'm too angry to speak to her.' After all the damage her meddling had done to him and his life, he wasn't about to let her off the hook that easily. 'Tell her to sort her own life out. She's an adult. It's not my problem she married a loser. You and I both knew she was making a mistake before she made it.' He paused. 'Well, good luck with that. I've got to go,' Damien lied, keen to get out of the call.

He hung up, feeling a mix of relief, empowerment and guilt surging through him. It felt good to not get sucked into Tina's web on her whim, to actually say no. He probably should be being more supportive, but what he'd said was right: it was her farm to do with as she wished. He'd be pretty devastated to have to find some-where else to follow his dreams, but that was no reason for her to be yanked about by Geoff the dickhead. *God, I could knock his bloody block off too.* But he could also see that Geoff the dickhead was also Poor Geoff, to some extent. Damien hadn't had Tina living with him twenty-four-seven for years – he could imagine that would send anyone over the edge. Or into the arms of another woman.

Damien could see that there wasn't much point worrying about the stuff he couldn't change and that life was a lot easier if he just focussed on dealing with each bridge he came to. That was what Jacqueline had taught him. Also, she was big on saying that opportunities always arose from seemingly hopeless situations if you took notice. He really hoped she was remembering all this for her own situation and not worrying too much. As he'd seen, good things really could come from bad.

If only his mother had let Jacqueline help her. He was sure she hadn't, otherwise they probably wouldn't be where they were and he wouldn't be having these conversations with his sister. He felt good about staying out of it, stepping away from Tina's manipulation. He hoped for Lucy's sake that she would stay true to form and not get sucked into the vortex. Being thousands of miles away would help.

Chapter Twenty-seven

Jacqueline tried not to be concerned about the lack of clients and instead be grateful that it meant she could close her office early and have a leisurely drive up to Charity Flat with her parents and look around. And if tonight went well, things might improve.

She put her key in the door. 'Hi, won't be a sec, just want to quickly change,' she called to her parents waiting in the lounge as she raced through the house, propelled by nervous energy.

'No rush,' Philip said.

It was nice to have someone to come home to; her parents' presence did well to distract her from too much worrying about the outcome of her case with the medical board. It was something she couldn't control – it was now in the hands of the universe; she'd done all she could, Doctor Squire was doing all he could. She'd counsel a client in the same situation to do their best to keep busy and distract themselves from thinking about it too much. Not bury their head in the sand, as such, but deal with the bits that could be dealt with and try not to dwell unnecessarily on those things that couldn't.

Her heart thudded and her hands shook as she tore off her clothes. When her fingers struggled to do up the small buttons on the shirt she'd chosen, she really began to wish she'd said no to Paul and was instead putting on comfy clothes and getting ready to curl up in front of the TV with a glass of wine. It briefly crossed her mind to plead a sudden bout of food poisoning, before she scolded herself for thinking it. She'd be letting people down; she couldn't do that. *Toughen up, princess*, she told her reflection in the mirror, *it's your job*.

No matter how many times she told herself that this would be just like any of the other talks she'd done, she couldn't shake the feeling that there was more riding on this one. A small part of her would have preferred it to be just her and Ethel making the drive, so things would feel the same. But how could she have expressed that without hurting Eileen and Philip? They were being supportive. They were always fully supportive, and rarely critical.

'Right, ready to go?' she called at the lounge room door, handbag over her shoulder, car keys and a few CDs in hand. She hoped if they got a singalong happening, like the other day, her nerves might be kept at bay.

'You look nice,' Eileen remarked.

'Yes, very professional but friendly and approachable,' Philip said.

'Thanks. I'll just run across and get Ethel.'

'She changed her mind, she's not coming,' Eileen said.

'Oh. Okay,' Jacqueline said, glancing across the road. Really? Since when did Ethel cancel, or cancel and not let Jacqueline know personally?

She drove in silence through town towards the turn-off to Charity Flat on the highway. Paul had warned it came up quickly after a series of bends and was easy to miss, and that it would be a long time until you realised you'd made an error.

'So, what's Ethel's story, anyway. What came up?' she asked when she'd successfully taken the turn-off, got back up to speed and set the cruise control. She could relax a little now. Paul had said after that turn there was no way she could get lost.

'Um, well,' Eileen said, fidgeting with the edge of her blouse.

Jacqueline's antennae shot up. Something was amiss. Her mother was the worst liar. 'What? Have you had a falling out, or something?' It wouldn't surprise her if the trio had overdone spending time together and got a bit crotchety with each other.

'Not exactly,' Eileen said.

'What's happened?'

'It's fine, just a little difference of opinion,' Philip called from the back seat.

'About what?'

'Damien,' Eileen said with a sigh.

'What about him?'

'Your mother and I don't agree with continuing to give him space, that's all.'

'So why haven't you just gone out there to see him?'

'Ethel knows him better than us – she is related to him, after all,' Eileen said.

'And we don't want to get her offside,' Philip added.

'But you have a legitimate reason – and every right – to be in touch, Dad, you're part of his enterprise. Why not go out on those grounds? And you've clearly got Ethel offside anyway, so you may as well.' Jacqueline knew she was more annoyed than she should be. She was stressed about her talk and frustrated at not being able to do anything herself about Damien. She was also now a little annoyed with Ethel too. 'At least call him.'

'I have. He didn't answer. I left a breezy message asking after the animals. Maybe Ethel's right.'

'It could be that we've just spent too much time together and got on each other's nerves a little,' Eileen said.

'Hmm,' Jacqueline mused, and turned the radio up, though there'd be no singalong today.

'Actually, would you mind if we put an audio book on?' Eileen said, pulling a box out of her handbag. 'Perfect for long drives, we've found.'

'Oh. Okay, what is it?'

'A Phryne Fisher mystery by Kerry Greenwood. We're loving the series on the ABC.'

'Sounds good. Just slide the disc in there,' Jacqueline said, pointing. She tried to ignore the narrator's voice and focus on running through the main points of her upcoming talk while Eileen and Philip were silent, but before long she was listening intently and engrossed in the story.

★

Jacqueline was surprised to see the big green sign to Charity Flat up ahead. It seemed like only minutes had passed, and her nerves had been kept at bay for all that time. She had never listened to an audio book before, but what a great idea for whiling away hours travelling. She'd have to get some. She slowed down to make the left turn at the T-junction, as directed by the sign and Paul's instructions. She wondered where this one local attraction he'd mentioned was. Oh, well, she'd just keep driving straight ahead. Paul would have told her if she needed to turn anywhere else to find it.

'What on earth is that?' Eileen said, pointing ahead and slightly to their right.

'Lordy, is that a big kangaroo?' Philip said.

'That must be the local attraction. Paul said we couldn't miss it,' Jacqueline said, checking her mirrors before turning in.

'He was right about that,' Philip said.

'Is it meant to be funny?' Eileen said.

'I'm really not sure.' Jacqueline frowned. She smiled at remembering Paul's wink and cheeky grin. 'Apparently it's made it onto *Sunrise*,' she offered, parking the car and pulling on the handbrake.

'I hope that's because someone was taking the piss.' Philip said.

'Philip!'

'Sorry, but there was no other way to put it. I'm finding this quite perplexing.'

'Perhaps that's the point,' Eileen suggested.

They got out and walked around the huge concrete structure, which Jacqueline estimated to be about two stories high. It was clearly depicting a kangaroo, but the proportions didn't quite seem right.

'Right, well, according to this,' Philip said, standing in front of an information plaque, 'it *was* a giant kangaroo, but a big wind took the top section off a few years ago and it got shortened during repairs. Now it's a big wallaby.'

'I think I would have been inclined to tear the thing down and start again,' Eileen said. 'Let's see what the shop has to offer.'

They stepped inside and the screen door shut with a loud metallic slap behind them. 'Oh dear,' Jacqueline heard her mother mutter. She followed Eileen's gaze to the sign announcing the best hot dogs in Australia – kangaroo hot dogs, no less. She exchanged wide-eyed expressions with her parents before moving through to where they could see tables of souvenirs – stubby holders, magnets, key rings – and a stand of postcards. Jacqueline was trying very hard not to laugh. She was now avoiding looking at Eileen and Philip, who were picking things up to show each other, clearly on the verge of laughter themselves. It was lucky Jacqueline couldn't quite hear their whispered, earnest commentary, she'd crack up for sure.

'I'm getting this as an olive leaf for Ethel,' Eileen said when they'd made their way right round the small room. She held up and shook a small plastic dome. 'See, it's the monument. And it's got brown dust instead of snow or glitter floating around.'

'Lovely,' Philip said, sounding less than impressed. 'And I think you mean olive *branch*, dear.'

'Yes, quite right, silly me,' Eileen said, chuckling, as she headed back to the counter. The place was eerily silent. It wouldn't surprise Jacqueline if the shop operated on an honour system. Though someone had to be there, if only to put together a hot dog made from the meat of the animal they were celebrating out front. She just couldn't shake how wrong that seemed. An image came to mind of Damien's cute little joey, and she shuddered. Though she supposed it was no different to eating lamb and seeing lambs frolicking in paddocks in spring.

They had a good drive around the town, marvelling at some of the lovely old homes, and then easily found the RSL hall and its car park. Jacqueline cursed the return of her nerves as she parked the car and got out. *Nothing you haven't done before*, she told herself.

'Here you are,' Paul said, suddenly materialising beside her.

'Hi,' she said, startled, when he pecked her on the cheek.

'Hello again, Mr and Mrs Havelock.'

'Oh, Philip and Eileen, please,' Philip said, waving a hand.

'We've got a great turnout,' he said, looking pleased.

'Brilliant. Thanks,' Jacqueline said.

'Don't worry, you'll do great,' Paul said, beaming at her, clearly picking up on her nerves.

God, I wish you were here, Ethel, she thought, as he led her up the steps with her parents trailing along behind.

'So, you found us okay?'

'Yes, no problems, thanks. You give good directions.'

'And the big question of the evening is, did you find the big wallaby-slash-kangaroo?' he said, grinning.

'We did indeed,' Philip said. 'Please tell me that's some sort of joke,' he added quietly, leaning in close to Paul.

'I think so, dreadful thing. But it's got the town divided: half love it and are very proud of it, the other half thinks it's the most hideous thing ever and should be torn down. There's even a family that's been split, thanks to their strong opposing opinions.'

'No, surely not,' Jacqueline said. 'That's crazy.'

'Yep. Better believe it.'

'Right. Got it. Don't mention the monument,' Philip said, grinning and tapping his head with his finger.

Like always, Jacqueline's nerves subsided after she'd got her first few sentences out. As she usually did, she started by introducing herself, explaining the role of a psychologist, how talking to someone could help with all sorts of things, and that a conversation with her would remain confidential. She expressed her sympathy for those who'd been affected by the recent devastating fire and then relief that no lives had been lost, which took her nicely into suggesting people take the fire as a bit of a wakeup call to get their affairs in order.

'It would be wise, as part of your fire management plan, if you haven't already done so, to put together a folder of documents that, if lost, would make life very difficult. People often think of packing clothes, photos and a few treasured items when preparing to flee. But what happens if you're not there or it all happens so fast you can't pack anything? You'd be standing there with just the clothes on your back and maybe your car keys and wallet – or handbag. You no longer have your filing cabinet with your documents for identification, your insurance policy details – who do you call? What about your bank details? It'll be a lot easier, and quicker, to start sorting through things and piecing your life back together if you've at least got the basic information. If you're computer literate, scan everything and save it to a cloud-based system so you can get to it anywhere on any computer. Backup your digital photos, scan your old ones. Perhaps the tech savvy can help those who aren't – maybe make it a community project. Perhaps the school computer science class could help,' she said a little excitedly, as the idea that had come to her gained momentum.

She shot a questioning glance across to Paul. He was nodding, a thoughtful expression on his face. A lot of other people were nodding too, and whispering animatedly to each other. Good, she was making sense, helping. But it was just common sense, not really anything to do with her role as psychologist. She was just hoping they'd take something away from tonight, even if they thought psychology was a load of bunkum, or word had got around about her predicament and they didn't trust her.

'Other than the obvious benefits, being prepared will help you feel more empowered if the worst happens,' she added. 'Taking charge of something – no matter how small it is – can sometimes be the difference between coping and not. When bad things happen, it's really easy to fall into a pattern of negative thinking and a feeling of helplessness, which can then easily turn into depression. But having something to focus on that will help you claw your way back really does help. And being aware of and acknowledging how you feel and addressing any negative feelings is really important. Don't let things fester. I know you country folk tend to not want help, and you like to keep things to yourselves. It's good to be strong and independent, but don't avoid seeking help because that's the norm. If you've been through a fire, for example, that's not normal, so throw any misconceptions or rules out the window. Having someone listen to you can really help. So don't bottle it up and deal with it alone.

'But it's also wise to be a little careful about where you seek help and who you open up to. Now, I'm not just drumming up business for myself,' she said with a wry smile, and was pleased to hear tittering and a few chuckles make their way around the room. 'But it's a fine balancing act. Well-meaning friends and family can sometimes do more damage than good with their words. For example, saying to someone who has lost their home and worldly possessions that at least no lives were lost isn't helpful to someone who's feeling completely bereft, which is a very valid reaction. Instead of cheering the person up, it can make them feel guilty for being devastated about their loss and in turn, make them reluctant to talk about it and how they're feeling, which is really important.

'So, as a friend or family member, be really mindful of your words. Choose them carefully. Try to imagine how you would feel if the situation were reversed. And for those of you who are suffering, be kind to yourself. Choose to spend time with those you feel understand you, those who say what you need to hear at that time. Don't feel pressured to be with people who make you feel worse, no matter who they are. What you feel is unique to you and your situation. No one has the right to judge how you feel. So, rather than have someone's words drag you down more, it might be best to politely excuse yourself from the situation. Also, I would say, be wary of those who think they know what you need because they've known you for a long time. With something like a fire or any other traumatic or highly emotive situation, as I've said, I think it's fair to say it's often a new playing field. Treat it as such and draw up new rules if you need to – whatever it takes to get you safely through something tough as intact as possible.

'And I think I'll leave it there. Thank you for listening, and please know there is help available if you want to reach out.'

Paul joined her on the stage. 'Thank you so much, Jacqueline, you've given us a lot to think about. Extra big round of applause, everybody, for the lovely Jacqueline Havelock, especially for giving up her evening and driving all the way up here from Wattle Creek,' he said.

'Thank you,' she said, accepting the cellophane-wrapped bottle of red wine he handed her.

Hearty applause erupted. Jacqueline hoped they weren't just being polite. She was pretty sure it was one of the worst talks she'd done – it had been disjointed and hadn't flowed well enough. But it was too late now, she thought, as she stood beside Paul, smiling out at the crowd below the stage.

'Oh, I forgot, are there any questions?' he asked when the noise had died down. He scanned the crowd.

No hands went up. *Wow, that's never happened before,* Jacqueline thought. She hoped it was a good sign.

'Well, clearly you're all feeling shy. Fair enough. I'm sure Jacqueline will be only too happy to answer any questions over a cup of tea.'

Jacqueline smiled and nodded in an effort to appear friendly and inviting, though she wouldn't mind the opportunity to have something to eat and drink – she was suddenly very hungry.

'Okay then, a lovely spread awaits us in the supper room, so feel free to head on through and tuck in, people.'

Jacqueline enjoyed hearing another healthy round of applause start up as Paul ushered her off the stage, down the steps and through to the supper room.

By the time the crowd started dispersing, Jacqueline had barely managed a sip of tea, thanks to, as usual, a constant stream of people coming up to her – mainly to tell their own stories and be friendly rather than asking actual questions. She was positively starving, and exhausted, when she and her parents finally made their way outside with Paul. She was very pleased to hand over her car keys to her dad when he said he'd drive.

'The supper was lovely. Thank you for a great evening,' Eileen said, getting in the car. Jacqueline's mouth watered at hearing the word supper. It was an hour until they would be home in Wattle Creek. She'd even eat a kangaroo hot dog, if the souvenir shop was still open.

'Your talk was fantastic. And thanks again so much for coming up,' Paul said, hugging Jacqueline and pecking her on the cheek. 'Maybe when everything is sorted out we can see if it would be worth you coming up once a month, or something.'

'Oh, well, I'd have to ask Doctor Squire – he's my boss.'

'Just something to think about.'

'Yes.'

'Well, I'd better let you go, you've got a bit of a drive ahead.'

'Thanks for inviting me.' *God, what a thing to say!* Clearly she was far too tired and it was starting to get far too awkward between them. She needed to get out of here.

Thankfully, Paul stepped back with a wave. 'Drive safely. I'll see you around.'

'Thanks. Yes, see you later.'

'You did really well. We're so proud of you. Aren't we, Eileen?' Philip said.

'We certainly are. You gave everyone a lot to think about, including us,' she added thoughtfully.

Jacqueline wondered if they were referring to Ethel, Damien, or both – well, they were connected, after all.

'Now, what would you like first, a sausage roll or a sandwich? I can recommend both,' Eileen said from the back seat. Jacqueline turned and saw that there was a foil-wrapped plate on her mother's lap.

'Oh, wow, and just when I'm starving. Mum, you're an absolute lifesaver!'

'As much as I'd like to take the credit, it's all Ethel and Paul. Apparently she texted him with strict instructions to do you up a plate.'

'Sausage roll, thanks.' *Oh, bless you, Ethel,* Jacqueline thought, almost weeping with relief and gratitude.

Chapter Twenty-eight

Damien stared at his coffee, dazed. He was dog tired from wrestling with his conflicting feelings towards his mother and worrying about the future. He thought he heard a vehicle pull up quite close outside, but ignored it, used to people coming and going over at the building site, which he'd all but lost interest in. It was his mother's place and by the sounds of it, she would be reclaiming it very soon – either to sell or to live in herself. The slam of a car door and then footsteps made him tilt his head. Damn it, the last thing he felt like was company. It wasn't Auntie Ethel, the footsteps were too light, and the series of gentle taps on the thin aluminium of his door confirmed it – Auntie Ethel always gave one hard rap before entering with a cheery, 'Hello, anyone home?'

He got up wearily, struggling to ease himself onto his feet. Squish was on the floor, tail wagging, ready to be the doorman. Damien opened the door slowly. A small, slim girl with red eyes and a tear-stained face stood before him. She'd obviously been crying, for hours by the looks of her. Damien felt his heart lurch slightly. He thought there was something familiar about her, but perhaps it was just the fact her wan expression was one he'd seen in the mirror before and would again, if he cared to look. She twisted her hands in empty belt loops.

'Hello. Can I help you?' Damien asked.

'Um. You said you take all sorts of animals and don't kill them?'

It was more a question than a statement. Damien experienced a brief moment of clarity: the girl from the supermarket. She *was* familiar, though he didn't know for the life of him which local family she belonged to.

'We sure do, and we certainly don't,' Damien said, fighting to sound professional. 'Do you have an animal you want to surrender?'

'No. Yes. Well ...'

Damien stood watching and feeling very awkward as tears ran down her face. She looked about twelve, but couldn't be. There was no one with her. He glanced over her shoulder to double-check if someone was waiting in the ute with horse float attached. She was alone. Should he put his arm around her? No. He was meant to be standing there as a business person, providing a professional service. Anyway, he had enough problems of his own, enough sadness of his own. He didn't need anyone else dragging him down. And if anyone wrapped their arms around him he might never let go. He was seriously running the risk of dissolving himself.

'I'm sorry,' she finally snuffled, dragging a sleeve across her face. 'I need to go. Where shall I put them?'

'What do you have?'

'Two horses. And an, um, emu.'

Damien felt a shiver creep down his spine. He hated emus – had ever since being pecked at Auntie Ethel's farm as a kid. Shit. He tried to pull himself together. The emu was not his only worry. Two horses? He hadn't had a thing to do with horses for years. Didn't want to admit it, but their size bothered him. *Businesslike, Damo, get a grip.* He couldn't leave this poor girl standing there sobbing. He had to at least say something.

'Would you like to come in? Talk about it?'

'I don't want to do it, but I have to. But they're my best friends,' the girl wailed.

'Come inside,' he said, holding the door open and stepping aside. He glanced back at the silent horse float as he closed the door. Hopefully the animals inside were okay to stay put for a bit.

He turned to get the girl a glass of water and when he turned back she was seated, patting Squish, who had his head in her lap. Damien felt a surge of gratitude to the dog for being his lifesaver.

'Thanks,' the girl said, accepting the glass and the box of tissues he'd taken from the bench.

'So, tell me what's going on.' The fact he almost sounded like Jacqueline wasn't lost on Damien. In different circumstances it would have made him chuckle, but the thought just made him feel bluer. If only she were here, doing this, with him. What did he know about dealing with a sad young girl who did not want to give her horses and emu up but apparently had to? His enterprise was animals, not people, though a quiet voice in the far depths of his mind told him he was dealing with people at the old folks' home every Wednesday. And that if it weren't for people, the animals wouldn't be needing the likes of him.

'I have to give them up,' the girl croaked. 'I don't want to, but I don't have a choice.'

'Look. Let's just go back a bit. Start at the start. I'm Damien. And that's Squish,' he said, nodding and trying to offer a warm smile. But he was really too tired to manage warm and what he actually offered was probably more along the lines of tight.

'I know who you are. I'm Alice. I'm sorry about all this, but I just thought I'd drop them off.' A new round of tears began.

'I don't think you're in much of a state to drive,' Damien said kindly. 'It's not safe.'

'I know.'

'So what's going on? Are you sure you want to surrender them? I mean, are you sure you have to? Is there really no other option?'

Alice shook her head and gulped back tears.

'Do you want to tell me the whole story? Maybe there's another way. Or maybe it might just help to tell someone.'

'You're being so kind,' Alice said. 'I feel terrible.'

'Of course you do. It's a tough decision.'

'Not only that. You don't know who I am, do you?'

'No. Should I?' Damien frowned. 'You work in the supermarket. You served me earlier, right? Have we met before that?' Damien racked his brain and came up empty, which wasn't surprising. He couldn't think straight about anything these days. The alarm on his phone rang in the silence. 'Sorry, that's me. Next feed is due,' he said, getting up and retrieving the box of kittens from the end of his bed and putting it on the table. When he opened the box to find four pairs of bright blue eyes staring up at him, he thought his heart might melt. They'd become quite active of late, scratching about, trying to escape. But now they were a picture of cuteness, all sitting there, still and quiet.

'Oh, aren't they gorgeous. Can I pat them?'

'Yep. They'd love a cuddle while I get their feeds organised.' Damien prepared the bottles with formula and then turned around and watched while the kettle boiled. Alice's tears had stopped, the tension in her features had eased, and she had a smile on her face as she held the four tiny bundles of fur to her chest, watched on closely by Squish. Damien felt himself choke up. He was overtired. This was what it was about. If only all the troubles in the world could be solved so easily. Perhaps they could – look what Squish had done for him. If only more humans could put their own problems and issues aside to appreciate and take care of those who couldn't take care of themselves.

Damien got a flashback to a time his parents had discussed selling one of Lucy's horses and her staunch vow to never speak to them again if they did. He remembered it had been his father pleading with his mother to keep the horse. It hadn't been successful enough at the recent show; that's what horses had been about for Tina – competition, not fun. It really was no wonder Lucy had no interest in horses these days. The horse had stayed and eventually passed away in the paddock from old age, if he remembered correctly.

The kettle burbled and then clicked off. He finished the bottles and tested their temperature against his top lip, like Auntie Ethel had taught him. It was just a habit, really, because he had it all down to a fine art.

'So, you were about to tell me the whole story when these little guys rudely interrupted,' he said softly when she'd handed the kittens back and they were in their box and busy with their bottles.

Alice took a deep breath. Damien was pleased to see she was calmer and seemed to have run out of tears. She stroked Squish, who was back in her lap.

'Oh, and where am I meant to know you from, other than the supermarket yesterday?'

'You don't know me and I doubt you'll want to, but I know you.'

'Sorry?' Damien blinked and frowned. 'What?'

'My mum is sleeping with your stepdad. Well, she was.'

'Please don't call him that. He's just the dickhead my mother married. Nothing to do with me,' Damien found himself saying.

'Sorry. I shouldn't be here. You have every right to not want to help. But ...'

'Now hang on. Firstly, I'm sure you have about as much chance of telling your mother how to behave as I do – Buckley's. They are their own people. And if Geoff couldn't keep it in his pants, well ... Sorry, that's a bit rude of me.'

Alice waved his embarrassment and apology aside.

'Look, what I'm saying is that we have no control over what other people do, we just have to manage the fallout as best we can.' Again Damien was reminded of Jacqueline. They weren't her words, he didn't think, but it was along the lines of what she'd advise. Well, he thought so. God, how he ached for her, even just to hear her kind, practical advice. 'What I want to know is why you have to give up your horses when you clearly don't want to.'

'Geoff's dumped my mum, her name's mud in town, and now we've both lost our jobs. I think we'll have to move back to the city. I can't afford to keep the horses.'

The situation struck Damien as odd yet so typical of the way things worked out here. It was all well and fine for the good people of the district to turn a blind eye to a straying husband, but now that he's been found out by his wife they pull rank and punish the one who – they think – led him astray. Of course they would be siding with Tina, she was a landowner. Geoff was a retired shearer and had little to no standing. Damien felt his blood boil at the fact that poor Alice was here in front of him, facing losing her horses all because of his mother and the dickhead she'd chosen to marry.

'Right,' Damien said, trying to both simmer down and buy time while he sorted through the details. He longed to be helpful. God knew, Alice was relying on him. He drummed on the table with his fingertips.

'It's all my fault,' Alice said, gathering herself. 'If I'd just kept my mouth shut … I should get going. Do you have yards I can put them?' Damien noticed her chin was wobbling again and her eyes brimming.

Damien blinked. 'Hang on, what did you say? What do you mean, kept your mouth shut? About what?'

Damien had the awful feeling he was about to hear something he didn't want to hear. 'What, exactly, is all your fault?'

'Everything.' Alice brought her hands to her face just as a new flood of tears began.

Damien waited her out. He didn't really have much choice – there was nothing he could say.

'If I'd just kept my mouth shut, kept out of his way,' she muttered through the sobs.

'Did Geoff do something to you, Alice?' he asked. He felt as if he had both hands over his eyes and his ears. He didn't want to know, but he felt he needed to, and Alice probably needed him to. He'd failed Lucy – back then and again yesterday. He'd apologise to his sister, beg for forgiveness, when he got the chance. Not that he deserved it. Remembering Lucy telling him their mother had laughed at her allegation made his blood boil all over again. God, he wanted to throttle Tina. It was damned lucky for her she was over six hundred kilometres away. If she'd taken Lucy seriously, then Alice might not be sitting here now. Somehow he needed to help her to make some sort of amends. And listening to her was a start. Again he was reminded of Jacqueline – God, he wished she'd get out of his head – and how much talking to her had helped him through a very, very dark period. His memory flickered to the gun and the incident in the shed. He shuddered and banished the image.

'I'm sorry, you've probably got heaps to do. I should be going,' Alice said, making to get up again.

Damien knew she was torn – felt the need to leave and not burden anyone, but the desperation to be unburdened. A problem shared is a problem halved; it was true, as he knew only too well. Had Alice's mother laughed at her too?

'Just tell me where to …'

'I've got nothing on. And I'm not letting you drive anywhere when you're so upset.' *God, I sound about sixty.* 'Do you want me to call your mum, or something?' he added helplessly.

Alice shook her head.

'I need a coffee. Do you want one? Or perhaps tea or Milo, or hot chocolate. Have you eaten, do you want some toast?'

'Coffee would be great, thanks. Just white with one. But I don't want to …'

'I wouldn't mind the company, to be honest. You'd be doing me a favour. My mother has got me into a pickle of my own, actually.' Damien was a little shocked at his candour. 'It seems our pickles are in the same jar.' He couldn't help smiling wanly, and was pleased to see Alice do the same, rolling her eyes at his attempt at humour.

Damien felt as if Alice was his little sister – he wanted to help her. Part of it, he thought, was that he and his real sister had drifted so far apart. He still cared about Lucy, of course he did, and would do anything for her. Trouble was, he knew nothing about her now she was in London. What did they have in common other than blood and DNA? Nothing; he was just a farmer who lived out in the sticks, planting a crop and harvesting it year after year, dealing with sheep, and always had been. And Lucy was a sophisticated city girl who, he assumed,

ate out at fancy restaurants, shopped, and worked in
some high-rise office doing something glamorous – he
wasn't exactly sure. He realised with a shock that he'd
never shown much interest in her life. He didn't even
know what she actually did for a crust, or even if she
currently had a boyfriend – a few had come and gone
over the years. Their occasional phone calls had all been
about the farm. She'd ask how the season was progress-
ing and, bang, he was off and running. It was a subject
he could talk about. Damien didn't do deep and meaningful, especially with his sister. Though, really, asking
what she did for a living and what that entailed and if
she enjoyed it was hardly deep and meaningful. He tried
to shake the guilt aside.

'Did you go to the police about Geoff?' Damien
blurted. God, he really wasn't any good at this sort
of thing. Where was Jacqueline when he needed her?
Should he just get Alice to empty the float and send her
on her way with a recommendation to book in to see
Jacqueline? Probably, but a part of him wanted to know
the details, if she wanted to tell them. Not wanted to,
needed to. It was part of his penance for being so clueless,
so dismissive when it came to his sister and her interactions with Geoff. Oh, of course he'd seen things. He was
now getting very vivid images: the lewd comments, in
the sleazy tone, about what Lucy was wearing; Geoff's
gaze raking up and down her figure while he licked
his lips. Damien's stomach turned and he almost gasped
when the scene of the last Christmas Lucy had been
home surfaced. She was taking two large platters of food
to the table. Geoff had leapt up to unburden her – ever

the gentleman – but now Damien clearly saw in his mind's eye Geoff's hand deliberately brushing Lucy's breasts. *Jesus. How could I have been so disloyal?*

Damien felt so disappointed with himself, so ashamed, that his face coloured. Even though it would be too little, too late, he owed his sister a massive apology. But not nearly as big as the one his mother owed her. He didn't think Tina could have hurt Lucy more, if she'd tried. She should probably be grateful her daughter spoke to her at all.

'No. He didn't really do anything much,' Alice said with a shrug, bringing Damien back to the conversation. 'He was too clever.'

'I don't mean to pry, and you don't have to tell me if you don't want to, but what did he do?'

'Tried to cop the odd feel, squeeze past at the bench and brush my butt or breasts. You know, the sort of things you'd tell yourself you imagined? So many times I just thought I was being paranoid. And he had a way of looking at me – not really looking at me, you know, in the eye, but kind of looking me up and down. And a few times I saw him licking his lips while he did. Just creepy stuff.'

'But it made you feel uncomfortable. That's no way to live.'

'God, he made my skin crawl,' Alice said, shuddering.

'So did you tell your mum? And did she, um, believe you?'

'Yes. Eventually. I didn't want to be the one responsible for them breaking up. She really did love him.' Alice looked at Damien a little sheepishly. 'God knows why.

I love my mum, but he belonged to someone else. She should never have gone near him.'

'So what did she say? When you told her?'

'That no man was worth her daughter feeling uncomfortable in her own home,' Alice said with clear pride. 'Huge relief. It could have gone either way. Plenty of mothers might have thought I was just attention seeking or something.'

'Hmm.' It was all Damien could say as he dealt with the overwhelming mixture of renewed rage towards his mother, sympathy for his sister, and disappointment and shame towards himself that was assaulting him. What sort of a big brother had he been? Useless. Bloody useless!

'Anyway, even if she hadn't, she wouldn't have been able to ignore catching him peeping through the bathroom keyhole when she came home early the other day.'

'God. That's terrible!'

'Yeah. But he didn't see anything. I had him pegged as creepy from the start, just hoped he'd prove me wrong. I always made sure there was nothing he could see through any keyhole. Though that didn't stop him trying for as long they were together. He's got patience, I'll give him that,' she said with raised eyebrows. 'Anyway, that's why I'm here. It all hit the fan, as they say. Mum threw him out, and then we got thrown out. We were on a few acres on the edge of town. Not sure where he went.'

'Back home, I think. He threw my mum out.'

'Oh. I'm sorry.'

'Don't be, it's not your fault.' *And it's nothing she doesn't deserve.*

'Thanks so much for this. I feel so much better.'

'I'm glad. Maybe you should go and see Bill, the local copper. He's a good bloke. Surely there's a law around what Geoff did – stalking, or something?'

'I'll think about it, but I don't want to cause a fuss.'

'Well, it's up to you.'

'Thanks so much for caring. I really don't have many friends,' Alice said shyly.

'What about the horsey set, don't you all hang out together?' That's what it had been like in his sister's day.

'Nah. I think the pony club closed down and, anyway, I'm not into competition. I had heaps of lessons when I was a kid. But I just have horses because I like them. Ben and Toby out there,' she said, tossing her head, 'are the only two I've ever owned by myself. I rescued them. They were at a disposal sale, all set to go on the truck. You know, *the* truck?'

Damien nodded. He knew all right. His mother had often mentioned the nearest abattoir, Peterborough, when storming inside after a horse hadn't pulled its weight.

'What about the emu? I've got a confession to make – I'm terrified of the bloody things. Got pecked as a kid,' he said with a shudder.

'Aw, don't worry about Sam, he's a sweetie. No idea what his story is, he just turned up one day. I guess you could say he adopted me. But you can see the problem, can't you? We'll have to head back to the city, and no city stable – even if I could afford it – is going to want an emu hanging around.'

Damien wasn't sure he wanted an emu hanging around either.

'Anyway, I don't think Ben and Toby would be keen on being pampered horses again. They're track rejects. And I don't want to split them up. Which is kind of why I thought you'd be prefect. Because you're all about the animals – all animals. I know you'll look after them. I saw the write-up about you in the paper the other week.' Alice dipped her head and coloured a little.

'Do you ride them? Can they be ridden?'

'Yeah. Quiet as. Do you ride?'

'Nah. Tried it once when my sister was into it. But it wasn't for me.' Damien had the strange thought that that was then and now is now. So much had changed. *He* had changed. Perhaps he might give it a go. It might be nice to wander around the stock, check on the kangaroos on horseback. Except, of course, the shed full of saddles and stuff had been swallowed by the fire. Damn. He drained the rest of his coffee.

'Come on, I think they're probably keen to be let out by now,' he said when Alice had finished her coffee.

As she left the van, Alice seemed suddenly sad again. Damien's heart wrenched. And then he had an idea. And wanted to belt his head against the van for not having it sooner and putting Alice out of her misery. Though he could barely believe he was about to say it.

'Hey, why don't you just leave Ben, Toby and Sam here until you're settled somewhere else? There's no need to formally surrender them. Maybe you won't need to go to the city. They'll be fine here for as long as you need, while your sort yourself out.' The words came out in a rush. It's what Lucy would have done. She was a huge animal lover – always had been. Damien had come to the party quite late.

'Really?'

'Yep.'

'Oh my God. Wow. Thank you, thank you, *thank you.*'

Damien was stunned to have Alice's arms flung around him suddenly and pulling him into a tight hug, a hug so forceful it nearly knocked him off-balance.

'This means so much to me. Thank you. Seriously,' she said when she released him.

'No worries. Happy to help.' He was sorry and a little embarrassed to see tears streaming down her face again, but consoled himself that these might be good tears. And that he was the cause. That thought gave him a warm feeling deep inside.

Damien stood back by the tailgate while Alice went into the front door of the float to untie the horses. He was surprised to see Sam, the emu, carefully step out of the small door, one long leg and then the other. If he wasn't frozen with fear, Damien might have laughed at the huge bird, which shook itself, looked around, and then stretched to its full height as if to shed its embarrassment and then assert its superiority. Damien stood rooted to the spot, quivering all over, as the bird walked straight up to him and stared him in the face, beady eyes just inches away. Damien held his breath. Alice popped her head out.

'All ready when you are. Oh. Sam, leave him alone. Not everyone wants you in their face.' With that, the bird seemed to give an harrumph before tossing its head and wandering over to where Bob and Cara, still in their runs, were taking turns cowering and trying to appear bold, with bouts of menacing barking. Damien saw Squish disappear under the caravan.

'Righto,' Alice called. 'Ready when you are.'

Damien undid the latches, carefully lowered the tailgate, and then stood out of the way. There was no centrepiece dividing the space between the two chestnut horses and no rails behind them. Damien crossed his fingers, hoping they weren't the sort who reversed at a million miles. But both horses backed out slowly and carefully and then stood quietly, with heads held high, to take in their new surroundings. Damien felt a bit jittery at their size and close proximity. God, he really was going to have to grow a spine.

'Ben, Toby, this is Damien,' Alice said, rubbing their faces. 'He's very kindly come to our rescue, so be nice. Ben has the star and two white socks.'

Damien held out a hand for them to sniff, like he would a dog. Was that what you did with horses? He couldn't remember. Horses up close and personal were a distant memory.

'They like their faces being rubbed and being scratched between their ears. Like this,' Alice said, and demonstrated. Figuring this was his cue, Damien followed suit with Toby. The horse lowered its head and closed its eyes before letting out a long, deep groan, which Damien took to be contentment.

'See. He likes you.'

Damien smiled and rubbed more vigorously. Ben gave his shoulder a slight nudge as if to say, *My turn now*. But before Damien could do anything, the horse had sneezed loudly and deposited several huge globs of snot down the front of his work shirt.

'Lovely, thanks very much,' Damien muttered.

Alice laughed. 'Sorry. They do that after being in the float on a dirt road. It's the dust.'

'Suppose you'll be next, Toby. Go on, go your hardest. What's a bit of snot between friends?' He and Alice stood rubbing the faces of both horses, and Damien leapt when the beaked face of Sam, the emu, suddenly appeared over his shoulder. 'Christ,' he said, putting a hand over his heart. 'You scared the shit out of me.' Damien wouldn't admit it in such polite company, but he really did feel something in his bowels shift slightly.

The beady eyes surveyed him. Could emus smile? This one looked like it was enjoying Damien's terror. Bloody hell, he was being teased, he was damned sure of it.

'Step back, Sam,' Alice commanded.

Damien wouldn't have believed it if he hadn't seen it for himself, but the animal stepped back and seemed to have a chastised look on its face.

'Right, where shall I put these guys?' Alice asked.

'Over in the sheep yards for now. Follow me.' Damien led the way, wondering what the heck he was going to do with Sam the emu following him. It was unnerving. Nothing like facing one's biggest fear, he thought, as he trudged on.

'Do we put them in together? What about Sam?' From memory, he thought Auntie Ethel's emus had roamed about the farm as they pleased, regardless of where they were put. They had a knack of silently moving about and popping up right beside you when you were least expecting it. Terrifying for a little boy, worse when the beasts pecked and chased you if you ran. Damien shuddered at the memories, the fingers of fear creeping down his spine just as they had back then.

'He likes to stay close, so put them all in together for now. He seems to be able to get out of any enclosure, so locking him up is pointless, though I reckon he'd be hard pressed to get out of there,' Alice said, pointing to Damien's newly constructed enclosures. 'He'll generally follow one of the horses if you need to move him and are afraid. Otherwise, just loop some string around his beak. He leads fine if you're a bit firm. There's nothing to be worried about. Though I do understand fear. I'm afraid of moths,' she said shyly. 'Ridiculous, I know. They can't even hurt you. The only thing with Sam is he's a bit friendly, if you don't like emus. Just push him away and tell him to step back. Be firm. Same with the horses.'

Damien thought he'd worry about trying to manhandle the emu another day. Right now he just wanted to get the horses settled and give his heart rate a chance to return to somewhere near normal.

'Do you mind if I leave the float and all my gear in it? There are a couple of stock saddles and everything else you need if you decide you'd like to give riding another go.'

'No problem. Sorry I don't have a shed for you to put it in under cover.'

'No worries. It'll be fine. Sorry you lost everything in the fire. That must have been terrible.'

Damien shrugged. 'It's been a weird time all right.' What else could he say? He didn't want to go into a sermon about discovering that, really, when it came down to it, he was just relieved no lives were lost. And, anyway, his mother was such a control freak that everything was insured to the hilt. He could sense Alice was starting to stall, not wanting to leave, and he wanted her to leave while she was still calm.

'And I'm really sorry I don't have room for you to stay with them. If I had a shed and a swag, or the house was finished, you could have ...'

'It's okay. Thanks, anyway. I really appreciate all you're doing. You've no idea how much ...' And then the tears started up again.

Damien was not much into hugging, but wrapping his arms around Alice felt like the most natural thing in the world to do.

'It'll all be okay, you'll see. These guys are safe, they're fine here with me for as long as you need. It's not goodbye forever. You can visit them whenever you want.' He felt her nod against him and mutter something he couldn't decipher.

Slowly she pulled away, dragged a tissue from inside her sleeve, and blew her nose. 'Sorry, I'm being so pathetic.'

'God, don't be sorry. And you're not. What you're doing is hard. They're special to you. But they'll be fine. I'll take really good care of them,' he said, laying a hand on her shoulder. 'Even the emu,' he added, giving a roll of his eyes and a crooked grin to lighten the mood. She smiled weakly. 'Now off you go and sort out whatever else you have to sort out,' he said, giving her a gentle brotherly shove.

Alice's chin wobbled again. She nodded. Damien put an arm around her shoulder and ushered her to the driver's side of the ute, opened the door for her and then closed it after she was seated.

'Take care. And I hope your mum's okay,' he said.

Alice nodded as she turned the key and croaked, 'Thank you so much, for everything.' She put the vehicle in gear and drove off.

Damien's heart lurched after her. He knew tears would already be flowing freely down her face again. He wished he could have taken away her pain and angst as well as the burden of the horses and emu.

Chapter Twenty-nine

Damien found he couldn't drag himself away from watching the horses. He was tired, but it wasn't just that – they were relaxing to watch. There was something quite magical about their elegance, their lovely kind eyes, long lashes, the slow, rhythmic chewing as they ate, and their long velvety ears flicking back and forth, taking in everything around them. He found himself sitting on the ground right beside the fence and crossing his legs. Squish pushed his way under his arm and into his lap. Damien smiled when he felt Jemima snuffle at the back of his neck and then lean against him.

As he sat there, the heavy burden of what he'd just taken on began to descend again. He'd told Alice these guys would be safe with him for as long as needed. But what if that wasn't true? What if the farm needed to be sold? It was one thing to send Jemima and the kittens elsewhere – sure, it would be hard and he'd be sad – but this was different. He'd made a promise. And not just to the animals and to the memory of his dead father, but to another human being; their owner. Damien McAllister was loyal and honest to the core. Perhaps he should have told her the truth about what was going on. God, what a mess. He buried his face in Squish's fur.

Jemima sat beside him and he rubbed her face and gave her a kiss on the nose. Out of the corner of his eye he noticed Bob and Cara also lower themselves to the ground nearby. But when Sam the emu plumped down beside him and peered at him with those expressive eyes, head tilted as if in question, Damien didn't know whether to laugh or cry.

He thought he might have just heard a car pull up but couldn't bring himself to go and check. While he was sitting here surrounded by animals who had everything they needed, he could ignore the world and the possible devastation that faced him. He reluctantly dragged himself to his feet. As much as he wanted to, he couldn't sit here all day doing nothing.

He wandered over to the building site, his little menagerie – Sam, Jemima, Bob, Cara and Squish – shadowing him. He stood staring at the timber framework. Things appeared to be at a standstill. No doubt he was meant to be making some decisions and was the reason for the hold up. He'd better pull his finger out and get onto it. He sighed deeply. Even if the farm was to be sold, the house had to be finished. It was definitely past the point of no return, and far too many people had been far too generous to call a halt. He sighed again.

He turned back, hearing the crunch of a slowly approaching car on gravel: Philip Havelock's Statesman. Shit. His heart started to race and he felt his underarms begin to dampen. He really wasn't up to speaking to Jacqueline's parents yet. But he didn't have a choice with them right here. He tried to straighten his shoulders, but they refused to cooperate. He walked over to where they'd stopped the car. Philip and Eileen were exiting and he nodded and offered a weak smile to Eileen. But then he realised she had stopped and was standing with the door still open, fear written right across her face. *Sam.* He'd forgotten about the bird. If he'd known they were dropping in he would have locked everyone up. He looked around. Sam was still beside him.

'Don't worry, he's friendly. I'm terrified of emus too. Well, I was until we met a while ago. Do you want me to lock him up?' Though as he said it, he wondered how he'd manage that. Alice's instructions were all well and good for her.

'No, I'll be fine. I've just never met one up close before.'

'Jemima will look after you,' Philip said, nodding at the roo, who was making her way towards Eileen.

Sam wandered over to Philip. 'Hello there, Sam, is it?' Philip said, and rubbed the top of the emu's head.

Apparently having satisfied his curiosity, Sam wandered off and Damien turned and accepted Philip's hand with a slight grimace, which he'd meant to be a sympathetic, knowing smile.

'How are you, my boy?' Philip said, pumping his hand and patting his shoulder firmly, as if nothing had happened.

'Hi, look, I'm sorry about … ' Damien began. About what? He was so sorry about so much: having a fuckwit of a mother, being gutless in facing them – so many things.

'Ah,' Philip said, waving a dismissive arm. 'How about a cuppa?'

'Yes, please. I'm parched,' Eileen said. She looked relieved to see the emu moving further away. She enveloped Damien in a tight hug, taking him by surprise. 'And I've just got to take a proper look at this van of yours.'

'Okay,' Damien said, vaguely waving an arm.

'I'll be mother then, shall I?' Eileen said, when they were inside and Damien had completed the five-second tour of his temporary home.

'Coffee, white with one would be great, thanks.'

'The usual for me, thank you, dear.'

'We've been to the cottage for a look-see,' Eileen announced.

Damien almost giggled at such ocker words coming from the very refined, almost prim, Eileen Havelock. He felt himself relax a little and smile weakly. God, it was good to see them. He'd been such an idiot to avoid them.

'Yes, and Eileen seems to think we can live in a caravan on site while the builders are at work,' Philip said. Damien noticed he was looking around with a doubtful expression.

'I'm wondering if it'll be an option. It might be a lovely adventure. Philip is needing a bit of convincing.'

'Dear, I'm right here, you know. And it is *very* small. No offence, Damien,' he added.

'Hey, no skin off my nose. It's on loan. I'm just really grateful to have somewhere out of the elements and away from the creepy crawlies.' Eileen put a mug in front of him. 'Thanks. So the house hunting didn't go so well then?'

'It was okay. There are a few viable options, but it just seems to make more sense to park something onsite, and it's much more cost-effective. And the power's already available.'

Damien thought six, eight or twelve months, or however long it would take to do the old stone place up – it was a dump, he wasn't sure he'd be bothering at all, but each to their own – was a long time for two adults to share such a small space.

'It'll be fun. We can have a large annex. It'll be just like camping,' Eileen declared gleefully.

'Might I remind you about the one time we attempted camping?'

'Er, no, thank you. But that was different, anyway.'

'Yes, dear. Eileen lasted one night, well, not even one. At midnight she demanded I drive her to the nearest motel – half an hour away – and wake up the owners to give us a room. We were damned lucky they weren't booked out! And that they answered their door at that hour.'

'It was raining,' Eileen explained to Damien. 'And *someone* hadn't stretched the guy ropes, or whatever they're called, wide enough, or something, so there was practically a river running between us.'

Now it was Philip's turn to flap a dismissive arm and look a little sheepish. 'I tell you, putting up a tent is a lot harder than it looks. Never again,' he said.

Damien was enjoying their friendly banter. They both had a glint in their eye, so he knew it was all in fun.

He didn't think they looked much like your typical grey nomads, but then wondered what a typical grey nomad looked like. While Philip was obviously good with his hands in the case of surgical procedures on animals, he didn't strike Damien as the sort to be too keen on hooking and unhooking trailers and changing tyres. He looked more the sort to drop his car off for a service or call the RAA to change a tyre.

'Now, Damien,' Philip suddenly said, full of seriousness. 'Eileen and I want you to stop avoiding us. We understand why, but it's not necessary, please. Ethel filled us in on everything – well, we assume everything – about your mum being the one to dob Jacqueline in to the authorities. I hope you don't mind her doing that.'

'It's fine,' Damien croaked.

'You've got enough going on without hiding yourself away. That's not healthy. I can only think you did that because you were concerned about what we might think.'

Damien nodded and stared down into his mug. He felt like he was in the principal's office at school all over again.

'We love our daughter,' Philip continued, 'we really do. But she's a grown-up and quite able of taking care of herself and fighting her own battles. Though, of course we'd do all we could to help. But what I'm trying to say, and making a hash of it, is that we don't hold you responsible for what your mother has done. And neither does Jacqueline.'

Damien looked up quickly. He tried to speak, but the words didn't come out.

'Yes, she knows,' Philip said.

'Oh no. God,' Damien said, rubbing his face with his hands. 'How will I ever face her now?'

'You're being too hard on yourself. And, I dare say, your mother,' Philip continued kindly.

'I'm sure she thought she was doing the right thing by you,' Eileen said, gently laying a hand over Damien's. 'Mothers don't set out to deliberately hurt their children, Damien. They do the exact opposite. Well, unless they've got a box of screws missing.'

Damien wasn't entirely sure his mother hadn't completely lost the plot – why else would she have ever thought what she did was a good idea? He stayed silent. They didn't know what a manipulative bully she could be. And he'd seen it through Lucy's eyes now too. It wasn't just him being a bit paranoid.

'And we've met Tina. She loves you, Damien.'

'Yes, look how she embraced your change of career and new venture. Sure, she shouldn't have done something so drastic, and definitely should have thought it through a bit more – spoken to you first – but we've all done things in haste that have turned out to be not such a good idea.'

'I hear what you're saying, but I could still just about wring her bloody neck,' he said with a tight smile and slow shake of her head. 'What was she bloody well thinking?'

'That Jacqueline was a threat to her son? However misguided that's turned out to be. I think that's what it was, at the heart of it,' Eileen said quietly.

'I really love Jacqueline,' Damien said earnestly, looking at each of them in turn.

'We know you do. And she loves you. You'll get through this.'

'One day I'm going to marry her. If that would be okay with you?' he added, searching their faces earnestly.

'We'd love to have you as our son-in-law, when the time is right, wouldn't we, Eileen?'

'We certainly would.' Damien noticed there were tears in her eyes. He felt emotion try to grip him too, but he swallowed it down.

'How is she?' he asked.

'She's fine. Sad – missing you – angry, disappointed, frustrated, afraid, desperate for it all to be cleared up and over and done with – probably everything you're feeling,' Philip said, smiling warmly at Damien.

'Hopefully it won't be too long and we'll at least know where things stand and what the future holds. Doctor Squire is quite confident all will be resolved,' Eileen added a little wistfully.

'Yes, he really is being very supportive of Jacqueline,' Philip added.

'Thank you so much for stopping in. You're right, I have been avoiding you. I didn't know how I'd look you in the eye again. And the rest of the world,' Damien said. 'My life feels like such a mess.'

'Is there something else going on?' Philip asked.

'Mum left Geoff.'

'Yes, she announced that at dinner that night at Jacqueline's,' Eileen said, looking baffled.

'And now it looks like the farm might be sold to sort out their financial settlement.'

'Oh,' Eileen and Philip both said at once.

'Just when I've finally sorted myself out.' Damien buried his head in his arms on the table. Tears filled his eyes. He just felt so overwhelmed, so damned useless. He'd nearly given in to the tears when Squish nudged him. He swallowed hard and concentrated on patting the little dog.

'Are you sure it will come to that? Perhaps there's another way,' Eileen said.

'I don't know. I don't know anything any more.'

'Have you sat down together and started working through the figures?' Philip asked.

'No. I only found out after I'd discovered that she was the one who dobbed Jacqueline in. I'm too pissed off to speak to her. Oh, I'm so sorry about the language,' he said, looking at Eileen.

Eileen waved his apology away.

'As I said, it's all such a mess. And I don't know what to do.' He hadn't meant to say that bit, it sounded so childish.

'You've got your own piece of land, haven't you?'

'Yes, but there's nothing there – no power, no water. Just a super shed. And it's too far out of the way for people to deliver unwanted animals. It's too inconvenient. I'm off the beaten track here as it is.'

'You can't think like that. It's defeatist. There must be a way,' Philip said, rubbing his chin thoughtfully.

'Yes,' Eileen agreed. 'If they're going to bring them at all, what's a few more kilometres? As long as it's well signposted and easy enough to find. You can't give up so easily.'

They went through all the pros and cons. While they didn't come up with anything concrete, Damien was beginning to see that while it wasn't ideal and would take a lot of work, Esperance could be relocated to his block. Unlike Eileen, he wasn't entirely convinced that people would be willing to go so far off the beaten track, but he had to get a grip, and start thinking more positively, otherwise he might slide right back into the hell he'd been in before. Anyway, it might not come to the farm being sold. Access wasn't the only problem, however: his block wouldn't support enough sheep or crop to bring in the income he needed so badly.

'Perhaps you could do something else a bit different to make ends meet?' Eileen suggested.

Damien had wanted to snap, *Like what? All I've ever known is farming.* But they were just trying to help. He could see that.

'It'll work itself out,' Philip finally said.

'Yes, you'll see. These things always do,' Eileen added.

Damien nodded. He felt much better for having discussed it; felt not quite so terrified of the future. He was grateful they hadn't once suggested he walk away from the animals, his dream. His mother would have, of that he was sure. That was another reason he didn't want to discuss all this with her: he couldn't bear to listen to her making it all about her, as she always did. And this was pretty much all about her – if it wasn't for her marrying and now wanting to divorce the dickhead retired shearer, Damien wouldn't be in this fucking mess. But there was a flicker of hope burning deep inside him. He wasn't sure what form it would take or even if it was just a feeling of relief that he'd unburdened himself, but he'd go with it for now. Everything would work itself out, he had to believe that. What else was there?

'We saw your Facebook post on the tax–deductible donation status,' Eileen said. 'Huge congratulations. And don't worry, as far as we know, Jacqueline still isn't on Facebook. We know all about the petition. It's amazing seeing the town come together.'

'So what's Sam, the emu's story?' Philip said. 'I'm curious to look him over. As I'm sure you can imagine, I've never had one in my city surgery before.'

Damien got up. 'Come and meet him properly. He's actually quite nice. I've had a fear of emus since I was a little tacker. Would you like to come as well, Eileen, or stay here? There are actually two horses as well.'

'Oh, actually, I wouldn't mind staying here. I'm a bit afraid of horses too. Can I feed the kittens, or something?'

'You can have a cuddle with them, if you like. There's still ten minutes until their next feed,' Damien said, checking the time on his phone. 'Though, knowing them, they'll be squawking any minute now.'

Damien and Philip made their way over to the yards and, as they did, Damien couldn't help smiling at the assortment of creatures surrounding them. While he felt better for having spoken to Philip and Eileen, the shadow of fear, dread and helplessness hung all around him.

'Hello there,' Philip said. 'You're a couple of fine looking pieces of horseflesh.'

'They've been well looked after. The girl who had them, Alice, lost her job and the rental where she kept them. I hope she can come back for them before too long, not that I mind having them. But she was distraught, poor thing. It really cut me up to see her go through that.'

'Well, thank goodness she had you.'

'Yeah. I suppose so.'

'Seriously, Damien, you're doing a lot of good here. You have to believe that. The animals need you, the people need you. Ethel told me about the two pups. I'm so sorry you had to go through that. It's shocking, but sadly all part of dealing with animals. It's wonderful that you care so much to be so upset, but you need to keep it in perspective. You're new to this, and unfortunately you've seen some tragedy early on, but you just have to remember that there are so many relying on you.'

'I think that's the problem.'

'Oh?'

'I'm scared of letting anyone down. And I will if the farm gets sold.'

'I think you have to put that out of your mind until you have some facts to work with. It's one thing to make contingency plans and be prepared, but worrying about things that might or might not happen will just do you in.'

'I'm going to have to phone Mum, I guess,' Damien said.

'Well, as tough a conversation as it will be, it'll probably help. You've certainly been through the wringer lately, haven't you?'

'It feels like it.'

The horses walked over and stood in front of them on the other side of the fence, putting their noses close to Philip's and Damien's faces. Sam joined them and they leant on the rail, patting the horses and emu in silence.

Damien was beginning to see the appeal of horses. He'd changed a lot recently and really wished he had Jacqueline to share these revelations with. Here he was thinking he was the one saving the animals, but he had the uneasy feeling that they were doing a lot more for him than he was for them.

'Jacqueline's amazing,' he said, and was shocked to realise he'd spoken aloud.

'Yes, she is.'

'She was incredible at the CFS debrief last week. The guys really took to her. We need her here. The town needs her.'

'Well, lots of people are working on resolving the situation.'

'Yeah, no thanks to my bloody mother!'

'It's done now, Damien. We just have to deal with it. Remember, she's going through something pretty big too. Everyone reacts to things in different ways. I'm sure she feels badly enough about it,' he said kindly, and put a hand on Damien's shoulder.

Damien nodded. Philip was right, of course. At that moment Damien's phone started its alarm jingle.

'Kitten-feeding time,' he announced, giving Ben's face a final rub and stepping back from the fence.

Chapter Thirty

Jacqueline was grateful for every one of her clients turning up on time in a steady stream that kept her busy listening to them, responding, writing notes in their files. A few new bookings even came in. She only took names and contact numbers until people turned up for the first time and filled out the form she'd devised, so she was never able to know where exactly they were from or if they were calling as a result of one of her talks. She hoped there would be a few calls coming soon after Charity Flat, but conceded it was unlikely; it was a very long way to drive. While she'd learnt that country people were comfortable driving long distances, she still doubted many would be inclined to drive so far for an appointment with her. It would probably prove to be a wasted evening in that respect, but at least it had been a good distraction from her own problems and her parents had certainly enjoyed it.

Jacqueline sighed. That morning, she'd hugged her parents goodbye, plastered a smile on her face, and waved as they backed out of the driveway with a little farewell toot. She hadn't wanted them to leave and had struggled to keep the sadness and tears hidden. She was meant to be an adult, for goodness sake! Once she'd pulled herself together, she'd gone inside, grabbed her handbag and keys, pulled the door shut behind her and got into her car. She'd driven the short distance to work not because she didn't want the fresh air or exercise, but because that way she had gear shifting, road rules and looking out for other drivers to concentrate on to prevent her from falling apart and dissolving into tears. While her parents had been there she'd had them to distract her from the disaster that was currently her life. And there was nothing like being taken care of by Eileen Havelock. Now Jacqueline had to fend for herself again, physically and emotionally, the stupor she'd felt since she'd received the letter was creeping back.

She checked her watch. Finally it was five o'clock and she was exhausted and looking forward to escaping back to her little cottage – her mother had left a chicken curry for dinner. It would feel strange going home to an empty house and while part of her wanted to be left alone, another part of her wanted Ethel to knock on the door and agree to stay and eat with her.

She was surprised and a little disappointed to hear a knock on her office door just as she was gathering her handbag. She really hoped it wasn't Louise or Cecile inviting her to the pub to cheer her up.

'Come in,' she called.

The door opened and Doctor Squire bustled in. 'Oh, I'm glad to catch you before you left, my dear.'

'Hello. Busy day?' she asked for something to say while he caught his breath.

'Yes, but no more so than usual,' he said, plopping down into a chair. She followed suit, and as she did, noticed he had a piece of paper in his hand. Could he have heard something from the board already? Her heart skipped a beat. No, it was too soon, she thought, feeling slightly deflated.

'I had a phone call from the mayor of Charity Flat.'

Uh-oh, am I in trouble again? 'Oh, I'm sorry I didn't … I just thought …' She felt heat rising in her cheeks.

'No, my dear, I'm not here to tell you off,' he said, waving her words away with his hand. 'I wanted to thank you for taking the initiative and giving up your time to travel so far. You were quite a hit, I hear. They're keen to discuss having you travel up regularly to consult – say a day a month – and are looking into grant options to fund your travel. Oh, and I wanted to give you this,' he said, handing over the piece of paper. 'It's a claim form for travel expenses. Popping over to nearby towns is one thing, but driving to Charity Flat and back out of your own pocket is unacceptable. It's a business expense. Just fill it in and return it to the girls on the desk. They have the forms there when you need more. I just wanted to let you know personally so there could be no misunderstandings.' He smiled at her. 'Speaking of misunderstandings, how are you coping with the waiting to hear from the board? I understand your parents left this morning, I hope you're not feeling too badly about that.'

'Thanks, but I'm okay.'

'You can be honest, you know,' he said.

'Well, it was wonderful having Mum and Dad here and I'll miss them, but I'm a big girl. And the cottage was starting to feel a little crowded,' she added, trying to lighten the atmosphere. She was afraid she might actually cry if things kept on the way they were.

'And the career situation, how are you coping with the wait?'

'Well, it's hard, I won't deny that, but I'm trying to keep busy and not think about it. If I do, it feels like it's taking forever and that the wait is slowly killing me,' she said with a tight smile.

'I feel the same. But, you're right, keeping busy is the best thing we can do. We've done what we can, we now just have to wait it out. Unfortunately, these organisations tend to move at a snail's pace. Fingers crossed it won't be too long until we hear. Well, I'd better get back to it – a few patients still to see at the hospital. I just wanted to check on you and thank you for all your efforts to keep drumming up business, despite the difficult circumstances you find yourself in. I'm sorry I'm such an absent boss, but please know you are appreciated.'

'Thank you, it really does mean a lot,' she said, her throat tightening.

After he'd gone, Jacqueline sat looking at her handbag, feeling both buoyed and a little stunned. How lovely of him to take the time to drop in, given how busy he was. It really was nice to feel appreciated and that they were in this career palaver together. Perhaps it really would work out okay.

As she pulled out of the car park she toyed with putting her foot down and driving out to see Damien – she was desperate to share Doctor Squire's visit with him. Her stronger urge was to see if he was all right, make sure he hadn't withdrawn to the point where he was sitting out there being miserable. But instead she sighed and put her indicator on and took the left turn to head home. Ethel was keeping an eye on Damien. She had to respect his desire that they not see each other until her career was sorted out, even if she thought he was being over-cautious. It stung a little that he seemed to care more about the town keeping their newly acquired psychology service than his own happiness. Or her happiness. But she couldn't help loving his loyalty and dedication, and his willpower. And it was a wonderful compliment to her skills that he believed in her. Maybe one day they would be lying in bed, entwined, and laughing about this time. She could only hope. Meanwhile she had to keep her head down, trust in Doctor Squire, and hope for the best.

And if it all went wrong, she thought as she turned her key in her front door, might Damien whisk her away to make a life together somewhere else? *Don't be bloody stupid. This is where he belongs, he's a part of this place.* He needs land to chase his dream. But what would happen if he lost his farm? She couldn't imagine staying here if she lost her qualifications and became the talk of the region for all the wrong reasons. God, how humiliating. But she had to stop thinking about what she couldn't control. Wasn't that what she told almost every patient who walked through her door? God, she was so much better at seeing the problems and solutions of people other than herself.

She really hoped that if it came to the crunch, Damien would put it all aside and seek help anyway. Suicide had never been mentioned by either of them, but Jacqueline knew enough now to suspect that he must have been pretty close to that point to have sought help from Doctor Squire and then get up the courage to see her the following week. All she hoped was he'd learnt enough in their sessions to stay well away from those destructive thoughts and be equipped to bat them away if they did creep in. But he had Ethel. And his CFS buddies. She hoped he wouldn't withdraw from them too.

He had her parents, too, she thought, brightening. She just had to believe he knew they would drop everything and drive the six hundred or so kilometres back if he picked up the phone and asked them to. But Damien was loyal to the core. She knew he'd worry how his friendship with them might make his insecure mother feel. It made Jacqueline furious – and actually queasy – to think how his loyalty and devotion to his mother had been repaid; not only with recent events, but basically his whole life. Jacqueline realised she was pacing back and forth across her bedroom, and stopped, focussing on getting changed into track pants and a T-shirt.

She ate dinner on her lap in front of the news. After trying and failing to settle into two shows and surfing the channels in the hope of something grabbing her attention, she gave up and turned it off. She thought she'd enjoy having her own space again, but instead she was missing the company and distraction of her parents. Her thoughts were again plaguing her and she'd never sleep in this state. Maybe a long, hot shower and half of an over-the-counter antihistamine sleeping tablet would help.

As she soaped herself, Jacqueline's frustration at her situation returned, namely feeling so damned helpless, since her fate rested in the hands of others. She wasn't one for sitting around waiting for things to happen. Well, she didn't want to be one of those people, but she was beginning to see she was a lot less independent and resourceful than she'd hoped. Was that one of the reasons she'd fallen for Damien? Farmers were so capable. Didn't the whole world know they could fix anything with the twine from hay bales and a roll of wire? Or was it gaffer tape? She knew the belief was tongue in cheek, but she'd been very impressed with how Damien nutted things out. And clearly his father before him had been the same. And that day moving the sheep during the fire – he'd been so calm, so capable. That's what you needed in a life partner: someone calm, capable, dependable. Pity she'd stuffed it all up, she thought, rubbing shampoo through her hair, shocked as tears sprang into her eyes.

Chapter Thirty-one

Damien was awoken by a thundering sound all around him, Squish huddled up close and trying to get even closer. He cocked an ear and concentrated. And then he laughed.

'Rain, Squish. It's raining.' Damien loved the sound of rain on a tin roof, but this was an entirely different sound – all around him the aluminium and plastic roared. It was like a freight train rumbling through. He couldn't detect pinging, so didn't think it was hailing.

He lay back down with his hands behind his head. God, it was a glorious sound when you didn't need to be out in it. Damien did a quick inventory as he always did when it rained – it was so ingrained. The ute wasn't undercover because there was no longer any cover for it. Its windows were definitely shut because it had been windy and he hadn't wanted any more fine black dust in there than there already was. Same with the caravan and its windows. The weather had been warmer than average for early autumn so he'd been using the air-conditioner most of the time. There were no field bins needing him to rush out and shut lids on, no tarps needing to be pulled over open truck bins. All the animals were shut up safely.

The horses. There hadn't been any thunder or cracks of lightning, so they should be fine, shouldn't they? He hoped so, he wasn't going out to check. He hoped Sam had found some shelter. He had considered locking the bird safely in a run, but wasn't prepared to put their new friendship at risk by trying to manhandle the creature. Damien was prepared to admit he hadn't completely conquered his fear of emus – that was a work in progress.

Hopefully the rain wouldn't hold up the fencing crew that was due to arrive today. Damien had asked the owner if he needed anything from him and he'd gruffly been told no, they were completely self-sufficient. He was secretly a little excited about being able to sit back and watch someone else do all the work. He wondered if he'd feel guilty when he saw them down in the paddock hard at it. And then he reminded himself they were being paid well – very well – so, no, he wouldn't be letting himself feel guilty. God, how good would it be to have nice straight, upright shiny fences and new posts? Some of the old fences had patches on patches. He'd never managed to keep up with the replacement schedule, nor had his father before him. Damien realised with a pang that he might not be here to enjoy the farm's new fencing. He sighed deeply.

He had to believe everything would work out okay in the end and that whatever shape okay took, he'd be fine and would adapt if need be. He had to keep telling himself that over and over, otherwise he'd completely fall in a heap and not be able to drag himself back up.

He'd spent most of the previous day in Mitre 10 looking at taps, toilets and basins with the help of Ethel and Doris, who seemed very pleased to be relieved from her counter duties to help a customer for a bit. He couldn't believe how long it had taken. He'd thought taps were taps and toilets, toilets. He'd run out of patience when they'd got to looking at tiles, and given up before making a choice. He thought they'd take the longest time to choose, but boy had he been wrong: everything had seemed to take forever. He'd come away happy with his other choices, which he'd made with Jacqueline becoming lady of the house in the back of his mind. So he hadn't chosen the cheapest beige taps, but the nice chrome ones – twice the price, but they looked a lot better. *Listen to you, Damo, you're sounding like you've almost got a bit of class.* Then he and Ethel had gone over to Hope Springs where the hardware store prided themselves on their range of lighting. Damien knew most places now had the little round lights that sat flush with the ceilings. He quite liked that idea, and being a little modern. Soon he'd have to venture down to Port Lincoln or up to Whyalla to choose carpet. He was not at all looking forward to that. He knew everyone was ripping up carpets and exposing floorboards or putting in that floating floor stuff that sounded hollow and plastic when you walked on it, and carpet was harder to keep clean and probably not hygienic when you had pets, but when he took his boots off in the laundry each day, he wanted his weary feet to walk on something soft. He hoped Jacqueline would agree. If only he could send her a text and check. But he'd dumped her.

Damien noted the change in sound on the roof above him. The rain was hammering even heavier. Squish squeezed up closer, trying to hide.

'It's okay. Just rain,' he said, rolling over and rubbing the belly the dog promptly presented for a scratch.

His alarm went off. He thought the kittens would probably be mewing by now. Perhaps he couldn't hear them over the din. He dragged himself out of bed. He was still pretty tired, which he knew wasn't helping his general disposition, and he'd got used to feeling heavy and a bit groggy all the time, not that he liked it. But you did what you did. Thankfully the time between feeds was gradually lengthening and he was getting a bit more sleep. And his body also seemed to be learning to take what it could when it could. These days he could often drop off as soon as he closed his eyes, whereas for years he'd spent hours tossing and turning, unable to fall asleep. It helped that he didn't have a massive, never-ending to-do list plaguing him. Everything on his list felt doable – no doubt only because it hadn't had long enough to grow into over-whelming territory.

Damien got dressed, got the kittens organised, put the TV on, and made himself a coffee. He couldn't even think of what he felt like for breakfast. He flicked between the two main morning shows and waited out the rain. He wondered if there was enough to wash away all the soot and black crap. Knowing his luck lately, it would just make it worse.

When the rain had stopped he headed out to check that everything was okay. As he opened the door he got a fright, finding Sam the emu sitting waiting below the steps. The bird eased himself onto his long legs and shook his feathers out. Squish bounded out and after encountering a puddle stood with one wet foot in the air, looking up at Damien with a stricken expression.

'What, don't you want to get your paws muddy, oh precious one?' he said and picked up the little dog. Probably best not to track it into the van anyway. Damien, followed by Sam, went over and let Jemima and Bob and Cara out. The two big dogs roared off like lunatics, splashing through puddles as they played their usual game of chase. Damien marvelled at how much more cheerful and alive he felt just from having the dampness and fresh smell of rain around him. It made his whole soul feel lighter. He felt himself smiling as he walked, taking in and letting out deep breaths.

He headed over to the house, followed by his menagerie. Half the roof had been put on, not that it helped: there was still only timber framing where walls would be, and rain rarely fell straight down around here; there were some pools of water lying on the concrete slab. He hoped it wouldn't do any damage to the building, but couldn't worry about it. He was sure half-built constructions got caught in the rain all the time and survived just fine. He had to hope his would too.

A vehicle was approaching and he looked up, standing where he was until it arrived. It was the fencing team.

'Morning,' said Dave, and extended a hand through the open window for Damien to shake.

'Morning,' he said, and nodded to the other two guys, whose names he didn't know. This needing to employ a fencing crew was all new to him.

'Right for us to start then?'

'No worries. I wasn't sure if I'd see you, what with the rain.'

'Bit of rain won't hurt. We're keen to get started.'

'Fair enough. Let me know if you need anything from me.'

'Thanks, but we shouldn't do. It's easy enough just replacing what was already there. Unless you've changed your mind about anything.'

'Nah, all good. Thanks very much.'

'No worries.'

As they drove off, Damien noticed builder Stan's vehicle coming in. *It's all go here this morning. And even better, nothing needing my involvement.*

'G'day.' He was about to add, 'Nice bit of rain,' out of habit, but stopped himself in time. Farmers usually rejoiced at rain, but no doubt builders hated the stuff because it held them up.

'Howdy,' Stan said. He eyed Sam warily and seemed reluctant to get out of his vehicle with the bird standing there.

'Don't worry, he's friendly. Just very curious. Sam, off you go,' he said firmly, and gave the bird a gentle shove. He held his breath to see what would happen. Sam seemed to give a harrumph of distaste before striding away. Damien nearly laughed. He'd never have believed it if someone had told him how expressive emus were. They were actually quite cute when you got to know them up close and personal – well, Sam certainly was.

Stan got out and they shook hands. 'How's it looking?' he asked as he gave Squish's ear a scratch.

'Fine, but I didn't go in – didn't want to walk all this shit in,' Damien said, lifting his boot – a mass of black soot clung to his tread.

'Good idea. It'll make a real mess. Don't worry, though, I've brought out some matting to put down. Now I'm really going to need a decision on the colour for the walls before the end of the day if you definitely still want to go with the stuff that comes already painted.'

'Righto.' Damien had been in a quandary about it for days. He didn't like the pressure of having to choose the colour for the outside of the house – a mistake there was around forever for all to see. Sure, it could probably be painted over if he didn't like it when it was up, but going pre-painted was more expensive, so it would be a waste and Tina would go ballistic if he wasted money. Though she'd also go ballistic if he got the colour wrong too. He wished he'd thought to go over it with Ethel, or even Eileen and Philip when they'd visited. But with so much plaguing him, he hadn't given it a thought.

'Here's another brochure,' Stan said, reaching into his vehicle. 'I rang them yesterday. The colours I've circled are what they have in stock and enough to do your place. Just a matter of putting it on a truck for overnight delivery. The other colours are available, but it could mean holding us up for a week or so.' It was clear to Damien that this is not what Stan would want.

'Okay, thanks,' he said, accepting the brochure. He liked the idea of having the choices whittled down. Though they were all nice enough – none of them were too in your face – he was having trouble deciding if he wanted to go with the greenish-grey that would blend in when more trees were planted or the buttery yellow that would stand out but which he quite liked. He also quite liked the pale grey. He had got as far as deciding he didn't want plain cream – it was too much like what he'd had before.

'Anyway, by five,' Stan said.

'Will do.'

'Well, I'd better get on.'

'Do you need a hand?'

'Nah, thanks, she's right.'

'Righto, I'll leave you to it.' Damien raised his hand in farewell and headed back towards the van. It felt weird to not lend a hand, especially when the guy was nearly old enough to be his father.

Damien tossed the brochure onto the table in the van on his way past before heading over to feed the horses. He hoped they were okay out in the weather. At least it wasn't too cold. He was actually starting to get a little warm under his jumper.

'Good morning,' he said, and rubbed the faces hanging over the fence. He tipped out the water that had accumulated in the feed bins and tossed in a biscuit of hay with a few pellets on top for a treat. Damien stood watching the horses eat, unable to tear himself away.

★

Damien was cuddling the kittens while trying to make a decision regarding the colour of his house when there was a friendly *toot toot* of a car horn. He popped the kittens back in the box and got up and joined Squish, who was whining at the door, already on the case, tail wagging so furiously his whole body shook. He smiled as he watched Squish launch himself off the steps and towards where Auntie Ethel stood beside her car a little way away. She raised her hand in greeting. That was odd – she usually bowled up to the door, gave a loud rap and entered. Damien followed suit and, with a puzzled frown, strode over.

'What's going on?' he asked as he gave her a quick hug. Ethel, looking a little concerned, nodded towards the house by way of an answer. Damien followed her gaze. There was someone who was not Stan making their way through the building, coming in and out of view as they passed behind the timber frame.

'She needed to see it,' Ethel said.

'Right. Fair enough.' Damien nodded thoughtfully. The big question was what the bloody hell his sister was doing here when just a couple of days ago she'd been in London. And more to the point, had made no mention of coming back. It wasn't Christmas and as far as he knew there were no family weddings, christenings, funerals or significant birthdays or other milestones being celebrated. Though it was entirely possible he'd forgotten something.

It seemed to take an age before Lucy was standing in front of him. They hugged in their usual awkward way, though Damien noticed they both hung on a little tighter and harder than before.

'Wow. Well hi, good to see you,' he stammered, a little shocked and lost for words.

'Surprise,' Lucy said, raising her hands and offering a tight smile.

'Not quite like the last time you were here,' he said with a shrug, indicating the building site with his head.

'No. God. It's awful. I didn't realise, didn't know what to expect.'

The words came out in a rush and then Damien watched, stunned, as she gulped for breath and two lines of tears began rushing down her face. He stood, frozen to the spot, as Auntie Ethel gathered his sister to her soft, ample chest and held her. Thank God for Ethel.

'God, I don't know what's wrong with me,' Lucy said a few moments later, wiping her eyes with tissues she'd dragged out of her pocket.

'It's a shock, I guess,' Damien said with a shrug. Though why it would be that much of a shock was a little beyond him. Did she think he'd lied when he'd told her their family home had burned down? If she found this upsetting, she was damned lucky she hadn't been here to see the smouldering remains. Now *that* had been shocking and heartbreaking. She'd left home years ago, so none of her stuff was gobbled up by the flames. Damien checked himself. He was being too hard on her. He'd been there on the ground, seen the progression, and he'd seen plenty of fires in his day. Sure, not many houses, but still, it must have helped him cope. Lucy hadn't had any of that exposure.

'Yeah, shit happens,' he said with another shrug. Shit, he hadn't meant to say the words out loud and sound like he didn't care. He did, very much, but what was done was done. Time to move on. *Christ,* he thought with a jolt, *I sound just like Mum: cold and unfeeling.* The look on Lucy's face told him she'd just had the same thought.

'You must be Squish,' Lucy said, bending down and making a fuss of the Jack Russell.

'Sure is. And this is Sam and Jemima,' he said, pointing to the bird and kangaroo who had just appeared.

'Golly, quite the menagerie,' Lucy said, clutching her chest and letting out a little nervous laugh.

'Don't worry, he's a friendly emu, aren't you, Sam?'

Bob and Cara rushed up to Lucy and gave her a cursory sniff before running off to carry on with their play fighting.

'And I see those guys are still lunatics,' she said, nodding after them.

'Sure are. Though they were amazing during the fire. Hey, you're never going to guess what else is here,' he said, changing the subject.

'What?'

'We also now have two horses.' He grinned.

'No, surely not.' Lucy put on a big show of clutching her chest and pretending she was about to fall over.

'It's true.'

'You've gone soft,' she said, grinning and poking Damien in the chest.

'Yes I have, and I'm proud of it,' Damien said, smiling back. 'Esperance takes care of all creatures great and small, sis.'

'What's their story? Can they be ridden?'

Damien opened his mouth to answer, but Lucy was no longer there. She was on her way to where the yards had always been, practically skipping, almost running.

Damien shared a grin with Ethel as they followed, much more slowly. When they caught up, Lucy was standing with both horses in front of her, whispering soothingly to them. She stepped back and took in a 360-degree view of her surroundings.

'The shelters and runs look amazing,' she said.

'Yeah. The working bee was fantastic, all because of Auntie Ethel, I reckon.'

'Lovely of you to say, but not true,' Ethel said.

'So, what are you doing here, anyway?' Damien asked as they slowly made their way back to the caravan.

'Just felt the right thing to do. With all that's going on with Mum, I kind of thought you might like some more moral support,' she said a little shyly. 'Especially since you don't have Jacqueline. I'm so sorry about that.'

'Yeah, well, me too. But thanks. And it really is nice to see you,' he said, reaching out and putting an arm across her shoulder. He'd have pulled her into a hug if they had that sort of relationship.

'Hey, Luce?' he said, stopping. She stopped too. He put his arms around his sister and embraced her, shocked by his actions as she seemed to be. He'd changed, he was changing. 'Thanks so much for being here. It means a lot.' Tears stung his eyes.

'You're welcome,' she whispered into his neck, giving it a kiss, before she extracted herself from his clutches.

As they walked on in thoughtful silence, Damien felt his heart soar a little. If he'd known losing everything would change his relationship with Lucy like this, he might have thought to light a match himself. If it weren't totally immoral and illegal, that is.

'This is nice,' Lucy said, looking around as they ushered her into the van first.

'It's home for now. A little on the small side, but comfortable enough. Though you should have heard the din the rain made.'

'Oh, kittens!' Lucy said, rushing to them.

Seeing her cuddling them made Damien think how odd it was that he was the one doing the animal rescue venture. Lucy had been a staunch animal lover from day one: she'd been bringing home baby animals and feeding them with an eye dropper for as long as he could remember. He wondered if she'd have stayed and fulfilled their dad's dream instead of him, if things had been different.

A sudden thought gripped him. Would Lucy be interested in joining him in this venture if the farm didn't have to get sold? Or maybe setting up with him somewhere else? Could it be a viable enough business to support both of them? But she was settled in London and this place wouldn't hold enough excitement for her. The mother issue complicated matters too … But the thought stayed with him like an itch he couldn't quite scratch.

'It really is good to see you, Luce,' Damien said again as he delivered mugs to the table. He'd said words to this effect many times to his sister when she'd visited over the years, but he'd never quite meant them like he did now. He always followed up with something a little cruel, like, 'So how long are you gracing us with your presence?' But this time he was too scared to hear the answer. Damien liked the feeling that reinforcements had arrived. Lucy was much smarter than he was, and so much better at standing up to their mother – well, he'd always thought so, anyway.

'What's this?' Lucy asked, pointing at the brochure.

'That's the choice of colours for the house cladding. I have to choose and let Stan know by five. The circled ones can come straightaway, so I want one of those. What do you guys think?'

'That one,' Lucy said at once, pointing to the buttery yellow one.

'Auntie Ethel, which one do you like?' Damien and Lucy asked at the same time.

'Looks good to me. Nice and bright and cheery.'

'And fresh. And different to what we had before,' Lucy said.

'Okay. Done. And here I was thinking I'd never make a decision. Hey, you wouldn't by any chance be able to come with me to Lincoln tomorrow – both of you – to help choose carpet and tiles, and bits and pieces for the house? Since you're so good at this. I've been putting it off.'

'Okay. You'll come too, won't you Auntie Ethel?' Lucy said.

'No thanks, but I will happily take care of the kittens for you.'

'Oh, I hadn't thought of them,' Damien said. 'Thanks very much.'

As they sipped on their coffees, slipping into silence as they stroked the kittens and Squish, Damien felt a little guilty at thinking how things were easier without his mother's presence. He could see how much more at ease Lucy was out of Tina's gaze. He too was definitely less on edge. He felt terrible for thinking ill of his mother, but he couldn't help being observant. It was what it was, there was no denying it. As much as Tina wanted to pretend she wasn't the problem, what Damien was seeing said otherwise.

'So, have you spoken to Mum again? Does she know you're here?'

'Yes. We spoke late yesterday. I had a few hours in the airport in Adelaide, but she couldn't make it to see me, said she had something else on. It was a bit weird, actually. She was quite cagey. Normally she'll tell you exactly what she's doing with all the detail under the sun.'

'Maybe she's giving you the silent treatment like she seems to be giving me. I rang and left a message and haven't heard back from her. But no, hang on, you spoke to her. So it must be only me getting the silent treatment. That'd be right. So how was she?'

'Weird. There seemed to be something not quite right about her.'

'Well, she's going through a lot. Maybe she's getting a bit depressed or she's freaking out about how she's going to cope financially, or something.'

'No, she didn't sound upset – which you'd expect her to, with all that's going on – she was just the opposite. She was actually upbeat. Cheery even.'

'Maybe she'd been drinking.'

'I don't think so,' Lucy said thoughtfully, shaking her head. 'She definitely wasn't slurring her words.'

'So what do you think's going on? Is it something we need to worry about?' Damien sent a prayer skywards that he wouldn't be required to intervene.

'I know this is probably ridiculous, but she sounded just like when she first got together with Geoff.'

'Well, I'm happy she's finally left the prick, except, of course, for the potential financial headaches it's causing. Maybe she's feeling relieved and becoming a little giddy with it all, as Grandma would have said. She's finally free.'

Lucy had an odd expression on her face, like she'd put two and two together and didn't like what she'd come up with, or didn't believe it, or something. And then it slowly dawned on him. *Like when she first got together with Geoff*, Lucy had said. *No.*

'What, you think she's met someone? A man? Already? No way. She left Geoff, like, thirty seconds ago.'

'Well, you know how she hates being on her own. Geoff was the first to take any interest after Dad, and she latched onto him like a piranha.'

'I still can't believe she couldn't see what we could.'

'Perhaps she did, but kept her eye on the prize of not being alone. Or perhaps she thought she could change him.'

'Hopefully she wouldn't be stupid enough to get involved with someone else while everything is such a mess. Or if she does, he's rich and will take care of her.'

'Maybe she'd just been to see her lawyer and found a loophole in her finances with Geoff. That would be good.'

'So, when's she coming back?'

'She was cagey about that as well. Said something about maybe getting a ride back, but seemed to be waiting to hear from someone.'

'I guess we'll find out soon enough.' Damien cursed the feeling that swept through him: that he didn't want his mother there in his orbit, making him feel tense, and especially ruining the good vibe he had going on with his sister.

'Hey, do you remember the number for the girl who brought the horses out – what was her name, Alice?' Lucy asked.

'Why? You're welcome to ride them. You don't need her permission – they've been surrendered. Well, kind of. There was no need to take her number. She handed them over, there'd be no need for me to call her. She has my number for when she wants to visit or take them back.' Damien knew he was going on and sounding very defensive, but he was a little annoyed with himself for not getting her details.

'It's not about the horses,' Lucy said quietly. Damien noticed she shared a quick look with their auntie Ethel, who had remained strangely quiet for ages. If they weren't all sitting at the tiny caravan table he'd have forgotten she was even there.

'What? What's going on?'

'Lucy wants to speak to her – since she's been through some, er, *awkwardness* at Geoff's hands.'

'Oh.'

'Yeah. I feel terrible. If I'd made people listen, believe me, all those years ago, maybe she wouldn't have had to go through it. God knows who else he's leered over or touched up along the way.'

'Luce, I'm so sorry I …'

'Damien, you have nothing to be sorry about. You weren't to know.'

'But if I'd been more observant ...' *Been a better brother, an approachable one, someone you could have confided in.*

'Let it go. Seriously. So she worked at the supermarket? Anything else you know about her and her mum?'

'No. Auntie Ethel? You'd know better than me.'

'I've got my feelers out. With luck they won't have left town yet. Bill might know where they are or be able to ask around,' Ethel added thoughtfully, as if to herself.

'Why would you get the police involved? That's taking it a bit far, isn't it? She indicated it wasn't something she was going to pursue. Maybe she just wants to forget it. I don't think he actually touched her.'

'Sorry, what? Police? Don't be ridiculous,' Ethel said quickly. Too quickly to Damien's mind. 'Not *that* Bill,' she added, even more hastily. Was there another Bill? Damien was pretty sure he didn't know one.

'Speaking of cagey, what are you up to? What's going on?'

'Nothing.'

'Auntie Ethel?'

'Seriously, Damien, leave it.'

The tone, which he rarely heard from Auntie Ethel, stopped him in his tracks. He had the strange feeling that Lucy had not flown halfway across the world merely to provide him with moral support, but he said nothing. There was definitely something going on that didn't involve him and that he didn't need to know about. Women's business, most likely. Fine, whatever, he had enough on his mind anyway.

Chapter Thirty-two

Jacqueline made her way swiftly up and down each aisle in the supermarket, perusing her list and looking for other items on the shelves she might need but hadn't realised. She quite enjoyed this sort of leisurely grocery shopping, not that she could dawdle – they closed at five-thirty, which was only twenty minutes away. She'd got used to doing her shopping Tuesdays and Thursdays to coincide with the two days fresh fruit and vegetables were delivered, but had missed yesterday and had spent way too long sorting through the limp lettuce. What she hadn't got used to was everything that was meant to be fresh looking like it had been sitting around for a week, and how much more expensive it all was so far from the Adelaide distribution centre.

She'd just thrown a pack of toilet paper into her trolley when she heard her name being called from behind her by a familiar voice.

'Jacqueline Havelock, is that you I see?'

A smile was on her face when she turned to see Ethel striding towards her and a younger woman – around Jacqueline's age – pushing a trolley and clearly hurrying to catch up. Jacqueline hung onto Ethel tightly for a moment before they separated, shocked at just how pleased she was to see her friend and neighbour; she'd knocked on her door after work the day before to see if Ethel wanted to come across the road for a drink and she hadn't been in. Jacqueline had been far more disappointed than she should have been.

'This is Lucy McAllister, Damien's sister,' Ethel said, stepping aside to introduce the younger woman.

'Lovely to meet you,' they said simultaneously as they shook hands.

'You're based in London, aren't you?' Jacqueline said.

'Yes. I don't come back very often, but I decided I'd better see first-hand just what sort of a mess my mother has got herself into.' She looked around before carrying on in a lower voice, 'I am so sorry to hear what's going on with you. I hope you don't mind, but Auntie Ethel's filled me in.'

'Thanks. I'm sure it'll work itself out,' Jacqueline said quietly, smiling warmly at Lucy. She liked Damien's sister enormously already. Damien had never spoken of her much at all, so Jacqueline hadn't been sure what to expect and was a little ashamed to admit that she had thought Lucy might be stand-offish and a bit cold. This was partly based on the fact that Damien clearly didn't have a very close relationship with his sister – silence tended to speak volumes in Jacqueline's experience – and also on Tina being so cold and abrupt. Perhaps, like Damien, Lucy was more like her father. Jacqueline wished she'd had the chance to meet him, she had the feeling they'd have got along famously.

'So you're staying in town with Ethel?'

'Yes. Mum's not here, so I can get away with it,' Lucy said, linking an arm through Ethel's. 'Mum would have a fit if I dared stay anywhere but with her. "Oh, what would people think?"' she mocked, rolling her eyes. 'Small towns. I'm sure you're getting a feel. Lovely one minute, can be toxic the next. Sorry, listen to me going on. I have a bit of a love-hate relationship with this place, I'm afraid.'

'Don't worry, we're all well aware of the wicked ways of Wattle Creek, aren't we, dear?' Ethel said. 'But our new psychologist is far too polite to say what she really thinks – in public, that is.'

Jacqueline laughed, not quite sure how else to respond. She took her own covert look around. There was only one other shopper – out of hearing up the far end of the aisle by the clothes detergents. She coloured slightly and hoped their voices weren't carrying through or over the shelves into the other aisles.

'We'd better get to the checkout before they lock us in,' Ethel said. 'Pop over for a glass of wine and cheese and bikkies and then stay for dinner. I've got a roast in the slow cooker. It'll be good to catch up properly – it's been ages. Sorry I wasn't home last night when you called. Oh, Olive told me. Not much escapes her,' she added, noticing Jacqueline's bewildered expression.

'Nosey old Mrs Caffey strikes again, eh?' Lucy said. 'You can't sneeze without that woman telling the whole town you've got a cold.'

'She's not that bad. And she has been known to be quite useful. Remember how she got to the bottom of that poison pen letter incident before Bill?'

'Just saying,' Lucy said, a little sheepishly.

'Right, so are we seeing you for dinner?'

'Yes, thank you, it sounds lovely,' Jacqueline said, her mouth already watering. 'But I'll bring the wine and nibbles.'

'See you a bit later,' Lucy said, smiling warmly. 'It really was lovely to meet you. I'm so looking forward to getting to know you better.'

'Likewise,' Jacqueline said.

'Cheerio,' Ethel called as she did an about-turn and headed to the front of the store.

★

'How long are you staying for?' Jacqueline asked when they were settled in Ethel's lounge room with a glass of wine and a small cheese platter on the coffee table.

'I haven't decided. A couple of weeks? I wanted to be here for Damien, with all that's going on and, well, Auntie Ethel thought there was something more practical I could help with.' She looked at Ethel, who gave a nod.

'There isn't much Jacqueline doesn't know,' she said. 'And anyway, she's practically family.'

Lucy looked down and fiddled with the stem of the champagne flute she held, as if arranging her thoughts before speaking.

Jacqueline sat, stunned and dismayed, as she listened to Lucy   explain how her mother had dismissed her very real concerns over Geoff. God, what damage would that have done to Lucy, and her relationship with her mother? But at the same time, Jacqueline was wondering why it would bring Lucy back now. Before she could ask, Ethel took over, telling Jacqueline about Alice and how her mother had dumped Geoff as a result of her allegations; luckily the girl had a supportive mother who wasn't completely self-absorbed. While Lucy appeared reasonably lighthearted, Jacqueline just knew she was covering up a lot of pain. She felt guilty about being a little tense with her own parents at times over the years and being unappreciative, but deep down she knew – and had always known – that they loved her and would always support her, no matter what. Her heart ached for Damien's sister. And for Damien. Not only had these two lost their father at a young age, but it looked like their mother had all but cast them aside emotionally. While she knew people did strange things out of grief and insecurity and she was trained to keep an open mind and not judge, right now she wanted to slap Tina McAllister. The worse thing was it didn't seem that Tina had learnt anything nor had a clue she was letting her children down. No doubt she was blaming Lucy for their estrangement. She could almost hear Tina: 'Oh, yes, that daughter of mine. So wrapped up in her own life I barely hear from her.'

Jacqueline had the startling thought that she wanted nothing to do with the woman, which was going to be very hard if Tina ended up being her mother-in-law. Not exactly something she needed to worry about happening in the near future, Jacqueline thought sardonically, taking a long sip of her sparkling wine in an effort to banish the negative thoughts threatening to swamp her.

'Anyway, we managed to track down Alice and she's coming with us to the police station tomorrow. Thank goodness she and her mother hadn't left town yet.'

'So are you having Geoff charged? And what with?'

'No, unfortunately I don't think there's a law against being a creep.'

Jacqueline frowned. *So what am I missing?*

'We're hoping that Bill will go and speak to Geoff and he'll leave town and not make a fuss over the settlement rather than run the risk of the truth coming out,' Ethel explained.

'We need Alice because otherwise it'll look like I'm making it up to help Mum or something,' Lucy added.

'I know what you're thinking,' Ethel said.

Jacqueline raised her eyebrows.

'You're thinking this sounds dodgy, that Bill will be doing something wrong. But Geoff's done the wrong thing and should pay for it.'

Jacqueline did think it all sounded a bit off, but conceded that perhaps this was another case of things being done differently out here. 'It's not for me to say,' she offered. 'I'm not involved. You have to do what you think is right.'

'Right, enough of the serious talk,' Ethel said, 'it's time we ate.'

Jacqueline enjoyed the evening and getting to know Lucy better. She seemed to have quite a dry sense of humour and was really fun to be with.

Later, as she crossed the road to go home, Jacqueline's thoughts returned to the conversation about Bill the policeman and Lucy, Alice, and Geoff. While it all still seemed a little off and she was concerned Ethel's meddling could well get her friend in trouble, Jacqueline couldn't help but marvel at Ethel's ingenuity. And her loyalty. There didn't seem to be any lengths she wouldn't go to to help her family or those she cared about. She really was a good one to have in your corner. *If only she could help me out of my situation,* she thought with a heavy sigh as she put her key in the door.

Chapter Thirty-three

Damien was pleased to see his aunt's car waiting beside the highway at the end of the dirt road with Ethel and Lucy standing beside it, clearly all ready to go. The cloud of pale limestone dust hanging behind his ute in the still morning was as good as a smoke signal – they'd have seen him coming from almost as far back as his boundary.

He looked along the seat, half expecting to see Squish, but he'd left the little dog at home, sulking in the run with Jemima. He couldn't risk leaving him roaming about and being run over by one of the building or fencing guys' utes. Squish had laid down on his belly with his chin on his paws and his nose pushed right up against the chicken wire with a pout so strong Damien nearly gave in and let him come along. But he'd stopped himself in time – he'd have to spend most of his time in the ute while they shopped, and all the extra traffic and people might terrify the little fellow. And the last thing they needed was Squish clambering all over them, making them hot and smelly and covering them in little white and brown hairs. As much as his sister had enjoyed meeting the little dog, she probably wouldn't welcome his slobber and hair all over her clothes.

He stopped and got out. 'Morning,' he said.

'Nice one, no wind for a change,' Ethel said, accepting the box of kittens and placing it carefully in her car. Damien realised he could have left Squish with Ethel too. He hadn't given it a thought.

'Old blankets and towels, as requested,' Lucy said, and handed him her armful. It was amazing the things he kept realising he'd lost in the fire, things like padding for when he needed to carry something precious in the back of the ute. He had plenty of rope because that was kept in the toolbox on the ute's tray, along with a few other farm essentials, but there was a limit to what he could cart around.

'Thanks for these,' he said, stuffing them into the toolbox so he could barely close the lid. 'And for taking care of the kittens.'

'No worries at all,' said Auntie Ethel.

'Right, ready to go?'

'Yep.'

They were silent as Damien turned onto the highway, both waving to Ethel, standing by her car. He went through the gears and got the vehicle quickly up to the one hundred kilometre per hour speed limit on the familiar bitumen road.

'So, have we got a list or are we just aimlessly wandering around?' Lucy asked when they had settled into their journey.

Damien dragged the pad of paper from the dash in front of him and handed it to her without a word. He might not know the name of his sister's boyfriend or much about her life in London, but he knew she was organised. And he was becoming good at making lists, too, thanks to Jacqueline. Damn it, he wished she'd stay out of his thoughts.

'Right. Okay. Um,' Lucy muttered, as she read down the page.

'Okay?' What he really meant was, *Does it meet with your approval?* Not only was Lucy organised, but she was picky and had a tendency towards being bossy. Though, to be fair, he'd spent very little time with her in recent years. She could have changed. He had. Or she might not have changed, but how he saw her might have. Again, because of Jacqueline. *Damn it! Stop.*

'Do you mind if I put it in order – like what to get in each shop?'

'Go for it,' Damien said with a grin and plucked the pen from his top pocket. The old Lucy would have just done it, taken over without asking.

They'd barely got to the coast by the time she had finished reorganising his list, just fifteen minutes into the hour and twenty–minute journey, and she put the pad back on the dash and handed him the pen with barely a word. Damien was soon wishing he'd done this differently. If only Auntie Ethel was there, chattering away about random stuff. Anything to ease the awkwardness and lack of free-flowing conversation. It was going to be a long, slow day.

It wasn't like he hadn't tried, though: 'So, have you heard from Mum again yet?'

'Nope.'

Silence.

In the old days he'd had his endless to-do list to whinge about, and the sheep and the ancient gear he had to keep patching up to keep going. Now he didn't have a thing to complain about. He had a team doing his fencing, another building his house, and someone else to do his cropping when the time came. It felt pretty damned good to be able to live his dream. He felt really free. Sure, there were a few niggles with his new venture, but he didn't feel like he was drowning as he once had.

But he couldn't crow about how great his life was now to Lucy. He felt a little guilty that she'd been fending for herself all these years while he'd been given a job and a roof over his head.

'Sing out if you need me to drive,' she said.

'Righto. Thanks. Should be right.'

'You must be tired from getting up all night for the kittens.'

'Getting used to it,' he said with a shrug.

'You'll have your body clock reset and then you won't need to do night feeds.'

'Probably. Murphy and his bloody laws.'

'Yeah.'

Silence.

'It all looks the same. Few more houses here and there, I guess,' Lucy said.

'Farms have been subdivided so all the hobby farmers and retired cockies don't have to have neighbours.'

'Fair enough.'

'Yeah.'

Damien instinctively put his hand by his leg to give Squish a pat. He missed the little guy. He could ease any awkwardness just by demanding attention. Damien knew he should be asking about Lucy's life, but couldn't bring himself to. He wasn't sure why.

'Hey, you don't have furniture on the list. You know you're going to have to fully furnish the place, right?'

'Oh. Hadn't given it a thought.'

'If we're efficient with the boring stuff, we might have time to do some of that as well.'

Damien almost pointed out it was *all* boring stuff to him. And then he brightened a little: he could have a big-screen TV, which he would especially welcome after the one in the caravan that was about as big as a cereal box. And he could have one of those modern recliner chairs. He felt a stab of sadness at remembering his father's recliner. He shook it aside. He'd go for leather so it didn't stick to him in summer like the vinyl had. He found himself shifting a little in his seat, sitting more upright, looking more keen. Shopping sure would be much better having Lucy's eye.

'So are you still with the advertising company?' he found himself asking.

'Yeah. Though I'm now a graphic designer, not just a lowly admin assistant.'

'Oh. Right. That's great. Well done.' *Why didn't I know this? Did I know this?* His brow furrowed.

'Mum didn't tell you, did she?'

'No. But it's my fault. I should have asked. Asked you, I mean. I've always been too wrapped up in my life and my own problems.'

'It's okay, it's not really something that would be of interest to you.'

'But I should still show an interest. You always ask about the farm.'

'Yeah, but that's because I know about it. I grew up here remember? Just because I left and have an office job doesn't mean I stop being interested. It's in my blood, I think.'

'It's weird, though, how Mum doesn't pass on some stuff but goes on and on about other things.' Damien had to be grateful to Lucy for letting him off the hook so easily. He knew he'd asked her stuff over the years and she'd told him, but he was always so distracted by his own worries. And since he'd seen Jacqueline and got a better handle on his head and the fog up there had cleared, he could see just how self-absorbed he'd been. Just like his mother.

'So, what else have I missed? Are you still seeing Rick, Richard, Robert?'

'Tom. Rob was the one before.'

'Oh. Right. Sorry.'

'My fault for being so disastrous at relationships,' she said with a smile.

Damien felt the urge to say, *And why do you think that is?* but kept it in check. He almost laughed out loud. There was Jacqueline in his head again. 'So, are you okay?'

'Am I heartbroken, you mean? Am I over here escaping it all?'

'Yeah. I guess.'

'Yes and no. And, probably. He wasn't the one. Though I'm beginning to wonder if such a thing exists. Tom actually ran off with his ex-wife's latest ex-boyfriend.'

'Oh. Right. Well. Shit.'

'Yeah, exactly. So at least I don't have to worry that I didn't wear high enough heels or not enough makeup. It's not like I can compete with a different gender.'

'No.'

'I'm so sorry again about Jacqueline. She seems really nice.'

Damien looked at her quickly. 'You've met her?'

'Yeah, she was over at Auntie Ethel's last night.'

'They're as thick as thieves, aren't they?'

'Yeah. How was she?'

'Good. Okay. Worried about things. You know,' Lucy added, a little helplessly.

'I dumped her.'

'But for the best.'

'Doesn't feel like it.'

'I know. But it'll work out.'

Damien wanted to scream at Lucy that he wished everyone would stop saying that – he was sick of hearing it. He wanted proof. Action.

'Auntie Ethel told me the whole story. I think you did the right thing. It's good of you to put the town ahead of your needs.'

'Yeah, well …'

'She loves you. She'll wait for you.'

'She said that?'

'She didn't need to. She knows why you did what you did. I got the impression she's pretty impressed. Especially after you spent that night out in your ute keeping an eye on her when that guy was stalking her. And she respects the choices you've made, what you're doing with your life. I think if you've got respect for each other, all the other stuff will come.'

I just hope she hasn't come to respect Paul Reynolds too much. Damien had heard Jacqueline had gone to speak at Charity Flat at Paul's invitation. He'd been trying very hard to not give it or anything on the subject of another man any airplay in his head. It would do him in for sure. She was a free agent. He just had to trust he really did mean that much to her, that *they* did. 'Did you respect Tom? You know, before you found out he was, um, gay?'

'Bi. And, no, not really. I thought I did, but looking back I didn't respect him for putting his job ahead of me. That sounds so selfish of me. It's a bit complicated, but he'd never turn his phone on to silent in a restaurant – it would always be on the table beside him. And he'd answer it. He was the manager of a stationery company for Christ's sake – nothing was ever going to happen that needed him twenty-four-seven. He used to spout about work-life balance – it was his mantra. But blind Freddy could see he was a slave to his job.'

'Haven't we all been?'

'Well, farming's a bit different. It *does* require you to be pretty much on call around the clock. Anyway, enough about my crap,' she said, waving an arm.

'So how long do you think you'll stay?'

'Not sure. A lot longer while Mum's not around. Sorry, shouldn't say that. She just frustrates me with the whole parading me around to all and sundry as if she's responsible for me doing so well. Especially when she tried to stop me going to London in the first place.'

'Why was that?' Damien didn't remember his mother talking about Lucy going to London at all.

'Not sure. Probably because I was doing something she hadn't had the chance or the guts to do herself. I know she's been good to you, but she's never been supportive of me. And she's very controlling.'

'Yes, she is that.' Damien knew it was the understatement of the year, and he was saying nothing new, but it *was* relatively new to him. He'd never fully realised just how in-his-face Tina had always been. So much for being self-employed.

'You've only just realised that, haven't you?' Lucy said quietly.

'Yes. And what a poisoned chalice the farm has been.'

'So why not move everything down to your block and cut her out completely?'

Damien shrugged. Such a move seemed to make sense to other people, but not only was this his mother, Tina relied on him for most of her income, more so now she was on her own again. And, yes, he owed her. She'd given him lots of grief over the years, but had also given him a job and a roof over his head. Although it hadn't exactly been free. He thought about how she just burst in whenever she chose and ordered him around. He knew they'd had what was technically known as a co-dependent relationship. He'd reduced his dependency, but he still needed to ease himself slowly from her clutches. He wasn't sure who needed the separation the most: him or her. It was change and change was hard, especially when something had been like it was for so long without question. It would take time.

'Maybe people might actually appreciate a drop-off point for animal surrender that's more off the beaten track. Maybe it would help,' Lucy offered with a shrug.

Damien stared at her for a moment before returning his eyes to the road. She might have a point; maybe he'd been looking at it all wrong. Maybe the farm being sold and him being pushed onto his own land to continue his venture wouldn't be the end of the world he thought it might be. If people had been generous with building his shelters once, maybe they would be again. And he was a fully-fledged tax-deductible donation entity – people, and maybe even businesses, would be much more willing to donate now, for sure. Not to mention the heap of followers he had on Facebook.

'Hmm.'

'But whatever happens, we still need to shop for the house – you're not getting out of that,' Lucy said, clearly misreading his thoughtful expression and vague response.

'I hate the idea of asking for help again. You should have seen how many turned up for the working bee.'

'I wish I'd been there. Damien, you do a lot for this community – of course people are going to return the favour.'

'But what they did was so much bigger than anything I'll ever do. I only turn up on a fire truck now and then or turn snags on someone's barbie.'

'And helping, and being a part of things, makes you feel good, doesn't it?'

'I guess.' Damien took a moment to think about it, flick through in his mind the various things he'd done over the years. 'Yeah, it does. Definitely.'

'Damien. Never underestimate the joy someone gets from helping you. I know it's hard to ask for help – and you've got the double whammy of being a man and being a farmer – but by asking for help, you're helping people feel better about themselves by letting them make a difference, do something real.'

'You should be in marketing,' Damien said, not sure what else to say. All this deep, heavy talk was a little uncomfortable. But maybe there was something in it – hadn't Philip Havelock said similar things?

Lucy laughed. 'I am. Sort of.'

'Yeah, well, you're clearly good at it.'

'Thanks. Don't laugh it off and deflect, though, Damien. I'm being serious. I see Esperance as being for the whole community, and I'm sure plenty of other people do too. And people like you because you contribute. Nothing's ever been too hard or too time-consuming for you, even though you've always been stressed by your own stuff and worries.'

Damien felt a jolt run thought him. She was right. He'd looked forward to being asked to do a working bee or something for someone in the district or a community organisation. And got a buzz out of being asked to go on the CFS truck. He'd always thought it was to escape his overwhelming life, but he genuinely liked to help people. He could see that now. Why else had he been willing to drop everything for a day, knowing he'd have to face his mother's wrath and work ridiculous hours to make it up?

Damien was surprised to see the outskirts of Port Lincoln looming ahead. The trip had gone a lot quicker than it had looked like it would when they'd set off. And he was feeling really good about things. It really was much better and easier being with his sister with his mother out of the picture.

'Do you want to take a drive around first, say out to the marina, to see how things have changed?'

'No, but I'd almost sell a kidney for a decent coffee.'

'Okay. I'll park on the front street then. I'm not sure where has really good coffee.'

'It only has to be better than instant. Anywhere will be fine. Hey, is that place that used to have the bright orange vinyl booths still here? Do you remember it?'

'Yep.'

'Do you remember how Dad always ordered a Kitchener bun?' Lucy said.

'Did he?'

'Yeah. And a cappuccino? And didn't it sound so exotic back then?'

'I don't remember.'

'Oh, I do. He'd always order the same thing. And the Kitchener bun had to be cut in half. And Mum would spend the whole time scowling at him.'

'God, you've got a good memory.' Damien was annoyed with himself for not being able to remember. Maybe he hadn't been there. Lucy had come to Port Lincoln for dentist and orthodontist visits while he'd been left back at school. He had the strange feeling of being left out of something important.

They found a park right out the front of the café and walked in. Damien had been in here heaps of times — he stopped in here with his mum during the trips they made down to visit the accountant once or twice a year. He liked it because it was simple and familiar.

'I'm going to have a Kitchener bun,' Lucy announced. 'Going to join me in my nostalgia? I'll even have a cappuccino rather than my usual latte. And it has to be in a cup, not a mug.'

'Um.'

'Come on, be a devil. Pity Mum isn't here to frown at us.'

'Yeah. Why not. You grab a pew and I'll get it.'

'You sure?'

'Yep, it's on the farm.' *Least I can do, since you've been so short-changed for so long,* Damien thought. He knew when he took over the farm it would have been fair to pay Lucy out. Thank Christ he hadn't had to. But it would have been the right thing to do. The daughters of farmers generally got a rough deal: some families paid them out, and equally, but usually only if there was a son who wasn't going to be on the farm as well. He wished his dad was here, especially to see them getting on so well. They'd fought a lot as kids and had plenty of harsh words and silent wars since. Their dad had been forever saying, 'If you don't stop that, I'll bang your heads together,' or 'I'm taking on the winner,' if their fighting was physical.

Damien wondered if he'd ever stop missing his dad. He was feeling it more since he'd discovered so much more about the man and felt a deeper connection to him. He wondered how Lucy fared – they'd been especially close. But he didn't want to go there while things were so good.

Chapter Thirty-four

Jacqueline woke up feeling lost and lonely. She'd been okay while she'd had the weekly routine to focus on, but now it was Saturday morning and she was on her own, she wasn't quite sure what to do with herself. She knew when she dragged herself out of bed that the house would feel too big and too empty.

She forced herself up. She went through the motions of preparing bacon and eggs for breakfast, more to pass some time than any great hunger. All the while she kept pushing the thought of 'then what?' to the back of her mind. If she was in the city, she might have taken herself off to the cinema to watch two movies in a row. The thought of curling up on the couch for pot luck with whatever was on the TV didn't hold the same allure. Nor did watching one of her DVDs. Her collection mainly consisted of movies featuring Julia Roberts, Hugh Grant and Colin Firth, but she was trying to forget how crap her life had become so the last thing she needed was to be reminded of what she was missing with Damien.

The way she was feeling there was no way she'd settle into reading a book either. She wished she'd arranged to catch up with Louise or Cecile, but she'd really thought she'd enjoy spending the day alone, pottering around the house.

After breakfast she forced herself to shower and dress. Then she grabbed her car keys. She'd get in the car, turn up the radio, and just drive – see where her meandering took her. As she left the house, she looked across the road and paused. Ethel's car was in her driveway. Maybe she could... No, it was time she started fending for herself. She would entertain herself. Yes, she could do this.

Left or right? Jacqueline asked herself as she looked both ways at the end of her street. She found herself turning left and then making her way to the lookout Paul had taken her to. She hadn't heard from him. A part of her was a little disappointed; another part told her it hadn't been that long since she'd seen him. The days seemed to drag by excruciatingly slowly while she waited for news from the board about her career. Anyway, she was glad he hadn't made a move on her, wasn't she? She was waiting for Damien. Wasn't she?

She cringed at her new car bumping and shuddering its way up the winding gravel road to the lookout, but reminded herself it was only a car. Once she'd parked, she took in the view and felt a peacefulness sweep through her. She let out a sigh. It really was a lovely spot. It wasn't so clear today, but she could still make out the huge white grain silos beside Pigeon Bay. Maybe she should drive down and see if Paul was there, surfing. A few hours in the water trying to master standing on the board would chase away her boredom and keep the demons at bay. And the exercise would ensure she slept well that night.

No. Paul would have called her if he was interested in seeing her. To contact him would sound desperate. And she didn't want him getting the wrong idea, did she?

'Not going there,' she said aloud, and turned the key in the ignition to start the car again.

At the end of the lookout road, she decided she'd check out Hope Springs. She'd only driven through the day she'd arrived and everything had been shut the evening she'd gone over there with Ethel to do her talk. But she wouldn't turn right to go back through Wattle Creek and risk talking herself into going home and resuming her moping, she'd head left and see if she could find a back way. She didn't have a map, but she knew what general direction the town was in. And she had a phone – if she got completely lost she could call Ethel. Not knowing exactly where she was going would keep her mind sharp and occupied.

'Let's go on a little adventure,' she told her car. She really needed to give it a name. She hadn't named the previous one, but she hadn't felt so connected with it as she did this one, most likely because she was feeling so unsettled and the little vehicle was providing so much comfort.

She cursed again when she ran out of sealed road. She found herself apologising for the rough road she was taking the car on, and then laughed at her ridiculousness. She must have been under so much pressure lately she was becoming completely unhinged. She drove, lost in her thoughts, looking at where the sun was every time she came to an intersection and letting that guide her. She was banking on Hope Springs being pretty much due east of Wattle Creek and figured if she came at it from the north, she couldn't miss it. She almost laughed – thinking that almost guaranteed she would miss it, which reminded her of Paul giving her directions to Charity Flat. For a split second she considered changing course and heading there instead, but reminded herself she'd already decided she was not going to spend her day hunting Paul down and behaving like a crazed stalker. She was supposed to be a professional, a psychologist, for Christ's sake!

She took it very slowly on the dirt and several times was passed by utes that left her in clouds of dust so thick she had to slow to a crawl while it settled.

It felt like she'd been driving for hours when she finally saw the outskirts of town in the distance. She'd done it!

She parked in the bare area under the trees just as Ethel had done and made her way to the art gallery.

'Hi there. Jacqueline isn't it?' asked the lady on the desk, looking up from her knitting.

'Hello. Yes, hi,' she said, smiling.

'I'm Bev. Welcome. All pieces have been done by our local art group, and are for sale,' she said proudly. 'Mine are the beanies and socks over there,' she said, sounding even more proud, and pointed over Jacqueline's right shoulder. 'We call ourselves an art group, but we do all sorts. Though, really, what isn't art? That's a bit too deep a question for a Saturday, isn't it?' Bev added with a tilt to her head. 'Oh, yes, far too deep.' She let out a hearty laugh.

'Yes, yes it is a bit,' Jacqueline agreed, also laughing.

'If you'd like to join the Hope Springs Art Group, new members are more than welcome. Oh, but we meet on the first Wednesday of every month so that wouldn't suit you with working full-time, would it?'

'No, it wouldn't. And anyway, I don't have an artistic bone in my body,' Jacqueline said.

'As you'll see when I stop nattering and let you browse, there's no criteria for exhibiting and none whatsoever for joining. We pride ourselves on being inclusive and, above all, sociable. Some members have bucketloads of talent, like Tracey over there.' Jacqueline turned to look where Bev was pointing. On the far wall was a series of paintings of animals. 'And then there are those, like myself, who have absolutely zero creative ability and attend meetings purely for a natter and to escape our husbands. Oops, did I say that out loud? Let's just say suddenly having my Joe under my feet all day thanks to retirement isn't all it's cracked up to be, and leave it at that. We have some male members and men are always very welcome,' she said demurely. 'Enough from me, you enjoy a wander.'

Jacqueline smiled warmly at Bev before moving away. On the whole she did enjoy her wander, which ranged from exquisite paintings and pottery she thought wouldn't be out of place in a city gallery to pieces she couldn't for the life of her interpret. Regardless, it was nice to look, and at least the wondering was distracting her and passing some time. And, it was really nice to see a friendly face and be welcomed so warmly. She felt terrible that she hadn't seen anything she really wanted to buy. One piece – a charcoal drawing of a seagull – she'd half considered, but until she knew what was happening with her job, she felt she really needed to save her money. If she lost her registration, a pay cut would almost certainly be on the cards. She couldn't go buying something just to make herself and Bev on the desk feel better.

'Thanks very much, Bev, that was lovely,' she said as she left.

'You're very welcome. We change the exhibition every month or so, so come back again. Actually, do you mind if we put your name on our list for invitations to openings? It's always a nice evening out.'

'Thanks, that would be lovely.'

Jacqueline couldn't resist going into the newsagent-slash-takeaway shop to order a milkshake, though she'd take it back to the car. She'd never enjoyed sitting on her own in public to eat, and the place was busy. People nodded in a friendly fashion to her as they came and went. Some seemed a little familiar, but she wasn't sure if they actually recognised her or they were acknowledging her just because.

Finally the place emptied and she was next to be served.

'Hello, Ms Havelock, isn't it?' said the same man who'd served her the last time. 'Ethel not with you today?'

'Yes, but call me Jacqueline. And, no, I'm on my own today. And you're Owen, aren't you?' she said, his name suddenly coming to her.

'I certainly am. You've got a good memory.'

'Not as good as yours, I'm sure,' she said, smiling.

'So, same as last time – chocolate milkshake with the lot?' he asked, beaming.

'Yes, that would be lovely, thank you. To take away, thanks.'

When Owen handed over the tall cardboard cup, she paid, thanked him, and made her way out, thinking how good it felt to have people remember her. As she put her hand out to open the door, it opened, almost upending her drink. She grappled to keep her milkshake from spilling before looking up and being startled to find herself staring up into the eyes of none other than Paul Reynolds.

'Sorry, are you okay?' he asked.

'Yes, perfectly fine, I think,' she said, looking down at her milkshake.

'So it seems the tables have turned and it's now me trying to tip food over you,' he said jovially, grinning at her. 'Where are you off to in such a hurry, anyway?'

'The car,' she said a little sheepishly.

'Are you on your own?'

'Yes, just having a day out, wandering around, seeing where the car takes me,' she said, trying to sound nonchalant.

'Fancy some company?'

Would I ever! 'Sounds great. Would you like to stay here or go somewhere else?'

'It's too nice a day to be inside. There's a lovely shady spot under the tree in front of the pub near the boat ramp. I only came in for the paper, but now I've seen that milkshake, I can't resist. I haven't had one for years,' he added, and strode to the counter. Jacqueline went to the small table where she'd sat with Ethel to wait.

'Caramel milkshake with the works to take away, thanks, Owen,' Paul said.

Soon they were sitting side by side on a bench under a sprawling Norfolk Island pine, sipping on their drinks and watching the comings and goings at the boat ramp.

'Sorry I haven't been in touch,' Paul said. 'I've been caught up with work – there's a mass sell-off of stock at the moment so it's been more hectic than usual. I know I've said it before, but you really were fantastic – a real hit.'

'Thanks, that's lovely of you to say. Though you don't have to sound so surprised,' she said.

'Sorry, I didn't mean to, it's just that sometimes newcomers, especially professional services, can be treated with a bit of suspicion. Any surprise you're sensing is not about you, it's about the fact that you were so well received. But the fire was the first loss of a house in nearly twenty years, so it's got everyone spooked.'

'It's okay, I was just teasing.'

'Fair enough. So how's everything going with your, um, problem? Any news yet?'

'No.'

'That must be doing your head in.'

'Yup. Hence me driving miles just for a milkshake. Actually, it's worse than that. I was keen to go anywhere. To be honest, I couldn't bear to be in the house. Mum and Dad have gone home. Not that I'm not used to being on my own. Normally I quite like it, it's just that …' *Shut up, stop rambling, Jacqueline.*

'It's okay, I get it. I hope it'll all be resolved soon – and with a good outcome.'

'I have my fingers crossed. Meanwhile I'm just trying to keep busy. The weekend sort of took me by surprise, to be honest.'

'I can imagine. Hey, we've taken up your suggestion and are looking into doing a community project, putting people's documents and photos in the cloud, just like you suggested. The council thinks there might be a grant we can get.'

'That's fantastic.' It felt really good to have been helpful in a truly practical sense. She was a little shocked by her next thought: *God I wish I could share this with Damien.* She wondered how his day with Lucy was going. The fact that he'd barely ever mentioned his sister told her they weren't close. Perhaps they'd become closer now things were so up in the air with Tina.

'So how are you going to keep yourself busy tomorrow? Fancy seeing if there are a few small waves? I haven't decided if I'll go down or not, but I definitely will if you'll come,' Paul said.

'Oh. That would be lovely, but I think I'd better clean the house.'

'Is that the royal brushoff, like "Sorry, but I have to wash my hair"?'

'No, I really do have to clean the house.' *Liar!* The truth was that thinking about Damien made her feel guilty about enjoying time with Paul. She cringed at feeling herself blush.

'I don't believe you, but it's okay. You're going through something big. As you said in your talk, you have to be kind to yourself at a time like this. Please don't feel pressured by me. But if you want to use me as a distraction or you just fancy a chat, you have my number.'

'Thanks, it really does mean a lot. And it really was great to see you.' *You've completely made my day.*

'Well, I'd better keep going. I've still got another client in the area to see.'

'Oh, sorry, I didn't realise.'

'Don't be. I was at a loose end with some time to kill. I was only going to sit and read the paper. This has been much, much better.'

Paul walked Jacqueline to her car and gave her a hug and a peck on the cheek. As she hugged him back, she wished it was Damien's arms that were around her.

Feeling much better about everything, and a little weary from all the driving, Jacqueline headed straight home. She'd pull a piece of lasagne from the freezer, read for an hour or so, and then it would be time for the news and dinner. Tomorrow she really would clean the house and keep herself busy that way. And then on Monday she'd have a busy work day to keep her mind occupied. As she drove, she wondered if she'd rather know what day to expect a reply from the board or if it was better not to know. Since she didn't know, it didn't really matter, did it?

Chapter Thirty-five

Damien woke feeling amazing, the best he'd felt in ages. Even better was not having to get up in a hurry. Not that he was lolling about, but seven o'clock was pretty late for him. He lay there beside Squish, luxuriating in the complete and utter freedom he felt. Then the horses called out, demanding to be fed.

'Oh, well, Squish, no rest for the wicked,' he said, giving the dog a final pat before getting out of bed.

He went through his morning routine, all the while humming and whistling to himself, and marvelling at how good he felt. He'd just finished his breakfast of toast and jam and a mug of coffee and was getting ready to consult his to-do lists – both daily and longer term – when he heard a vehicle approach. He cocked his head to listen. He frowned. He could now hear voices – female voices – quite close, but no one was knocking on his door. Then he thought he heard what sounded like the door of the horse float parked nearby. He went to investigate.

A ute was parked a little way away. It seemed vaguely familiar, but he couldn't quite place it. Not surprising, given all sorts of vehicles were regularly coming and going these days. But what was Lucy doing with it?

'Hiya,' she said, coming towards him carrying a large box. 'Auntie Ethel says they needed a bigger box and you need to cut back on their feeds. They're taking advantage. And getting too fat,' she said, thrusting the box into his chest.

'Are they now?' he said, grinning. 'Whose ute?'

But before Lucy could answer, Alice popped out of the float. So he *had* heard the float door. He hadn't imagined it.

'Hi, Alice.' Damien was perplexed. He looked from Lucy to Alice and back again. They didn't know each other, did they?

'Hey, how's it going?'

'We're going riding,' Lucy announced.

'Oh. Right. I didn't know you knew each other.'

'Do now,' Lucy said cheerily. 'We met in the supermarket.'

'I've got my job back,' Alice said.

'That's great.'

'And it looks like I might be getting closer to being able to take the horses back. If that's okay?'

'Of course. I'm pleased things are working out for you.'

Damien felt a little sad. In just a few days, the horses and emu had started to really feel a part of the place and it wouldn't be the same if they went. He was hoping to have the oldies from the home out to visit but there'd be no point if there were no interesting animals to see.

'I'll leave you to it, then. Have fun.' He went inside, unable to shake the feeling there was something odd going on. Clearly Ethel had found Alice and introduced her to Lucy. But what was she up to? Because Damien had no doubt Auntie Ethel was up to something. He sighed. No doubt he'd find out soon enough. Or perhaps it was best he didn't know. He thought Auntie Ethel had a tendency to push the moral envelope at times.

He looked up when the door opened. Lucy's head appeared in the gap.

'Alice says that Sam will probably follow too, so not to worry if you can't find him.'

'Okay. Thanks. The big dogs will probably tag along, so I hope the horses will be okay with that. They haven't minded them hanging around them so far.'

'They'll be right.'

'Have fun.'

'Thanks, will do.'

Damien went out and watched Lucy and Alice on the horses as they made their way south from the house followed by Sam the emu and Bob and Cara. Everyone looked calm and content enough. He picked up Squish, who was sitting dutifully beside him.

'You're a good, loyal friend,' he said, kissing the dog on the forehead. 'Thank you,' he said, in response to the wet kiss he received in response. 'Come on, we've got tiles and stuff to unload.'

Damien was putting boxes in the partially built house and carefully writing in thick black marker what was for what – *laundry floor, laundry walls, bathroom floor, bathroom walls*, etc – when he heard another vehicle pull up. He peered between the timber uprights through where the walls would one day be and his heart gave an extra beat. There was Geoff's car – Geoff and another man were inside. He toyed with remaining hidden, until the men got out and began poking about the front of the house as if they belonged there. His blood started boiling. Thank goodness Lucy and Alice weren't here. He strode out and around to where the men were.

'Geoff, what can I do for you?'

'Hi, Damien. I've brought Richard Brown from Stockman Real Estate to take a look around to do a valuation for our settlement. I'm sure your mother has told you we've separated. Well, we need to …'

Damien held his hand out to the man he didn't know. No point being rude.

'Well, you've made a wasted trip. Geoff, you're not welcome here.'

'Now, come on, Damien, we've always got along okay, haven't we?'

'Until I found out what a creep you are. I always thought you were a loser and my mother made a poor choice, but that was her business. But spying on and trying to touch up women – and women young enough to be your daughters – well, that's just plain disgusting.'

The other guy was doing a lot of staring at the ground where his foot prodded the dirt. Damien felt for the bloke. He was clearly only trying to do some business. It was just a pity he'd got himself involved with Geoff. Damien gained some satisfaction in noting how red in the face and neck Geoff was.

'I suggest you leave now. Sorry you've got caught up in this, Richard, but you've made a wasted trip. The farm is in my mother's name and hers alone,' he said, more for Richard's benefit. 'So you're not going any further without showing me a written and signed request from her.'

'But it's a joint asset by law.'

'That's not my problem and nothing to do with me. Now, you've got five seconds to get back in that vehicle and leave before I call Bill Hanson.'

'Yeah, I know how buddy-buddy you are with him. You'd better call him off, if you know what's good for you.'

What? But Damien was distracted by Squish, who started up a deep growl that he'd never heard before and would have found quite unnerving if he didn't know the dog so well.

Richard got straight back into the vehicle. Geoff hovered, looking at Squish as if trying to work out how serious the threat was. Damien got out his phone and made a show of scrolling through contacts. He had Bill's mobile number and the station number in his list. Holding the phone up, he raised his eyebrows at Geoff.

'All right, all right. I'm going,' Geoff growled – though not nearly as impressively as Squish, Damien thought – and got into the car. 'But don't think you've heard the last of this.'

'Make sure it's in writing and signed by my mother, then,' Damien said, forcing his tone to be cheery, and walked away with a wave of his hand. He kept an eye on them to make sure they were leaving.

Damien fumed. At Geoff, but also his mother. He found her mobile number in his contacts, selected it, and pushed the button to connect.

'Damien, lovely to hear from you.'

Damien frowned at how upbeat she sounded. Had she been drinking? It wasn't nine o'clock in the morning yet.

'Mum, I've just had Geoff here with some real estate bloke to look over the farm. Did you know about this?'

'Um, yes, it'll have to be looked over sooner or later for valuing. I can't see any other way around it. I'm sorry.'

'You bloody well could have told me! I'm part of all this, in case you've forgotten – we're meant to be business partners, even if it is only your name on the title.'

'Look, I know you're upset about Jacqueline ...'

'Did I mention Jacqueline just now? No! This isn't about her. It's time you stopped burying your head in the sand and dealt with a few things. Don't you think you at least owe me a discussion about where things stand?'

'I don't know where things stand. I'm trying to ...'

Damien was stunned to hear a male voice in the background: 'Oh, sorry, I didn't realise you were on the phone.' Maybe Lucy was right and their mother really had met another man.

'Fine, Mum, whatever. I get it, it's none of my business. But if you want me to let Geoff or anyone else on the place then bloody well put it in writing!' Damien slammed the phone shut, grateful to still have an old flip one that he could take out his frustration on. What the bloody hell was she playing at? Didn't she care about losing the farm, about taking Damien's future away? Jesus, how bloody self-centred could you get? And how could she be off having an affair, starting a new relationship, while everything was going to shit?

By the time he'd finished unloading the ute, Damien was feeling a little calmer, but he couldn't shake the curiosity over what Geoff had said about calling off the cops. He felt a few cogs fall into place. Ethel had asked if he had Alice's details. She'd clearly found her because she and Lucy were here together now. And the one thing that Lucy and Alice had in common, other than a love of horses, was that Geoff had been creepy towards them. Ethel must have gone to see Bill. But why now? He felt like there was something he was missing. Oh well, perhaps it was best he didn't know. He had to forget it or else he'd send himself mad trying to nut it out. Maybe it was what it was and there was nothing more to nut out. He'd ask Ethel next time he saw her.

Meanwhile he was still pissed off with his mother. That clearly wasn't going to be put aside so easily. What he'd said about the farm being none of his business hadn't just come out through anger, it was what he felt, and it was the truth. His next move dawned on him like a slow-moving storm rolling in: it was time to cut the ties. This having to always be answerable, especially to someone as controlling as his mother, was not on. Sure, she'd been fine with his new venture, but he suspected she might be on her best behaviour and that it would only be a matter of time before she went back to her old ways.

And what if he got married? Would he be exposing his wife, no matter who it was, to God only knew what intrusion? His mother had always come and gone from the house with no regard for his privacy. It hadn't bothered him too much – the fact she tended to tidy the place up while she was there outweighed the inconvenience of her just rocking up unannounced. If he lived there again, it would go back to how it had always been. And Tina couldn't be told anything and she didn't get hints. He was kidding himself if he thought she'd stop barging in even after he was married. It would always be her house, her farm, and she would always feel free to intrude whenever she liked.

Well, she could have it. She'd need somewhere to live if she ever came back. She could lease out the farm or make some share-cropping deal with someone. But he was done.

*

Damien drove down to where the new fence stood, its fresh-looking posts and shiny wire gleaming in the sunlight. He got out and ran his hands along it and took a whiff of the earthy timber. He almost laughed at how he must look – like someone admiring a piece of art or a prized possession. To him, this fence was both of these things. He'd never had a whole new fence before; parts had always been recycled, reused or purchased second-hand at clearing sales, and fences as a whole were rarely replaced. Money had always been tight. And his dad had been the king of innovation, recycling and making do. While Damien had admired him, respected his frugality, he'd also always envied their richer neighbours with their bright new fences and flasher, more reliable equipment. He felt a little guilty and disrespectful towards his father now for admiring this fence so much. But, man, it was a beautiful work of art. And, better yet, it hadn't been his blood, sweat and tears that had put it here. He laughed out loud as Squish and Bob chose a post each to christen with pee.

'Nice one, boys!'

He chained the two kelpies back into the tray and got in the ute to drive home. He detoured to the rise above the gully where the family of kangaroos liked to congregate. He got out the binoculars and panned around. They all looked the same. If the young buck he'd saved was there, he could no longer pick him out. Good for the roo, a little sad for Damien.

At that moment a roo on the far edge of the group turned and bounded a few metres towards him, stopped and rubbed its face with its paws. Was that the young buck giving him a sign? He'd take it as such. He smiled and waved. There was no one to tell him otherwise.

He put the vehicle back in gear to return to the van. But at the track home he found himself turning right instead of left and heading out to his block.

Damien parked in the gateway that joined his land with their original place – what he was now thinking of as his mother's farm. He looked around, his gaze settling on the group of magnificent native pines way down at the boundary beside the road. They were quite superb, even from this far away. And a hell of a lot nicer than all the charred remains back at home. It was as if he was seeing them, appreciating them, for the first time. He'd driven over this land plenty of times in his ute, moving sheep, and in the tractor, sowing, spraying and harvesting crops. But the land was bought purely to increase their acreage, to make their business more viable. It had some of the heaviest, best dirt, but it was the fact it was for sale at a reasonable price and joined their land that had sealed the deal. Other than a super shed, it was bare.

Over near the trees was a bit of a rise that might make a good site for a house, if one was so inclined. It wouldn't have the far-off view of the ocean that his dad's had, but the patchwork of farmland and scrub was picturesque, and the blue of the distant hills and mountain ranges was quite beautiful. Perhaps that was the reason someone had planted the pines. And they'd definitely been planted – they were in nice straight rows. He'd never considered the place for its aesthetics.

He drove down to the trees and parked. The super shed was far enough away to not be a blight. There was no reason why this couldn't be a nice spot for a house. Except for all the extra distance on dirt roads to get to town. Damien frowned. That was the fly in the ointment. And it was a big fly. He sat there feeling deflated and not even sure why. And then something started tugging at his brain, like the thread of a memory he couldn't quite grasp.

Something about a boundary? Or perhaps it was just the disappointment that the boundary was so far away from anything. It wouldn't work – he couldn't be driving that far to town. And it was all dirt roads. Damien knew he was probably being spoilt, but he knew he'd resent the travelling. There was no point going any further. Oh well, he'd at least considered it as an option. Time to head back, though he figured he may as well go right around and check on the whole place while he was over here.

He headed east towards the small paddock surrounded on all sides by scrub, with just a gap to enter. He only tended to venture into it to check for sheep during muster. It was cleared but was too small for him to be bothered putting the tractor in to crop it. What you wanted was big open spaces for cropping and enough areas of shelter for stock. This was a pain – a waste of twenty acres of good soil. The effort and cost to clear it and add it to the adjoining paddock wouldn't have been worth it. But now he was looking at things through different eyes, looking for different areas of potential, he could see how much of an asset this small, secluded paddock could be to a few horses, donkeys, or even camels – whatever needed a home. He could easily have solar-powered electric fencing installed to keep stock from getting near the barbed wire.

He drove on along the boundary and up onto the next rise, where he stopped to take in his surroundings, get his bearings. He was so rarely over here that he now felt a little disoriented. He looked around. Before the fire, he would have been able to see the top of his big implement shed. But it had definitely been over there to his right, because he could see the line of Stobie poles. He looked to his left. Two paddocks intersected with his on the other side of the fence. One was the northern boundary to the piece of land the Havelocks had bought.

His heart rate quickened. If Jacqueline's parents let him put a track through here to the council road – put in an easement – he'd only be a kilometre from his current driveway. And the old cottage was on the other side of the scrub, so they'd still have their privacy.

Damien's dad had fought all those years to get his road in from the bitumen. He'd wanted it to go right past his place, through what was now Damien's block, and join up with the back road – to make carting grain easier for all those out that way. Maybe Damien could go some way towards making that dream of his come true too …

No, hang on. He didn't want grain trucks rumbling too close to his home. His own private track to meet up with the end of the current council road and get straight out to the bitumen highway would be enough. God, it might actually work in Esperance's favour to have two entrances, he suddenly realised. It would be like serving two sides of the district without people having to drive so far. God, why could everyone else see it and he couldn't? If he could get the council to start grading and taking care of the five hundred metres of road beyond his current driveway that ran alongside Tina's boundary and put down five hundred or so metres himself, he'd be set.

He turned the ute around and headed back the way he'd come. His brain was firing with creativity and his pulse was racing with excitement. He pulled up on the rise facing north and took in the view. Then he got out and faced west and took in that view. He did the same for the remaining two directions and all the angles in between, taking careful note of what he could see, where the prevailing wind would travel in each season. When he'd finished, he sat in quiet contemplation.

And then another thought struck him like he'd been hit over the head with a sledge hammer: it didn't matter where he put his house. There was no power, no power lines to take into account – he could stay off-grid. There was water laid on to the paddocks, but not near here. He should be able to be self-sufficient with that too by collecting enough rainwater off the roof, and cart some if not.

Just like all those weeks ago, when he'd realised his destiny lay in Esperance, Damien buzzed with the slightly overwhelming feeling that the world really was his oyster. He ran his hand rhythmically along Squish's belly. He heard the metallic rattle of the big dogs' chains hitting the tray as they settled down for a snooze. He stared out through the bug-speckled windscreen framed in dirt. His brain raced a mile a minute, but he felt calm. He'd build his own house here on his land, cut the apron strings for good. His dad had always wanted to build a mudbrick house. He'd also toyed with straw bales. But back then it hadn't been done often and involved too much trial and error. Now it was a completely different story.

But maybe having a transportable arrive on a truck was a damned sight easier. Or one of those two-storey weatherboard or corrugated iron houses with the garage underneath could be the go. The view might be quite spectacular from another level up.

As for income, he'd get a contractor to crop what he could here, run some sheep himself, and make up any shortfall with working for other farmers during the busy times. He was licensed to drive semi-trailers, so he could even do some truck driving to make ends meet if necessary.

Damien was surprised at how little the thought of getting work away from his property bothered him. He'd heard of other farmers doing it, but he'd always seen it as a sign of failure, total humiliation, and admitting defeat. No doubt he'd got that view from his judgemental mother as well. While she was all about impressions, now he could see that life was more about whatever it took to keep your dream afloat. Some things were worth doing and some compromises worth making. With or without Jacqueline, he was going to do this. He had to. He hoped Tina wouldn't get her nose out of joint and withhold the proceeds of their partnership, including the insurance money. But if she did, he'd find a way around it. He'd heard about a farmer's son suing his parents for unpaid wages. He didn't think he'd go down that path, but if his mother did get difficult he'd damn well fight for himself and his future.

He took a deep, slightly tentative breath to see how his decision felt. He was calm and rational, driven. And the longer he stayed here, the more he liked the feel of the place, especially the whisper of the wind through the pine trees. He dragged the pad of paper from the dash and began drawing a rough map of where everything was, marking up plans for his future.

Damien became engrossed in shifting between his hand-drawn map, which had on it what he wanted and where, and his to-do list. He needed to get his priorities right and just focus on the crucial things for now. Moving himself was fine, easy – he just had to hook the van to the ute – but to move the animals he needed enclosures down here. He'd decided that south of the house was best. That way the hot north winds would blow any odours and dust away.

It actually felt quite good to be starting over, though he did feel a little guilty that the working bee would essentially be rendered a waste of time. But he couldn't worry about that. He had a blank canvas on which to work and would think it all through carefully before doing anything permanent.

Damien was startled when his phone started vibrating and ringing on the dash, very loud in the silent cab.

'Christ, scared the crap out of me. How 'bout you, Squish?' he said, putting a reassuring hand on the little dog while he picked up. He frowned at the unknown number displayed.

'Hello, Damien McAllister speaking.'

'Hey, it's me,' a muffled voice hissed. Whoever it was must be whispering.

'Sorry, who am I speaking to?'

'Lucy, your sister, remember me?'

'Where are you and why are you whispering? I can barely hear you.' Damien almost laughed, realising his voice had gone quiet to match his sister's.

'I'm hiding in the loo at Auntie Ethel's.'

'Why?'

'You're never going to believe this, but Mum's turned up.'

Damien felt the calmness he'd been experiencing seep out of him and tension sneak in.

'But I only rang her not long ago.'

'She was on her mobile, wasn't she? Well, she could have been anywhere.'

'Great. All good things must come to an end, apparently.' Damien felt decidedly deflated.

'Yes, well, anyway ...'

'So, what's the story?'

'This is something you're also not going to believe ... Well, no, actually, you probably won't be surprised.'

'Lucy, just spit it out.'

'She swanned in here on the arm of a bloke, like she's just come back from a holiday.'

'You're right, I'm not surprised. She hates being on her own. So, what's he like, a creepy loser like the last one?'

'No. Actually, he seems really nice. And there's a nice shiny Merc out the front.'

'Oh, won't the old ducks in the street be all in a fluster? I hope he's here looking for a farm to invest in.'

'I don't know what's going on. Look, I'd better go before they send out a search party for me. I'm just warning you. Act surprised when you get a call from your mother in a few minutes. I suspect you'll be summoned to a family meeting, or at least dinner.'

'Okay. Thanks.'

'Hey, are you okay?'

'Yeah. Well, as well as can be expected under the circumstances.' Damien found himself smiling at having used one of his father's common phrases. Lucy took it as the dismissal it was meant to be and they hung up.

'Never a dull moment around here, Squish,' he said after he'd closed his phone.

Concentration now broken, he put his papers back on the dash and put the vehicle in gear. The tension was still within him and he could feel the frown in his face.

He was annoyed at letting his previously buoyant mood be upset. He'd head home to feed the kittens – a cuddle with them was sure to make him feel better. He hadn't actually meant to be out so long, he suddenly realised, opening the phone up to check the time. He cancelled the alarm he'd set before driving off.

The phone rang again. He stopped the vehicle and retrieved it from the dash. Auntie Ethel's home number was lit up on the screen, though chances were it wasn't Auntie Ethel on the line.

'Hello, Damien speaking.'

'So how come you don't know it's me today?' Auntie Ethel said, with her usual cheerfulness.

'Hello there,' Damien said, smiling and relaxing slightly. 'I wasn't sure if it might be my mother using your phone. Lucy called me.'

'Ah, I thought she might have. Either that or my egg sandwiches for lunch disagreed with her,' Ethel said with a chuckle.

'So, how is she?'

'Top of the world – she's the centre of attention.'

'Who is he?'

'You'll find out. The reason I'm calling is to invite you in for tea tonight. No, Jacqueline will not be here. I think your mother will be enough to deal with with.'

'So, I'm being summoned, then, am I?'

'Yes. This is compulsory. You're not leaving me and your sister to deal with her. You know how she is when she's met a new man.'

'Like a giggling teenager, I know,' Damien said with a groan.

'Yes, only it's worse this time.'

'Why's that?'

'You'll see.'

'Righto. I've got a few things to tell her, myself, actually.'

'Sounds ominous. Do I need to hide the knives?'

'Not from me, you won't,' he said with a laugh.

'Good to hear. See you later then.'

'Yes, because I apparently don't have a choice,' Damien said, still feeling a little jovial. Bless Ethel, she really was the tonic.

'No. You don't. Cheerio then.'

'We have a dinner date, Squish. And a date with destiny,' he added. He put the vehicle back into gear and carried on home to see to the animals and have a shower before heading into town.

Chapter Thirty-six

Damien arrived at Ethel's and pulled up behind a navy blue Mercedes. He sat for a few moments taking it in. In a different lifetime he might have owned such a stunning beast.

'Well, this is it, Squish, time to face the music,' Damien said, and got out.

He snuck a look in the side windows of the vehicle as he passed by. Probably best he had his hands full of chocolates and wine, else he might not have been able to stop himself running a hand over the impressive piece of machinery.

He was still thinking of the car as he lifted his hand to knock on his auntie Ethel's door. As expected, his mother answered. She had a tendency to take over. And, also as expected, she turned her nose up at seeing Squish standing beside Damien.

'Hi Mum,' he said, moving forwards.

'Damien, lovely to see you,' Tina said, and hugged her son vaguely. She was just as Lucy had said: happy, and looking around ten years younger. Annoyance stabbed at him. He hated how she was so good at glossing over things, pretending they hadn't happened. She was an expert at putting on a happy face — should really have been an actress. Sometimes he wondered if she actually forgot things or whether it was all just a very good act. If he hadn't sorted out his life, essentially planned on cutting her out of a large chunk of it, he might have been more angry right about now. But now he could see her for what she was: an insecure person desperate to control, desperate to appear perfect and part of a well-adjusted family. Damien thought if Tina stopped pretending long enough, she'd realise just how damaged her relationship with Lucy was, and she'd have a fit. Damien pitied his mother for her lack of insight, but he wasn't about to enlighten her. He loved his mum, it was just that more and more often lately he really didn't *like* her all that much. Like now, when she was standing there all nice as pie, doing her we're-the-perfect-family skit in front of this new bloke.

'Damien, this is James Telford.'

'Hi, James.' Damien put out his hand to the man dressed impeccably in a tailored striped shirt and navy chinos. He seemed a decent enough fellow. And he had a firm handshake, which was always a good sign. 'Nice car.'

'Thanks. I think it's part of a late midlife crisis. I've wanted a Merc forever, but have only recently managed to make it happen.'

Damien liked his humility and honesty.

'James is a partner in a large city law firm,' his mother said, stroking James's arm as if he was her pet. She was practically purring and was clearly very pleased with herself for bagging this one.

'But not Tina's lawyer, I might add. That would be unethical,' James added. Damien watched, impressed, as he carefully unhooked Tina's hand from his arm. Clearly he was onto Tina – or just not as into her as she'd like to think. 'Come on, we can't be standing here in the hall all night, leaving Lucy and Ethel to do all the work in the kitchen. Damien, I want to hear all about your venture. Tina has been a little sparse with the details.' James stepped aside to let them pass.

I bet she has, Damien thought, *most likely because she's feeling guilty that she's about to pull the rug out from under me by selling the farm.*

'Our firm's proud of its community involvement – perhaps we might be able to give some legal assistance, or contribute in some other way – at least let's talk about it,' James said as they made their way down the hall.

'That'd be great.'

In the kitchen, Lucy was busy at the bench chopping vegetables and Ethel was at the stove, peering into a large steaming pot, holding a wooden spoon in one hand and a shiny metal lid in the other.

'Good evening, something smells good,' Damien said, raising an arm in greeting to his sister and his aunt.

'Lamb shanks. Lucy's request. Thank goodness for the cooler weather,' Ethel said.

'Sounds good to me. These are for you,' he said, holding up a box of chocolate-coated almonds before putting them on the bench.

'Oh, scorched almonds, yum,' Lucy said.

'Thank you, that's lovely. They'll be great with coffee later,' Ethel said.

'… and a bottle of red and one of white,' he said, taking the brown paper bags from under his arm and holding them out.

'Crikey, we've got grog coming out of our ears,' Ethel said. 'James and Tina brought some too.'

'Well, I can't guarantee how good these are. I know squat about wine, as you know. But Ralph at the pub reckons they're okay.'

'Shall I do the honours?' James asked, pulling the bottles from their bags and scrutinising them.

'If you like, though feel free to have yours if you prefer.'

'Yes, yours are probably much better quality, James,' Tina cooed. 'And these are screw caps,' she added with a slight sneer.

'Nothing wrong with either of these,' James said. 'And at least with screw caps you know it's not going to be corked. Perhaps you didn't notice, but the bottles I brought also have screw caps.'

Damien thought he really shouldn't enjoy seeing Tina put in her place quite as much as he was. He managed to catch Lucy's eye and exchange raised eyebrows and smirks.

'Okay, who's for red and who's for white?'

'Red for me, thanks,' Damien said.

'White for me, thanks,' Lucy said.

'And me,' Ethel said.

'I don't mind having white if that's what everyone else wants,' Damien said.

'I'll have a red with you,' James said. 'Tina?'

'Red for me, too, thanks.'

'We're all set here for about half an hour, so let's go through to the table,' Ethel said when the drinks had been poured and distributed. 'You too, Squish. Come on.'

'So, how did you two meet?' Damien said. 'I'm sure you've already told the story, but I'm keen to hear it.'

'Well, I was waiting to see my lawyer – who actually can't really help, by the way. If Geoff wants half the farm, he's entitled to it. Anyway, James walked past and we recognised each other immediately.'

'Do you know each other?'

'Oh, didn't I say? We were at school together,' Tina said.

'A lot of water has passed under the bridge since then,' James added. 'My dad was in the bank here many moons ago. We were here for around eight years.'

'Oh. Right. That's nice.' Damien gulped his wine. He was itching to stop this polite small talk and get down to business.

'Now, sorry, James, to bring up family business in front of you, but there's something you should know.' Damien immediately felt the heat rise under his shirt and his palms began to sweat. He wiped them on his jeans under the table. The red wine he'd been enjoying now tasted bitter and metallic in his mouth. He swallowed against a suddenly dry throat. 'I'm out of the farm,' he blurted.

'Sorry?' Tina blinked and frowned at him from across the table. He hadn't given a thought to where he'd sat, but now he realised it was probably quite telling to have Lucy beside him, his mother directly across and James across from Lucy, with Ethel at the head of the table between them. The referee.

'I'm moving everything down to my block. Once the house has been rebuilt, you can live there, or lease the farm or sell it. What you do is up to you.'

'Damien, now come on, surely this isn't because you're still angry at me about Jacqueline? There's no need to be silly and childish about things. You need to get over it now, Damien, put it behind you.'

Damien felt the rage build inside him. He focussed on breathing slowly and deeply. He started counting. He wouldn't lose it in front of James, he was too well brought up and conditioned. No doubt that was why James was here. Fuck, he wanted to slap his mother's face. His eyes burnt with the pressure of holding the fury at bay and his head started to pound. He looked down, feeling Lucy's hand on his thigh. Squish, who'd been sitting by his chair, chose that moment to jump into his lap. The dog sat up, looked at Tina, and growled. Damien noticed amusement twitching at the corners of James's mouth and the disgust clear on the face of his mother.

'All I'm doing, Mum, is taking control of my life. You are free to sell the farm, with no objection from me. We'll need to wind up the partnership – maybe you could give us some advice there, James, or point us in the right direction.'

Tina was looking very pale. 'But …'

'Mum, you're free to sort things out with Geoff and make a fresh start, you should be happy.'

'But there's no house there, no power – it's just a block.'

'And a fresh start. I'm sick of feeling obligated.'

'Since when have I …? I've been very supportive of your new venture, haven't I?' And there it was, the tone of affront, the tone that said Tina thought this, as usual, was all about her. Damien had to stop himself from rolling his eyes and shaking his head.

'Yes, you have, Mum, and I'm grateful. But it's my venture and I need to make it completely mine by moving it to my own block. Being at the farm is too tenuous a position – you splitting up with Geoff has brought that home to me. That's all.' He shrugged in an effort to lighten things. He didn't say what he really wanted to – he didn't want to antagonise his mother, and was hoping to keep her onside long enough so he might do okay financially out of splitting the partner-ship. But he wasn't in control of her and what she chose to do. And, if it came down to it, he'd live in a tent for the rest of his life rather than change his mind now. Though Tina would most likely do the right thing by him financially, if only to prevent word getting around about her.

'Wow. Well, I didn't see that coming,' Ethel said, downing her half-full glass of wine in one gulp, and holding out her glass to James for a refill.

'Well, I'm shocked. After all I've done.'

'Tina, darling, it's really not about you. If Damien wants to cut the ties, then that's up to him, isn't it? I say, congrat-ulations. Onwards and upwards. To independence,' James declared, raising his glass. 'All the best, mate.'

'Thanks, James,' Damien said, returning his smile. He felt a little bewildered.

'Yes, well done,' Lucy said, putting her arm around his shoulder and squeezing.

'But it's so far out of the way,' Tina persisted suddenly after a few moments of silence.

'I'm going to put a track through, join up with the road that goes to the Pigeon Bay road.'

'Well, I might not agree to you going through my land,' Tina said haughtily. True to form, Damien thought. He hoped James was taking note.

'Nice to know how supportive you *really* are,' he bit back, and then wanted to kick himself. He'd allowed himself to sink to her level. 'It's the Havelocks' place I'd need to go through, not yours.'

'Well, have you asked them? I bet they won't want a road going near their cottage.'

'No, I haven't asked them yet. And if they don't, then that's fine. I'll take that as a sign I'm meant to carry on driving the long way around.'

'The novelty of that'll soon wear off,' Tina said with a harrumph. 'You'll see.'

'I thought you'd be pleased to be able to do what you want with your farm without worrying about me. But whatever you think doesn't really matter. This is what I'm doing. I'm telling you, not asking your permission. It's not up for discussion.'

'Right, well, I think it's dinner time,' Ethel said, getting up and breaking the silence when it became uncomfortably long.

As Damien sipped his wine, he thought about his mother's reaction. It was sad that she couldn't be happy for him, see what a big, important step this was. She was terrified of losing her grip on him. It was sadder still that she couldn't see that the tighter she tried to hold onto people, the more she pushed them away, as she'd done with Lucy. He wondered what excuses she gave herself and others for the sparse contact she had with her daughter.

He could see now just how tactful Jacqueline had been in her comments about his mother. He hadn't realised how bad being in a co-dependent relationship was, how toxic. The word sounded so benign. It had only been when he'd looked it up on Wikipedia that he'd seen what she'd really been trying to tell him. Well, he was certainly starting to get it now, and doing something about it. *Oh Jacqueline.* It hurt to think of her sitting alone in her little house right across the street. He'd give anything to have her beside him or be there curled up beside her on her floral couch. He couldn't wait to tell her his latest revelations and decisions. He knew she'd approve.

'I'm so pleased for you, and proud of you,' Lucy whispered, while making a big fuss of Squish in Damien's lap.

'Excuse me, I need to powder my nose,' Tina said, getting up abruptly. James half rose like the true gentleman he was.

'Who powders their nose these days? Certainly not our mother,' Lucy scoffed quietly. 'I'll go help Auntie Ethel,' she said, and also left the table.

'Sorry about that – airing the dirty washing,' Damien said to James, feeling the need to say something since it was only the two of them left in the room.

'Not at all. I think it sounds very exciting. And your mum's been telling me about how things stand. I'm a bit of a non-conformer myself, so I like someone who stands up for themselves and what they believe in.'

'But you're a lawyer, and a partner in a big firm at that.'

'Yes. I show my independence in other ways.'

'So you and Mum are an item, then?' It had to be asked. The more Damien was seeing of James, the more their relationship didn't make sense.

'Oh no,' James said with a laugh.

Damien looked at him with wide eyes, the bewilderment clear on his face.

'I'm gay. Camp as a row of tents,' he said with another laugh, and raised his glass theatrically.

'Oh. Right.' Damien had never met an openly gay man before. It wasn't something you'd admit to, living in a place like Wattle Creek, even if you were. He had no idea what he should say. He racked his brains for something appropriate. 'Well, each to their own,' he said, raising his own glass, again grateful for the distraction. And then he paused. 'So, um, Mum knows, right?'

'I've told her. We're just friends. But she clearly still sees me as worth parading around town. She always was both insecure and a drama queen. Haven't seen her in over thirty years, but she hasn't changed a bit. And I'm really sorry to hear about your dad. We weren't friends, but I knew him.'

'Thanks. So do you think Mum's trying to fix you, then?' Damien mused aloud.

'I think so. Good luck with that, eh?' James said with a laugh.

'Yeah, cheers to that,' Damien said, grinning and raising his glass and holding it across the table. They clinked while smirking.

Damien marvelled at how much he liked this bloke and was almost disappointed he wouldn't be around as Tina's partner.

'So, your mother tells me you saved a kangaroo joey and nursed it back to health. I'd love to come out and see it.'

'Yes, Jemima. She's great. Sadly she couldn't be re-released because of all the handling. I've got an emu now, too. You're welcome to come out and visit, but I'm not having you taking that nice car of yours on my crappy dirt road. I'll come in and get you.'

'Thanks, but it is only a car.'

'I insist.'

'Okay. But I warn you, I'm not too keen on emus. They give me the heebie-jeebies.'

'Me too, but Sam's all right. How long are you around for?'

'Just a few days. Your mother needed to get back and I was feeling nostalgic and keen to check out the old stomping ground.'

'Dinner is served,' Ethel called as she and Lucy entered, carrying plates piled high with food. Tina reappeared and silently took her seat at the table, placing her napkin back on her lap.

The conversation over dinner was polite but the atmosphere a little tense. Damien took special note of how his sister interacted with their mother. He'd remained blissfully ignorant for too long. Lucy was polite, but a lot quieter than she'd been recently. She answered her mother's probing questions, which Damien now suddenly realised were not intended to politely ask after Lucy's life out of interest, but designed to make her daughter feel uncomfortable, put on the spot. Anyone who didn't know Tina very well wouldn't pick it, but the snide tone and emphasis on specific words were a giveaway. Damien's breath caught and he had to cover up his shock with a sip of wine as what he'd missed for so long became obvious.

'And how is the *office* job?' Tina asked.

'Great, thanks,' was Lucy's simple reply. At least she wasn't going to fuel the fire. Why would she tell her mother anything about her life but the barest essentials?

'Where do you work?' James asked.

'KYOM Advertising – in London.'

'Oh, wow. They're huge. And do incredible work.'

'Yes, but it's still just an office job. It's not as if you do any of that,' Tina said primly.

Damien's brow furrowed as he tried to think what Lucy had ever been interested in, had been encouraged to do. His dad and Lucy had spent ages together in the shed woodworking. She'd had a better knack and more patience for it than Damien had. At one point he remembered she might have mentioned becoming a cabinet-maker. But he couldn't remember any talk of that since their father had died.

'I'm a graphic designer, Mum, so, yes, I do do some of that.'

'Don't tell me you were involved with that hilarious men's underwear ad for the Super Bowl last year. That was KYOM, wasn't it?' James asked.

Damien was having to forcibly keep his mouth from dropping open. Even he'd heard of the Super Bowl ads. He'd never watched the game, but he knew how famous it was for its ads. Wow, his sister was doing that?

'Yes. And I was, actually. The Bright Eyes Optical two years ago was mine too.'

'I don't remember that one. But this is fantastic. Wow. I've met a celebrity.'

'What do you mean *yours*?' Tina asked.

'My work, Mum,' Lucy said with a weary sigh.

Damien wondered just how many times Lucy had explained to their mother what she did for a living, and felt ashamed all over again for also being clueless.

'Well,' Tina said, in the tone she used whenever she was beaten or not the centre of attention.

'I don't think you understand how talented your daughter is and just how well she's doing, Tina. KYOM is one of the largest advertising firms on the planet.' James turned back to Lucy. 'So how long are you over for?'

'I'm not sure. I might move back and settle in Melbourne or Adelaide. Perhaps start a business.'

'Oh, you won't want to be taking that sort of financial risk if you've already got a good job.'

'My financial situation really isn't any of your business, Mum.'

'And I'm sure Australia would be terribly boring after the London high life.'

Sneers all over the place, Damien observed, his blood starting to boil. 'Why can't you ever just be supportive,' he suddenly found himself saying.

'I am being supportive. Of course I'm being supportive.'

'How? Not once have you said, "Well done, that's great, whatever makes you happy" – and without a sneer, I mean. You should be very proud of Lucy, not trying to tear her down or belittle her. She went to London with barely a cent and not knowing anyone …' Damien refrained from adding *to get away from you* '… and has studied and worked hard to get where she is. I know I'm proud of her. And I'm sorry I haven't ever said it properly before,' he said, now turning to Lucy. His sister gave him a weak smile.

'Of course I'm proud of her, I'm her mother.'

You could never win. Tina was the way she was and would never change. She was a self-centred bully who would never understand anything where anyone else's feelings were concerned. He could see why Lucy just steered clear. Tina had regularly pissed him off, but he didn't tend to hold onto things for long. Maybe it was being male that made all the difference. Or maybe Lucy was just supersensitive – wasn't that one of the things they said about creative types? He so wished he could go and ask Jacqueline about it. He sighed to himself, careful to not let it out.

'God, Tina, from where I'm sitting, you're nothing but a bully,' James said quietly, shaking his head. 'Give the girl a break. And Damien. You should be pleased your kids have done so well despite you clearly trying your best to drag them down.'

'I have not.'

'Oh really?' James stared her down with arched eyebrows. 'They're doing too well for you, but you make out the exact opposite because you're so disappointed in yourself and hate the thought of them doing better than you. But what have you ever done? Tina, you need to deal with your own insecurities and stop manipulating, emotionally blackmailing and bullying people. I think you're damned lucky they still speak to you at all. They're both a lot more tolerant than I'd be. You spent the whole six hours in the car telling me how difficult they are, but now I'm seeing who the difficult one is.' He stood. 'Look, I'd better go before I say something I regret. Thanks for the offer to stay, Ethel, but I'll see if the motel has a room.'

'Yes, good idea,' Tina said acidly.

Damien wanted to leap up and throw his arms around the man and tell him how wonderful it was to hear someone standing up to his mother, not to mention figuring her out in a heartbeat. He could see Lucy was looking enormously grateful too.

'Hey, no, don't do that,' Damien said, leaping up. 'You're welcome to stay with me. I have a couch and table that turns into a bed. I'm in a pretty comfortable caravan. The reception for the motel will probably be closed anyway.'

'Oh. Okay, if you're sure.'

'No problem at all.' *Are you kidding? You've just stood up to my mother and uttered words I've probably wanted to say for years and hadn't quite realised, and if I had, probably wouldn't have found anyway.*

They all trooped up the hall to the front door, leaving Tina at the table, her jaw tight with rage.

'I'll just get my bag,' James said, going to his Mercedes.

'I'm so proud of you, Damien, for going out on your own. As usual, your mother managed to steal the lime-light. I hope you won't change your mind,' Ethel said, giving him a tight hug.

'Thanks for standing up for me. It really means a lot,' Lucy added, surprising Damien with a hug moments after Ethel had let him go.

'Well, you can come and help me build pens tomorrow if you're so grateful,' he said with a laugh. All this emotion and being deep and meaningful was getting a little awkward and embarrassing.

'Okay.'

'Come on, Squish,' Damien said, bending down and picking the dog up.

As he went around to the driver's side of the ute, he glanced across at Jacqueline's house. Light was glowing at the edges of the curtains in the lounge room. His heart lurched. *God, I miss you.* He'd love nothing more than to be going over there and curling up together and analysing tonight's happenings. And he so desperately wanted her to say it was okay that he really didn't like his mother. Was it okay? He realised with a jolt that life would be a lot calmer and easier without Tina in the picture. Clearly Lucy had come to that conclusion years ago and these days very carefully managed her interaction with her mother. *Oh well, better late than never, Damo.*

You're doing it, you're standing up for yourself by moving onto your own place. And then you can padlock the gates and not let her onto the property if you choose.

Damien took a deep breath of the fresh evening air. It was a little sad to think it had come to this, but it was what it was. And he really did feel quite liberated. And a little scared. No, he'd hold onto feeling liberated. He reckoned this was the real freedom he'd been searching for since his dad had died. Esperance Animal Welfare Farm had only been halfway there, he could see that now.

'Right, got everything?' Damien said as James got in after placing an RM Williams–branded duffel bag in the back of the ute.

'Yep. Thanks for this.'

'No worries.' It seemed so inadequate, but Damien had no idea where to start to explain just how much what he'd said tonight had meant.

Chapter Thirty-seven

Jacqueline forced herself back into the habit of taking long morning walks and also walking the few blocks to work. The exercise helped to keep her head clear. This waiting for the board to make their decision and notify her really would do her in if she let it. While she was learning to enjoy her own company again, Jacqueline was also loving getting out in the car. She'd even taken herself down to Pigeon Bay the last few evenings for a walk along the jetty and beach, and to dip her toes in the ocean before the weather got too cold. She'd hoped to see Paul, but hadn't. She was definitely settling into the district. Sure, she would have preferred Damien's company, but as it was, life was pretty darned good – well, while she could block out the dark cloud looming overhead, that was. Would it dump its rain on her or keep on moving and reveal blue sky? She would have to wait and see.

As Jacqueline left the house for work, she wondered who owned the lovely dark blue Mercedes at the kerb in front of Ethel's that had arrived while she'd been at work the day before. Something was going on with her friend – more to the point, she was up to something – and it was clear she didn't want to share it with Jacqueline. No doubt she'd hear soon enough. Most likely from one of her clients – nothing stayed a secret around here for long. She really hoped her own secret had managed to stay hidden – she didn't like to think that people sat in her office knowing she'd made such a mistake in her own life. And it wasn't as if she could say to them, 'Do as I say, not as I do.' Picturing herself saying it to a client made her smile broadly as she unlocked the door to her office.

Regardless of the outcome of the board's review into her relationship with Damien, she would be okay. She thought she'd stay here and adapt if she needed to, especially as her parents were set to make the move over. They'd rung, full of excitement, to tell her they'd found a builder who specialised in working with stone and blending the old with the new. Apparently he was from Melbourne and had moved to the district for love. Wasn't that nice?

At lunchtime, just as she'd finished eating her ham, cheese and mustard sandwich at her desk, there was a gentle tap on her door – too gentle for it to be Ethel, she lamented. She was really missing her friend's company.

'Come in,' she called.

The door opened to reveal Doctor Squire. Jacqueline's heart seemed to freeze for two beats before racing to catch up.

'Hello.' She was pleased she managed to sound bright.

'Do you mind if I sit?' the older man said, pointing to the two chairs.

'Go right ahead.'

'It looks like we've had word,' he said, handing her one of what she now realised were two envelopes in his hand. No need to ask word from where or whom.

Jacqueline's heart pounded as she read her name on the front of the envelope and then turned it over and slid a nail under the seal. She noticed that on the other side of the desk, Doctor Squire was doing the same and felt a surge of renewed respect, realising he'd waited to open his own letter with her.

'Right,' she said, taking a deep breath as she pulled the contents out and unfolded the crisp letter.

She tried to take in the words, commit them to memory, but her brain was feeling addled. She started again.

Dear Ms Havelock, Regarding … blah, blah, blah.

And then there it was:

Having carefully considered the matter and your response, the board has concluded that you have no case to answer. This matter will be taken no further.

It went on to wish her all the best with her career.

She was off the hook. It was over. Jacqueline was engulfed by relief so intense her chest filled with a ball of anxiety. It floated up, lodging in her throat and causing her eyes to fill. She bit her lip.

'Good news,' Doctor Squire said.

She nodded, fighting the tears. *Hang on, was that a statement or a question?*

'It's over, Ms Havelock. Well done,' he said, smiling warmly at her and reaching across the desk to clasp her hand in such a touching gesture that Jacqueline nearly sobbed.

'I wouldn't have believed it if I hadn't seen it for myself,' he said, shaking his head slowly. 'Finally, a little win for the country. We get to have our cake and eat it.'

'Sorry?' Jacqueline's brain really wasn't working properly. Relief was consuming her, cutting off all other thought processes.

'You get to keep your qualification, I get to keep you – if you want to stay, that is – and you get your man, I think is the way to put it.'

'What?' The word came out in a whisper. Or had she spoken at all? Her mouth was certainly open. She closed it.

'Here, read for yourself,' he said smiling and handing her his piece of paper.

She frowned as she read. Loud white noise roared in her ears.

Dear Doctor Squire, Thank you for your submission in response to … blah, blah, blah. Jacqueline skipped forwards.

… while we could never condone a breach of ethics, we understand certain leeway might be awarded in light of the circumstances you outline.

As there is no evidence of wrongdoing on Ms Havelock's part and thus no case to answer, we consider the matter closed.

Never before have we seen this level of support for a practitioner. You have made a compelling case for an exception to be made in this instance and we request that the highly unusual decision remain confidential.

We thank you for your, and your community's, input into this matter and wish you all the very best ...

'So, I can ... Damien and I can ...?' she asked.

'Yes, my dear, you are completely off the hook – your career and relationship are both safe.'

'Oh, thank you, thank you so much.' Jacqueline wasn't sure how she'd got there so quickly, but suddenly she was embracing a startled Doctor Squire. He was momentarily stunned, but then held her firmly as she dissolved into tears. God, how embarrassing! But she couldn't help it.

Finally she pulled herself together. 'Sorry about that,' she said meekly.

'It's quite okay. It's been a very difficult time. But it's over now. And the result is better than we could have hoped for.'

'Thank you so much for going in to bat for me and Damien. I didn't expect ...'

'Well, someone had to, dear. Blind Freddy can see you and Damien are good for each other. And I couldn't have you leaving and him following – the CFS, and the whole community for that matter, would have had my guts for garters.'

'Well, again, thank you. It means so much to me,' she croaked.

'I know we had a bit of a rocky start, you and me, but I hope we've put that behind us. I hope you'll stay on and learn to love the place and all of us, with our little quirks and quaint country ways.'

'Oh, I already do.'

'Okay, well, no rest for the wicked, as they say. I'd better get back to the grind. I'd like to celebrate properly. I'll speak to Nancy about what evening would suit for dinner and see what we can arrange.'

'That would be lovely. I really can't thank you enough, for everything.'

'It's my pleasure. And my motivations were not entirely selfless.'

He left the room with a wave of his hand.

Jacqueline collapsed back into her chair. Her heart pounded heavily but slowly. It was hard to believe it was over after all the weeks of angst. Just like that. Things were very different now. While she couldn't have hoped for a better outcome, it was a bit of an anticlimax, really. Though what else could she expect? It might have been nice to take the day off to celebrate, to draw an immediate, definite line in the sand. But Doctor Squire couldn't have dropped everything and taken her to the pub to celebrate – they both had patients to see to. Life went on. She itched to tell Ethel, but held back. Her friend was busy with whatever was going on – she had Damien's sister, Lucy, there, as well as whoever owned the Mercedes. And she had something going on involving Bill the policeman; Jacqueline had seen his divvy van outside her house, too.

Jacqueline also itched to phone Damien with the news. But he'd dumped her – yes, because of this, but still. Perhaps he'd moved on, wasn't interested in picking up where they'd left off. No, Damien had to be handled more delicately than picking up the phone. She'd loved to have driven out there right now, but she had a client arriving in around half an hour. And, anyway, it would be selfish of her to disturb his work without warning. She was fully aware that his world did not revolve around her and he certainly hadn't stopped his life to sit waiting to hear the outcome. Jacqueline thought about phoning Paul, but that didn't feel quite right either. She finally picked up the phone and dialled her parents' number.

'Mum, Dad, it's me. Just calling to say hi,' she said, once the message had ended. She was surprised at how calm she sounded, but the click of the answering machine activating had taken the wind out of her sails. She almost didn't bother phoning her dad's mobile and was a little relieved when that too went to voicemail. She'd just hung up when there was a loud three-beat rap on the door. *Oh, well, back to work.*

'Come in.'

She was shocked to see Ethel enter.

'I've heard the news. Well done. Just brilliant,' Ethel cried, bustling in with her arms open wide to accept Jacqueline, who leapt up and rushed into her friend's embrace.

'Oh, Ethel, I'm so glad to see you. God, I've missed you,' she said, breathing in her dear friend's comforting scent of Lux soap and a faint hint of lavender.

'News certainly travels fast around here,' Jacqueline said as they broke away.

'You don't know the half of it,' Ethel said.

Jacqueline was surprised when Ethel made no move to sit. She clearly had somewhere else to get to.

'Come on, grab your handbag, I'm kidnapping you. We need to celebrate.'

'I'd love to, but I can't. I've got three clients still to see this afternoon.'

'No, you don't. Doctor Squire's had one of the girls phone them to postpone. He called me.'

'Oh,' was all Jacqueline could say, her head starting to spin again. She didn't like letting people down, but if this was Doctor Squire's doing, well, who was she to argue?

'So, are you coming?'

'Where are we going?' she asked, dragging her handbag out from under her desk and getting up.

'You'll see.' Ethel hurried her out of the door and across the car park to her car. 'Damien has decided to move Esperance over to his block — cut ties with his mother. It's a bit of a long story,' she said as they drove. 'Anyway, there's an impromptu working bee. It's all happened very quickly, and not quite on the same scale as last time, but we need to get some food down to them. I need you to get changed and come over and help me put together a stack of sandwiches. They'll be starving, so we'll have to hurry. Okay?'

'Okay.' Jacqueline's head swam. She hoped Damien was all right. Something pretty big must have happened for him to make such a decision.

'You skedaddle,' Ethel urged when they pulled up in her driveway. Jacqueline leapt out of the vehicle while resisting the urge to put her hand to her head in a salute.

In less than five minutes, she had changed into jeans and a T-shirt and was entering Ethel's open door to make her way down the hall to the kitchen, calling, 'Ethel, it's just me.'

And an hour after that she was feeling a little nervous, setting off to Damien's block with the boot of Ethel's car laden with food and beverages. She was quiet, the whirlwind that her day had turned into silencing her. She hoped Damien would be pleased to see her, but was wary of making assumptions. To do so was to set oneself up for disappointment.

Chapter Thirty-eight

Damien watched as a collection of fully laden utes, including some with trailers piled high, arrived. He could hardly believe what he was seeing and was still a little dazed and vague when he showed everyone his hand-drawn plan and what he needed to achieve that day in order to completely move himself and the animals down here. With so much help, it might just be possible.

'Ah, we can do better than the mere basics, can't we fellas?' Keith Stevens said. Damien was pleased to have Keith involved; being CFS brigade captain meant he was a wiz with mobilising people and getting stuff organised. Keith was in his element, and was taking over.

'Right, Stan, you and Bob finish the enclosures – all of them as shown here. Dave, how about you and your team do what you do best, and fence off the couple of small paddocks?'

Everyone scattered to get to work and Damien and James found themselves standing alone and with nothing to do.

'Right, well, I don't ever want to hear anyone say country folk are slow,' James said, clearly both amused and impressed.

'God, my head is spinning,' Damien replied. 'I don't believe it. The community already built the enclosures back home and tidied everything up after the fire.'

'Well, I'd say you deserve it. They obviously want to help you, so accept that it's karma.'

'But twice?'

'Why not? They believe in you and your venture. And never underestimate the buzz they'll be getting from being a part of it.'

Lucy appeared beside them. 'God, can you believe this?' she cried.

'Amazing isn't it, though nothing on the scale of last time. Thankfully we don't need all the heavy machinery cleaning up the mess,' Damien said. 'Makes life a lot easier.'

'It must be a bit weird for you – kind of like déjà vu; unsettling.'

'A bit, yeah.' While she was right, there was one major ingredient missing: Jacqueline. He thought he'd give his right arm to have her standing beside him. And her parents, they'd been there last time. And Ethel, she'd been a huge part of it. Whenever something was going on, she was usually in the thick of things.

'So, is there anything I can do?' Lucy asked.

'I don't think so. There's not even anything left for *me* to do, by the looks of it,' he said with a laugh. They turned and cast their eyes around at the various groups of workers.

'Maybe it's time you moved yourself, brought the van down,' James suggested.

'And how about I borrow a ute and move the horses?' Lucy said. 'They'll happily stand tied up at the float for a bit. And of course there's Sam. I'm sure he's smart enough to hang around them and stay out of the way. Best to get them down here and settled before dark. What do you think?'

'Good idea. I'll bring Jemima too. By the time I make sure everything is safe in the van and get it here those enclosures will be finished and all the noise will have stopped.'

'Right, sounds like a plan. Come on then,' Lucy said.

'I'll just let Keith know,' Damien said. 'He seems to have appointed himself foreman.'

★

Damien hooked the float to Keith's ute and then waited to help load the horses. Not that any was needed; they were perfectly behaved and seemed to have the routine down pat. They stood back as Sam strode up the tailgate first and settled himself on the floor in the front, out of the way.

'Who would have thought?' Lucy said, chuckling as she sent Ben and then Toby up the ramp.

'Are you sure you're right to drive? It's been years since you towed a float.'

'No worries, I'll just take it very slowly.'

'Righto then, see you soon,' Damien said with a wave before joining James, who was readying the caravan for transportation. Apparently his parents had had a van and he knew all about what to secure and how. Damien was grateful for his expertise, as he didn't have a clue and, if left to his own devices, might have ended up with a pile of smashed plates and glasses. And he certainly wouldn't have known to take the TV off the bracket and lay it face down on the bed.

In less than half an hour, James, Damien, Squish, Jemima and the box of kittens were ready to go. Damien had wanted to linger to silently say goodbye to his father's legacy and apologise for leaving. Thankfully, it wasn't as hard as it would have been if all was as it had been before the fire. As it was, it was barely recognisable. But Damien could picture all his dad's hard work, cobbling everything together out of scraps and what most people discarded as rubbish. Damien was grateful for having grown up with knowing how precious things were and having to save and strive for what you wanted. And yet for most of his life, he'd resented it. It was only recently he'd seen what a great lesson he'd been given, and just how clever and resourceful his father had been. At least he could take his memories and his father's teachings and wisdom wherever he went.

They drove part of the way in silence. It was as if James was giving Damien the peace to be with his memories and say goodbye. But coming over the rise and seeing the vehicles and activity spread out below them was too breathtaking not to comment on.

'It's an amazing sight,' James said. 'We need a photo of that for your Facebook page.'

'Oh. I haven't even thought about photos,' Damien said, becoming disappointed with himself as he slowed the vehicle. 'Bugger.'

'Don't worry, I've taken heaps. I'll send them through to you.'

'Thanks, that'd be great.' Damien halted the vehicle and waited while James took some shots.

'Got a couple of good ones,' James said, leaping back in and shutting the door.

'Thank you,' Damien said, as he put the vehicle back in gear and carried on.

He was glad everyone had parked close to the road as it left the space where he wanted to put the van clear. It didn't really matter where he parked it, but he wanted it where he thought his house should go. That way he could get a feel for the spot and know for sure.

As they arrived, they noticed the workers were wandering towards the parked vehicles. There in the centre of things was his Auntie Ethel – handing out sandwiches and drinks.

'God, I'm starving now I've seen there's food on offer,' James said.

'Well, you've certainly earnt it.'

'What do you reckon about waiting until we've eaten to unhook this and set it up? We need to make sure it's fully level, which might take a bit of patience,' James said.

'Good idea.' Damien pulled up where he thought he wanted the van and got out with the box of kittens. It was too warm to leave them in the vehicle, so he'd put them in a shady spot where he could keep an eye on them. He looked up from telling them where they were going and what he was doing, and froze. Standing beside Ethel was Jacqueline, head bent, pouring liquid from a water bottle into a cup. God, she was the most gorgeous woman he'd ever seen. Pity she couldn't be his. He'd love nothing more than to throw himself at her feet and beg for her forgiveness. It didn't really matter, he thought with a depressed sigh. Nothing had changed, they were still a no-go zone.

Just as he was about to look away, she looked up. They locked eyes. Her face lit up as a beaming smile overtook it. Damien smiled weakly in return. Luckily he had his hands full, or else he might have thrown his arms around her and totally embarrassed both of them, not to mention getting her into more trouble. What a fucking mess.

'I'll just find somewhere to put this – it's the kittens. It's too hot in the ute and ...'

'Can I have a look?'

'Sure. Just let me put them down – they're starting to get a bit heavy.'

He put the box in the open boot of Ethel's car, trying to ignore the close proximity of Jacqueline and her gorgeous scent. His fingers shook as he prised open the lid and lifted it.

'Gosh, they've grown,' Jacqueline exclaimed.

'Yep, they're doing well.'

'Can I have a cuddle?'

Can you ever. Oh, you mean the kittens. Damn it. 'Sure.'

She eased the ginger one out of the tightly packed group and brought it to her chest. Damien nearly melted. She'd make the perfect mother to his children. Jesus, where had that come from? He plucked the tabby grey kitten out to hide his awkwardness. They stood there looking at each other as they silently stroked their kittens. Damien wondered if it could get any more awkward.

'I got some good news earlier,' Jacqueline said, a little shyly.

'Oh, what's that?'

'I'm off the hook. *We're* off the hook. The board has decided there is no case to answer and have closed their investigation.'

'Oh, wow, that's great. Good for you.'

'Good for us, Damien. Doctor Squire received a reply too. Apparently he put in a submission including results from a petition …'

Damien concentrated on looking down at the kitten and his fingers stroking its soft fur. He hated keeping secrets from Jacqueline, but if Doctor Squire, Ethel, or anyone else for that matter, hadn't told Jacqueline everything, then he wasn't about to be the one to do it. Not now, anyway.

'Well, anyway, the board, in a never-before-heard-of move, has decided to bend the rules. There's nothing stopping us being together now, Damien. I won't get in any trouble.'

'Oh. Wow. Really?'

Jacqueline nodded.

Damien felt like a dumb teenager standing in front of a girl for the first time after the hormones had set in and made him realise boys and girls were different. Regardless of what she'd just said, he wasn't about to make some huge public declaration – he'd learnt his lesson on that front.

'If you, um, want us to be together again, that is,' Jacqueline continued awkwardly. 'I'll understand if you …'

'Are you kidding? No way. I mean yes. I want you. I've … Oh, hell.' He quickly but carefully put the kitten back in the box and threw his arms around her and held on, breathing in the gorgeous apple scent of her hair and her fresh skin. He reluctantly released her after a few moments, held her back from him and looked into her beautiful face. His heart swelled.

'Oh, Jacqueline, you've no idea how much …'

'Oh, Damien, I've missed you so much,' she said, her eyes glistening.

They looked into each other's eyes another beat before locking lips, drinking in each other's love.

After what seemed hours, but was only probably minutes, they were roused by a round of applause, followed by a couple of whistles.

'Yeah, righto,' Damien said, letting Jacqueline go. 'Nothing to see. Move along now,' he said, blushing and laughing with embarrassment.

And then all the kittens started squawking, even the one Jacqueline was still cuddling.

'Okay, okay, message received loud and clear, you guys.'

'I'll sort these out while you eat,' Ethel said, appearing beside them.

'Okay, thanks.' Damien was disappointed to have the spell broken, but told himself he might have the rest of his life to gaze upon this incredible woman. Could life get more perfect?

★

Eventually Lucy, James, Damien, Ethel and Jacqueline were sitting squeezed around the caravan's table, enjoying a cup of tea and marvelling at what a day it had turned out to be. Damien silently noted that he had all those he loved the most right beside him. He included James in that group – he'd taken a real shine to the bloke and knew they'd become firm friends, even though James was so much older. It was just such a pity he lived so far away, though he had promised to visit and come and help out at the farm from time to time.

Damien thought about ignoring his phone when it skittered on the bench and started ringing, but found himself reaching for it out of habit. He'd at least see who it was. 'Mum Mobile' was lit up on the screen. He so didn't need his perfect day to be ruined, but it was usually just best to get these things over with. Otherwise he'd just have to phone her back.

'Mum, hi, what can I do for you?'

'I'm at the farm. You're not here. And someone's stolen the caravan.' There was the affronted tone. She wasn't worried about the van. This was the tone that said that it was unacceptable that something was going on without her knowing all about it – better yet, without her being the centre of things.

Damien was sick of his mother's insecurities. He wasn't going to play along any more. 'I'm down at the block. So is the van. I told you I was moving down here.'

'But I thought …'

'You thought what?'

'Well, I didn't realise you were moving straight away.'

'Well, I have. What can I do for you?'

'I wanted to talk to you.'

'I'm listening.'

'In person. I've been to see Geoff. I need to discuss …'

'Well, we're on our way in to Auntie Ethel's, you can meet me there,' Damien said, shooting Ethel a grimace that he hoped was both apologetic and questioning. She shrugged nonchalantly in return. A split second after Damien had heard his mother's voice, he'd realised he didn't want her turning up here. She was bound to cast her critical eye over things and give some caustic remark. He didn't need that today – or ever. He'd even put a padlock on the gate between the two properties. The last thing he needed was her barging in as if his block was still an extension of her property.

'Who's we?'

'Me, Jacqueline, Lucy, Auntie Ethel and James.'

'Well, aren't we having quite the little gathering?'

'I'll see you at Auntie Ethel's. Bye.' Damien felt a perverse amount of satisfaction in hanging up on his mother.

'Sorry about lying and putting you on the spot, Auntie Ethel.'

'No worries, I completely understand. You don't need her coming here and raining on your parade, right?'

'Thanks. You're really are the best, you know.'

'How 'bout you take me to the pub for tea to prove it?'

'Good idea, we should at least celebrate your move,' Lucy said.

'We'd better get cracking if we're to beat her home,' Ethel said.

★

'I'm off to book into the motel. I'll save us a table,' James called to Damien and Jacqueline as he got into his car outside Ethel's.

'Okay, see you soon,' Damien called.

'Good luck.'

'Thanks.' He walked inside holding Jacqueline's hand. He hadn't wanted to let it go at all since she'd shared her news, but driving a manual vehicle had made things a little difficult.

They'd barely got in the door when the doorbell rang. Damien, Jacqueline and Lucy went through to the dining room while Ethel answered it.

'Hello, Jacqueline, lovely to see you,' Tina said curtly as she joined them.

'And you, Tina.'

'Tina, would you like to sit, or are you happy to stand there making the place look untidy? Cup of tea, maybe?' Ethel said.

'No thanks, I can't stop.'

'Mum, don't you owe Jacqueline an apology?' Damien ventured.

'What for?'

'Are you kidding me? How about for nearly ruining her career.'

'Damien, I'm sure Jacqueline is mature enough to see it as a little misunderstanding made by a mother and concerned citizen doing her duty.'

'You don't see what you could have done, do you?' Damien was aghast.

'Damien, stop being melodramatic. It's not my fault Jacqueline did the wrong thing, broke the rules. I'm sure it will all turn out just fine, if it hasn't already.'

'It already has, no thanks to you.'

'See, all's well that ends well. What did I tell you? Now, I need to talk about the farm. Geoff and I are back together so there's no problem. Nothing will change. Isn't that wonderful?'

'What?' Damien frowned and blinked. 'But he's been cheating on you, Mum, he's a ...'

'No, he's assured me that's in the past.'

'God, Mum, open your bloody eyes for once,' Lucy said. 'He's a creep.'

'Oh Lucy, just because you don't get along, there's no need to slander the man's name. He's got a good heart. He makes me laugh and he's very good to me.'

Damien blinked again. Where the hell had his mother gone – the strong version who was only just the other week declaring the man a lying, cheating prick?

'It's not just me, Mum,' Lucy said calmly.

'Yes, I know all about your little vendetta. Geoff's told me. You should be ashamed of yourself, Ethel, for being hoodwinked by two silly girls.'

Damien almost exploded. He could feel the heat of rage burning his face and neck.

'I think you'd better leave, Tina,' Ethel said quietly.

'Fine, I'm leaving. Anyway, I only came to say that the farm is fine and ...'

'You'll have to get someone else to run it, then,' Damien said.

'What?'

'I'm out. I told you. I've moved everything down to the block.'

'But ...'

'Yes. And I hope you'll be reasonable in dividing up the bank account and insurance. Here's what I've come up with,' he said, pulling a sheet of figures from his pocket and handing it over.

Tina snatched it up and stuffed it in her handbag without looking at it. 'Well, so much for holding onto the farm all these years so you have a job. Where's your loyalty?'

'And where's yours – to Lucy? You've been dreadful to her over the years.'

'Oh for goodness sake, Damien, Lucy has always had a very vivid imagination.'

'Excuse me, don't talk about me as if I'm not here.'

'Sorry,' Damien said.

'Not you,' Lucy said, glaring at her mother.

'Was there anything else you needed to say before you left, Tina?' Ethel asked calmly.

'Yes. Geoff and I are moving to Adelaide. He wants a fresh start. And I agree.'

'Get your head out of the sand, Mum. He *needs* to leave, otherwise he'll be run out of town.'

'Oh Lucy, you've had your head buried in too many novels. People don't get run out of towns – it's the twenty-first century! If Geoff's having any trouble in town it will be down to your vindictive little crusade. Whatever that was in aid of, I'll never know. Ethel, you really should stop meddling in things that don't concern you.'

'These kids do concern me. And you wonder why Lucy has so little to do with you. Yep, you're a self-centred, manipulative, emotionally blackmailling bully all right.'

'Well, it takes one to know one,' Tina said haughtily and strutted out with her chin held defiantly high.

'What is she, twelve?' Damien asked when they heard the front door slam behind her. '"Takes one to know one"? For God's sake.'

'Wow,' Lucy said. 'Thanks for saying that and defending me.'

'You know I only speak the truth, Lucy, dear,' Ethel said, sitting down and patting her hand.

'Sure you want to be a part of this?' Damien said, putting an arm around an obviously stunned Jacqueline. She hadn't said a word, had sat calmly and stony faced.

'She's certainly a piece of work. Classic narcissist behaviour,' she added, as if to herself.

'I'm sorry she didn't apologise to you,' Damien said.

'Damien, you need to understand that no matter what she says and how cruel she is, she'll never apologise, even if pulled up on it. A narcissist will never believe they've done anything wrong. Any problem perceived is the fault of others, not them. It's best to avoid interacting with them, or at least limit your exposure. Lucy, you probably did the right thing by leaving. Mother and daughter relationships are known to be difficult at the best of times, but when one person is a narcissist, it can make life hell.'

'So what Tina is has a name? Interesting,' Ethel said.

'Any magic cure, then, doc?' Damien asked.

'I'm afraid not. You can't help anyone who doesn't want help or doesn't see a problem. And with a narcissist ...'

'They don't think there's anything wrong with them,' Damien cut in. 'I get it. God. These last few weeks sure have been an eye opener.'

'You could escape inside your tractor or header and get enough peace before, I guess.'

'You've got nothing to be sorry about. I needed to know. I don't want her treating Jacqueline badly.'

'Oh, don't you worry about me,' Jacqueline said. 'I'm a big girl.'

'Well, thank God I know she's moving to Adelaide,' Lucy said. 'I'm definitely not going to consider moving there now!'

'Are you seriously thinking about moving back?' Damien asked.

'Sort of. Maybe. But I'm scared if I give Mum an inch, she'll try to take a mile, and then next thing I know she's phoning every day for a chat and popping around for coffee.'

'Yes, and if you work from home it'll be all that more difficult,' Jacqueline mused. 'People tend to think those working from home aren't really working, certainly not keeping strict business hours.'

'Especially narcissists, right?' Damien said.

'Yes, especially narcissists.'

'And I wouldn't mind betting if you're living in Melbourne or Sydney she'll see that as free accommodation for week-long shopping trips,' Ethel chimed in.

'There is no way in hell I'm having my mother stay with me!'

'Well, better start practising saying no, sis, while you're deciding what to do with your life. You'd be welcome to stay with me, if I had the space.'

'The spare room here's available for as long as you want it,' Ethel said.

'Thanks, I really appreciate it. I don't know what I'm going to do. But for one thing, I'm glad I came back. It's been good to see it's not just me who has issues with her. And she'll never change. I just have to manage our interactions as best I can, right, Jacqueline?'

'Yes. Exactly.'

'It's sad,' Lucy continued. 'I love her because she's my mum, but I really don't like her very much.'

'Hmm,' Damien agreed.

'Well, they say you can choose your friends ... I need a serious drink after Tornado Tina's visit,' Ethel declared. 'Poor James will be wondering if we're ever going to turn up.'

'I'm really proud of the way you stood up to your mother,' Jacqueline said quietly.

'Thanks. I can't believe how clueless I've been for so long. She's well and truly played me over the years,' he said, shaking his head.

'Don't be too hard on yourself. Narcissists are prime manipulators.'

'Oh well, better late than never, I guess. And she won't be bothering me much if she's six hundred kilometres away. And I'll have you to steer me right. She can do her worst, as long as I have you. Ah, Jacqueline, it's been a great day,' he said with a contented sigh.

'The best,' she said, pulling him that bit closer to her.

Chapter Thirty-nine

Jacqueline wished she and Damien could just go across the road to her cottage and make up for what they'd missed out on these past few weeks. Oh, to be alone with him. She didn't feel like being sociable, bumping into clients, smiling and nodding politely, pretending she didn't know any of their private business. She was starting to feel very weary now all the tension she'd been holding onto had been released. She felt as if she could sleep for a week, given the chance. But James was waiting for them and Ethel was keen to go – it was the least she could do after all her friend had done for her, not to mention all the meals she'd cooked for Jacqueline and her parents. She really was a very special person and Jacqueline was so lucky to have her to call her best friend. What a rollercoaster her life had been since she moved to Wattle Creek. At least she could look forward to good times ahead.

'Right, all ready to go?' Ethel said as she pulled her front door shut.

Damien, Lucy and Jacqueline murmured their agreement. Jacqueline was pleased she wasn't the only one feeling a little unenthusiastic.

'Don't worry, you two, you'll get to be alone together soon. I know you've got a lot of catching up to do.' Ethel's tone caused Jacqueline to blush. Oh, yes, the whole town would most likely know what she and Damien would be doing later, though she was fast running out of steam. She'd be asleep before nine o'clock, the rate she was going.

Ethel and Lucy strode off ahead while Damien and Jacqueline ambled along behind, arm in arm. They were mostly silent, no words necessary for either of them.

'No matter how close I am, it still doesn't feel close enough,' Damien said at one point, taking the words right out of Jacqueline's mind. 'God, I've missed you – us,' he added with a long sigh.

'Me too. I can't believe it's actually over. I know it's only been days – a couple of weeks – but it feels like we haven't seen each other for months.' She squeezed his arm.

'Jacqueline, I'm really sorry for being so hard on you – for drawing such a deep line in the sand. I just …'

'Damien, I understand. I really do. And for the record, I love and respect you all the more for it,' she said and then gulped as intense emotion gripped her. She was shocked at the force of what she was feeling. She almost gasped, and reached out to gain support from the brick fence they were passing. She felt like sitting down and having a long, hard weep. Everything still felt so raw, so new.

Damien stopped and sat on the wall and pulled her into him. They faced each other, smiling. Damien's smile was warm, but as Jacqueline stared at him, a shot of fear caught her heart that the smile could have been one of sadness just as easily as contentment or happiness. He kissed her on the nose and then held her a little away from him.

'I love you so much, Jacqueline Havelock. Marry me. Not this year and maybe not next, but promise that when I've got everything sorted and can provide for us, you'll marry me.'

'And I love you too. So, so much.'

'So …?'

'Yes. Oh Damien, yes!' She threw her arms around his neck and hugged him. And then the tightness in her chest erupted and she cried, great racking sobs rushing from her in a torrent. He held her to him, his face buried in her hair.

'It's over now, let it all out,' he whispered while stroking her hair with one hand and rubbing her back with the other.

A moment later Jacqueline felt his shoulders begin to shake and then tears dampen her neck. Gradually all the pent-up emotion from the stress and uncertainty of the past few weeks left her, draining to her feet and into the ground. She didn't want to let Damien go. She didn't want him to let her go. He was her rock. Together they could do whatever they needed, whatever they wanted to do.

She felt him gently take her by the arms and ease her from him. He studied her face for a moment before cupping it in his hands and kissing her passionately. She responded, and it became a kiss the likes of which Jacqueline had never known, had never thought existed.

They'd kissed before, and it had been wonderful, but it had nothing on this. Never would she have thought it possible to feel your soul actually join with another's at a particular point in time. But if asked to describe what she'd just experienced, that was what she'd say. As naff and clichéd as it sounded, she really did think they – and their pact – had been sealed with that kiss. It was such a powerful thing, perhaps even more intimate than making slow, sensual love. A little buzz went through her as she thought of what still lay in store for them. If kissing could do this to her, well …

They eventually broke away and half-sat, half-stood against the low wall, gazing into each other's eyes.

'Come on, you two, enough canoodling,' Ethel called. They looked up, startled, to find Ethel and Lucy waiting for them at the corner about a hundred metres away.

'Oops, sprung,' Damien said, grinning, took Jacqueline's hand and resumed their walk. Jacqueline beamed and felt like swinging her arms and skipping. But she restrained herself to just a quiet, '*Wow!*'

It turned out to be not at all the quiet meal and early night she'd been hoping for. The hotel dining room slowly filled up and Jacqueline was stunned when Doctor and Nancy Squire arrived and sat down beside her. From Ethel's greeting, it was clear she'd invited them. That was nice.

Jacqueline was even more surprised when people started coming over to her and Damien in the corner and uttering congratulations and smiling at them approvingly, while saying what good news it was. She nodded and thanked them very much while hoping her confusion didn't show. How could anyone possibly know of their engagement when it had happened less than an hour ago and they hadn't told a soul? Even Ethel's radar wasn't that good!

But Damien was strangely silent beside her. Did he think they weren't talking to him? And then some words she'd recently read came back to her slowly and it all started to make a little more sense. In the board's letter to Doctor Squire they'd mentioned something about the community. Had the townspeople known of her plight? How embarrassing. She frowned a little, unsure if she was pleased or deeply concerned. She felt herself go pale.

Jacqueline looked down, feeling a hand on hers. Doctor Squire squeezed gently.

'Don't worry, my dear, no one knows why they were asked to provide letters and sign a petition of support. Your secret is safe.'

Jacqueline looked up at him and almost cried again. He was looking at her so kindly.

'Thank you. Thank you so much for everything. I won't let you down,' she said, willing the tears to stay unshed.

'I know you won't,' he said, and patted her hand before removing his to resume eating.

The rest of the evening passed in a bit of blur for Jacqueline. At times it was noisy, verging on raucous, and often she felt herself fading out and her attention leaving the dining room and returning to the doctor's words. *People wrote letters in support of me, signed petitions, even though I'm new and they're not too sure about seeking help or talking to an outsider?* She felt warmth and comfort flow through her. It didn't matter where she lived – hell, she'd live in a tent if she had to to be with Damien – what mattered was the people around you, the support. She'd seen this banding together of communities, but to be the cause, to be at the centre of it, well, this was something else entirely. Feeling incredibly honoured, Jacqueline thought she could now see why farmers and their families battled the elements, struggled through floods and droughts and low wool, lamb and grain prices year after year. She knew they weren't quick to embrace newcomers, yet they'd embraced her. She was hit with another wave of emotion, which she only just managed to swallow down in time. She was so grateful to everyone, especially Doctor Squire for taking a chance and bringing her to Wattle Creek.

This was home, she felt that with every fibre of her being.

Here is a sneak peek of

Leap of Faith

by

Fiona McCallum

AVAILABLE NOW

harlequinbooks.com.au

Chapter One

Jessica warmed Prince up just behind the starting line. She'd studied the plan well and walked the cross-country course twice today and three times the day before. She had all the twists and turns and best places to steer Prince into the fences memorised. He wasn't as light and quick on his feet as most eventers, so if she had any chance of capitalising on her good dressage score, she'd have to keep him to a tight line. Thankfully the course was dry – a damp, slippery track made for a treacherous, slower round.

Her first Adelaide International Horse Trials. *God, I'm nervous*, she thought, *a lot more than usual*. Her stomach was churning, trying to find food she hadn't eaten. Nothing new: she never ate until after the cross-country round. Her husband, Steve, often wondered why she put herself through all this. How much fun was it if she almost made herself sick with nerves every time? Fair comment, she reckoned. It wasn't really about having fun, but about the drive to be the best you and your horse could be.

For Jessica, there was no better feeling than winning. Well, that and making her father proud. She didn't like to admit it, but she was fully aware that much of what she'd done in her life and what continued to push her was all about gaining her hard-taskmaster father's approval.

And today her nervousness was exacerbated by Jeff Collins' absence. He'd been her coach as well as her father and she hadn't realised it would be this hard to go on without him. This was a huge event, so much bigger and more important than any of the others she did throughout the year – had ever done, actually. In the past few weeks since her father had passed, she'd begun to question if she was losing her edge, her guts and her determination to tackle the fences, and the will to keep up with the high standards necessary to succeed. For the first time, she hadn't had him beside her walking the course, discussing the options and choosing the best one, pointing out overhanging tree limbs, where she could cut corners, where it wasn't safe to, etc. Two knowledgeable heads were always better than one.

Yesterday, on her first walk around, she'd been sad to be doing it alone. She'd nodded to other competitors she knew, but they all tended to walk the rounds in concentrated silence. And then her feelings had turned to guilt as she'd contemplated how much she actually quite liked the silence and being able to carefully consider the many aspects to the round without her father muttering and imposing his views on her or demanding to know her every move, over and over.

Training for this event had been different, and so many times she'd doubted what she was doing. Realising just how much of a crutch her father had been had come as a shock. Now, almost daily, she had moments where she didn't believe she could do this on her own, before she reminded herself that she had always done all the riding – her father had just stood on the ground or sat on a rail – and, towards the end, in a deckchair – issuing orders and criticism.

The problem was she'd always had the comfort of knowing that if something went wrong, her dad was usually there to sort it out, to issue instructions or phone someone for help. Now she was all alone. But she had to suck it up; she was a big girl. She felt kind of liberated. She had to keep believing in herself – and Prince. He was ready, they were ready. Anyway, her father would be furious if he could see her being so insecure. He'd probably say something like, 'We didn't spend all this money and all this time, all these years, just to have you be so pathetic.' Yep, her dad had been pretty hard on her. But he'd also been fair. She wouldn't be where she was if it hadn't been for him. And her mother, before she'd died a couple of years ago.

Jessica thought about the advice her dad used to give her on competition days, and how he'd always question her instincts and decisions – sometimes over and over. It used to drive her mad. She so didn't miss that. The really annoying thing was that he hadn't actually been on a horse in twenty-odd years, so he couldn't begin to know her mount's fears, how long his stride really was, when he preferred to take off well out from a jump or go in deep. But that didn't stop her father thinking he knew best and forcing his opinion on her. And she'd learnt early on that you didn't contradict or argue with Jeff Collins. It was easier to just pretend you agreed and then do your own thing. Nonetheless, over the years she'd done pretty well. And today she would too.

Saddling up, she'd felt very sad and alone, and had wished she hadn't been so quick to urge Steve to go and play tennis.

Her husband didn't share her love of horses and competition, but he was supportive. Yet Jessica didn't like to take advantage of his kind nature and have him traipsing all over the place with her when it really wasn't his thing. In addition to his tennis and golf, he had his Country Fire Service; the CFS regularly took up a lot of time. And there was only so much someone could do.

Jessica watched as the horse before her went through the start gates and approached the first fence. Her heart was pounding and felt high up in her chest, as usual, but she also had a lump lodged in her throat that was threatening to upset her breathing. Normally her dad would be there just off to the side. While she never saw him scurrying across the course to keep watch on her, it was always a comfort to know he was out there some-where. She was starting to feel quite melancholy and found herself gasping. God, she really had to pull herself together.

Jessica took a few deep breaths and patted the neck of the large bay thoroughbred-warmblood cross beneath her. He was still calm and didn't seem too affected by how tense she was. But she had to get herself together; she was the one in charge. Prince had to follow her direction; if her messages were mixed or indecisive over jumps this size, it could end in disaster and serious injury – for one or both of them. It was a warm day with little breeze, so she'd also really have to keep on him to up the pace, stop him slacking off.

'Righto, mate, that's us. Let's do this,' she said, gritting her teeth and turning him towards the starting area as her number was called. Her heart flipped, but she gathered up her reins and stared down the course at the first jump – a nice solid log – twenty metres away.

'And ten seconds to go,' the starter called.

Jessica tightened her reins and applied more leg to wind Prince up like a spring ready to go. He responded perfectly: head up, ears pricked, his powerful hinds well underneath him.

'… four, three, two, and go!' the starter said.

Jessica gave Prince his head as they leapt across the start line and bounded towards the log. She stared hard ahead, feeling the length of Prince's stride below her. She tightened him up around eight strides out from the jump so she could carefully count her last four strides and shorten or lengthen him so he'd be placed to take off perfectly. The type of jump determined where she placed him, except with the first, where she always tightened him up a lot more so as to leave nothing to chance. Prince's approach and leap over the first obstacle usually gave a good indication of how the whole round would pan out. If he was unsettled and a bit spooked by spectators or the shadows, and hesitated at all approaching the first fence, she knew she'd have a battle on her hands to keep him focussed. She always held her breath until they were safely on the other side and on their way to the next fence.

Today she let out her breath and relaxed a little as they landed beautifully and headed on to the hay bales.

'Good boy,' she whispered.

They bounded along, Jessica picking her track just as she'd walked it. She continued to count her last four strides into each obstacle in her head, adjusting Prince as she went. He was responding perfectly. A third of the way around and she was still clear and travelling well.

But Prince's breathing was more laboured than she would have liked, and he was sweating more heavily than usual. It was a tough course, and her first at this higher standard. She had to do her best to keep him up and energetic. No matter how hard she pushed him, though, he didn't seem to have any more pace to give. He was moving along okay, not so tired that she'd pull him up and retire, but she certainly wouldn't be anywhere near the top of the leader board at this rate unless everyone else bombed out. All she could do was her best to keep them safe and go for a clear, slow round with time penalties.

The water jump was next. Around the jump was a sea of colour. *Jesus, look at all the people. Crikey. Concentrate, Jess!*

Did Prince have the legs to go straight through or should she go the safer, longer route? It was coming up fast. She was through the trees and on the approach and had to make a split-second decision. She hesitated, her mind clouded. Prince was on track to go right through. She gathered him up, but it was too late – she'd missed the first of her four strides. Three, two … Shit, she wasn't going to make it. He was half a stride out and badly placed – too far for one stride on such a fence and too close for him to get an extra one in. All she could do now was just hope to hell he'd get her through this. She gave the horse his head, grabbed onto the martingale strap with both hands, sat back in the saddle and held on tight with her legs. She'd let them down.

He leapt. But not high enough. Among the sound of flapping leather and the heave and grunt of the big horse beneath her, she heard a collective intake of breath from the crowd. *Oh shit. Shit!*

There was an almighty thud as the tops of Prince's legs hit the solid timber of the jump.

Everything became a slow-motion whirl as the horse struggled over, Jessica still in the saddle and clinging on. Then she could feel them tipping sideways, falling. It was deathly quiet around them.

A loud splash shattered the eerie silence. Jessica felt herself hit the water, and then the heavy weight of Prince was on her. *Ow! Oh Christ.* She wanted to scream, release some of the agony in her leg. But if she opened her mouth she'd probably drown. Her helmet was full of water. She was too heavy. It was all too hard. If Prince was dead on top of her, she'd rather be dead too.

She closed her eyes.